THE GIRL AT MIDNIGHT

The GIRL at MIDNIGHT

MELISSA GREY

✳

DELACORTE PRESS

Text copyright © 2015 by Melissa Grey
Jacket art copyright © 2015 by Jen Wang

All rights reserved. Published in the United States by Delacorte Press, an imprint of Random House Children's Books, a division of Random House LLC, a Penguin Random House Company, New York.

Delacorte Press is a registered trademark and the colophon is a trademark of Random House LLC.

Visit us on the Web! randomhouseteens.com

Educators and librarians, for a variety of teaching tools, visit us at RHTeachersLibrarians.com

Library of Congress Cataloging-in-Publication Data
Grey, Melissa.
The girl at midnight / Melissa Grey.—First edition.
pages cm
Summary: "A girl, who's adopted and raised by a race of creatures with feathers for hair and magic in their veins, becomes involved in an ancient war and a centuries-old love, discovering startling truths about the world she lives in"—Provided by publisher.
ISBN 978-0-385-74465-2 (hc)—ISBN 978-0-375-99179-0 (glb)—ISBN 978-0-385-39099-6 (el) [1. Fantasy.] I. Title.
PZ7.G872Gi 2015
[Fic]—dc23
2014008700

The text of this book is set in 12-point Fairfield.
Book design by Claudia Martinez

Printed in the United States of America
10 9 8 7 6 5 4 3
First Edition

TO THE MIDNIGHT SOCIETY

PROLOGUE

The Ala had gone to the library in search of hope. She walked through the stacks, one hand tucked into the pocket of her trench coat, the other trailing over the cracked spines of well-loved books and through the dust collected on those lesser-loved ones. The last patron had departed hours earlier, yet the Ala kept her sunglasses on and her scarf wrapped tightly around her head and neck. The dimness of the library made her black skin appear almost human dark, but the feathers she had in place of hair and the unrelieved blackness of her eyes, as wide and glossy as a raven's, were pure Avicen.

She was fond of books. They were an escape from responsibilities, from the other members of the Council of Elders, who looked to her—their only living Seer—for guidance, from the war that had raged for longer than most could remember. The last great battle had been fought more than a century ago, but the threat of violence lingered, each side waiting for the other to slip up, for that one tiny spark to ignite a blaze beyond anyone's control. Her fingers stopped their slow dance as a title caught her eye: A *Tale of Two Cities*. It might be nice to read about someone else's war. Perhaps it would make her forget her own. She was about to pull the book off the shelf when she felt a feather-light tug on her coat pocket.

The Ala's hand shot out to grab the pickpocket's wrist. A girl, skinny and pale, clutched the Ala's coin purse in a tight, tiny fist. She stared at the Ala's exposed wrist, brown eyes unblinking.

"You've got feathers," said the girl.

The Ala couldn't remember the last time a human had seen her plumage and been so calm about it. Dropping the girl's wrist, the Ala pulled the sleeve down over her forearm, straightening her coat and scarf to hide the rest of her.

"May I have my wallet back?" It wasn't a wallet, not really. In place of money, it held a fine black powder that hummed with energy in the Ala's hand, but the girl didn't need to know that.

The thief looked up at her. "Why do you have feathers?"

"My wallet, please."

The girl did not budge. "Why are you wearing sunglasses inside?"

"Wallet. Now."

The girl looked at the small purse in her hand, seemed to consider it for a moment, then looked back at the Ala. Still she didn't relinquish the item in question. "Why are you wearing a scarf? It's June."

"You're very curious for a little girl," the Ala said. "And it's midnight. You aren't supposed to be here."

Without a moment's hesitation, the thief replied, "Neither are you."

The Ala couldn't not smile. "Touché. Where are your parents?"

The girl tensed, eyes darting around, scouting an escape. "None of your business."

"How about this," the Ala said, crouching down so she was level with the girl's eyes. "You tell me how you came to be in this library all alone in the middle of the night, and I'll tell you why I have feathers."

The girl studied her for a moment with a wariness at odds with her age. "I live here."

Scuffing the toe of one dirty white sneaker against the linoleum floor, the girl peered at the Ala from under thick brown lashes and added, "Who are you?"

A multitude of questions wrapped in a neat little package. Who are you? What are you? Why are you? The Ala gave the only answer she could. "I am the Ala."

"*The* Ala?" The girl rolled her eyes. "That doesn't sound like a real name."

"Your human tongue could never hope to pronounce mine," the Ala said.

The girl's eyes widened but she smiled, hesitantly, as though she wasn't quite used to it. "So what should I call you?"

"You may call me the Ala. Or Ala, for short."

The little thief scrunched her nose. "Isn't that like calling a cat 'cat'?"

"Perhaps," the Ala said. "But there are many cats in the world, and only one Ala."

The answer seemed to satisfy the girl. "Why are you

here? I've never seen anybody else in the library at night before."

"Sometimes," the Ala said, "when I'm feeling sad, I like to be around all these books. They're very good at making you forget your troubles. It's like having a million friends, wrapped in paper and scrawled in ink."

"Don't you have any normal friends?" the thief asked.

"No. Not as such." There was no melancholy to the Ala's answer. It was merely truth, stripped of adornment.

"That's sad." The girl slipped her hand into the Ala's, one small finger stroking the delicate feathers on her knuckles. "I don't have anyone either."

"And how is it that a child has escaped the notice of everyone who works here?"

A little shyly, the girl said, "I'm good at hiding. I had to do it a lot. Back home, I mean. Before I came here." With a determined nod, she added, "It's better here."

For the first time in as long as the Ala could remember, tears stung at the corner of her eyes.

"Sorry about taking your wallet." The girl held the coin purse up to the Ala. "I got hungry. If I'd known you were sad, I wouldn't have."

A tiny thief with a conscience. Would wonders never cease?

"What's your name?" the Ala asked.

The girl looked down but kept her hold on the Ala's hand. "I don't like it."

"Why not?"

Shrugging a single bony shoulder, the girl said, "I don't like the people who gave it to me."

The Ala's heart threatened to crumble to ashes. "Then maybe you should choose your own."

"I can do that?" the little thief asked, dubious.

"You can do anything you want," the Ala replied. "But think carefully on it. Names are not a thing to be rushed. There's power in names."

The girl smiled, and the Ala knew she would not be returning to the Nest alone that night. She had gone to the library in search of hope, but what she'd found instead was a child. It would take her many years to realize that the two were not so different.

CHAPTER ONE

10 YEARS LATER

Echo lived her life according to two rules, the first of which was simple: don't get caught.

She stepped gingerly into the antiques shop nestled deep in a back alley of Taipei's Shilin Night Market. Magic shimmered around the entrance like waves of air rising from hot cement on a sizzling summer's day. If Echo looked at it dead-on, she saw nothing but an unmarked metal door, but when she angled her head just right, she caught the faint gleam of protective wards, the kind that made the shop all but invisible, except to those who knew what they were looking for.

The neon light that filtered in from the market was the only illumination in the shop. Shelves lined the walls, packed with antiques in varied states of disrepair. A dismantled cuckoo clock lay on the table in the center of the room, its bird dangling from a sad, limp spring. The warlock that owned the shop specialized in enchanting mundane objects, some of which had more nefarious purposes than others. The darkest spells left behind a residue, though Echo had been around magic long enough to be able to sense it, like a chill up her spine. As long as she avoided those objects, she'd be fine.

Most of the items on the table were either too rusty or too broken to be an option. A silver hand mirror was marred by a crack that divided its face in two. A rusted clock ticked away the seconds in reverse. Two halves of a heart-shaped locket lay in pieces, as if someone had smashed it with a hammer. The only object that appeared to be in working order was a music box. Its enamel paint was chipped and worn, but the flock of birds that graced its lid was drawn in lovely, elegant lines. Echo flipped the top open and a familiar tune drifted from the box as a tiny black bird rotated on its stand.

The magpie's lullaby, she thought, slipping her backpack off her shoulders. The Ala would love it, even if the concept of birthdays and the presents that accompanied them was all but lost on her.

Echo's hand was inches from the music box when the lights flared on. She snapped her head around to find a warlock standing in the shop's doorway. His chalky white eyes, the only thing that marked him as not quite human, zeroed in on Echo's hand.

"Caught you."

Crap. Some rules, it would seem, were meant to be broken.

"It's not what it looks like," Echo said. It wasn't her finest explanation, but it would have to do.

The warlock lifted a single eyebrow. "Really? Because it looks like you were planning on stealing from me."

"Okay, so I guess it's exactly what it looks like." Echo's eyes darted to a point behind the warlock. "Holy— What *is* that?"

For just a second, the warlock glanced over his shoulder, but it was all Echo needed. She grabbed the music box and shoved it in her bag, slinging the pack over her shoulder as she rushed forward, slamming into the warlock. He crashed to the floor with a shout as Echo bolted into the market square.

Rule number two, Echo thought, snagging a pork bun from a food stall as she sailed past it. *If you do get caught, run.*

The pavement was slick with the day's drizzle, and her boots skidded as she turned a corner. The market was teeming with shoppers packed in shoulder to shoulder, and the rich odors of street cuisine mixed in the balmy air. Echo bit into the bun, wincing at the steam that burned her tongue. Hot, but delicious. It was a universal truth that stolen food tasted better than food that wasn't stolen. Echo hopped over a murky puddle and nearly choked on a mouthful of sticky bread and roasted pork. Eating while running was harder than it looked.

She squeezed through the crowd, dodging rickety carts and gawking pedestrians. Sometimes being small paid off. The warlock on her tail was having a tougher time of it. Tourist-grade china clattered to the ground as he crashed into the pork bun stall and let loose a flurry of curses. Echo's Mandarin was sparse, but she was pretty sure he'd just lobbed a barrage of colorful insults at her and her parentage.

People got so touchy when their things were stolen. Especially warlocks.

Echo ducked beneath a low-hanging awning and glanced over her shoulder. The warlock had fallen behind, and there was a respectable amount of distance between them now. She took another bite of pork bun, crumbs flying. A magic-wielding psycho with a grudge might have been hot on her heels, but she hadn't eaten since the slice of cold pizza she'd had for breakfast. Hunger waited for no woman. The warlock shouted for a pair of policemen to stop her as she blew past them. Fingers glanced against her sleeve, but she was gone before they found purchase.

Fan-flipping-tastic, Echo thought, fighting the ache building in her muscles. *Almost there.*

The brightly lit sign for the Jiantan metro station came into view, and she gasped with relief. Once she was in the station, all she had to do was find a door, any door, and she would be gone in a puff of smoke. Or rather, a puff of sooty black powder.

Echo dropped the remainder of the pork bun into a nearby bin and rummaged in her pocket for the small pouch she never left home without. She catapulted herself over the turnstile, tossing a cursory "Sorry!" at the flummoxed station attendant as the stampede of booted feet closed in.

There was a utility closet on the platform less than fifty yards ahead that Echo knew would do nicely. She dug her fingers into the pouch to capture a handful of powder. Shadow dust. It was a generous amount, but the leap from Taipei to Paris was hardly a modest one. Better to be safe than sorry, even if it meant running perilously low for the trip back to New York.

Echo smeared the dust against the doorjamb and hurtled through it. The warlock shouted at her, but his cry, along with the sound of trains pulling into the station and the buzz of conversation on the platform, died as soon as the door shut behind her. For a brief moment, all was darkness. It wasn't nearly as disorienting as it had been the first time she'd traveled through the in-between places of the world, but it never stopped being strange. In the empty space between all the heres and all the theres, there was no up, down, left, or right. With every step, the ground shifted and warped beneath her feet. Echo swallowed the bile rising in her throat and thrust her hand out, deaf and blind in the vacuum of darkness. When her palm connected with the peeling paint of a door beneath the Arc de Triomphe, she sighed with relief.

The Arc was a popular way station for travelers of the in-between. With any luck, the warlock would have a hell of a time tracking her. Tracing a person's progress through the in-between was difficult but not impossible, and the warlock's dark magic would make it that much easier for him. As much as Echo loved Paris in the spring, she wouldn't be able to stay for long. It was a shame, she thought. The parks were lovely this time of year.

She made her way to the opposite end of the Arc, scanning the crowd for the familiar sight of a cap pulled low to hide a shock of vibrant feathers coupled with a pair of aviators worth more than her entire wardrobe. Jasper was one of her more mercurial contacts, but he was usually true to his word. She was about to give up and pick a door to ferry her back to New York when she saw it: a flash of bronze skin and the glare of sunglasses. Jasper waved, and Echo broke into a grin before cutting through the crowd at a brisk clip.

Her voice was breathy with exertion when she reached him. "You got the stuff?" she asked.

Jasper slid a small turquoise box out of his messenger bag, and Echo noticed that the door beside him already had a smear of shadow dust on its frame. Jasper could be thoughtful when he tried, which wasn't very often.

"Have I ever let you down?" he said.

Echo smiled. "Constantly."

Jasper's grin was equal parts dazzling and feral. He tossed the box to Echo with a wink strong enough to penetrate the reflective glass of his aviators. Echo popped up onto her toes to press a quick kiss to his cheek. She was through the door and into the in-between before he could summon a witty retort. She'd once told Jasper that he could have the last word when he pried it from her cold dead hands, and she meant it.

Crossing the threshold into the in-between was less jarring the second time around, but the contents of Echo's stomach still gave a mighty heave. She groped through the black, grimacing when her hands made contact with something solid. The doors leading to Grand Central Station were always grimy, even on this side of the in-between.

New York, she thought. *The city that never cleans.*

Echo exited into one of the corridors branching out from the main concourse. She paced around the information booth at its center, weaving between gaggles of tourists taking pictures of the constellations on the ceiling and commuters awaiting their trains. Not one of them knew there was an entire world beneath their feet, invisible to human eyes. Well, to most human eyes. As in the warlock's shop, one had to know what one was looking for. She'd give the warlock a handful of minutes to make an appearance. If he'd managed to follow her from the Arc, she wanted to make sure she didn't lead him to her front door. Echo had no proof, but she was certain that warlocks made terrible houseguests.

Her stomach rumbled. A few bites of pork bun wasn't going to cut it. She spared a thought for the hidden room in the New York Public Library that she called home, and the half-eaten burrito she'd left sitting on her desk. Earlier that day, she'd swiped it from an unsuspecting college student as he napped, head pillowed on a battered copy of *Les Misérables*. There had been poetry to that minor act of thievery. It was the only reason she'd done it. She didn't need to steal food to survive, as she had when she was a child, but some opportunities were too good to pass up.

Echo rolled her neck, letting the tension that had built up in her muscles work its way down her arms and out her fingers. Inch by inch, she let herself relax, listening to the rumble of trains in and out of the station. It was as soothing as a lullaby. With a final glance around the concourse, she hefted her bag over her shoulder and headed toward the Vanderbilt Avenue exit. Home was a scant few blocks west of Grand Central, and there was a stolen burrito with her name on it.

CHAPTER TWO

Two kinds of people camped out in the New York Public Library so late at night. There were the scholars: Caffeine-addled college students. Obsessively meticulous PhD candidates. Ambitious academics angling for tenure. And then there were the people who had nowhere else to go: People who sought solace in the comforting musk of old books and the quiet sounds of other humans breathing, turning pages, and stretching in their creaky wooden chairs. People who wanted to know that they weren't alone while being left alone. People like Echo.

She moved through the library like a ghost, feet quieter than a whisper over its marble steps. It was late enough that no one bothered to raise their eyes from their books to take notice of a young woman, dressed in head-to-toe black, slinking around where she had no business. Echo had long ago established a route that led around staff members counting the minutes until they got off work. She didn't need to worry about security cameras. America's librarians fought valiantly to keep their readers' privacy protected, and the library was a camera-free zone. It was one of the reasons why she'd chosen to make it her home.

She slipped through the library's narrow stacks, breathing in the familiar smell of stale books. As she climbed the darkened stairwell leading to her room, the air thickened with magic. The wards that the Ala had helped Echo set up pushed back at her, but the resistance was weak. They were designed to recognize her. Had anyone else stumbled upon the staircase, they would have turned back, remembering that they'd left the stove on or were running late for a meeting, but the spell rebounded off her.

At the top of the stairs was a door, as beige and plain as any other utility closet, but it too had magic all its own. Echo slipped her Swiss Army knife from her back pocket and flicked it open. She pressed the tip of the small knife into the pad of her pinkie and watched a bead of blood well up.

"By my blood," Echo whispered.

She touched the drop of scarlet to the door, and the air crackled with electricity, raising the fine hairs at the back of her neck. A quiet click sounded, and the door unlocked. Just as she did every time she entered the cramped room overflowing with treasures she'd liberated over the years, she kicked the door shut behind her and said, to no one in particular, "Honey, I'm home."

The silence that answered was a welcome change from the shrill symphony of Taipei and the cacophonous crowds of New York at rush hour. Echo slung her bag onto the floor beside the writing desk she'd salvaged from the library's recycling pile and collapsed on her chair. She flicked on the fairy lights strung around the room, casting the cozy space in a warm glow.

Before her lay the burrito she'd been dreaming about, surrounded by the odds and ends that decorated every available surface of her room. There were tiny jade elephants from Phuket. Geodes from amethyst mines in South Korea. An original Fabergé egg, encrusted with rubies and trimmed with gold. Surrounding it all were stacks of books, crammed on every available surface, piled on top of each other in teetering towers. Some Echo had read a dozen times, others not at all. Their mere presence was a comfort. She hoarded them just as eagerly as she hoarded her other treasures. Her seven-year-old self had decided that stealing books was morally bankrupt, but since the books hadn't left the library—they'd merely been relocated—it wasn't *technically* stealing. Echo looked around at her sea of tomes, and a single word came to mind: *tsundoku.*

It was the Japanese word for letting books pile up without reading them all. Words were another thing Echo hoarded. She'd started that collection long before she'd ever come to the library, back when she lived in a house she preferred not to remember, with a family she'd have been happier forgetting. Back then, the only books she'd had belonged to a set of outdated encyclopedias. She'd had few possessions to call her own, but she'd always had her words. And now she had a trove full of stolen treasures, some more edible than others.

She raised the burrito to her lips, poised to take a bite, when the sound of fluttering feathers interrupted her. Only one person had the ability to bypass her wards without raising a single alarm, and she never bothered to knock. Echo sighed. *Rude.*

"You know, I've heard that in some cultures," Echo began, "people knock. But then, that could just be idle gossip."

She swiveled in her chair, burrito in hand. The Ala sat on the corner of Echo's bed, black feathers ruffling gently, as if caught on a breeze. But there was no breeze. There was only the Ala and the slight charge to the air that accompanied her power.

"Don't be moody," the Ala said, smoothing her arm feathers. "It makes you sound positively adolescent."

Echo took an exaggerated bite of the burrito and spoke around a mouthful of rice and beans. "Truth in advertising." The Ala frowned. Echo swallowed. "I *am* adolescent." If Echo had abysmal table manners, the Ala had only herself to blame.

"Only when it suits you," the Ala said.

Chewing with her mouth open was a perfectly reasonable response as far as Echo was concerned.

"Anyway," the Ala sighed, surveying the shelves overflowing with shiny knickknacks of every variety, "I'm glad you've returned, my little magpie. Steal anything nice today?"

Echo pushed her backpack toward the Ala with a toe. "As a matter of fact, I did. Happy birthday."

The Ala tutted, but the sound was more pleased than disappointed. "I don't understand your obsession with birthdays. I'm far too old to remember mine."

"I know, and that's why I assigned one to you," Echo said. "Now open it. My bacon was almost burned by a warlock getting that thing."

"Just one?" The Ala's words were tinged with laughter. She slipped the music box from the backpack, handling it with more care than it looked like it deserved. "I wouldn't think a single warlock would be a problem for such a talented thief. You did, after all, boast of your ability to—what did you call it—'B and E' with the best of them."

Echo scowled, though the effect was mitigated by the shredded cheese dangling from her lower lip. "Throw that back in my face, why don't you?"

"If I didn't, how would you ever learn the folly of your arrogance?" A gentle smile softened the Ala's chiding. "The young always think they're invincible, right until the moment they learn otherwise. Usually, the hard way."

Echo's only response was a half shrug. The Ala cast a glance about the room, and Echo wondered what it looked like to someone besides herself. Books piled precariously high on every surface. Pilfered jewels worth enough to pay for college twice over. A riot of crinkled candy bar wrappers. It was a mess, but it was her mess. From the wrinkle forming between the Ala's brows, Echo didn't think she appreciated the significance of that.

"Why do you stay here, Echo? You can come to the Nest and live with us. I know a fair few Avicelings that wouldn't mind having you near."

"I need my space" was all Echo said.

What she didn't say was that she needed space away from the Avicen. Her own smooth skin, bare of the colorful feathers that decorated their limbs, was enough to signal that she didn't belong. She didn't need their sidelong stares to remind her that she was among them but not of them. And stare they did. As if her presence disrupted the natural order of things. They might have gotten used to Echo over the years, but that didn't mean they had to like her.

The library was her home. Books didn't give her dirty looks or whisper snide comments under their breath. Books didn't judge. Books had been her only friends before the Ala had found her, alone and hungry, and whisked her away to the Avicen Nest. These books were her family, her teachers, her companions. They had remained loyal to her, so she would remain loyal to them.

The Ala's weary sigh was as familiar a sound to Echo as the beating of her own heart. "Fine. Have it your way." She looked down at the music box in her hands. "This is lovely."

Echo shrugged, but she couldn't fight the pleased grin that found its way to her face. "It was the best I could do, given the circumstances."

The Ala cranked the knob at the base of the music box a few times before lifting the lid. The little bird spun in place as the tinny melody wafted into the air.

"The magpie's lullaby," Echo said. "That's why I picked it." She lazily waved her fingers in the air as though she were conducting a tiny orchestra. *"One for sorrow, two for mirth."*

The Ala smiled fondly. *"Three for a funeral and four for a birth."*

"Five for silver, six for gold," Echo sang. They finished the last line together. *"And seven for a secret not to be told."*

Just as the last note rang out, a compartment slid open near the base of the box. It had blended so seamlessly with the lacquered wood that Echo hadn't even noticed it. The Ala removed a folded piece of paper from the compartment. "What's that?" Echo asked.

The Ala unfolded it with careful fingers. She cocked her head to the side, gaze still locked on the paper. "What made you choose this music box?" she asked. Her voice was low and cautious, as if the words were chosen with the utmost care.

"I thought it was pretty," Echo said. "And it played our lullaby." She leaned forward to peer at the paper, but her view was blocked by the Ala's hands. "What *is* that?"

The Ala rose to her feet, folding the paper once more, movements quick and precise. She tucked it into one of the pockets hidden in the folds of her gown. "Come. We can discuss it at the Nest."

"Can it wait?" Echo asked, waving the burrito at the Ala. Little bits of rice and cheese plopped onto her lap. "I'm about to go to town on this burrito."

The Ala's arched eyebrow was all the answer Echo needed.

"Fine," she mumbled, placing the burrito back in its foil. It looked so sad, alone and half eaten. It was downright mournful. She stood, brushing off her jeans and picking up her backpack. "But this had better be worth it."

"Oh, it will be," the Ala said, sprinkling a handful of shadow dust into the air around them. The inky black tendrils of the in-between snaked around her legs, and Echo's stomach gave a preemptive lurch. Traveling through the in-between was never fun, but without the anchoring solidity of a doorway, it was a wretched experience. The Ala held out a hand to Echo. "Remind me, child, have I ever told you the story of the firebird?"

CHAPTER THREE

Even through the thick stone walls of Wyvern's Keep, Caius could hear the sounds of the ocean pounding against the rocks below. A wicked Scottish wind beat at the outer walls, and the sea roared with it, crashing against the fortress's foundations with unrelenting fury. He envied the waters their passion, their rage, their unmitigated frenzy in the face of such an immovable object. He closed his eyes and imagined for a moment that he could feel the spray of the ocean on his face, that he could steal from it even the smallest fraction of its strength. But Caius was not the ocean, and the obstacles he faced were as sturdy as any stone edifice.

"Your loyalty is commendable," he said, turning to the two prisoners behind him. "Truly."

A pair of Avicen scouts knelt on the floor of the keep's dungeon, wrists shackled behind their backs with heavy iron manacles. Their plumage might have once been richly colored, but their feathers were now matted with a thick layer of filth and blood. The one on the left, feathers speckled like those of a tawny owl, swayed on his knees as he struggled to stay upright. The Avicen next to him reminded Caius of a falcon, small and sleek, with sharp yellow eyes. That one refused to tremble. He was a rock, steady and still. Thinking of them in terms of the birds they looked like was simpler than asking their names. If Caius saw them as animals, then it would make it easier to do what he knew he must. The falcon spat at his feet, flecks of blood mingled with saliva spattering Caius's boots.

"We won't tell you anything." The falcon remained defiant, even in the face of the Dragon Prince himself. Commendable indeed.

Caius nodded to the two guards standing behind the Avicen. They were Firedrakes, the most fearsome regiment in the Drakharin army. A pair was overkill for two half-starved prisoners, but sometimes a point needed to be made. The Firedrakes seized the owl by his arms while the falcon looked on in horror.

"You won't," Caius said, "but he will."

Half-mad pleas for mercy fell from the owl's cracked lips as the Firedrakes hauled him to his feet. Their golden armor glinted in the low light of the dungeon's torches, and the dragons emblazoned on their breastplates danced in the flames. The owl's babbling continued as he was dragged before Caius. It was a shame the roar of the sea wasn't loud enough to drown it out.

Caius laid a hand on the owl's cheek, careful not to press into the bruises there. The owl shuddered at his touch and went silent.

"Tell me what I want to know." Caius's voice was low and

soft, as if he were coaxing a frightened animal out of its hiding place. "And I promise I will be merciful."

The falcon fought to scrabble to his feet, but one of the Firedrakes kicked the back of his knee, sending him crashing to the floor in a heap of feathers and rage.

"Dragons don't know the first thing about mercy," the falcon hissed, eyes aflame with barely checked fury. The Firedrake pressed his heel into the falcon's throat, silencing him.

Caius ignored him, steady gaze never leaving the owl. "Why were you in Japan? The Drakharin hold that land, and have for nearly a century. What business did you have there?"

The owl licked his cracked lips, eyes flicking from Caius to his comrade on the ground.

That won't do, Caius thought. He tightened his grip just enough to bring the Avicen's attention back to him.

"Despite what you may have heard," Caius said, "I am a man of my word. Speak now, and I will show you and your friend the mercy you deserve."

The owl swallowed, blinking rapidly. His too-wide pupils dilated and retracted with alarming speed. When he spoke, his words were so quiet Caius had to lean in to hear them.

"The general sent us."

Caius ground his teeth so hard, his jaw clicked. "The general. Altair."

The owl nodded, head bobbing in short, quick jerks, so like the bird he resembled.

Caius stroked the owl's cheek with his thumb. A fine tremor worked its way up from the Avicen prisoner's feet to the ruffled feathers at his temples. "And what did Altair ask of you?"

"Traitor," the falcon spat at his companion. The Fire-drake ground his boot down again, and the Avicen's next words were nothing more than a pained gurgle. The owl's trembling evolved into a full-body shake, the feathers on his arms quivering. He tried to look back at his comrade, but Caius held his head in place.

"Go on."

The owl licked his lips again, worrying the bottom one with his teeth. "The general . . . he sent us to Kyoto. To a teahouse. There was an old woman living there, but she didn't know anything about what Altair is looking for."

Caius's hand stilled, resting on the curve of the owl's neck. He stroked the skin above the owl's fluttering pulse with his thumb. "And what is that?"

"The firebird."

Caius had to fight to keep his face as blank and placid as the mask he wore at court. So long had he waited to hear another speak that word.

"And did you find anything else besides an elderly human woman?"

"No," the owl said, shaking his head in little birdlike twitches. "Nothing."

"Nothing," Caius repeated. Of course it was nothing. It was always nothing.

Releasing the owl from his hold, Caius stepped back. He resisted the urge to wipe his palm on his thigh.

"Thank you. Your cooperation will be rewarded." Caius nodded to the Firedrakes once more. They pulled the owl back and yanked the falcon to his feet.

"Kill them."

The owl's eyes flashed with the first bit of fire Caius had seen in him. "You promised us mercy."

"This is mercy," Caius said, already turning away. "Your deaths will be quick."

As the two Avicen were dragged deeper into the belly of the dungeon, Caius let his eyes fall shut. He could still see the owl's strange, wide eyes as clearly as he had seconds before, but the image disintegrated as his audience broke her silence at last.

Clap. Clap. Clap.

Caius turned to the sound. His sister, Tanith, stood before him, resplendent in her gilded armor, even with a layer of soot and rust-colored blood adorning it. A few locks of blond hair had fallen loose from her braid, framing her face with soft gold. Her crimson eyes gleamed with mirth. It had been her Firedrakes who had intercepted the two Avicen, and she'd paraded them, bloodied and broken, before Caius with a zeal that made his stomach turn. A bloody Tanith was a happy Tanith. A happy Tanith was the last thing Caius needed. It was the last thing anyone needed. Anywhere. Ever.

At least one of us enjoyed the show, he thought.

"Well done, Brother. I was beginning to think you'd lost your touch." Tanith stepped forward, armor clinking as she walked. The heavy scarlet cloak fastened around her shoulders dragged along the stone floor with an audible hiss. "But as amusing as that demonstration was, it was still a colossal waste of time. You can't find the firebird because there's nothing to find. It isn't real, no matter what some crackpot Avicen general thinks."

Caius dragged a hand through his dark hair. It had grown long in the past several weeks, and he wondered if his courtiers found him too scruffy for a prince. "All I need is more time."

"You've wasted all the time you have," Tanith countered, "chasing a mythical beast that doesn't exist. A mythical beast that might not even be a beast at all, mind you. Time grows short, and your nobles grow weary."

"I am their prince," Caius said sharply. "For me, they will make time."

"You're only their prince so long as they want you to be. So long as you deserve that title." Tanith shook her head, golden braid brushing against one of her epaulets. They were twins, but aside from their high cheekbones, dusted with a smattering of dragon scales, they had little in common. Caius had always been the quiet one, stoic and studious, while Tanith was fire and passion and rage. "You would do well to remember that."

"Is that a threat?" Caius asked. He never quite knew with his sister.

"No. Merely a statement of truth." She smiled, but it was dry and joyless. "Dragons aren't known for their patience. This hunt for the firebird . . . it's folly, Brother."

Caius turned from Tanith and paced to the ornate fireplace that dominated the far wall of the dungeon. It was flanked by two stone dragons, mouths open wide so they would have looked like they were breathing fire had the flames not died down to embers hours ago. He could hear Tanith shifting behind him, impatient as ever. It was petty, but he made her wait a few moments before speaking.

"Are you questioning my judgment?" Caius asked, wiping

the mud off his hands with a scrap of cloth left on the mantel. The owl had been filthy.

Tanith snorted, indelicate as ever. "It wouldn't be the first time I've had to. Or have you forgotten . . . oh, what was her name?"

Caius turned back to the stone dragons with their blank, emerald stares. He did not supply a name. Tanith had not forgotten it, and neither had he. The silence between them was heavy with the weight of all that remained unsaid.

"That was a long time ago," Caius said softly. "Hardly worth remembering." He wondered if Tanith would be able to detect the lie in his voice.

"Those who forget their history," Tanith said, moving to his side so she could gaze at his face, "are doomed to repeat it." She held her hand up, and a tongue of fire sprouted from her palm. She flicked her fingers toward the hearth, and the embers sprang back to life with a searing heat. "This firebird is going to be another mess of yours I'll have to clean up."

Caius rested his hands on the mantel, dropping his head so his long bangs obscured his view of Tanith. He was tired. Tired of this conversation, tired of trying to convince Tanith of the burning certainty he felt about his course of action, tired of ignoring the pointed glances and curious whispers of his own people as the days came and went with little to show for them.

"The firebird is real." He had been singing this song for a hundred years, and still Tanith refused to be swayed. "It's real, and it's our only hope of ending this war."

The hand that came to rest on his shoulder was small but strong from years of handling a sword. He hadn't heard her remove her gauntlets, but she must have. He was tired, and it was making him slow.

"The firebird is a myth, Caius. A fairy tale. Nothing more. You've lost sight of what's important."

The absolute gall of her. He turned to face his sister. "If this isn't important, if finding the firebird is a waste of time and resources, then what is important? What's important to you, Tanith, if not ending this war as quickly as possible?"

"Victory," she said, without a hint of hesitation. It was so easy for her. It always had been. He envied her that simplicity. How comforting it must be. "You know as well as I do that this cease-fire is a farce, and it's only a matter of time before open war erupts, especially if they keep sending spies into our territory."

"Like we send spies into theirs?" Caius asked.

"You say that like war is supposed to be fair."

"I'm not that naive."

"Could have fooled me," Tanith said. "Tell me again how much time, how many resources you've wasted on this fruitless search?"

"I don't consider the expenditure a waste. I'm trying to help our people by putting an end to this war. The firebird is prophesied to do just that."

"I'm trying to do the same, but prophecies aren't worth the paper they're written on. Our people need tangible results, Caius. Not fairy tales."

Fairy tales, Caius thought. *If I never hear those words again, it'll be too soon.* "Have you ever asked yourself why you fight?"

Tanith shrugged, firelight glinting off her soiled armor. "I fight because I must. The Avicen began this blood feud.

I'm going to end it. Their greed for power stole ours. The Drakharin once had enough magic to transform themselves into dragons. Real dragons, Caius. We once soared through the skies and breathed fire on our foes."

Caius's lips twitched into a ghost of a smile. "Now who's quoting fairy tales?"

Tanith cupped her palms and blew into them. A tiny ball of flame erupted, hovering over her skin like a will-o'-the-wisp. "Some of us still breathe fire, Brother."

"You summon it," Caius said. "A fine distinction. And even if that old tale were true, destroying the Avicen won't bring back what we've lost."

Tanith clapped her hands, and the fire extinguished. "Believe what you want. I believe in what I can see and touch. Even if destroying the Avicen won't restore our magic, it'll make me feel better. I want justice for our people and an end to the Avicen threat. Those are the things that should concern you, Caius. Not a magical bird you read about in a book."

Caius rolled his neck and arched his back, stretching. He needed rest and soon. "I did not read about it in a book. I read about it in several books, thank you very much."

"Yes, and half of them were written by Avicen. Mind your sources, Brother. They aren't to be trusted."

"I'm sick of fighting." Caius's voice was quiet, but he knew Tanith would hear him perfectly well, though whether or not she would listen was another matter entirely. "Aren't you?" It was a foolish question, for he knew what her answer would be, but still, he had to ask.

Tanith canted her head. Torchlight caught the delicate iridescence of the scales that trailed along her cheekbones.

She blinked at him, red eyes gleaming in the firelight, and said, simply, "No."

The word hung in the air between them, a neat and tidy summation of the rift that had been growing for years. It hadn't always been like this. Once, they'd been inseparable. They'd galloped around this very same fortress, carried aloft on invisible horses, clashing blunt wooden swords as they played at a war they hardly understood. But the girl with the unruly golden curls and chubby hands made sticky from sweets was a far cry from the woman who stood before him now, magnificent and terrible, proudly stained with the blood of her foes. His sister had grown into something beautiful and savage and absolutely foreign to him. He missed her sometimes, the girl she had been before years of battle and bloodshed had forged her into steel.

Tanith's eyes softened around the edges. For a moment, she was his sister again. Not his general, but his sister. "We need to act before the Avicen do. If we wait any longer, I fear what it would mean for the Drakharin. I want the best for our people, same as you."

With a heavy sigh, Caius stepped away from her. He'd had enough of her and her doubts. "Thank you, Tanith, that will be all."

Tanith studied him, her expression hard and unreadable. Caius waited for her to protest her dismissal. As the highest-ranking officer in the Drakharin army, Tanith was more accustomed to giving orders than taking them, but there was one person she did not outrank, and that was Caius. He was the Dragon Prince—the youngest ever elected to the position—and had been for a century. He'd proved himself worthy of the title through years of battle and politics. His sister occasionally needed reminding that it was his head, not hers, upon which the crown of the Drakharin sat.

After a full minute, Tanith extended her arms, sketching out a shallow bow. "As my prince commands."

If Tanith's insincerity were gold, Caius thought, *I'd be a rich man indeed.*

CHAPTER FOUR

Echo was glad she'd skipped the burrito. As the dark of the in-between gave way to the soft, golden glow of the Ala's chamber, the contents of her stomach roiled as if she were at sea, even though they hadn't traveled far. The Nest lay right below the library on Fifth Avenue, but as far as Echo knew, she was the only human aware of its existence. It always felt this way, traveling with the Ala without a man-made threshold to anchor her passage. The Ala remained as unruffled as ever. Her black feathers were smooth and silky, as dark as the in-between itself. Maybe the Ala carried a little bit of it inside her. It would explain how she could wrap it around herself like a cloak and travel wherever she pleased, threshold or no. Echo gave herself a moment to adjust as the last lingering tendrils of the in-between faded in the air like smoke on the wind.

"What's this about a firebird?" Echo asked, rubbing soothing circles on her stomach. "I thought that was just a human fairy tale. Pretty sure I read about it in a book of Russian folklore."

"Every good fairy tale has a kernel of truth to it." The Ala led Echo to the heart of her little nest, with its odd array of mismatched furniture, tapestries, and pillows. Bowls of assorted sweets were strategically sprinkled about the room. The Avicen sweet tooth was the stuff of legend. Echo had many a memory of losing herself in that sea of pillows as she begged the Ala for just one more story—and one more cookie—before bed. "And more than a few human myths are pulled from our own legends. You should hear the things they say about me. In certain parts of Serbia, they believe that a demon named the Ala eats babies and controls the weather. Baby-eating." She punctuated the word with a short, sharp laugh as she settled on a wicker chair in the center of the room and beckoned for Echo to join her. "Preposterous."

"I always knew there was something fishy about you." Echo set her backpack on the floor and grabbed a whoopie pie from the plate atop the small wooden end table before collapsing face-first onto a chaise longue upholstered with a burgundy velvet that smelled faintly of lavender. No nausea was so great that it couldn't be cured with a whoopie pie. Voice muffled by the couch, Echo added, "Now, are you gonna tell me about the mystery paper you pulled out of that box or what? The suspense is killing me."

The Ala slipped the parchment from her pocket and unfolded it with careful fingers. "This, Echo dear, is the most important map you're likely to see in your lifetime."

Echo sat up and propped her feet on the ancient cedar chest that doubled as a table. As was the Ala's style, it matched nothing else in the room. She reached out a hand

and wiggled her fingers. After a moment's hesitation, the Ala relinquished the map. It was small, with ragged edges, as if it had been torn from a larger whole, creases gone as soft as cotton where it had been folded. The colors had faded to a range of sepia tones, but the barest hint of blue clung to a river that laced through the center of the map, interrupted by a phrase written in neatly drawn kanji. Circled in brown ink that must have once been red was a modest home in the district west of the river. Echo ran her fingers along the kanji, and though her grasp of written Japanese was only slightly better than her Mandarin—which wasn't saying much—she recognized the words. She'd seen them often enough on her own maps, tucked away with the atlases she kept in a dedicated corner of her room in the library. The slash of blue was the Kamo River in Kyoto. Near the bottom edge of the map, someone had written a few lines of text in neat block letters, along with what Echo assumed was a date: 1915.

She squinted at the text and read, "'Where flowers bloom, you'll find your way, through the darkness and the flames, but beware the price that you must pay, for only the worthy will know my name.'" She scrunched her brow and looked up at the Ala. "I don't get it. What's so important about a hundred-year-old map of Kyoto with a weird rhyme on it?"

The Ala took the map with reverent hands. "I know the Avicen who wrote it," she said. "And I believe I know why it was written." She stood, placing the map on the coffee table between them and went over to the bookshelf nestled in a corner of the room. Books were squished along its length, packed in tighter than they should have been. Echo remembered pulling them off the shelves after the Ala had taken her in and reading the ones she could understand. Some were written in Avicet, a language that still eluded Echo after all these years, but the Ala had read to her at night, translating as she went. They were mostly historical texts, detailing the development of Avicen culture over the years; some covered the Avicen's migration to the eastern part of North America and the reasons why they'd stayed even when human metropolises began to boom along the coastline, forcing them below ground. When Echo had asked why the Avicen stuck around, the Ala had merely tutted and said, "We were here first." A few books detailed the Avicen's political structure—an oligarchy headed by a Council of Elders comprising six of the community's oldest members, of which the Ala was one—while others, like the one the Ala took off the shelf, dealt with esoteric mythology. About three inches thick, the leather-bound tome was written in a form of Avicet so old that few could read it.

"Wait a minute. If an Avicen left this map behind, then why is the rhyme written in English?" Echo asked.

"As with so many of the young ones, English was her first language," the Ala replied. "Avicet is so rarely spoken these days."

"Young?" Echo took another look at the date. "This is a hundred years old."

"Youth is a relative concept." The Ala returned to her seat, flipping through the book's weathered pages. "Here." Her fingers landed on an illustration near the center of the book. She angled it toward Echo. Without knowledge of old Avicet, Echo couldn't make sense of the words, but the image caught her attention. A bird, outlined in bloodred ink, hovered on the page, as if frozen in flight, its golden wings upraised, feathers transitioning to flames at their tips. Tendrils of black smoke clung to its clawed feet as it rose above a pile of ash, beak open in a silent screech.

"This," the Ala said, "is the firebird." She pointed to the words scribbled beneath the illustration. "'When the price is paid,'" she translated, "'the worthy will know my name. When the clock strikes midnight, the end will come.'"

"The end?" Echo frowned, looking between the Ala and the book. "This is starting to sound ominous. I don't know if I can handle ominous on an empty stomach."

The Ala leaned toward Echo, serious and somber. "According to our prophecies, the firebird will bring about the end of this war with the Drakharin, but the nature of that end is up to whoever controls it." With a swat at Echo's boots, the Ala added, "And get your feet off my table."

"Pause," Echo said, putting her feet on the ground. "Rewind. Explain to me how a bird is supposed to end a war."

"The firebird isn't exactly a bird."

"No, of course not, that would be too obvious," Echo mumbled, biting into the whoopie pie. "So what is it?"

The feathers on the Ala's arms ruffled in frustration. "We don't know. Not exactly. Some say it's really just a single golden feather capable of granting wishes. Others claim it's the name for a creature that became extinct long ago. There's even a small subset of scholars who believe it's a bird that can breathe fire."

Echo quirked an eyebrow. "Kind of like a dragon?"

Pride gleamed in the Ala's eyes. "Clever girl. Avicen and Drakharin mythologies have been known to overlap on occasion. What we do know is that, whatever its form, it is neither good nor evil. It can be used to accomplish great things. But greatness is not always good."

"Yeah, yeah." Echo picked at the bits of cream filling drooping over the sides of the whoopie pie. "One ring to rule them all, I get it. But I'm still not clear on why the Avicen and the Drakharin have been at war for so long. I mean, they hate each other, but like . . . why?"

The Ala leaned back in her chair, running a hand through the long, soft feathers on her head. "The Drakharin blame the Avicen for their slow fade in power over the years—a spurious charge. As if such a thing were even possible, but desperation makes people believe crazy things. Magic courses through this world like an unseen ocean. It flows, in and out, like a tide. When the Drakharin felt that tide receding, they wanted someone to blame. Animosity has simmered between our people over petty grievances for millennia, so the Avicen made a convenient target. I doubt it was as calculated as that, but the seed of that idea grew until no one questioned its validity. Now fighting fuels more fighting, and hatred breeds more hatred. It almost doesn't matter why the war began. We've fought for so long that I fear we've forgotten how to do anything else. But I know, in my soul, that the tide is changing. The firebird is no simple legend told to little Avicelings before bedtime. It is rising. I can sense it like the surge of a wave on the horizon."

"You got some good mileage out of that sea metaphor. I'm impressed," Echo said.

The Ala sighed. "Is everything a joke to you?"

"Only the things that matter." Echo shrugged. "So, let's say this firebird thingy is real. What are we going to do about it?"

"*We* are going to do nothing." The Ala shook her head, peering around the room. Her eyes came to rest on the dark walnut sideboard so loaded with candles of every size and shape that their combined flames emitted as much light as a roaring fire. "For now, just keep this to yourself. I don't need the general finding out I have it."

"Altair?" Echo asked. "What does he have to do with anything?"

The Ala pursed her lips and huffed out a frustrated breath. "Let's just say that Altair has been interested in the firebird for some time now. He's what one would call a true believer, and searching for the firebird has been a priority of his for over a century. At one time, the other members of the Council of Elders agreed with him, and he managed to sway even the most ardent of skeptics. A vote was held about a hundred years ago that determined the hunt was worthy of a military operation."

"Really?" Echo said. "I can't imagine the councilors in charge of things like food distribution and living arrangements would be game for military shenanigans."

The Ala's expression hardened. "Five of the six councilors voted to send out an operative whose sole mission was to find the firebird. I was the lone dissenter."

"Why?" Echo said. "Wouldn't finding the firebird be a good thing?"

"Finding it wasn't what I took issue with," the Ala said. "I didn't—and don't—believe that Altair is the best person to control it. The Avicen government is run by the council, but he can be persuasive when he wants to be. I fear that in his hands, the firebird would become a weapon. I hope that one day this conflict finds its resolution, but I prefer to seek out peace, not more death." She motioned toward the map. "The notes on that map were written by that operative." She paused. Sadness flitted across her face for the briefest second before she schooled her features. Echo wanted to ask what was wrong, but the moment passed and the Ala continued. "The last communication we received from her was sent from a safe house in Kyoto that was Avicen-controlled until the Drakharin won that territory from us in the 1920s. After the operative disappeared, the trail of the firebird went cold, and the council lost interest in Altair's zealous quest soon after. He has sent spies into Kyoto once or twice since then, but the Drakharin have strengthened the wards around their territory so much that it's practically impossible for Avicen to sneak past them undetected."

Echo nodded. The Ala had always been candid with her, but she'd never before shared this much information about the inner workings of the Avicen government. "Okay, my lips are sealed, but if Altair asked you about it, couldn't you just tell him to mind his own damn business?"

The Ala sighed. "Unfortunately, dear, that's not how a government by committee works. Altair and I are both members of the council, and as such our word holds equal weight."

"Yeah, but someone's word should lose a little weight if he's an asshole," said Echo.

The Ala tutted, but she couldn't hold back a tiny smile. Her long-standing dislike of the general was a poorly guarded secret. "Ah, if only we were a dictatorship like the Drakharin."

"Well, I think you'd be a benevolent dictator," Echo said. "At least for a few years. Before your inner Stalin kicked in." She took a final bite of whoopie pie. "Power corrupts."

"I appreciate the vote of confidence," said the Ala. "But

what I would appreciate more right now is a little silence while I figure out how to proceed. This message was left behind like this—and not sent to Altair—for a reason."

"Do you think the firebird is in Kyoto?" Echo asked.

The Ala shook her head. "No, if it were, Altair would have found it years ago." She heaved a weary sigh and waved in the general direction of the door. "I need time to think. Go, run along."

"Works for me." Echo pushed herself up from the chaise longue. "I've got a bag of stolen candy that's not gonna eat itself." She hefted her backpack over her shoulder and made her way to the door. With one hand on the knob, she turned back to look at the Ala, stooped over the map. There was so much she wanted to ask, but she'd never before seen such sadness on the Ala's face. Prying didn't feel quite right.

"Hey, Ala?"

The Ala hmmed in response but didn't look up from the map.

Echo tapped her fingers against the knob. *One for sorrow, two for mirth.* "The person who was sent after the firebird . . . did you know her well?"

The Ala tore her eyes away from the map, blinking up at Echo as though she were surfacing from the bottom of a pool. When she spoke, her voice was far away, as if weighed down by sadness. "I thought I did," the Ala said. "But sometimes I wonder if it's possible to ever really know anyone."

CHAPTER FIVE

Echo was no more than two steps beyond the Ala's door when she was besieged by a pack of children. They might as well have been raised by wolves, for all the supervision they received from the elder Avicen. Like frenzied urchins, they clung to Echo's legs, clamoring for her attention. The downy feathers tufted on their arms and heads came in all hues. They were the sapphire shades of bluebirds, and the vivid red of cardinals, and even the soft bubble-gum pink of flamingo feathers. And each of the children was vying to be heard over the rest.

"Echo, Echo!"

"What did you bring us?"

"—is there candy, you said there'd be candy, last time there was no candy—"

"—Echo, Flint pushed me, and then I pulled on his feathers, but then he—"

"Enough, enough!" Echo shouted with a laugh. "Yes,

I brought you candy"—a cheer rose through the tiny crowd—"and, Flint, you shouldn't push people, if you have a crush on Daisy, you'll stand a better chance if you just tell her nicely"—a small red-feathered Aviceling grumbled in protest—"and, Daisy, good girl, somebody hits you, you hit 'em back, just like I taught you."

Echo pulled a paper bag full of colorful rock candy from her backpack. "Here, you fiends." She tossed the bag into the cluster of Avicelings. "Eat it all at once. Make yourselves sick. That'll teach you the dangers of your gluttony. Little beasts."

A quiet laugh came from one of the archways leading deeper into the Nest. Echo broke into a grin when she spotted an Avicen with familiar white feathers and the jet-black eyes of a dove.

"Greetings," Echo said, bending into an exaggerated bow, "my sister from another mister."

"Greeting, Echo, queen of the orphans." Ivy curtsied. They'd been best friends since the day Echo had arrived at the Nest as a child, bonding the way only two seven-year-olds could. Ivy waved at Daisy, who pushed Flint aside long enough to wave back, grinning toothily around a bright pink chunk of rock candy. "You're like Oliver Twist to those kids."

Echo extracted herself from the gaggle of children that had lost interest in her the second she'd relinquished her candy. She skipped over to Ivy, linking their arms together.

"I always saw myself as more of an Artful Dodger." Echo pulled Ivy down the stone hallway that would take them to the heart of the Nest. It was designed a bit like a wagon wheel. All roads led to the center, which housed the massive gateway that acted as the Avicen's primary point of access to the in-between and the world beyond. "You're Oliver Twist."

"Whatever you say, Artful Dodger." Ivy laughed. "I take it you stole that candy."

"I liberated it." Echo rummaged through her bag once more, fingers closing around a carefully wrapped honey cake. "I also liberated this." She handed the cake to Ivy, whose efficient fingers made quick work of the pink paper wrapping before she took an obscenely large bite.

Around a mouthful of half-chewed cake, Ivy said, "Please, sir, may I have another?"

"Ew." Echo wrinkled her nose. Someone had to maintain an air of civility. "It's almost like you were raised with a deficit of adult supervision."

"Been reading your big fancy books with their big fancy words again?" Ivy swallowed the cake in a single gulp. It was like she hadn't even bothered chewing. "And yeah, it was exactly like that, actually."

Echo had not been the first lost child the Ala had taken in, nor, she suspected, would she be the last. War had a way of making orphans. Like Daisy. Like Flint. Like Ivy. They walked along the warmly lit corridor, and Echo nodded at the few passing Avicen she recognized. There was the green-feathered Tulip, who made a living selling odds and ends like buttons and mismatched tea sets. An older Avicen named Willow, who draped herself in brightly colored scarves and crooned for dollars in the subway. The blue-eyed Fennel, who obsessively collected purple straws.

"I'm feeling decidedly celebratory," Echo said.

"Thievery go well, then?" Ivy asked.

"*Well* might be an exaggeration. I had a run-in with a warlock and some cops and just barely made it out by the skin of my teeth."

Ivy's brows drew together in concern. "Echo—"

Echo took Ivy by the hand and twirled her. It was just as Fred Astaire had twirled Ginger Rogers. Echo's knowledge of dancing was almost entirely informed by the library's collection of old movies. "Chill, Ivy. Don't lay an egg."

Ivy twirled away from Echo, moving to a tune only she could hear. "That wasn't funny the first five hundred times."

"Yes, it was," Echo said. "But anyway, I got the booty, made it back in one piece, and I'm thinking victory drinks are in order."

Ivy snorted. "Ha. Booty."

"You're a disgrace."

"Whatever," Ivy said, spinning to a wobbly stop in front of Echo. They'd reached the gateway, an architectural wonder that never failed to take Echo's breath away. Two black swans, fashioned from delicately rendered iron, held their necks aloft, beaks meeting at the very top and forming an arch. On their backs sat two massive cast-iron braziers holding fires that burned perpetually. Echo and Ivy joined the queue. Two Avicen stood in front of them: one as wide as he was tall, which was not very, and a stately older woman with hair-feathers that were a lovely shade of dusty pink.

"You were saying something about victory drinks?" Ivy stepped forward as the Avicen woman threw her handful of dust into a bowl of fire. The air between the swans' necks shimmered as she stepped into it before a cloud of black smoke rose. When the cloud dispersed, the Avicen was gone. "I hear London is lovely this time of year."

Echo weighed the pouch of shadow dust in her pocket. Just enough to make the trip. "Maison Bertaux?"

Ivy nodded. "Maison Bertaux."

CHAPTER SIX

Maison Bertaux sat on a narrow side street in Soho, sandwiched between an Indian restaurant and an old-fashioned British pub, a neat microcosm of modern-day London. Its display case, decorated with cheerfully fluttering Union Jacks, was bursting with pastries of every kind. Delicate marzipan sculptures. Cream puffs overflowing with custard. Sinfully rich chocolate cakes. Fruit tarts so sweet, they exploded on the tongue.

Ivy pored over the decadent array of desserts for precisely three and a half minutes before placing her order, even though she always got the same thing: a pot of peppermint tea and a chocolate éclair. But every time, she dawdled before the display, weighing the benefits of each and every pastry Maison Bertaux could boast, which was endearing, if a touch annoying. Echo ordered a cream puff to go with her single-serving pot of tea. Pastries in hand, they marched up to the second floor, which was blissfully empty. They sat at their favorite table in the far corner, the one with the hand-painted chessboard on its surface, nestled against the window looking down on the street below.

Across from Echo, Ivy wrapped her gloved hands around her steaming teacup, inhaling the sweet aroma wafting from it. Echo knew Ivy's lids would be drooping in pleasure behind the sunglasses she wore to hide her inhuman eyes. She had piled spoonful after spoonful of sugar into her tea—Echo had stopped counting after four—to the point where Echo wondered if there was, in fact, any tea left in the cup at all. How Ivy managed to swallow that down with the massive chocolate éclair she had ordered, Echo would never know. Her own Earl Grey was blessedly devoid of sugary interference. She dribbled only the smallest hint of milk into her cup, swirling around the clouds of white until her tea was a smooth sandy beige. *Perfection.*

"Uh-oh," Ivy said, taking a delicate sip of her sugar water. She pointed her chin at something over Echo's shoulder. "Incoming."

Before Echo could turn around, two hands were placed ever so gently over her eyes. The voice that accompanied them was a perfect match: warm, solid, butterfly-inducing.

"Guess who?" the disembodied voice asked right in her ear, breathy and delicious and far too close. A featherlight kiss was dropped on her cheek.

"Hmm," Echo mused, "is it . . . Abraham Lincoln?"

The soft puffs of his laughter sent shivers up Echo's body, from the tips of her toes to the roots of her hair. It was excruciating how easily he made her insides topple like dominoes, even after two months of dating. *He must never know.* They'd known each other since the age of seven, just like she and Ivy. Their relationship was new, but occasionally, the weight of their friendship overwhelmed it, and he would act more like a *friend* than a *boyfriend,* ribbing her about the crazed butterflies in her stomach, even if he delighted in their presence.

"Nope," he said.

Echo didn't need to see Ivy's face to know that she was rolling her eyes so hard she could probably see her own brain.

"Is it . . . Spider-Man?"

The hands disappeared, and Echo blinked away the bright afternoon sunlight. Ivy was, rather dramatically, sprawled on the table, facedown, gagging.

"Nope," the owner of the disembodied voice replied, plopping down next to her. "Just your friendly neighborhood Rowan. Though I *do* think I'd look cute in spandex." He reclined on the bench, long legs kicked out and crossed at the ankles, elbows resting on the table behind him.

The golden glow of his tan was made for the late-afternoon sun. Echo had always thought it was a shame he had to hide so much of it under his many layers. London might have been a liberal city, but Rowan's tawny feathers would have caused quite a stir, even in Soho. The short, sleek plumage he had in place of hair was tucked up under a charcoal-gray beanie, and a pair of fingerless knit gloves hid the light dusting of feathers across his knuckles. His jacket was zipped up nearly to his neck, leaving just a triangle of golden skin exposed at the throat. Echo zeroed in on it like a hawk. His hazel eyes—as human as her own, courtesy of some mixed genetics in his ancestry—twinkled, and she knew that he'd noticed. She wasn't sure when she'd transitioned from believing he had cooties to nursing a crush so catastrophic it could level whole cities, but it had worked out rather nicely, since, as luck would have it, he'd developed his own city-destroying crush on her. The past eight weeks had been the happiest of her life, though the dynamic among their trio—once as inseparable as three peas in a pod—had altered somewhat. Tensions had been running high between Ivy and Rowan, and Echo knew her budding relationship was to blame.

Ivy pretended to heave all over the table. "Hi, Rowan. Why, hello, Ivy, how nice to see you. Have a seat. Don't mind if I do. Ah, why don't I help myself to your fiendishly expensive éclair," she said as Rowan did just that.

He smiled as he bit into the éclair, and Echo cursed herself for noticing the way a stray bit of cream caught on his lower lip. She cursed herself doubly for noticing the way his tongue snaked out to catch it. If her hormones had a face, she would slap it.

"What brings the Avicen army's most promising recruit to this fine establishment?" Echo asked. Rowan's *aw-shucks* faux-humble preening wasn't fooling anyone, but she liked it anyway.

"Swung by the Ala's to see you." He smiled at Echo, all straight white teeth and effortless charm. His hand inched across the table to cover hers. The feel of his skin against hers was electric; she wondered if the novelty of it would ever wear off. "And she said I might find you here. Warhawk training was suspended for the day." He released Echo's hand to wash the éclair down with a sip of her tea. How he managed to make food thievery endearing, she would never know. "Some guys were talking about a recon team that disappeared a couple of days ago, and Altair's been busy dealing with that. It's kind of nice having a break."

His fingers were long and elegant, and they cradled the teacup as if it were the world's finest china. Echo extricated the cup from his hands to refill it. "I didn't think Altair knew what a break was," she said.

Rowan shrugged, reaching for Ivy's éclair again. She poked his hand with her fork, wearing a scowl that didn't quite work on her delicate features.

"He's tough but fair," Rowan said, rubbing the back of his hand. He cast his puppy-dog eyes at Ivy, but she was immune. She always had been, unlike Echo, even when Rowan had made a habit of stealing their scratch-and-sniff stickers when they were little. His thievery had been marginally less charming then.

"Ugh, spare me," Ivy mumbled. "I see their brainwashing has started to take hold. You've been in the army for, what? Two weeks? You just turned eighteen, and you've already drunk the Kool-Aid."

Echo buried her face in her hands. "Please don't start this again, you two. I would like to go one afternoon without having to remember there's a war on. Even if it is a cold war or whatever. Just one afternoon. Just. One." She waved a hand at the cramped tearoom, with its Basquiat-inspired crayon drawings, and relief sculptures made of yarn and pushpins, and brightly colored carnations dotting each table. "I would like, just once, to be able to enjoy victory drinks with my best friend and my gentleman caller"—she waved her teacup in the air, sloshing Earl Grey down its side—"in peace." Calling him her boyfriend, out loud, when people could hear it, still felt a bit too real. The word never escaped her mouth without the accompaniment of a giggle, and Echo did not giggle. She chuckled. She cackled. Occasionally, she even chortled. But giggling? Heavens, no. For good measure, she added, "Your bickering is ruining my appetite."

"As if anything could," said Ivy.

"Hey, man," Echo said, scooping a dollop of cream off her plate, "once you know what it's like to go hungry, you never turn down food."

The hand Rowan rested on Echo's knee was warm, even through her jeans, and his eyes went that soft shade of green-ish gray she loved. His left eyebrow twitched upward, his way of silently asking, "Are you okay?" Echo smiled in response, letting him know she was. The day the Ala had introduced them all those years ago, he'd been eating a cupcake, and a significant amount of the frosting had found its way onto his face. When he'd caught her staring at the cake crumbling in his hand, he had—without the slightest hesitation—offered her the remaining half. Food, Echo thought, was the founda-tion upon which the very best friendships were built. Rowan gave her knee a single quick squeeze before resting his el-bows on the table and turning back to Ivy.

"Look, Ivy," he said. "Not all of us have the luxury of cushy healer apprenticeships. If I'm going to have to take or-ders from someone, I'd rather it be Altair. He's not a bad guy, despite what you tree-hugging hippies might think."

"Tree-hugging hippies?" Echo asked, dabbing at a few renegade drops of tea on the table. "Did hippies ever actually hug trees?"

Ivy opened her mouth, no doubt to say something unkind

to Rowan. Echo kicked Ivy under the table, digging the toe of her boot into the other girl's shin. Ivy's sunglasses did nothing to mitigate the force of her glare, but that was fine. Echo could handle a dirty look, so long as it was silent.

Rowan sighed, hands held up in mock surrender. "I didn't come here to fight, Ivy."

"Apology accepted," Ivy replied. Haughty was not a look she wore well, so Echo knocked her boot into Ivy's shin once more.

The remainder of Ivy's éclair was swiped from her plate before she could react. Rowan's megawatt grin could have lit an entire nation. "I also didn't come here to apologize."

Echo nudged her elbow gently into his side, making little grabby hand gestures at the éclair. Rowan broke it in half, offering her the slightly bigger portion. She took it with a smile, certain it tasted sweeter because it had come from him. Ivy looked as though she was ready to choke on the betrayal.

"Then, pray tell, why did you come here?" Echo said, ignoring the daggers Ivy was shooting from her eyeballs.

"Like I said, to see you," Rowan answered, darting in to press a quick kiss on Echo's lips. He stood and stretched, arms reaching high above his head. His shirt rode up, exposing a sliver of skin between his jacket and the top of his jeans. It had to have been deliberate, but Echo was strangely at peace with that. Rowan smiled as he said, "And to tell you the Ala was looking for you. She said she needs you for something."

He pulled a battered leather wallet from his back pocket and tossed a fiver on the table. It was the wrong amount, from the wrong country, but Echo appreciated the gesture nonetheless. "You heading back?" he asked Echo. "If you are, I'll go with you."

Ivy shook her head at Echo behind Rowan's back. Echo studiously ignored her.

"Yep," Echo said. "Don't you have to do that thing, Ivy?"

Scrunching her nose in puzzlement, Ivy asked, "What thing?"

Best friends, Echo thought, *should be able to read minds better than this.* All she wanted was some alone time with Rowan, but Ivy needed to get the telepathic memo first. "That thing you told me about that you have to go do. You know . . . that *thing.*"

With a slight sigh, Ivy acquiesced. "Oh," she said. "Right. That *thing* I have to do. That's . . . elsewhere."

Echo shot Ivy a grateful smile. She owed her, but the friend economy would balance itself out sooner or later. She added her own money to the pile on the table, making sure to include enough to cover both the stolen éclair and Ivy's tea.

"In that case," Rowan said, "I'll wait outside." With a wink and a wave to Ivy, he sauntered away. Echo watched him go, denim clinging to his form in all the right places. Ivy slurped down the rest of her tea, as noisily as she possibly could, before saying, "Honestly, Echo, he's still that sticky brat who'd steal all of the Ala's cupcakes. I don't know what you see in him."

Callipygian, Echo thought, watching Rowan depart. *Having a nice butt.* She took a moment to appreciate the scenic view before saying, "Honestly, Ivy, I don't know what you *don't* see."

CHAPTER SEVEN

Caius was in a bed, but not his own. His head rested on a fluffy pillow, soft and sweet-smelling, and not the dark mahogany desk he had the vague memory of falling asleep on. The cry of seagulls outside the window and the warmth of sunlight on his face were signs enough that he was dreaming. The sky above Wyvern's Keep was perpetually cloudy, and birds had not been seen over the northernmost tip of Scotland for years. The few that made it through the wards—the same ones that blocked it from the view of humans—were struck down by Drakharin archers. One never knew what form an Avicen spy would take.

The sheets beside Caius still held the warmth of the body that had rested next to his. Laying his palm flat against the soft linen, Caius rolled over, pressing his face into the pillow beside his own. The faintest trace of her scent lingered there. She had laughed when he'd buried his nose in the feathers on her head and told her they smelled like pears. It was a strange thing, he'd said, to smell like pears, with a name like Rose.

"I hate pears," she'd replied, but she had smiled, and that was all Caius wanted.

Here, he was warm. He was happy. The sun was shining, and the birds were singing, and they were safe. Caius needed nothing more than that to know none of it was real.

He cracked open his eyes, flinching at the onslaught of bright morning light. He couldn't see her, but he knew Rose was there, sitting by the window. A gentle breeze rustled her hair-feathers, with their contrasting streaks of black and white. She was singing quietly, so as not to wake him, and it brought a sleepy smile to his face. He hummed along, just barely in tune. Rose turned to him then, a small, secret smile dancing at the corners of her lips. The moment was beautiful, like her, and as tranquil as still waters.

Naturally, that was when the world erupted into flames.

The firebird will be another mess of yours I'll have to clean up.

This was how Tanith cleansed. With fire and blood and death.

"Caius!"

Stumbling from the bed, Caius reached out for Rose, but he faltered on the glass that had shattered as wind and flames screamed through the windows, littering the floor with broken shards. Jagged edges cut into his skin, but he hardly noticed the pain. How could he notice anything when she was screaming, burning, dying? He tried to grab her, but she was beyond his reach. The curtains were on fire, and she was lost to view. Caius shouted her name, but he couldn't reach her. The room was engulfed in flames, and Rose was dying.

"Caius!"

A strong hand wrenched him from the nightmare. Caius's head shot up. The captain of his guard knelt next to his chair, one hand gripping Caius's shoulder like an iron vise.

"Dorian," Caius said, scrubbing at his face, wiping away the dream.

Silvery-gray bangs just barely brushed the top edge of Dorian's ever-present eye patch. His one good eye was the cerulean of a Caribbean sea, mingled with the navy of a starlit ocean. Specks of teal danced in his iris if he stood in the right light. It was a shame about the other eye, for more than just his lost depth perception. Though the eye patch was stitched in a sapphire hue that complemented the blues and silvers of his tunic, the perfection of his face had long ago been marred by the injury sustained during the last open battle between the Avicen and the Drakharin. Dorian's lips quirked up in a lopsided smile, tugging at the pale scars on his cheek. The smile didn't quite reach his eye, but Caius took what he could get.

He needed a moment to orient himself. There was no cabin by the sea. No burning curtains and screaming ghosts. He was seated behind the mahogany desk in his library, right where he'd fallen asleep, surrounded by soaring shelves piled high with books he'd spent centuries collecting. Leather-bound atlases crowded against yellowing rolls of parchment. Slender volumes of spells rested atop chunky guides on every subject from medieval alchemy to modern cosmology. The room was silent save for the popping of the fire in the library's elaborately carved stone hearth. Fanged wyverns danced around the flames, along with salamanders breathing little puffs of smoke, nagas crawling along a shore, and nixes swimming beneath marble waters. If Caius squinted, the undulation of the flames made the carvings look as if they were moving.

"Caius." It was Dorian's voice, but an echo of Rose's scream hid behind it. Caius closed his eyes and focused on breathing. In and out. In and out. It was all in his head. Dorian was speaking, just Dorian.

"Are you all right?"

Caius nodded. "Yes," he said, voice cracking. The dream clung to his skin like a film. The fire blazed in its hearth, and the smell of burning wood was a special kind of torture. "Yes, I'm fine."

He was not fine.

"You don't look fine," Dorian said. They'd been friends for too long. Caius hadn't heard him enter the library. He hadn't even heard the door swing shut, and he knew for a fact that its hinges were incurably rusty.

"You called for me," said Dorian, brows drawn together. "Remember? Not going senile in your old age, are you?"

"We're practically the same age, Dorian." Two hundred fifty was hardly what the Drakharin would consider old, but Dorian was three whole months younger and never let Caius forget it. It seemed fitting for the youngest prince in Drakharin history to have the youngest captain of the guard, so Caius had arranged for Dorian's appointment as his first order of duty.

Caius stretched, spine popping. When he tilted his head back, he could see the mural painted on the library's ceiling. It depicted the tale of some long-forgotten battle, colors faded as surely as the memory of the heroes who'd fought in it. Bright swathes of orange and gold cut across the ceiling as a green-scaled dragon breathed fire on a cluster of birds. Caius wrenched his eyes away. The nightmare clung to him with stubborn wisps of smoke and the whisper of a scream on scorched air.

He hadn't dreamed of Rose in ages. If there was one thing he'd learned to do in his years as prince, it was compartmentalize. A century ago, when he'd been elected, he was young and stupid, a foolish prince barely out of his adolescence. But now he knew better. The memory of Rose refused to be erased, but Caius had locked it away as well as he could. Or he thought he had. Evidently, Rose was as adept at picking locks in death as she had been in life.

"Caius?" Dorian asked, voice hushed in the silence of the library. "Are you sure you're all right?"

Caius avoided Dorian's concerned gaze, choosing instead to rummage through the chaos on his desk for the map he'd torn out of one of his contemporary atlases before falling asleep. "Here," he said, holding the page out to Dorian. "Look."

"Ah, a map." Dorian took it with a curious glance and hesitant hands. "Yes, I have heard of these."

"Don't be funny. You're no good at it." Caius snatched it back. "It's what the map leads to that concerns me and, by extension, you. Because you're the one who's going to find it."

"And what, pray tell, am I going to find?"

"The firebird." He paused. "Or at least a clue that might tell us where it's hiding."

Dorian's eyebrow inched closer to his hairline. "Sorry, I thought I just heard you say the firebird, but that can't be right. That would be insane."

Caius let his glare speak for him.

"Right," Dorian said, slipping the map from Caius's fingers. "And you want me to go find it . . . but why me? Doesn't Tanith normally run this sort of errand for you?"

"Because I trust you." It was the only answer Caius had and the only one Dorian needed.

Dorian was silent for a handful of moments, studying the map. "Are you sure about this?" he asked, looking back to Caius.

"As sure as I'll ever be. I would like to see this war end in my lifetime, and if the firebird is the way to do that, I will find it. We've all lost enough."

Dorian's hand rose halfway to his eye patch before he let it fall to his side again. "The Avicen believe it'll end the war in their favor. Couldn't they be right?" The word "Avicen" clawed its way from Dorian's throat as if he were expelling a demon.

"Whoever controls the firebird decides how it's used," said Caius. "The fact that those two Avicen scouts were sent to look for the firebird concerns me. It makes me think they might be on to something, but if we find it first, then we control it. We can end this war on our terms."

"And if I may be so bold," Dorian said. "What exactly are our terms?"

It was the exact question Caius had feared Dorian would ask. For Caius, finding the firebird was unfinished business. Not his own, but Rose's. She'd searched for it, chasing peace, but death had brought her mission to a premature end. Caius had vowed, by the smoking remains of her cabin by the sea, that he would finish what she'd started. Dorian, on the other hand, wanted revenge. For his eye, for their friends who had fallen in combat, for every loss he could lay at the Avicen's feet. Caius knew he wouldn't be able to sway Dorian, so he simply said, "Our desired outcome is a clean end." He'd let Dorian interpret that as he would.

Dorian nodded absently, but remained silent, eye focused on the map in his hands.

Caius sighed and asked, "Do you think I'm sending you off on a fool's errand? Honest opinion."

"My opinion hardly matters," said Dorian. He might even have meant it.

"You're my closest friend, Dorian. Of course it does." Caius was rewarded with a small smile, and he was glad of it. Dorian was notoriously sparing with those.

"I'll admit," Dorian said, trailing a finger along the lines of the map, "the idea of a firebird sounds a bit far-fetched."

Caius pinched the bridge of his nose and tried to will away the headache he felt blooming behind his eyes. It didn't work. "Which is simply a much nicer way of saying the same thing Tanith did. And if she did come around, I don't know that any of us would like what she would do with something like the firebird. You know how she feels about escalation."

"Well, Tanith certainly has her . . . opinions." The disdain in Dorian's tone was almost thick enough to walk on. Tanith was fire to Dorian's water, and there was little love lost between them. Dorian raised his gaze from the parchment to meet Caius's. "But you are my prince, and I would follow you anywhere. Even on a fool's errand such as this."

Caius grinned. "I knew there was a reason I kept you around."

"I thought it was for my roguish charm and devilishly good looks."

"Well, yes, but I assumed that went without saying."

"So," Dorian said, holding up the map at an angle. "Where am I going? I can't read this."

"That's because it's in Japanese," Caius responded. "I took it from one of my atlases. You're going to Kyoto. I did you the favor of circling the location our Avicen prisoners had visited prior to their capture."

"Oh, excellent, I might just catch the cherry blossoms." Dorian folded the map and tucked it away in his pocket. "Any idea what I'm looking for specifically?"

And that was the rub. "No," Caius said. "We have the where, but not the what. They said there's some elderly human woman living at the teahouse they were sent to and that she didn't know a thing, but there has to be more to it than that. Altair's too smart to waste resources on dead ends. Interrogate her. Find out whatever you can. If Altair has a lead on the firebird, I want to chase it down."

"You want me to terrorize a fragile old lady?" Dorian asked. "What kind of monster are you?"

Caius punched him on the shoulder. "That's no way to speak to your prince."

Dorian bowed deeply, but with a hint of a laugh dancing at the edge of his lips. "Forgive me, my liege."

Caius knew the gentle teasing was for his benefit, and he appreciated the effort. With tensions rising in his own court, it was nice to be reminded that he still had friends, even if they were in short supply these days. "You flatter me with your sincerity, Captain. Now get going. Round up a few of your best guards and make haste. I want whatever this is in my possession by morning."

"Then have it by morning you shall," Dorian said, straightening. With a brisk nod, he turned to leave.

Caius knew, beyond a shadow of a doubt, that he could trust Dorian with anything and everything, but some things still needed to be said. "And, Dorian?"

Dorian turned, eyebrow arched.

"Tell no one."

CHAPTER EIGHT

It was an easy jaunt from Charing Cross Road to Grand Central, and Rowan was the consummate gentleman the entire way, opening gateways to the in-between and holding Echo's hand as they crossed them. He was only a few months older than Echo, but there was something about him that made him seem more mature than his years. Confidence was a second skin he wore as comfortably as his own. It hadn't always been that way, though. Echo had been there to witness his awkward adolescence, when his limbs were gangly and he flopped around like a puppy that didn't know how to use its oversized paws. Over the past year, he'd blossomed like a beautiful flower—not that she would ever, *ever* say that to him. Unless, of course, she felt like making him cringe.

They made their way to the Nest, passing through the wards in one of Metro-North's abandoned tunnels. The Nest's main gateway was located almost directly beneath the busiest part of the station, where commuters gathered around the clock at the center of the main concourse. Magic, the Ala had explained to an awestruck seven-year-old Echo, was powerful there. The comings and goings of millions of feet and thousands of trains thinned the veil between this world and the world between, constantly pouring magic into the Nest's gateway.

"So," Rowan said, slinging an arm around Echo's shoulders, "any idea what the Ala wants with you?"

"Maybe." Echo reached up and twined her fingers with his. Rowan's half smile blossomed into a full one, and it summoned a matching grin from Echo. "But I can't tell you." She mimed zipping her lips shut.

"Oh, come on." Rowan twirled her around to face him, maneuvering her so that she was walking backward. Gentle hands on her waist guided her so she didn't miss a single step. The farther they got from the crowd around the main gateway, the more affectionate they could be. Even the Avicen who didn't mind Echo's presence among them had a tendency to frown on a relationship between one of their own and a human. The few drops of human blood that coursed through Rowan's veins were easily overlooked. They didn't blame him for the sins of his ancestors, but they did blame Echo for leading a nice Avicen boy astray. "What could be so important you can't tell your"—he glanced around, dropping his voice to a loud stage whisper—"boyfriend?"

There it was. That word. Echo wasn't sure she'd ever get used to it. She stopped walking and popped up on her toes, hands balanced on his shoulders, forehead resting against his. She remembered when they'd been the same height as children. The only fight they'd ever gotten into had been about who had reached five feet first. Six days of angry silence had stretched between them until Rowan had relented, conceding that Echo had cracked that milestone.

"Nope," she said. "It's all very hush-hush."

Rowan tilted his head to the side. He'd taken off the cap the second they'd passed into the safety of the Nest, loosening his feathers with a playful shake of his head. They were a thousand shades of gold and bronze, speckled with copper and cropped short. They shimmered faintly, lit by the glowing torches lining the stone corridors leading to the Ala's chamber.

"Have it your way," he said, letting his hands fall from Echo's waist. She frowned. It wasn't like him to drop something so quickly. They'd gone only a few steps before his fingers hooked around hers again, though his grip was tense. As they approached the residential section of the Nest, the doors became less uniform. Some had welcome mats in front of them, others had pots of herbs arranged on their windowsills. The Ala's chamber was located at the very end of the path. Rowan peered down at the gravel of the stone and wooden walkway, slowing his pace. He was uncharacteristically quiet. The Rowan Echo knew was all smiles and sunshine. This Rowan was veering dangerously close to sullen.

Echo stopped, pulling on Rowan's hand to prevent him from walking any farther. "Are you okay?" she asked.

Rowan jerked his head up. He glanced at her, nibbling on his lower lip. Any other day, Echo would have been transfixed by the way his lip was pillowed between his teeth, but there was a tightness to his shoulders that spoiled the moment. "We're still friends, right?" he asked quietly.

"Of course we are." Echo squeezed his hand. He kicked a loose stone, sending it clattering ahead of them. It bounced on the broken bits of wood that lined the ground at uneven intervals.

"I just—I don't want this"—he gestured at the space between them—"to change us, you know?" He took a step closer to Echo, and her heart fluttered against her rib cage. She was beginning to think that maybe this was what relationships did to people. They hurt and felt good, at the same time.

Echo brought his hand up to her lips to press a gentle kiss along the ridges of his knuckles. He'd tucked his gloves into his pocket, and the soft feathers on the back of his hand tickled her nose. "You're one of my best friends," she said. "You and Ivy are my family. You know that." She poked him in the side, making him jump. He'd always been incurably ticklish. "Besides . . . our dynamic hasn't changed that much. I still think I'm smarter, prettier, and funnier than you are, so there's that."

Rowan let out a small laugh. "Please. You wish you were this pretty."

Echo shoved him lightly. "Beauty fades." The moment the words escaped her lips, she regretted them. Sometimes it was easy to forget that Rowan wouldn't age the way she would. He would reach full maturity, and then, like all Avicen, his aging process would slow until it almost stopped. The Avicen could live for hundreds of years; human life spans seemed paltry in comparison. It was something they never discussed. Talking about it would require thinking about the future—*their* future as a couple—and Echo wasn't quite ready for that conversation.

Rowan settled his hands on her hips and pulled her closer to him. "Sorry," he said, pressing his lips to her forehead. "I'm just stressed out, and it's making me overthink just about everything."

Letting her eyes droop closed, Echo rested her cheek against his shoulder and breathed in his soapy scent. Boy smell. It was magic. She tilted her head up to meet his eyes. "What's got you so stressed?"

He huffed, as if he was breathing out his frustration. "Training's been pretty rough. My partner is kind of . . . intense."

Warhawk training operated on a buddy system of sorts. New recruits were assigned partners, and Echo had heard that Altair liked pairing up conflicting personalities to better teach the recruits the power of teamwork. Rowan was one of the most laid-back people Echo had ever met, which meant his partner must have been the opposite of mellow.

"Who is it?" she asked.

Rowan stopped walking. They'd reached the door to the Ala's chamber, with its trio of iron ravens glaring down at them from the lintel. A tense few seconds passed before he said, "Ruby."

Echo stepped back, dropping Rowan's hands as if they were hot coals. "Ruby? As in, the Ruby who hates me with the fire of a thousand suns? The Ruby who's tried her damnedest to make my life miserable since I got here? The Ruby who's been crushing on you since she knew what a crush was? That Ruby?"

Rowan winced. "Yup. That Ruby."

A small group of Avicen rounded the corner at the end of the corridor. Their glances slid between Rowan and Echo, taking in the palpable tension between them. Two of them bent their heads together, whispering. One hid a giggle behind her hand. Echo waited until they'd passed, turning left at the end of the hallway. When she was sure they were out of earshot, she said, "Why didn't you tell me?"

Rowan lifted his shoulders in a helpless shrug. "I didn't say anything because it doesn't mean anything. All she cares about is impressing Altair. Besides, it's just for training, and I know how much you hate her."

"I don't hate her." Echo knew she didn't sound convincing, but her dignity demanded the denial. Rowan looked at her, but it wasn't just a look. It was a *look*. "Okay, fine, I totally hate her. But she likes you. Like . . . *likes* you."

"Yeah, but . . ." Rowan stepped into Echo's space, crowding her against the wall. "I like *you*. Like . . . *like* you." With a small smile gracing his lips—which were entirely too perfect—he brushed Echo's ponytail from her shoulder, leaning down to nuzzle her neck. It was more of a resting of lips against skin than a proper kiss, but it sent tingles shooting down Echo's spine. He always knew just how to distract her. When they were kids, he'd tug on her ponytail or hide bugs in places he knew she'd look. This was much better. She brought her arms up to wrap around his shoulders, hugging him tight.

"Look, I'm sorry. I should have told you earlier," Rowan said softly, voice muffled by the collar of Echo's jacket. Her mouth felt curiously dry. Talking about feelings wasn't a strong suit for either of them. He sighed, breath ghosting across Echo's skin. "I just didn't want you to worry about anything. You have enough on your plate as it is."

"My life is virtually stress-free," said Echo, fingers carding through the soft short feathers at the nape of his neck.

"Is that so?" Rowan asked with a soft chuckle. He stepped back, putting a few inches between them. Echo wanted to reach out and crush his body to hers, but she resisted the urge. "You spend your days gallivanting all over the world stealing stuff, *and* I heard you had a run-in with a warlock."

Echo puffed out a breath of air that sent the strands of hair that had fallen out of her ponytail fluttering about her forehead. "Jesus, news travels fast."

"Too many Avicen, not enough gossip to sustain them." Rowan smiled again, and it almost reached his eyes. "Deadly combination. But you know . . . I worry about you."

It took entirely too much effort to meet his gaze. "Really?"

"Of course I do, dummy." With his free hand, Rowan brushed an errant lock of hair behind her ear. Echo's insides did all sorts of stupid things that she would deny under threat of torture. "Just be careful out there, okay?"

"Careful is my middle name."

Rowan's chuckle was nice and soft. Like how the feathers on his head felt when she ran her fingers through them. "I thought your middle name was danger," he said.

"That was last week."

"Of course."

"Of course."

Rowan slipped his hand from hers, though his fingers lingered a touch longer than they needed to. "I should go," he said. Echo didn't think she was imagining the note of wistfulness in his voice.

She had the unacceptable urge to ask him to stay. Instead she said, "Altair awaits."

"Yup." Rowan tucked his hands back in his pockets. "Wouldn't do to get on his bad side right out of the gate." He leaned down, closing the distance between them. His mouth was mere inches from Echo's, but he waited for her to make the first move. Ever the gentleman, no matter what Ivy said. Echo wrapped her arms around his neck and pulled him down to her. She could feel the curve of his smile against her lips as they kissed.

Kalverliefde, Echo thought. *The euphoria you experience when you fall in love for the first time.*

For a word that contained only four letters, love felt like a monumental leap, so she kept the thought to herself. Her fingers slid into the fine feathers at the base of Rowan's neck, causing him to grin against her mouth again. When he pulled away, Echo felt as though he were taking little bits of her heart with him. He dropped a tiny kiss on her nose and said, "I'll see you later, okay?"

With that, he turned back the way they'd come, heading to the barracks on the other side of the Nest. Echo raised a hand to her mouth. She could still feel the phantom touch of his lips on her skin.

"If you're quite done, Echo dear, I have a task for you."

Echo spun around, blushing with a vengeance. The Ala was standing in her now open doorway, eyes alight with silent laughter.

Echo's blush felt as if it were powered by lava, simmering just beneath her skin. "How long were you standing there? Were you watching? How much did you see?"

The Ala held her hands up. "I'm a thousand years old, Echo. It's nothing I haven't seen before. Now, come along so I can fill you in."

Without waiting for a response, the Ala retreated into her chamber. With a last glance back at the corridor—Rowan was long gone—Echo followed her inside. The chamber was exactly as she had last seen it, except for the whoopie pies.

They'd been replaced with a bowlful of coconut macaroons. A vastly inferior cookie.

The Ala walked to a table in the center of the room and picked up the map from the music box. She offered it to Echo. "I have a favor to ask of you."

There was a somber quality to the Ala's voice that settled deep in Echo's stomach. After a tense few seconds, Echo took the map, cradling the fragile paper in tentative hands. The Ala cleared her throat and settled onto the chaise that Echo had sprawled across earlier. A few crumbs of the whoopie pie she'd eaten littered the velvet, and the Ala brushed them off. It was as if she was stalling.

"Ala?" Echo sat down next to her and placed a hand on the Ala's arm. "What's going on?"

The Ala finally looked straight at Echo. "I want you to follow that map. If it leads to a clue about the firebird's location, I want to find it before Altair—or anyone else—does, but I can't exactly saunter into Japan myself. Kyoto is in Drakharin hands, but you're human. Your presence will go unnoticed." She cleared her throat and smoothed her skirts. "If you don't want to go, I won't force you. You are just a child after all."

Echo knew the Ala meant well, but hearing those words strengthened her resolve. If Rowan could be sent off to war, the least Echo could do was go on a little scavenger hunt behind enemy lines. She glanced down at the map, eyes roving over the words written in neat block letters at the bottom. *Beware the price that you must pay.* Echo shook off the sense of dread that snaked around her. It would be a simple job, straightforward in and out. She'd be fine. With a nod, she said, "If you need me to steal something, I will steal the crap out of it. You know that."

A smile graced the Ala's face, though her expression remained serious. "This task will require the utmost discretion, even from our own people. No one must know about your involvement. Especially not Altair or any of his Warhawks. And when I say any of his Warhawks, I mean *any*." The Ala pinned Echo with a hard look. "Not even the pretty ones." Echo blushed furiously. "Whatever you find there, retrieve it, and then come straight back to me."

As much as Echo hated keeping secrets from Rowan, she would do it. The Ala had given her so much—a home, a family—and asked so little in return. Echo could do this one thing for her. She placed her hand over the Ala's. "I've got this, okay? I may not be feathery, but you're the only real family I've ever known. If whatever this is, is important to you, to the Avicen, I'll find it. I'd take on the Dragon Prince himself if I had to."

With a small smile, the Ala patted Echo's hand where it rested on her own. "Let's hope it doesn't come to that." She let out a long sigh. "I know you must be exhausted, but do you think you'll be able to depart as soon as possible?"

"For you? Anything." Echo spared a thought for the nearly empty pouch of shadow dust in her jacket pocket. "I just need to swing by Perrin's shop to pick up a few supplies."

Echo leaned in to place a quick kiss on the Ala's cheek, as black as the rest of her but absent of feathers. She was nearly at the door when the Ala spoke again.

"Oh, and Echo?"

Echo spun on her heel, walking backward. "Yeah?"

"Try not to be reckless this time."

With a laugh, Echo pushed the door open with her hip. "I make no promises."

CHAPTER NINE

Dorian's scar itched. It did that when he was agitated, or angry, or experiencing anything one might call *emotion*. Or when rain was on the horizon, but he didn't think that was entirely relevant to why it was itching now. He fought the urge to rub it as he watched three of the guards under his command assemble on the rocky shore outside the keep's walls. Normally, the green and bronze of their armor—Caius's colors—would be gleaming in the fading twilight, but Dorian had ordered them all to wear civilian clothes and make sure their scales were hidden. They needed subtlety, not a show.

He could have used the massive archway on the grounds of the keep to transport them all to the shores of the Kamo River in Kyoto, but he preferred the natural threshold between land and sea. Water had always called to Dorian as if beckoning him home, and the ocean sang a sweeter song than the cold iron of the keep's main gateway.

He slipped a finger under the patch he wore to hide his scarred eye socket. When he touched the gnarled tissue where his eye used to be, the itch only worsened. No matter how long he lived with the loss, he didn't think that he would ever get used to how it felt. The eye patch itself was largely symbolic. Every Drakharin and their dog knew he had lost his eye to the Avicen, and he only kept the wound hidden because it itched most ferociously when they stared. It was vanity, but there were far worse sins than that.

You are my prince, and I would follow you anywhere.

Dorian could have laughed at his words, but being the punch line of one's own joke was a hollow humor. He had long since perfected the art of saying precisely what he meant without saying anything at all. It was true, he would follow Caius anywhere, even into the fires of hell if only Caius so much as hinted that he desired the company.

The memory of their first meeting was as raw as an open wound. It was the day Dorian had lost his eye. He'd been a fresh recruit, plucked from the ranks of Drakharin orphans, eager to prove his mettle the way only the young and disposable could. Battle, he'd thought, would be a marvelous affair. He'd imagined that he would earn glory and honor, but all he'd gotten was a knife in the eye. Lying on a rocky shore, so like the one he stood on now, in the middle of a godforsaken, abandoned spit of land in Greenland, Dorian had found a place beyond pain. His entire being had been reduced to the throbbing absence where his eye had been. Strands of silver hair had clung to his forehead, tacky with his own blood. He could barely see anything past the veil of red obscuring his remaining eye. The river by which he lay had gone pink and frothy with the blood of the fallen. The water was cold and it stung where it licked at his wounds, but he didn't have the strength or the will to move.

The Avicen who had taken Dorian's eye—a beast of a man with the piercing gaze of an eagle and white and brown feathers speckled scarlet with blood—had left him there to die, surrounded by bodies. Some were still writhing in agony, moaning out their last tortured prayers. They would die soon, as Dorian would. Cold and alone. Just as Dorian's own parents had. He could barely remember what they looked like. His mother had silver hair, so like his own, but the memory of her was a phantom, fuzzy around the edges. He knew, in that moment, that he would see her soon enough.

And that was when Dorian saw him.

A solitary figure picking his way through the dead and dying, turning over bodies with his boot. Looking for feathers or scales. Deciding who to kill and who to save. He was a lonely spark of life in a killing field. Dorian had opened his mouth to plead for rescue or death. He hadn't quite decided which. All he got for his trouble, though, was a mouthful of blood. He managed to croak out a single word.

"Help."

The figure's dark-haired head snapped around. When their eyes met, Dorian could have wept. Green eyes—rare among the Drakharin—shone through a layer of sweat and dirt that just barely covered a smattering of scales high on his cheekbones. The soldier made his way to where Dorian lay, gingerly stepping over broken bodies and shattered shields. It was strange to think that it would all be gone come morning. Mages, both Avicen and Drakharin, would sweep the battleground like maids after an unruly party. It was the one thing both sides agreed on. They fought. They died. They left no trace for human eyes.

By the time the soldier reached him, Dorian was convinced he was already dead. No one could look that good after a long and brutal fight, but there the stranger knelt, breeches stained by the pool of blood that surrounded Dorian's head like a halo. A gentle hand brushed Dorian's bangs off his forehead. He tried to turn away, to hide the ruin of his face, but the stranger didn't allow it.

"What's your name?"

Dorian had been taken aback. Who asked for names at a time like this?

The thought must have shown on his face, because the stranger managed a weak smile and added, "I'm Caius."

The more Caius spoke, the more Dorian's awareness returned. He noticed the insignia on Caius's armor and the green and bronze dragon pin that held his cloak around his shoulders. The mark of the Dragon Prince. Dorian had one foot through death's door, and he was face to face with a prince. Through some wild magic, he was able to mumble his own name.

Caius gave a terse nod. "Can you stand?"

Dorian shook his head.

"Take my hand."

Dorian took his hand.

Caius's smile was weak, but it was the grandest thing Dorian had ever seen. "Do you trust me?"

It was the most ludicrous question Dorian had ever heard. Caius was his prince, and so long as there was blood in Dorian's veins, he would follow him anywhere. Dorian answered with a shallow nod. With Dorian's hand gripped tight, Caius closed his eyes and took a deep breath. The familiar tug of the in-between pulled at Dorian's aching body, and soon enough, they were gone. They left the unforgiving rocky shore behind them as they fled to Wyvern's Keep, a place that Dorian had only dreamed of seeing.

Nearly dying in his first battle wasn't the most illustrious moment of Dorian's military career, but it had been the most significant. He had found the person to whom he had pledged his sword and his soul, and every step he had taken since then had been by Caius's side.

He was still rubbing at the empty socket that had once held an eye when a tap on his shoulder pulled him from the memory. Dorian turned. When he saw who it was, he looked skyward and asked the heavens, *Why?*

"Deep in thought, I see." Tanith was still wearing her golden armor, and it made her shine even in the twilight. "Try not to drown."

"Ah, Tanith," Dorian sighed. "Please, observe my sincere laughter."

Silence.

"Cute," said Tanith. "Too bad my brother doesn't see it."

Despite his rank and station, Dorian was not, by nature, a violent man, but his hands twitched into fists at his sides. It would not do to strike the general of the entire Drakharin army. It simply would not do.

"Can I help you with something?" he asked. It was that or start swinging.

"Oh, on the contrary." Tanith smiled. "I came to ask if you needed any help for your trip to . . ."

And there it was. Strange how some people did nothing without an ulterior motive.

Dorian shook his head, turning his attention back to his guards. They were ready, waiting patiently along the shore for their captain to open a gateway to the in-between, watching with thinly veiled curiosity. It was the Drakharin way. If you wanted a conversation kept private, you had it in private. Public displays were fair game.

"If Caius had wanted you to know," Dorian said, "he would have told you."

"Right," Tanith chuckled. "Far be it from me to interrogate his errand boy."

"I am the captain of his guard," Dorian said. "I do what he asks me to do."

Tanith stepped forward, red cloak brushing noisily over the pebbly shore. Her blond hair fell freely about her shoulders, and a few long strands were picked up by the evening breeze. Dorian eyed the billowing folds of her wool cloak. She could have hidden a blade or two in those depths. Knowing her, she probably had.

"You are the captain of the royal guard, it's true," said Tanith. "And so long as Caius is the Dragon Prince, you are his."

Dorian went as still as stone. "What are you implying?"

Tanith stood before him now, close enough for him to feel her warmth. Fire was her element to call, and the scant few inches between their bodies radiated with her heat.

"I imply nothing," said Tanith. "I'm merely stating that as captain of the royal guard, your allegiance lies with the Dragon Prince, whoever he—or she—may be."

So that was her game. She had always envied Caius. People may have loved him, but they feared her. It was no secret that she thought she would make a better Dragon Prince than Caius, but this was brazen, even for her.

"Caius may be blinded by the brotherly love he inexplicably still harbors for you," Dorian said. "But you're no sister of mine."

"No, of course not." Tanith smiled, slow and poison sweet. "Rumor has it that it's another kind of love that distracts you."

Dorian tensed, and Tanith's grin widened. "I don't know what you're talking about," he said. The words rang hollow, even to his own ears.

"Methinks the lady doth protest too much."

Dorian chose not to dignify her statement with a response. He stepped forward, one foot an inch deep in the water, another firmly on dry land. Half in the sea, half on the sand, he sprinkled a handful of shadow dust, summoning an opening to the in-between. Wisps of darkness arose from the ground and within seconds, his guards were gone.

"Have a safe journey," Tanith said. Her face disappeared from view, swallowed by black smoke. Dorian didn't need to see the look in her eyes to know that she didn't mean a word of it.

CHAPTER TEN

Echo threaded her way through the midafternoon crowd on Saint Mark's Place, swerving around packs of female students from the Catholic high school nearby, plaid skirts rolled up past the point of propriety, cigarettes dangling artlessly from their fingers, filters tinged pink with cherry lip gloss. They glared at her as she walked past, as if she were a threat to their prime real estate in front of the falafel joint. Echo didn't bother glaring back. In another life, she might have been one of them.

The street was an eclectic mix of old and new, gentrification clashing against a past that stubbornly clung to the dirty sidewalks of the East Village. A tattoo parlor that doubled as a crepe café was sandwiched between a brilliantly illuminated frozen yogurt bar and a store that seemed to sell nothing but ironic T-shirts. Above her head hung a three-foot-long plastic hot dog, marking the entrance to Crif Dogs, home of the trendiest frankfurters in the city. Echo pushed open the door and smiled at the girl behind the counter with booted feet propped up near the register, a long strand of blue hair twirled around her finger. The girl didn't smile back. That was fine. Echo wasn't here for hot dogs.

She made a beeline for the old-school phone booth at the back of the restaurant, its black wood and glass doors harking back to a New York that Echo was too young to remember. Once she stepped into the cramped square and pulled the door shut behind her, the clickety-clack of laptop keys and the rattle of dishes from the kitchen fell away. Echo looked through the glass at the patrons seated near the phone booth, but no one looked back at her. If anyone had bothered to tear their eyes away from their glowing screens, they would have seen nothing more than an empty phone booth, good for little beyond ambience. But even if anyone had noticed a girl disappearing into the booth, they'd soon forget. The aversion spell cast on it was simple but effective.

Echo picked up the receiver and waited. When a click sounded on the other end of the line, Echo said, *"Ingrediatur in pace. Egrediator in pace. Nisi legum aurum est."* The password had been the same for as long as she could remember: Enter in peace, leave in peace. The only law is gold.

The line clicked again, and Echo hung up. The back wall of the phone booth swung open, revealing a flight of stairs that would take her into the Agora, the underground market where Perrin's shop was located. She kept her hand on the wall to her right. Echo knew the way as well as she knew the layout of her library, but there was something about the darkened labyrinth that unsettled her. The wall acted as her anchor until she reached the market square.

It took her eyes a moment to adjust to the dim, greasy light of the Agora. Gas lamps swung overhead, casting a yellowish glow over the carts and stalls packed into a space as long and as wide as the main concourse at Grand Central. Down here, beyond the wards that shielded the marketplace from the outside world, the sound was almost deafening. Avicen traders shouted out bargains as warlocks haggled over bleached bones that looked suspiciously human. Trolleys overflowing with a strange mix of cooking utensils and weaponry clattered over cobblestoned paths that had been worn down to slippery smoothness by years of trampling feet. A few warlocks glanced Echo's way, their pupils erased by a sea of sickly white, and she dropped her gaze. Warlocks had been human once, but dark magic came with a price, and their humanity had been the cost of their power. The first time the Ala had brought Echo down here, to show her the bustling market beyond the Nest, she had made sure Echo understood that it was best not to make eye contact with that sort. A cluster of them crowded around a stall, arguing over the price of stillborn fetuses in jars. At least, Echo hoped they'd been stillborn. It was hard to tell with warlocks.

Perrin's shop was at the other end of the market, occupying one of the highly coveted storefronts that lined the walls. Echo wove through the crowd, waving at a few vendors she recognized. An Avicen with golden skin and deep scarlet feathers nodded back, his table piled high with clockwork gears and brass doorknobs. Another Avicen with brilliant purple plumage waved a bottle of something that was most certainly not a legitimate love potion under Echo's nose. She ducked so as not to inhale any of it and made her way to the other end of the Agora where a familiar sign—PERRIN'S ENCHANTING ESSENTIALS—dangled.

Pushing the door open, Echo was assaulted by the pungent scent of mixed incense and whatever potions Perrin was brewing behind the counter. The staticky crackle of a baseball game drifted from the small stereo sitting on the counter. Most of the Avicen were wary of human electronics, but Perrin's stereo was as much a fixture of the shop as his stacks of atlases detailing gateways to the in-between and the curio cabinets bursting with oddities from all over the world.

This far below the streets of Manhattan, there was no reception, but Perrin never missed a Yankee game, even if he had to listen to it on tape. It was old-fashioned, but the Avicen weren't the most technologically savvy people. Sometimes, Echo would record the games for him on a small radio she'd found at a flea market, trading the cassettes for shadow dust. The tinny sound of the commenter's voice announced the score—bottom of the ninth, 5–4 Boston—and Perrin's short, sharp feathers stuck up in irritation. He was not a Red Sox fan.

Perrin glanced up as the bell above the door jingled a chipper tune. "Ah, Echo," he said. "My favorite human friend."

"I'm your only human friend," Echo said, slapping her nearly empty pouch of dust on the counter. "I need to restock."

"Everything in this world has its price," said Perrin, head cocked toward the stereo. Yankees at bat. Bases loaded. Two balls. One strike. He made no move to pick up the pouch and wouldn't until she paid up front.

"Yeah, yeah." She slipped the small teal box out of her backpack's side pocket and placed it next to the pouch. "Here are your macarons."

Perrin eyed the box but made no move to accept it. Swing and a miss. Two outs. Two strikes. "Did you get the special seasonal flavors? And the chocolate one with the vanilla cream filling?"

"Yes," Echo replied. "I made sure your painstakingly detailed directions for the long-suffering staff at Ladurée were followed to the letter."

Curveball. High and inside. And a grand slam. With a soft chuckle, Perrin opened the box to reveal a neatly packed row of pastel pastries. He took out a single delicate macaron and waved it under his nose, closing his eyes in bliss. "A flawless combination of chocolate and vanilla. It is a symphony of flavor. One cannot have light without darkness to temper it."

"Simmer down, Socrates, it's just a cookie." Echo pushed the pouch toward him. "Can we get this show on the road? I have places to go, people to steal from, you know how it goes."

"Patience is a virtue, my child," Perrin said, but he took her pouch anyway, refilling it from the large barrel of shadow dust behind the counter. The Ala had once explained to Echo that the dust was the darkness of the in-between made tangible, and creating it was a highly specialized skill. Perrin was one of the few shopkeepers in the Agora who could boast of having his own blend.

"Why is patience a virtue?" Echo crossed her arms, leaning her elbows on the counter, mostly because it bothered Perrin when she did it. "Why can't 'hurry up' ever be a virtue?"

Perrin chuckled again, the gray feathers at his neck ruffling. "Ah, youth. Where are you off to next?"

"Official Avicen business," Echo said, tapping her fingers on the glass countertop. The long case was full of an assortment of oddities: rough-cut jewels, silver pocket watches, and more than a few ornate weapons, some of which Echo herself had bartered off. "Top-secret. I'm just that important."

"Secret? Nonsense." Carrying the pouch, now full of shadow dust, Perrin returned to the counter. He held up a hand near his knees. "I've known you since you were this tall."

"I was never that short," Echo said, pocketing her shadow dust. "I simply materialized just as I am now."

Perrin huffed, indignant, and smoothed down the graying feathers on his forearms. "You know you can trust me, right?"

Echo smiled at him. "Of course I do. But duty calls, and I have to run." She waved at the shopkeeper as she turned back to the entrance. "Later, Perrin."

She was halfway to the door when Perrin called out to her. "Before you go, Echo, take this."

He shuffled around the counter and pressed a woven leather bracelet into her palm. The elaborate braiding was punctuated with small rounded crystals and shot through with a single feather from Perrin himself. "For help, just in case you need it. If you're in trouble, I'll be able to find you." He pointed at the feather woven in with the leather. "Think of it as my Bat-Signal. It's not right that you should be out there on your own without knowing there's backup if you need it."

Something twisted deep in Echo's chest, and she would later swear that her smile had not wobbled quite so much when she took the leather band. It was nice to be reminded that she had an extended family, even if it was a weird one. "Thanks, Perrin. Wish me luck."

With a flick of his feathered hand, Perrin waved her off. "Good luck," he said. "And try not to need it."

CHAPTER ELEVEN

Kyoto was one of Echo's favorite cities in the world. The first time she'd visited—on an errand for Perrin to pick up a specific type of seasonal mochi—she'd marveled at the clash of old and new. Temples sat beside glass skyscrapers, while certain streets, like the one she currently stood on in the Pontocho district, were so well preserved that they were like portals back in time. A hundred years had passed, and still the teahouse to which the map had pointed stood, exactly where Echo had expected it to be. But as she stared at the sentries posted outside the building, her confidence shriveled up. The day had been so lovely, too, with the sun shining down on the narrow alleys of Pontocho, glimmering off the blue-green surface of the Kamo River, and illuminating the paper lanterns that swung gently in the breeze.

"Crap," she whispered. She'd been standing across the street, half hidden by the trunk of a cherry blossom tree, for a solid fifteen minutes. The line from the poem scribbled on the map ran through her mind. *Where flowers bloom, you'll find your way.* Echo huffed. *More like you'll find your untimely demise.* She'd almost waltzed right into the teahouse before spotting the sentries. They looked human enough, two eyes, two legs, no visible scales. She'd never seen a Drakharin in the flesh before, but there was something off about the way they moved, as if they were on alert. It didn't take a genius to put two and two together. She was in their territory, after all.

Guards, Echo thought. *Great.* She'd watched the sentries long enough for them to have rotated a full three times. The teahouse was being watched by no fewer than three of them, maybe four.

"One does not simply walk into Mordor," Echo mumbled. But that was what she was about to do. Steeling her nerves, she stepped around the tree and marched toward the front door. The guards shared a look as she approached, but the door to the teahouse slid open before they could intercept her. A wizened old woman, back stooped and face as wrinkled as tree bark, stood on the threshold, flashing a mostly toothless smile. She inclined her head in a shallow bow as Echo climbed the stairs.

"Welcome," the old woman said in lightly accented English, voice rough with age. "Come in, come in."

Echo's response fizzled before she could muster a greeting. Over the old woman's shoulder, she saw the most beautiful and terrifying creature she had ever seen. A young man stood in the main room of the teahouse, out of place in his dark blue jacket and rugged leather boots. A fall of silver hair brushed against the faint smattering of scales at his temples. From a distance, they almost looked like uneven skin, but Echo knew them for what they were. The air shimmered around the scales; he was using low-level glamour to hide them, kind of like magical concealer. The single blue eye not covered with an eye patch raked over her from head to toe with a haughty disinterest that was almost comforting. She was human, and he suspected nothing.

"Very rude, that one," the old woman muttered. "Wouldn't take off his shoes."

Act casual, Echo thought, swallowing down the sudden fear that seized her. *Because that's not hard at all.*

"Um" was all she got out. Not her finest performance. The silver-haired Drakharin slid his gaze away from her, as though he'd already written her off as some hapless human stumbling into his operation. A bit insulting, but she'd take it.

The old woman walked into the main room, beckoning for Echo to follow her. Her slippered feet shuffled against the tatami flooring. "Don't worry about your shoes." She leveled a glare at the Drakharin. "Nobody else did. Sit, sit. I made tea."

Echo sank to her knees on the tatami mat, and the Drakharin followed suit, giving her a curious but mostly uninterested look. *Nothing strange to see here, nothing at all.*

As the old woman filled two tea bowls with thick green matcha, Echo tamped down the hysterical laughter threatening to bubble to the surface. She was having a tea party with a Drakharin. She could hardly wait to tell Ivy all about it, if she lived to tell the tale. As it was, that was looking like a mighty big if.

The old woman's voice pulled Echo from her thoughts. "You know, you're not the first to come knocking at my door. Two boys came by just a few days ago. They had feathers, though. *And* they took off their shoes. One of them had eyes just like a falcon." She turned to the Drakharin, head tilted to the side, as if she was sizing him up. His single blue eye narrowed in suspicion, and his body went still, like a viper waiting to strike. The woman smiled, the weathered skin around her eyes crinkling. "No need to waste magic hiding your scales, boy. I can see right through your glamour. It's a skill my family has passed down through the generations since we inherited this teahouse. My grandmother told me that the previous owners had feathers, too. But you can only see them if you know what you're looking for." She winked at Echo. "You know what I'm talking about, don't you?"

Echo choked out a few syllables that were distant cousins of coherent words. The old woman saved her from responding by placing the tea bowls in front of them. "So," she said, sitting back on her heels. "What brings you two to my humble teahouse?" She angled her head to look at the Drakharin. Her eyes were the only thing young about her. They were bright and sly, like a fox's. "You first."

The Drakharin arched an eyebrow, as though he wasn't used to being told what to do by humans. "Information." His voice was rich and deep, with a slight accent that Echo couldn't identify. She'd never heard Drakhar spoken, but his native tongue must have been what colored his speech so.

The old woman chuckled. "Wrong answer." She turned to Echo. "And you?"

This is it, Echo thought. *Do-or-die time.* She could still escape this situation unscathed. All she had to do was feign ignorance. She could lie and say she'd honestly stopped by for tea. But the map from the music box was burning a hole in her pocket, and she knew she had to see this through. With the Drakharin's steady gaze locked on her, she pulled the map out of her jacket pocket. She unfolded it and slid it across the tatami mat. "This is what brought me here."

The old woman picked up the map and squinted at it. After a few seconds, she reached a wizened hand into the folds of her kimono. When she uncurled her fingers, Echo's entire field of vision narrowed down to what the old woman held. A jade pendant, large enough to fit comfortably in her palm, dangled from a thin bronze chain. A seam ran along its side—it was a locket. A bronze dragon with emerald eyes and outstretched wings huddled around the locket's circumference, as though hoarding treasure. Clearly, it was Drakharin in origin, but something deep and visceral within Echo called out for it.

"*That* was the right answer." The old woman reached for Echo's hand, arthritic fingers pressing the locket into her palm. "This is for you."

The Drakharin looked from the locket in Echo's hands, with its dragon insignia, to her. Echo could almost hear the gears in his head turning. The old woman curled Echo's fingers around the necklace, squeezing her hand with surprising strength. Her toothless smile was withered but lovely. "Take it," she said. "And be strong."

Before Echo could ask any of the multitude of questions she had, the Drakharin hissed, "You work for the Avicen."

Crap. Echo tightened her fist around the pendant and sprang to her feet, knees knocking over her bowl of matcha. The old woman threw herself between Echo and the one-eyed Drakharin, using her body as a shield as the tip of a long knife—Echo hadn't even noticed him carrying one—emerged from the back of her kimono, red with blood. Echo hesitated. It was so bright, so impossibly red against the cold gray steel. The old woman pointed a trembling finger toward the back door as the Drakharin struggled to free his blade. "Run," she croaked.

The Drakharin barked out a command, and the sentries from outside poured through the front door. Echo leaped over broken bits of china and spilled tea, and ran into the garden. When she saw what the old woman had left her, she almost wept with relief.

A pair of cherry trees stood in the garden, their twisting branches meeting like lovers in a perfectly formed arch. Echo assumed that their roots were doing the same beneath her feet. A naturally formed threshold. Her hands trembled with adrenaline as she scooped up a handful of shadow dust. The pouch slipped from her fingers, falling to the ground, but she had just enough shadow dust to open the gateway. She ran, smearing a messy trail of it down the trunk of the tree on her right. Echo spared a look over her shoulder as she skidded beneath the tree's entwined branches. She met that single, impossibly blue eye as the Drakharin rounded the corner, shouting out an order to his sentries before everything was dark, and she was gone.

CHAPTER TWELVE

Caius stared at Dorian, the sounds of the armory's training room—steel singing against steel, the scuffing of
boots along worn stone—shielding their conversation from
curious ears. Caius could have sworn that the captain of his
guard had just admitted to being outsmarted by an elderly
woman and a teenage girl—both human, no less—but that
couldn't be true. It simply couldn't.

"You lost her?" he asked, chest heaving from exertion.
He nodded at the guard with whom he'd been sparring,
dismissing her. She bowed and walked away, sheathing her
sword as she joined a cluster of other guards cooling down
in the corner.

Dorian opened his mouth to offer whatever disgrace of
an explanation he'd scrounged up between Japan and Scotland, but Caius wasn't interested in excuses. "One human
girl and you lost her?"

A pale pink flush crept up Dorian's neck, though the

scarred flesh on his left cheek remained as white as ever. At least he had the good grace to look embarrassed. Caius wiped the sweat from his brow with the back of his sleeve, hands still holding the two long knives with which he'd been practicing. They lacked the reach of a broadsword, but they made up for it in speed and precision. The blades were relatively plain, unadorned save for the long, elegant etchings of winged wyverns. Caius breathed deeply, allowing his pulse to slow. Dorian waited for him to speak, silent and shamefaced.

"Please tell me we have something to go on," Caius said, walking to the corner of the room farthest from where Tanith's Firedrakes were training. Every Drakharin in the room had sworn an oath of fealty to him, but the Firedrakes were staunchly loyal to his sister.

Dorian pulled something small from his pocket and held it out to Caius. It was a leather pouch, soft and supple from years of handling. It might have been purple once, but the leather had long since faded to a soft black. The cluster of stars embroidered on its front had gone gray from use. Caius reached inside, and his fingers came away stained with a fine black powder.

"Shadow dust," Caius said. "How in the name of all that's holy did a human girl come across shadow dust?"

"She used it to escape through a gateway the old woman had in the garden." Dorian shook his head, sighing a long, ragged breath. "Damn trees."

Caius closed his hand around the pouch. "A human traveling through the in-between. I never thought I'd live to see the day."

"Just tell me what to do." The blues in Dorian's eye

swirled like a maelstrom. Caius had never seen another Drakharin with eyes that varied with his mood. "I can set this right."

"I want her found. Round up our Avicen informants. Call in the warlocks if you have to. If there's a human running errands for the Avicen, if she's close enough to know about threshold magic, someone is bound to know who she is."

Dorian nodded. "There was one other thing," he said, casting his eye to the side. The Firedrakes had gone silent. When Caius looked their way, not one made eye contact. He waited until they raised their swords and resumed training before he spoke.

"What is it?"

Dorian stepped closer to him, voice pitched low. "The woman gave her something. A locket. Jade, I think, with a bronze setting. It bore your crest." He drew a small piece of paper from his pocket and unfolded it. "The girl showed her this."

When Caius saw what Dorian held in his hand, it was as though time slowed down around them. His heart became a rusty wheel, sputtering to a tortured crawl. He was painfully aware of every tiny movement of his joints as he took the map from Dorian. He knew that handwriting. He hadn't seen it in nearly a hundred years, but he *knew* it. Rose had never been careless enough to write him love letters, but she'd been an obsessive notetaker. Her cabin had been full of scribblings, from half-remembered song lyrics to vegetables she needed to pick from her small garden out back. There wasn't a single doubt in his mind that Rose—his Rose—had written the words on the map. But how had the girl come across it? He swallowed, mouth gone dry. "And you're absolutely sure it was a jade locket?"

Dorian wrinkled his brow and nodded, slowly. Caius looked away. He had no desire to see the confusion written on Dorian's face. There was only one piece of jade jewelry bearing his seal that had gone missing from his possession. It had been lost in a fire, a lifetime ago, along with so much else. His sister was the only person who knew about Rose, and that was a secret they would both take with them to their graves. Caius closed his eyes, and for a moment, he smelled nothing but acrid smoke and the salt of the ocean.

"She has no right to it." The words felt thick in Caius's mouth. Unwieldy. "Track her. Hunt her down."

Dorian was staring at him with concern, and maybe something else, something Caius couldn't respond to. It tugged at his heart, but not in the way he suspected Dorian might want it to. Every friendship had its secrets, and he was willing to play the oblivious fool if it meant Dorian got to keep his. Dorian looked like he wanted to ask Caius about the slight hitch in his voice, about the haunted look Caius feared was in his eyes.

"And when I find her?" Dorian asked.

"Do nothing," Caius said. If he wanted something done right, he would do it himself. "Report back to me."

"What are you planning, Caius?" Dorian's tone was not that of an obedient guard, but that of an old friend.

Finding the map, written in Rose's hand, and the locket Caius had given her meant that she'd been involved, somehow, in Avicen business in Japan, and he'd never known. He had told her everything about himself, every secret, every embarrassing story, every wish and dream he'd ever had. She'd known it all, and he was beginning to think now that he had only begun to scratch the surface of her. He remembered the feel of her skin against his lips as he kissed the side of her neck, admiring the way the locket had gleamed in the soft glow of the candles on her dressing table. The road to the firebird had led him here, picking up traces of the girl he'd loved and lost so long ago. He had to know how Rose fit into all this, had to make sense of the scattered puzzle pieces she'd left behind. "I'm going after the girl myself," he told Dorian, "but not as the Dragon Prince. This is personal. She has something of mine, and I'm going to get it back."

CHAPTER THIRTEEN

Echo emerged from the Astor Place subway station, the locket weighing heavily around her neck. She didn't dare go back to Grand Central, not when there was a chance that the Drakharin had been able to track her through the in-between. Her hands still shook from adrenaline, fingers sooty with the remnants of shadow dust. Before she did anything else, went anywhere else, she needed more. If they found her, she needed to be able to make a break for it through whichever gateway was nearest. Zipping her jacket against the wind, she started down Saint Mark's Place. One quick stop at the Agora to get more dust from Perrin, and then onward to the Ala.

She sucked in a deep breath, losing herself in the crowd of anonymous pedestrians. She was afraid that if she closed her eyes she would see the bright red of the old woman's blood gleaming on the one-eyed Drakharin's blade. It had been so shiny, like liquid rubies. Even with the blaring horns of rush-hour traffic, Echo could still hear the woman's last, rasping breaths.

Echo fumbled for the locket, slipping the chain over her head. There had to be something in it, something the Drakharin wanted badly enough to kill for. She tried to pry it open at the seam, but the clasp was old and warped, as if it had been smashed shut. It was jammed. Whatever secrets it held would stay secret until she or the Ala managed to coax them free.

With the locket clutched tightly in her fist, Echo shoved her dirty hands in her pockets as Crif Dogs' cheerful sign came into view. The blue-haired girl was still behind the counter, feet propped up, as if she hadn't moved since Echo had last been there. Echo didn't bother smiling this time, breezing past the crowded tables to the phone booth, speaking the password into the receiver on autopilot. She was halfway through the labyrinth when she heard voices. Voices she recognized. Biting back a curse, Echo ducked back behind a corner, praying to every god there was that she hadn't been seen.

"She's planning something. I can feel it in my bones," the speaker hissed. It was Ruby. Teacher's pet to Altair. Training partner to Rowan. Mortal enemy to Echo.

Crap. Echo pressed herself against the wall, the edges of an alcove digging painfully into her back.

"I can't bring the Ala herself before the rest of the council without evidence of wrongdoing, Ruby."

The second voice was deep, with a hint of rumble, like thunder. Altair. *Double crap. Triple crap. Infinity crap.*

Daring a glance around the corner, Echo swore silently. It was just the two of them, but it was enough. Altair, white feathers smooth against his head, matching the white of his Warhawk cloak. The deep brown feathers on his arms were almost black in the dim light of the labyrinth. Ruby's cloak, dark and shiny as an oil slick, blended with the black plumage on her arms and head, and she was all but lost in shadow. When she was in armor, she had to wear Warhawk white, and the brightness of it made her look sickly and sallow. Echo had heard that Ruby had learned to bend shadows to her will, but she'd never seen her actually do it before. It was one of the reasons she was among Altair's favorite recruits. Magic came easily to the Avicen—far more easily than it did to Echo—but Ruby was unusually talented for someone her age.

"After what you just saw?" Ruby asked. "How much more proof do you need?"

"You forget yourself, Ruby. I'm your commander, not your friend."

Embarrassment laced its way through Ruby's voice. "I'm sorry, sir. What would you have of me?"

Echo's stomach performed an impressive bout of calisthenics. If Altair started digging into the Ala's business, he wouldn't stop until he uncovered their plans to find the firebird. Calling Altair persistent would be a massive understatement.

"All I know is that the Ala has been sending that human girl of hers out," Altair said. "She's running errands for the Ala that no one else knows about. Keep an eye on her. The Ala may trust her, but she's not one of us."

"I never understood why we let her stay," Ruby said. Echo bit the inside of her cheek so hard she was in danger of drawing blood.

"Sentiment." Falling from Altair's lips, the word was profane.

Ruby said something that Echo didn't catch, but she didn't need specifics to hear the snideness in her tone. She needed to get out of there before they found her hiding in the dark like this, yet she couldn't go back, not without more shadow dust. Zipping the locket into her pocket, she squared her shoulders and rounded the corner. At the sound of her footsteps over the mess of loose planks that made up the labyrinth's floor, two pairs of eyes snapped to her.

Echo wiggled her fingers at them, silently relishing the way Ruby's lip curled in a sneer. The feeling was mutual. "Howdy."

Altair stared at her, the orange and black of his eagle-like eyes as sharp as ever. "Echo" was all he said before nodding at Ruby once and turning to leave. He walked down a corridor that would lead him to the tunnels beneath Astor Place, shadows swallowing his retreating form.

When Echo turned back to Ruby, she was greeted to the least amicable smile she had ever seen. She felt small, alone with Ruby like this. As much as Altair considered her an inferior being, she'd felt safer when he was there. He was a by-the-book sort of guy. Echo wasn't so sure about Ruby.

"Echo." Ruby's voice was cloyingly sweet and so fake that Echo wanted to scream. "And where have you been?"

Being chased around Japan by a bunch of Drakharin, Echo thought. But she couldn't exactly admit to that, so she lied. "Human doctor." She clasped her hands around her stomach. "Digestive woes."

Ruby scrunched up her nose as if she smelled something foul. "And where are you off to now?"

"Perrin's. I told Ivy I'd pick a few things up for her." Not the truth, but close enough. Maybe she ought to make that her life motto.

"I'll walk with you." Ruby said it as if it were the most natural thing in the world. As if their mutual dislike weren't so thick Echo could have scooped it up with a spoon.

Echo hesitated a few seconds before nodding. They proceeded in silence through the rest of the labyrinth and into the yellow light of the Agora. Echo smiled at a few Avicen who looked their way—the baker who carried the smell of flour and butter with him everywhere, the seamstress who bore a striking resemblance to a bird of paradise Echo had seen in a book—but the smiles she got in return were tight and cautious. They must have made a strange sight. Ruby with her black-feathered cloak, so like a shadow, walking side by side with Echo—small, featherless, human.

When Ruby spoke, she kept her voice pitched low enough that Echo knew the words were meant for no one's ears but hers. "Altair would see you handled with kid gloves, but I know the Ala is up to something, and you're involved."

Echo tensed. "I don't know what you're talking about," she said, keeping her voice as neutral as possible.

Ruby took Echo by the arm, fingers tight as a steel vise. "Whatever it is you're up to, you leave Rowan out of it. He has a bright future with us. Don't drag him down with you."

Echo wrenched her arm free, fighting the urge to rub the spot where she knew she would find finger-shaped bruises later. There wasn't a strong enough word in the English language to encapsulate how much she despised Ruby. She glanced at the Avicen milling about the square. Half a dozen heads snapped around, as though they'd just been staring.

She knew they were still straining to hear the conversation. Ruby's feelings about humans—Echo in particular—were public knowledge, and seeing the two of them together was probably the juiciest thing to happen all week. It was like Rowan said: too few Avicen, not enough gossip to sustain them. Echo turned back, meeting Ruby's steady gaze. Her eyes were the sickly pale blue of a vulture's. Echo hated them. She hated her stupid eyes and her stupid black feathers and her stupid milk-white skin. She hated everything about her.

"*Backpfeifengesicht,*" Echo said. It was one of her favorite words. *German. A face made for punching.* It suited Ruby perfectly.

Confusion flitted across Ruby's face for half a second. It was the sweetest half a second of Echo's life.

"What does that mean?" Ruby said. Echo could almost taste how much it pained her to ask that.

Echo smiled, saccharine sweet. "Look it up."

Ruby narrowed her eyes. "All I'm saying is if I were you, I would be careful in whom I place my trust."

"Gee, Ruby, I didn't know you cared."

"It's not you I care about," Ruby said.

In the time it took for Echo to blink, Ruby was gone. Echo scanned the crowd, but it was as though Ruby had simply faded into the shadows. Echo wouldn't have been surprised if Ruby had still been there, watching. Waiting for her to slip up. With the feeling of phantom eyes on her back, Echo walked the last few yards to Perrin's shop. Go in, grab the shadow dust, get out. First the Drakharin, now Ruby. She needed to get to the Ala. The Ala would know what to do.

Banging the door to Perrin's shop open, Echo's greeting died in her throat. The place had been ransacked. Jagged shards of glass littered the floor where Perrin's curio cabinets and display cases had been smashed open. Shadow dust had scattered everywhere, some of it lingering in the air. Broken wooden beams stuck out from where it looked like a body had crashed through the bookshelves, and heavy atlases and rolled-up parchment were strewn across the floor.

And right in the midst of all the chaos and debris lay a single white feather, as familiar to Echo as the hair on her own head. It was Ivy's. Echo's stomach dropped like lead through water.

"Shit."

CHAPTER FOURTEEN

"Ala!"

Echo burst through the door to the Ala's nest, her muscles screaming in protest. She'd run all the way from Perrin's shop, barely registering the people—Avicen and human—she had shoved out of her way as she flew through the crowded tunnels of Astor Place and Grand Central, barging through thresholds as if she were on fire. "Ivy's gone, they've taken her—"

"We know." Altair's voice was a steely rumble, its bass vibrating straight through to Echo's core. He and the Ala were deep in conversation. The Ala stood behind him, meeting Echo's frantic gaze with a guarded expression. The whites and browns of Altair's short, sharp feathers were almost pretty against the warm earth tones of the Ala's furnishings.

Echo's mouth opened and closed. She could imagine what the Ala would say, had these been normal circumstances. *Catching flies, are we?* But these were not normal circumstances. The Ala and Altair could hardly stand one another, and the latter never, ever made house calls.

"Uhhh . . ." Sometimes Echo had the sinking realization that she was not nearly as quick on her feet as she liked to believe. "It's Ivy. . . . She . . ." The words stuck in her throat, refusing to come out.

The Ala brushed past Altair. She took Echo's hands in her own, giving them a squeeze that was just this side of too hard. "I know. Altair's just told me. We have reason to believe it was warlocks."

"I went to Perrin's shop," Echo said, words tumbling out in a rush. "It's a wreck, and there's glass everywhere, and everything's broken, and"—Echo slipped her hand from the Ala's to reach into her pocket and pull out the single white feather she'd picked up off the shop floor—"I found this." Hot tears stung her eyes, but she did her best to blink them away. She would not cry in front of Altair. She absolutely, resolutely would not cry.

The Ala's hands flitted to her mouth as her carefully neutral mask crumbled. "Oh, Ivy. My sweet girl."

"We think the warlocks were hired by the Drakharin," Altair said, one hand resting on the pommel of his sword. He never went anywhere unarmed. "An attack inside the Agora would be too risky to attempt without the right motivation. Warlocks are a greedy lot. Easy to bribe and brutal when they want to be."

Echo opened her mouth to respond, but the Ala beat her to it. "But why would they take Ivy? Few would dare lay a finger on a healer—and an apprentice, at that."

It's because of me. The thought settled like heavy stones in Echo's stomach. She reached into her pocket to wrap her fingers around the locket. *They took her because of me. Because I have the locket and they want it.*

In that moment, she felt hopelessly young in a way she hadn't since she'd first run away. The Ala reached for her, but Echo pulled back. She would be strong, if not for her own sake, then for Ivy's. The thought that the hunt for the firebird had brought the Drakharin to the Avicen's doorstep coiled its way around Echo's heart and squeezed. If Ivy had been hurt, or worse, and if it had been Echo's fault, she would never be able to live with herself.

"A very good question, Ala." Altair's voice was quiet, but it carried a weight that sent Echo's heart pounding. "I was hoping the two of you might be willing to shed some light on the situation."

The Ala didn't bat an eye. "I don't know what you're talking about, Altair."

"Don't play dumb," Altair said. "It doesn't suit you." He stepped toward them, and Echo had a sudden appreciation for his formidable size. He was six and a half feet of battle-hardened warrior, and better women than she had fallen at his feet in fear. She felt every inch of her fragile humanity as she stood before him. He met Echo's eyes as he went on. "I have more ears in the Nest than either of you realize. I know the two of you have been plotting something behind my back, and I came here to find out what it is. The timing of the attack can't be coincidence. If it is related to whatever scheme you've been working on, you need to come clean."

The Ala placed a hand on Echo's arm, pulling her away from Altair. "Echo has nothing to do with this. You will leave her out of it."

The corners of Altair's mouth pulled into a frown. "If the

two of you are keeping secrets that might be relevant to rescuing Ivy and Perrin, I need to know." He inclined his head to peer around the Ala's shoulder at Echo. "You will tell me what you know, child, or we'll find out if a night in the cells loosens your tongue."

The Ala nudged Echo aside, placing herself between Echo and Altair. Echo was short enough for her view of Altair to be blocked by the Ala. The Ala kept one hand behind her back and wiggled her fingers at Echo. She seemed to know, without being told, that Echo had returned with something. One of the many perks of being a Seer, Echo supposed.

"How dare you?" the Ala spat, voice loud enough to guarantee she had Altair's attention. Echo slipped the locket into the Ala's palm. With a flick of the Ala's wrist, it disappeared into the folds of her gown. "Echo is my charge, which means she's under my protection. You have no right to come in here and make threats. She's but a child herself and has broken no laws."

"Broken no laws?" Altair laughed, hard and cold. "She's a thief. Any Aviceling could tell you that. The girl's hardly innocent."

The girl. As though Echo weren't standing right in front of him. No matter how long she lived among the Avicen, Altair would always see her as other. As lesser. She pushed in front of the Ala, wrapping her resolve around herself, donning it like a suit of armor.

"What are you going to do about Ivy?" Echo said. She would not hide behind the Ala because she was afraid of Altair. Not now, when her friend had been taken from her. Not when it was her fault. "And Perrin?"

Altair cocked his head, eyes blazing with restrained anger. "I don't owe you an explanation. If the Ala deems you a child, then you will be treated like one. Run along." Altair turned away from her to face the Ala. "This is none of your business."

"Excuse me, but my friends are my business." Before she had time to think about what she was doing, Echo grabbed Altair's arm, yanking him around to face her. Altair stared at her hand, so small against the thick, corded muscles of his forearm, and she fought not to flinch under that steady gaze.

"I've had it with you, girl," Altair said, towering over her, the deep brown and brilliant white of his feathers as breathtaking up close as they were from afar. "One more word out of you and I swear, I will toss you into a nice comfy cell, child or not."

Echo stared at him, hands twitching into fists at her sides. As children, she and Ivy had taken to raiding the Ala's closet and parading about in her long, flowing gowns. More often than not, they were returned worse for wear. The Ala had given them both a stern talking-to and told them to never do it again. Naturally, Echo convinced Ivy to double their efforts. The Ala had figured out very early on that the fastest way to get Echo to do something was to tell her not to do it. Altair had never paid her enough attention to learn that same lesson.

Leaning forward, chin angled upward, Echo met Altair's orange eyes, still hard and cold despite the warmth of the torchlight around them.

"Try me."

CHAPTER FIFTEEN

The dungeons of Wyvern's Keep were an unforgiving place. Dark stone walls, stained with the grime of years, swallowed light whole until only the faintest illumination was left to guide Dorian's steps. A metallic odor hung in the air, with a hint of something wet and cloying. Sort of like blood mingled with moss. Dorian breathed through his mouth, and he could almost taste the stench of burnt flesh and charred feathers. Tanith's interrogations were nothing if not thorough.

He stopped by the shopkeeper's cell first. Perrin, that was his name. Dorian strained to see the figure that lay prone on the floor of the cell, pressed against the far wall as though he'd fallen when cowering before the last person he had encountered. Tanith had that effect on the weak. On most people, really. The light was dim enough that Dorian had difficulty detecting the rise and fall of Perrin's chest. A few moments passed without the slightest inhalation to break the silence. The shopkeeper lay there with the perfect stillness of death. Dorian frowned. Perrin had little honor to speak of, but Tanith's methodical attentions were something Dorian would have wished only on his worst enemy.

The sound of rattling chains came from the cell at the other end of the dungeon. The Avicen girl. The one who'd been in the wrong place at the wrong time. She'd refused to give him her name, and Dorian wondered if Tanith had met with better luck. He walked to her cell door, making sure his footfalls were loud in the disquieting silence of the dungeon, so as not to spook her. She was crouched low in the corner of her cell, huddled to make herself as small as possible, but even the darkness did nothing to hide the fine tremors that shook her body. Her white feathers were stained with soot and blood, and she tensed as he approached.

Dorian rested his hands on the thick iron bars of her cell. "What's your name?" he asked, voice as soft as he could make it.

The girl did not so much as raise her head. Dorian sighed and reached into his pocket to retrieve his master key. At the sound of the door being unlocked and opened, the girl pressed herself more tightly against the wall. As if she had anywhere left to go. She buried her face in her knees and shivered.

Dorian knelt before her. "I won't hurt you," he said. Not that she had any reason to believe him, but faced with her sorry state, he didn't know what else to say.

The girl peered at him over her knees, large black eyes reflecting the glow of the torch outside her cell. She blinked, long and slow, before hiding her face in her knees once more.

"What's your name?" Dorian asked. "I'm not going any-where. I might as well call you something."

The girl mumbled so quietly, he couldn't catch it. "Come again?"

She spoke, only slightly louder, but it was enough for him to make out a single word. "Ivy."

"Ivy," he said. "That's a lovely name."

"Are you supposed to be the good cop?" the girl asked, voice raw and cracking.

"Excuse me?"

"The good cop." The girl—Ivy, he reminded himself—looked up. She coughed, and a few droplets of blood spat-tered on the dirty white feathers of her forearms. "The blond one, with the red eyes. She was the bad cop. So you must be the good cop." She coughed again. "I watch movies."

Dorian had no idea what she was talking about, so he let it go. "It doesn't need to be this way," he said.

Ivy raised her head higher. "Is this the part where you tell me that if I talk, you'll let me go, just like that?"

"No," he said. There was little point in lying to her. She might have been young, but she wasn't an idiot. "I won't let you go, but I can make sure that Tanith never returns. I can keep you safe from her."

The girl studied him for a moment, blinking owlishly in the darkness. "Liar," she said quietly.

"Believe what you will." Dorian rose to his feet, brushing off his breeches. "We aren't all monsters. That's what you Avicen call us, isn't it?"

He could feel her eyes on him as he turned away, key in hand. When she spoke again, her voice was scarcely louder than a whisper, and her words were lost to him. He turned back to her, dropping to his knees.

"I didn't catch that," Dorian said, leaning in as far as he dared. Her hands might have been chained, but one of the warlocks who'd brought her in bore a neat row of teeth marks on his arm. She hadn't been taken without a fight.

She cleared her throat before speaking. "How did you lose it?"

Dorian raised a hand to his eye patch, aborting the motion halfway. Her trembling had all but ceased, and she looked at him with a steady gaze, the tightness around her eyes the only sign that she was still frightened.

"Altair." He had no idea if the name meant anything to her, but when a humorless grin tugged at the corners of her lips, something black and venomous settled in his gut.

"Good." She spat blood and saliva on the floor beside her. "I hope he kept it. I hear he loves a good trophy."

Dorian's hand flew out before he even realized what he was doing. He struck the side of the girl's face, knocking her against the wall. Tears trickled down her cheeks, though her weeping was soundless. The fine tremors that had seized her body before returned, stronger this time.

The urge to apologize was almost overwhelming, but Dorian quashed it. He would not explain himself to an Avicen prisoner. He stalked out of the girl's cell, slamming the door shut behind him. He locked it and strode out of the dungeon, not bothering to acknowledge the Firedrakes on the door.

Once he was far enough away that the smell of blood and moss was nothing more than a rotten memory, Dorian paused, sagging against the corridor wall. The rough stone was blessedly cold on his skin. Bile rose in his throat. He felt as though he might be sick. Such obvious weakness disgusted him, and though he would have liked to think that it was the girl's weakness that sickened him so, he knew, without a shred of doubt, that it had been his own.

CHAPTER SIXTEEN

The only light in the Nest's cells came from the quivering glow of sconces mounted on the walls. Echo rested her head against the wall behind her for a split second. The stone was damp, as if it had things growing on it. Or at least the potential for things to grow.

She leaned forward, hands resting on her knees, butt numb from sitting on hard stone. A single tattered blanket, marked with stains whose origin Echo was happier not considering, was all that separated her from the cold stone floor of her cell. Her current lodgings were positively medieval, and not in a way that was even remotely charming, like the time she had bundled Ivy up in layers upon layers of knitwear and dragged her to Medieval Times in New Jersey. She'd had to swipe at least a dozen wallets to pay for the bus fare and their tickets, but they'd eaten turkey legs with their bare hands, and the Green Knight had given Ivy a rose after defeating the Black and White Knight in a joust.

The cell's odor was positively medieval, too. Echo couldn't tell where the smell was coming from. Maybe it was coming from the floors. Or the walls. Or everywhere. She took a deep breath, and all she smelled was damp soil.

Petrichor, she thought, flicking a loose clump of earth across the small cell. *The smell of dirt after rain.*

Without light, it was hard to tell how much time had passed. So far, a pitiful plate of bread and cheese and a tin cup of water had been pushed through the bars of her cell twice. Hours, then. No more than a day. It felt like an eternity. The Warhawks who'd tossed her in had refused to respond when she peppered them with insults. Hardly sporting of them. At least Ruby would have given as good as she got.

Echo tried to distract herself with thoughts of places more comfortable than this. She thought of the first time she'd ever slept peacefully, curled up on a mountain of throw pillows in the Ala's chamber, while the Ala sang her a lullaby about a magpie and sorrow. She thought of the warmth of Maison Bertaux's tearoom, where she'd laughed with her friends and felt young and invincible. She thought of Rowan. What would he think of her? He was one of them now. Their most promising new recruit. He liked Altair. Respected him. And Altair had just chucked her in a cell. In Rowan's eyes, would she be disgraced? The thought hurt, but only a little. Like a paper cut. She'd always been a bit of a disgrace. It was really only a matter of time before Rowan figured that out.

Echo wished she had paper. Writing would break up the monotony. She thought about what she'd write on her theoretical paper with her hypothetical pen. Her prison memoirs. A letter, maybe. But to whom? Rowan? Ivy? Thinking about

Ivy made the pit in Echo's soul expand, like a black hole devouring matter, so she tried not to. Though not thinking about Ivy, and where Ivy might be, and what Ivy was doing, and whether or not Ivy was afraid was like asking herself not to breathe. She might be able to redirect her thoughts, to hold her breath, but eventually her mind would rebel, and her lungs would demand oxygen, and she would be plagued with thoughts of Ivy again. Ivy alone. Ivy scared. Ivy hurt. And all because of Echo and that stupid goddamned firebird.

She sniveled, and wished she hadn't. It was a sorry noise. A pathetic noise. She had learned when she was a very little girl to cry without making any sound, but the thought of Ivy in pain, maybe even dying, her white feathers matted with blood, was too much to bear. She bit the inside of her cheek hard and willed herself to become steel. Sniveling wouldn't save Ivy, but swords were steel, and she swore to every god on high that she would run one through the first person who harmed a single feather on Ivy's head.

Echo sighed. She was going to rot down here. The knowledge was almost comforting. The matter of her rotting was wholly out of her hands. She rested her head against the wall and couldn't even be bothered by the dampness. Eventually, sleep took her, and as she fell into its embrace, she prayed it would be dreamless.

Echo woke to the sound of a gentle tapping against the bars of her cell. She bolted upright, scrubbing a hand over her face and wincing when a cascade of cracks and pops accompanied the roll of her spine. The stubborn spiderweb of sleep clung to her, and the remnants of her dream evaporated like wisps of smoke on the wind, forgotten.

"Psst. Echo."

Echo scrambled to her feet, squinting through the dark. "Who's there?"

A figure emerged from the dark, half in shadow, but Echo would have recognized those tawny golden feathers anywhere.

"Rowan," she breathed, hooking her fingers through the bars. "I've never been happier to see you."

He wore the same armor as the Warhawks who had locked her in the cell, and Echo hated it. She hated the shiny newness of the bronze breastplate, and the pristine white cloak that hung from his shoulders, and the little chains dangling from his epaulets signifying his rank as a new recruit. It wasn't him. It wasn't him at all. This war had wormed its way into her world, swallowing her friends one by one.

Rowan reached through the bars, lacing his fingers with hers. His hazel eyes were full of worry, and the feel of his skin on hers made something inside her twist into an elaborate knot. He rested his forehead against the bars. "I heard you were down here, and I came as fast as I could. I told the guards on the door I'd take their shift. What the hell happened?"

Echo closed her eyes and let her forehead fall against the bars. Their faces were so close that they were breathing the same air. His breath smelled of hot cocoa, and it made Echo want to laugh and cry and smash the walls of her cell with her bare fists.

"I got into it with Altair," she whispered. "Ivy's been

taken, and it's my fault. I can't tell you why. I want to, but I can't."

"Hey," Rowan said, freeing a hand so he could wipe at her cheeks. She hadn't even realized she was crying. "You can tell me anything. You know that."

Echo shook her head, mussing her hair against the bars. She couldn't tell. A promise was a promise, especially one made to the Ala. She worried her chapped lips between her teeth, biting back the words she so desperately wanted to speak.

Rowan's soft sigh ruffled the flyaway hairs at her temples. "It's going to be okay."

Echo squeezed his fingers, tightly enough to know it must have hurt. "We have to find her, Rowan."

He ran his thumbs over her knuckles, tracing the bumps and ridges, and it was so gentle, Echo thought she might start crying again.

"Altair's already organized a rescue team," he murmured into her hair. "Don't worry. We'll find her."

He was so sure, so confident. Echo wanted to believe him. She wanted to place her trust in him and the War-hawks to bring Ivy and Perrin home, but the firebird hung over her head, taunting her. She had placed her friends in danger. She had brought the fight to them. "You don't understand. It's my fault."

"But how? The other 'hawks are saying it was warlocks, probably hired by the Drakharin."

Echo banged her head lightly against the bars. "It was, but"—she sighed—"I think they went to Perrin's looking for me. I have something they want."

Rowan pulled back, his hands falling away from hers,

brows drawn together. The inches between them stretched into miles. The damp air chilled Echo's skin without his to warm it. After several agonizing minutes, Rowan seized the bars again, sighing heavily in frustration.

"What the hell were you thinking, getting mixed up with Drakharin crap?" he said.

"It was the Ala. She sent me to go find this thing and they're after it, too."

"What thing?" Rowan hissed, eyes nearly black in the dull light. "If you don't tell me, Echo, I can't help you."

"A locket." It wasn't a lie. Just a slim version of the truth.

Rowan shook his head. "I don't get it. Why is a locket important enough for"—he gestured at the cell—"all this?"

Echo hesitated. *Oh, screw it.* "The Ala thinks it's connected to the firebird."

Rowan stared at her for several seconds before saying, "Isn't that just some fairy-tale thingy that can magically fix everything?"

Echo's laugh was bitter and sharp. "Fairy-tale thingy," she said. "That's one way of putting it."

Rowan's hands were back, sliding over hers once more. "But seriously . . . isn't the firebird just a myth?"

"That's what I thought," Echo said. "But apparently, it's real, and it's important, and everybody wants it, and I have to pick up its trail before the Drakharin do."

"The Ala thought you might say that."

"The Ala? What are you—"

Rowan slipped a black bundle out from beneath his cloak. It was her backpack.

"The Ala asked me to bring this to you," he said, shoving it between the bars. "She told me to spring you and to make sure you did your job. She also said everything you need is in the bag, including another map, this one from the locket. I have no idea what she's talking about, but I'm guessing you do."

After a long blink, Echo said, "And you waited this long to tell me that because . . . ?"

Rowan's eyes softened around the edges. He held her gaze for a moment before ducking his head to stare at his feet. "I needed to know that it was worth it. I needed to know that the Ala wasn't throwing you in harm's way for no good reason." He swallowed thickly, eyes glued to the ground. "I don't want this war to get any worse, Echo. I don't want good people to get hurt. If the firebird can stop this—all of this—then we have to take a shot at it." He laughed, dry and brittle and joyless. "You'd be safer in the cell."

Echo clutched the backpack to her chest, feeling as if the weight of the world was slowly but surely settling itself on her shoulders. "But what about Ivy?"

"I'll make sure Altair takes me with him. I'll find Ivy. You find . . . whatever it is you have to find." Rowan pulled a chain from the neck of his armor. A skeleton key swung from its end. He shoved the key into the cell's lock, yanking the door open faster than its hinges could squeal. "I need you to promise me something."

"Anything," she said, stepping out of the cell and breathing deeply. She knew it was in her head, but the air on this side smelled that much sweeter, that much freer.

Rowan tangled his hands in her hair, pulling her close. His mouth crashed into hers, their teeth knocking together. The kiss was fast and artless, and Echo's heart hammered in her chest. When he pulled away, there was a fierceness there that she had only dreamed about seeing. The reality was more than she could have imagined. He drew her hand to his lips, kissing the backs of her fingers. Her skin tingled where his lips touched. When he spoke, she felt every syllable against her flesh.

"Come back to me," Rowan mumbled against her knuckles, his eyes shiny with something dangerously close to tears.

A lump lodged itself in Echo's throat, and it took every ounce of strength she had to say, "I will. I promise."

CHAPTER SEVENTEEN

*B*less your fine feathery soul, Ala, Echo thought as she rummaged through her backpack. Along with her lockpick and glass cutter, the Ala had packed a small book of spells, a full pouch of shadow dust, a change of socks, a pair of leather gloves, and a Tupperware container full of oatmeal raisin cookies. The Louvre was known for many things—the *Mona Lisa,* the Winged Victory of Samothrace, the glass pyramid out front—but its cafeteria was not one of them. Besides, it wasn't even open at midnight. Kind of like the rest of the museum. It was just Echo, the guards, and the tiny slip of paper the Ala had found in the locket, which had been tucked into the bag's side pocket, along with the locket itself. She slipped the locket on, studying the piece of parchment in her hand. It was another map, or rather, part of one. Just like the map of Kyoto, it had been torn from a larger whole. The same hurried hand had scribbled a note—this one in English—in the bottom right corner, most of which obscured the faded blue of the Seine as it cut through central Paris.

> *Found again, what once was lost,*
> *But nothing earned without a cost.*
> *This token of love will guide your heart*
> *To a pointed end, where all things start.*

The words "pointed end" were underlined with a thick stroke of ink. Right beside the Seine, the Louvre's recognizable shape had been circled in brownish-red ink. There was clearly some kind of methodology to the maps and their rhymes, but how they would lead Echo to the firebird—*if* they would—she had no idea. After slipping through the Nest as slyly as possible, she had used her shadow dust to jump straight from Grand Central—avoiding the Nest's main gateway—to the Louvre-Rivoli metro station connected to the museum. Even if the map were a dead end, it wouldn't hurt to have a few thousand miles between herself and Altair's wrath.

The gate that separated the station from the museum's lobby was overcome with a sprinkling of shadow dust to ferry Echo from a door on one side to a supply closet on the other. She nibbled on a cookie and thumbed through the spell book before landing on a well-worn page, its dog-eared edge permanently creased. She crouched down behind a column in the lobby, just out of view of the security cameras. She swallowed the rest of the cookie and wiped her hands on her jeans. With a single finger, she traced an Avicet rune on the marble floor.

Drawing in a deep breath, she steeled her nerves and said, "By the shadows and by the light, may I pass beyond all sight. From here to there, as quick as air, as I will it, so shall it be." Once she uttered the final word of the spell, she felt the familiar drain of energy from the very core of her being. Magic required some form of payment to work, a sacrifice to balance the scales of the universe the spell upset. It cost Echo more than it would a naturally magical creature, like the Ala, but it was a small price to pay if it meant strolling through the Louvre without anyone noticing. A dull, throbbing ache settled at the base of her skull. She'd have a wicked headache in a few hours, but that was a problem for later.

Overhead, the security camera whined a tiny electric protest before powering down. The meaty sound of bodies hitting the floor let her know that the night guards had collapsed, struck by a sudden and overwhelming sleep. The museum was hers and hers alone. She stood, slinging her backpack over her shoulders. She'd promised Rowan and the Ala that she would see her mission through, and that was exactly what she was going to do.

Echo ran a gloved hand over a glass case in the Near Eastern Antiquities section of the Richelieu Wing. It couldn't be a coincidence that the words "pointed end" had been underlined on the map. It had to mean something. Perhaps it was a reference to a sword or something else sharp and pointy that had been in the Louvre for at least a hundred years. The Near Eastern department—home to an impressive collection of Mogul weaponry—was her best shot at finding whatever she was looking for, but as she gazed at the sea of artifacts before her, her heart sank. It would be like finding a needle in a stack of needles. The map had narrowed down the location to the Louvre, but it hadn't come with a convenient catalog number.

"Crap," Echo whispered, pausing in front of one of the display cases she'd studied a dozen times over. Nothing jumped out at her. None of the placards held any information even tangentially related to firebirds. She was at a loss.

With a heavy sigh, she wrapped her fingers around the locket. The moment she touched it, her breath caught in her chest, and an electric current coursed through her body, the hairs on her arm rising with it.

In that moment, she knew what it was she sought.

This token of love will guide your heart, Echo recited to herself. Just like the rhyme on the map. With the necklace clasped tight in her fist, she followed the strange, persistent tug she felt deep in her belly to a modest glass display case tucked into a corner. The case held a single item, with a placard that said only PROVENANCE UNKNOWN.

It was a dagger, complete with pointed end.

Echo pressed her palm to the case, and the locket in her other hand blazed through the leather of her gloves. A row of small birds were set in the dagger's hilt, wings angled upward as though in flight, their black and white feathers detailed in delicately carved onyx and pearl. Magpies. The design was simple, the blade unadorned steel, but the dagger was the most beautiful thing she had ever seen.

Echo slipped the locket back on, freeing her hands to work on the case with her glass cutter, tracing out a circle large enough for her hand to fit through, careful not to cut too deep lest the entire thing shatter. It would have been cleaner and subtler to remove the top of the case, snatch the dagger, and replace the glass, but that would have taken too long. Her heart beat in time with the soft pulses of energy from the locket against her chest. She needed to feel the weight of the magpie dagger in her hand the same way she needed air in her lungs. Urgently. Undeniably.

She tapped at the circle in the glass, and it fell inward with a satisfying pop. After tucking the glass cutter into the side pocket of her backpack, Echo reached a hand through the hole. Her fingers brushed the metal of the dagger's hilt, and a surge of heat flashed through her body with a ferocity that knocked the breath from her lungs. She wrapped her hand around the hilt and once it was secure in her grip, the energy from the locket quieted.

The room was silent, but the skin on the back of her neck prickled with gooseflesh. She wasn't alone.

"It's rude to sneak up on people, you know," Echo said, fighting to keep her voice steady. She slipped the dagger through the hole, careful not to snag the bracelet Perrin had given her.

A soft chuckle. "Next time I'll be sure to wear a bell."

Echo turned to find a young man standing not twenty feet from her, half in shadow. He never should have been able to get that close. Few people in this world could have gotten the jump on her like that, but there he was, leaning against a pillar as if he hadn't even tried. His nonchalance was more menacing than outright violence would have been.

"And you are?" Echo asked. *Stay calm. He isn't threatening you. Yet.*

He stepped into the beam of moonlight streaming through the gallery's high windows. He was sickeningly handsome, verging on beautiful. The light threw the angled planes of his face into sharp relief. He was tall, with just the right amount of muscle for his height. Hair so dark it was all but black brushed the faint dusting of scales on his cheekbones, and his eyes were the kind of green that would make emeralds weep with envy. There was a savage sort of beauty to him.

Like a snake, Echo thought. *A pretty snake waiting to strike.* Her second Drakharin in as many days. *Lucky me.*

"What is this?" Echo said. She gripped the dagger tightly. "First One-Eye, now you. Am I being stalked by the cast of *America's Next Top Dragon?*"

The Drakharin simply blinked at her, silent.

"Tough crowd," she said.

"Who are you?" he asked, voice softly curious, as if he wasn't expecting an answer. That was fine by Echo since he wouldn't be getting one. "Why do the Avicen have a human child running errands for them?" His accent was hard to place. There was a faint thread of something almost-but-not-quite Scottish hiding beneath his words, like the slight rumble of *r*'s simmering just under the surface.

"Excuse you," she said. "I'll have you know that I am this close to being a legal adult, thank you very much." She held out two fingers, about an inch apart.

The Drakharin made a noise that was almost a laugh. "You're not what I expected, Echo."

Her blood ran cold. There was power in names. That was why the Avicen chose their own. And if there was power in names, then the Drakharin standing before her had just stolen a little bit of hers.

"How do you know my name?"

"A little birdie came and told me." His smile was a punch to the gut. "What kind of a name is Echo anyway?"

A little birdie . . . Ivy and Perrin. Echo's anger flared, bright and true. "It's mine, you scaly son of a bitch."

"I hear you have something of mine, Echo," the Drakharin said. "I would like it back." She hated the way he kept saying her name.

"What? This old thing?" Echo said, twirling the dagger between her fingers. Moonlight danced along the birds on the hilt, and for a second, it looked as though their wings were moving.

The Drakharin squinted at the dagger, and his mouth tightened into a hard line.

"Among other things," he said.

The locket, Echo realized.

She gripped the hilt of the dagger tightly enough that she knew she would have magpie-shaped indents on her palm. She hadn't eaten a proper meal in days, and she would be slow, but she was fresh out of options. Fight or flight. Judging by the confidence of his stance, he knew how to handle himself in a fight. She wouldn't stand a chance.

Echo grinned and said, "Finders, keepers, asshole."

And then she ran.

CHAPTER EIGHTEEN

Caius wasn't certain what he had expected when he found the human girl who'd managed to evade the captain of his guard, but it hadn't been this. One minute Echo was there; the next she was gone. It would have been impressive if it hadn't been so annoying. She was human, and he had underestimated her because of it. Cursing under his breath, he ran after her. He wouldn't make the same mistake again.

The girl didn't seem particularly strong or fearsome, but she was fast. With surprising agility, she vaulted over a marble bench, flying past rows of armor. She was flashy—impetuous, even—and that would be her downfall. And though she might have been quick for a human, Caius was not human, and she could not run forever.

"Stop!" Caius called out. Not that he expected her to listen. "I didn't come here to hurt you."

"Bull!"

He didn't know what bulls had to do with anything, but

he had the distinct impression she was calling him a liar. He swerved around cases full of ceremonial swords, hands itching to unsheathe his own blades. But he wasn't lying when he said he had no intention of hurting her. She was in league with the Avicen, but she was human, and that made her different. The normal rules of engagement didn't apply. He couldn't just kill her and be done with it. Killing her would be sloppy at best, unethical at worst.

Echo swung around a balustrade near the staircase leading to the main entrance. Caius leaped, grabbing the back of her jacket like the scruff of a kitten's neck. Her legs gave out under her, knees smashing to the marble floor. She twisted as she fell, taking Caius with her. One bony knee angled toward his groin, but he tangled his legs with hers, pinning her down and trapping her wrists above her head. They were slender enough to fit in just one of his hands. He snatched the dagger she held, tucking it into his belt.

"Like I said," Caius bit out, binding her wrists with a leather tie. She whipped her head around, trying to catch his hand with her teeth. She was feisty, he would give her that. "I don't want to hurt you."

Echo gave one final lurch, attempting to dislodge him. He didn't budge. She heaved a sigh, sagging against the floor.

"But you will," she said, flexing her fingers to test her bonds. Caius had tied them tight. She wouldn't be breaking free unless he wanted her free.

"If I must," Caius said, rising with a hand on her arm. She struggled to get to her feet, but when Caius used his free hand to steady her, she flinched, withdrawing as far from him as she could. It wasn't very far, but she had made her point. She didn't want his help. "You've got a lot of fight in you, girl."

"'Though she be but little, she is fierce,'" Echo quoted. Shakespeare. It was almost interesting. She pulled at her binds once more. "I have a name, you know."

"Yes, and a ridiculous one at that," said Caius, dragging her along after him.

For someone of his talents, the museum's lobby would be as good a gateway as any. The energy of thousands of visitors coming and going each day made it the perfect point from which to access the in-between. Echo dragged her feet, intent on making this difficult even if she had no hope of escape.

"Speaking of names, you never gave me yours," she said.

Caius shrugged a single shoulder. "You never asked."

The name of the Dragon Prince was kept secret after the election to make it difficult for the Drakharin's enemies to latch on to a specific target. Not even the Drakharin born after Caius was crowned prince knew his given name. It wouldn't mean anything to the girl, or so he hoped. It was a gamble, but the best lies were always salted with a sprinkling of truth.

"It's Caius," he said.

The girl mumbled something under her breath about sucking an appendage he was rather certain she did not have. He guided her down the steps leading toward the lobby, careful not to let her fall. When they reached the center of the room, with the apex of the glass pyramid directly overhead, he stopped.

"Where are you taking me?" Echo asked, nodding toward

the hallway leading to the metro station. "The exit's that way." She paused. "Jerk."

"Don't need it," Caius said. He couldn't not smile at her confusion. "My sources tell me you know all about the in-between."

"Yeah, but . . ." Echo looked around, shaking her head. "There are no decent gateways in here. You'd have to find a threshold near transport or a natural one or something."

"You might have to. I don't." He looked up, appreciating the shine of starlight through the glass above, and Echo's eyes widened. There weren't many who could travel without the aid of magic powders and carefully chosen thresholds, but there was a reason Caius had been chosen to be the Dragon Prince. The Drakharin respected power, and he had more than his fair share. He pushed outward with his mind, and energy surged from the center of his body. A swirl of shadows erupted at the top of the pyramid, drifting down to surround them. The girl tried to pull away, but Caius kept his grip on her arm.

"Come along, Echo," he said. "I'm sure your friends would love to see you."

Darkness fell, and they were gone.

CHAPTER NINETEEN

As the darkness of the in-between faded, Echo's spirits faded with it. Before her, black flames danced in ornate braziers on either side of a massive archway, so like the one in the Nest, but the iron beasts that formed it were no swans. Huge black dragons, with heads raised and teeth bared, puffed smoke from flared nostrils and gaping maws, necks entwined at a point high above Echo's head. This had to be Drakharin headquarters.

I am so screwed, Echo thought. *Or I passed screwed five miles back.*

Two guards flanking the archway nodded at Caius as he dragged her through it. She swallowed. She'd never met a Firedrake before, but there was no mistaking those red cloaks and golden armor. When they crossed the threshold into the castle's main hold, the wooden planks beneath her feet gave way to uneven stone, and Echo stumbled. Caius tightened his grip, hard enough that the delicate bones in her wrist shifted. She gasped, and he eased off, just enough so that he wasn't crushing her.

She tried to keep track of where Caius was taking her, but the twisting corridors and spiral staircases of Wyvern's Keep—it had to be Wyvern's Keep, no other Drakharin fortress would be this grand—began to blend together. Everywhere she looked, there were dragons. Ostentatious marble sculptures with burnished gold detailing. Roughly carved wooden reliefs, worn smooth with the passage of time. Tapestries depicting hellish massacres of birds. She wondered if he was leading her in the most roundabout way possible just to confuse her. It would certainly complicate an escape, should she have an opportunity to try for one. She had the craziest hunch that she wouldn't.

Desenrascanço, she thought. *Portuguese. To MacGyver oneself out of a sticky situation. See also: a thing that will not be happening.*

"So," Echo said, voice an octave higher than she would have liked. "I don't get the grand tour?"

"You know, you're awfully cheeky for a prisoner," Caius said, shooting her a wry smile over his shoulder. At least one of them found her predicament entertaining. "The person who hired me to find you would be amused."

"Must be my natural charm." *When in doubt, bravado. Always bravado.* Perhaps Caius would be kind enough to inscribe that on her tombstone. "And can I ask who hired you, or would that be too cheeky?"

After a moment's hesitation, Caius said, "The Dragon Prince."

Crap. When she'd told the Ala she would take on the Dragon Prince himself if she had to, she'd been trading in pure hyperbole. The universe was being entirely too literal for her liking.

"Well, don't I feel all important now," she said, struggling to keep her voice light. "So, what? Are you a mercenary or something?"

Caius yanked Echo up a flight of stairs, and she entertained the notion of throwing herself down them just to see if she could take him with her.

"Or something," he said, pulling her up the last few steps. "There is a . . . private matter I'd like to discuss with you before you meet him."

"A private matter? Are you flirting with me? Because you're cute enough, but you're not really my type." Echo wasn't sure she had a type, but if she did, it wouldn't be him.

Caius came to a stop in front of an elaborately carved door so abruptly that Echo stumbled into him. She bit back an automatic apology. No need to waste perfectly good manners on some jumped-up Drakharin mercenary. The cherrywood door had a tableau of dragons carved into it. There were creatures rising from the sea, scaled tails twisted in delicate curlicues, beasts soaring through the air on batlike wings, and what looked like mermaids playing harps on the ocean floor.

He pushed the door open, dragging Echo into a lavishly appointed library. Books covered every surface, wall to wall, floor to ceiling. Shelves overflowed with them. The room itself smelled like old paper, the air rich with the scent of well-loved books. Echo closed her eyes and, for the briefest moment, she was home again, surrounded by her own books, in her own library. The door clicked shut behind her, and she opened her eyes to find Caius standing before her, pupils dilated in the dim light of the fireplace, eclipsing the green of his irises. It had been a pretty thought, but this was not home, and she was less and less certain that she would ever see home again.

Caius studied her for a few quiet moments. The only sound in the room was the soft crackling of the fire burning in the hearth. Had the entire situation not been so awful, it would have been cozy. Caius stepped toward her, raising his hand to trace the chain at her throat with a featherlight touch. He wrapped his fingers around it and yanked the locket from her neck. The force of it made Echo stumble forward. It looked so easy when people did that in movies, but having a necklace ripped off *hurt*.

"Do you know what this is?" Caius's voice was low and soft, but there was an edge to it, a hardness. Crushed velvet stretched over steel. He dangled the locket by its broken chain, firelight casting a warm glow over the bronze dragon on its front.

Echo had a feeling that the real answer to that question was not at all what she was about to say. "A locket."

"And do you know who the owner of this locket is?"

Again, a question with an answer Caius knew and she did not. This game was no fun at all.

"Me?" she asked. *Bravado, bravado, bravado.*

"You're funny," Caius said, cupping the pendant in his palm. "But no." He studied the smooth jade and scratched bronze, expression unreadable. Echo stood there, feeling superfluous. "It's mine," he said. "Or it was. Long ago."

She didn't know what to say, so she said nothing.

Caius raised his eyes to hers and said, "And you stole it."

Typical, Echo thought. The one time she got in trouble

for stealing was the one time she hadn't actually stolen anything. "In my defense, the old lady gave it to me. Freely, I might add."

Caius cocked his head to the side. The scales on his cheeks shimmered faintly in the firelight. "Did it occur to you that it was never hers to give?"

Without waiting for a response, he grabbed Echo's bound hands with one of his own, the other sliding the magpie dagger from where he'd tucked it into his belt. She fought to pull her hands back, but he was too strong. She closed her eyes, expecting to feel the sharp sting of the knife cutting into her flesh. Instead, the tie snapped, and her wrists fell free. Her hands, numb from lack of circulation, flopped limply to her sides. She opened her eyes. He had cut her bonds.

"There," Caius said, still with that soft, steely voice. "Now we can talk."

Rubbing her wrists, Echo waited. If he wanted to talk, he could talk.

"Who sent you to retrieve these items?" Caius asked.

She was pretty sure she didn't have the right to remain silent, but she was going to exercise it anyway.

Caius leaned against a leather chair large enough to be called a throne. "I know you didn't go looking for them on your own. I want to know who sent you and why."

Still Echo held her peace. She might have been captured, but she wasn't about to give up any information on the Avicen without a fight. She owed them—Ivy, Rowan, the Ala—that much. She pressed her lips together and let her eyes wander about the room.

"Tell me, Echo. What do you know about the firebird?"

She tensed, and judging from the sharpness in his eyes

and the slight tilt of his head, she knew that Caius had noticed.

"What's the firebird?" *When bravado fails,* she thought, *play dumb.*

Caius pushed away from the chair to stand before her, far too close for comfort. Echo took a step back, cursing herself for it but unable to fight the compulsion to put space between them. Caius crowded her against the door, the point of the magpie dagger resting between her collarbones.

"Don't lie to me, Echo." He leaned in, face mere inches from hers. He tapped the blade against her skin, too lightly to pierce it, but firmly enough that she was well aware of how close the dagger was. "I don't like being lied to."

Echo swallowed, and the blade pressed harder against the soft skin of her throat. "I don't know what the firebird is. That's not a lie." Caius stilled the knife's tapping but kept it against her neck. "I was sent to find the locket and the dagger, but I don't know why. It's bad for business if I ask too many questions, so I don't. Surely a man like you understands."

Caius studied her for a moment. Echo hoped there was enough truth mixed in to hide the taste of the lie.

"A man like me," he murmured. "Fine." He stepped back, twirling the blade away from her neck. "Let's say I believe you. Just tell me one more thing: why are you, a human, helping the Avicen? Such a secretive people would never accept you as one of their own. There must be another reason."

"How did you—"

Echo pressed her lips together, but she'd already said too much. This hired gun had found her deepest insecurity and poked at it. *Damn him. Damn him to infinity and beyond.*

She was ready to lie, to tell him that the Avicen had bought her loyalty with genuine green American dollars when the door behind her burst open. It slammed into her back, and the force of it sent her careering into Caius's chest. He caught her by the biceps, and, for a brief moment, their faces were so close she could see little flecks of gold in his green eyes. He spun her behind him to face whoever had hurtled through the door.

A guard leaned heavily against the doorframe, sagging to the floor, hands clutching his side. Blood trickled between his fingers, and Echo thought that maybe he was holding his intestines in. Her stomach heaved.

Caius knelt by the guard, steadying him. "Ribos," he said. "It's Ribos, isn't it?"

The guard nodded, beads of sweat clinging to his sallow skin.

"What happened?" Caius asked. He pressed his hands above the guard's, but there was so much blood, it hardly made a difference. "Who did this to you?"

Echo thought about making a break for it, but looking at the freshly spilled blood pooling around the guard's torso, she wasn't sure that outside would be any safer. Caius, at least, seemed calm.

The devil you know, Echo thought.

"Tanith," Ribos croaked. "Her Firedrakes." He coughed, blood peppering Caius's face. Caius didn't so much as flinch. "A vote's been called. She's killing those who stand against her. She's going to make herself Dragon Prince."

CHAPTER TWENTY

Caius debated washing Ribos's blood off his hands after he'd called in another guard to take Echo to the dungeons. He wasn't done with her, not by a long shot, but he had more pressing matters at hand. He was torn between two urges, one infinitely more reasonable than the other. He wanted to storm the great hall, covered in the blood that Tanith had spilled to secure votes from nobles who had sworn their allegiance to him. He wanted to show them what she had done, what their own cowardice had wrought.

But he left Ribos crumpled on the floor of his study, and he washed his hands. This was not a battle that would be won with emotionally charged theatrics, no matter how loudly, how viciously his heart howled for justice. He would keep a level head. If he didn't, Tanith just might try to separate it from his neck.

The Firedrakes on the door didn't want to let him in.

He'd had to remind them that Dragon Prince or not, he was still a noble of the court, and he would enter the great hall to pay his respects, as was his right. The falsehood was sour on his tongue, but Caius swallowed his bitterness with a cordial smile.

Denied entry into my own court, Caius thought. *Honestly, the very notion.*

He wanted to be surprised by what he saw when the Firedrakes finally opened the doors leading into the great hall, but all he felt was a terrible, sinking resignation.

Tanith reclined on the throne that had been his, the crimson silk of her gown pooling around her feet like blood. Her hair was arranged in several thick braids piled atop her head, with a few curling strands framing her face. The gold cloak fastened around her shoulders perfectly matched the thin diadem she'd donned for the occasion. Caius had no doubt she'd picked the cloak for that very reason. His sister had always had a flair for the dramatic. How many times had he lounged on that throne, one leg thrown over the arm, as if he owned it. As if it were his by right. As if no one could take it away from him. But there was Tanith, as lovely as ever in her signature colors. The throne wasn't his anymore. Perhaps it never had been. Perhaps he should have paid more attention to the enemy within rather than scanning the horizon for the one he only imagined was there.

"That seat's taken," he said. The words were empty. He knew it. Tanith knew it. The courtiers cowering behind their layers of finery knew it.

"Yes," Tanith said. "But not by you. Not anymore."

"You work quickly." Dozens of eyes bounced between him

and Tanith, as though this were nothing more than a sporting event. There were fewer nobles present than there should have been, but the only sign that there'd been a disagreement over Tanith's call for a vote were a few scattered bloodstains and black burns on the stone floor. Trust his sister to handle her dissenters with fire and death. The rest huddled together, silent as mice. *Cowards. All of them, cowards.*

"I'm gone for a few hours, and you have yourself elected Dragon Prince. I'm impressed, Sister, really, I am."

Tanith rose, long skirts cascading to the ground. The epitome of royal elegance. "It was a free and fair election, Caius, as is the way of our people."

"I'm not so sure that's what Ribos would call it."

"Is that name supposed to mean something to me?"

"It should," Caius said. "He was one of my guards, and you killed him."

"The ends have justified the means among the Drakharin since the age of the first Dragon Prince." Tanith walked down from the dais with careful steps. The gown was lovely, but she'd always been better suited to armor, much like she had always been better suited to battle than statecraft. She would learn that soon enough, and if she didn't, then the Drakharin who voted her in would, when it was their own blood spilled across her killing fields.

"Still," Caius said. He was pushing his luck, but Ribos had been loyal. He deserved to have that loyalty returned. "It hardly seems fair that he should die so that you could gain a crown."

Tanith paused halfway between Caius and the throne. "Fair?" She laughed. "This is what you never understood.

It isn't about right or wrong. It isn't about good or evil. It's about power. Who has it, who doesn't. And now, Caius, you don't. And I do." She nodded at the Firedrakes that flanked the inner doors. "Take him. Let him cool his temper in the dungeon until he sees the error of his ways."

Caius held up a hand, and the guards halted. Tanith's mouth tightened into a firm line. They were her Firedrakes, but he had been their prince for a century. Old habits died hard.

"That won't be necessary," Caius said. From the corner of his eye, he spotted four more Firedrakes within the hall, in addition to the two behind him. If this went south, he could take out four of them, maybe five. But if Tanith was to jump into the fray, the odds would be stacked against him. There was only one way out, no matter how much it pained him to admit it.

"You're right," Caius said. "If you've won the vote, then you are the rightful Dragon Prince. I've always done my best to honor the wishes of our people, and I will do no less now." With a graceful sweep of his arm, Caius cut a deep bow, eyes downcast, as was right and proper. "You've won, Tanith. Congratulations."

Tanith was a master of many things. Few swordsmen could hope to best her in combat and fewer still had her keen eye for strategy on the battlefield. Her acts of bravery and feats of daring were known far and wide. But there was one skill that Tanith had never been able to master, and that was the art of spotting a lie, even when it was presented before her, bowed in a pretense of humble prostration.

"Thank you, Caius." Tanith closed the distance between

them. She placed a hand on his shoulder, urging him to stand. Her hand was warm, even through his tunic. "I was hoping you would see things my way."

"Of course," Caius said. He forced a small smile. "You are my only sister, and no matter what, you have my support."

Tanith smiled, and it was almost genuine. "Your loyalty does you credit, Brother." She gathered up her skirts and turned her back to him, a show of confidence among the Drakharin. Giving someone your back meant you trusted them not to stick a blade in it. Caius's hands itched to reach for the long knives he still wore, but Tanith was right. By Drakharin standards, it had been a fair and free election. *Laughable,* he thought. *Absolutely laughable.*

"Thank you again, Caius," Tanith said as she ascended the dais. She sat down on the throne that was now hers. "That will be all." It must have been a unique pleasure, throwing Caius's words back in his face.

With another bow, low and reverent, Caius took her words for what they were: a dismissal. They nodded to each other, across a distance more vast than the great hall itself. It was all so terribly civilized, and that, too, was pretense. If he wasn't gone by morning, the next body the Drakharin found bearing the marks of Tanith's sword would be his own. The Firedrakes opened the doors for him, and he left, his twin's crimson eyes burning a hole in his back.

CHAPTER TWENTY-ONE

The darkened corners and moldy stench of the Drakharin dungeons were the only company Ivy had as she sat on the stone floor, arms wrapped around her knees, shivering with cold. Perrin had been silent after the blond Drakharin left, her golden armor stained red with his blood, and Ivy wondered if he was dead.

There was a leak somewhere in the dungeons, and she'd been counting the drips to pass the time. She reached five thousand before she started to worry that she was slowly going mad. Her cheek still stung where the one-eyed Drakharin had struck her. She rubbed her face, sticky with tears and blood and snot. Maybe madness wouldn't be so bad. So long as her sanity anchored her to this hell, there would be no hope for her. Madness might be the only escape left, even if it was only in her mind.

The drips persisted, and Ivy persisted in counting them,

clinging to the tattered remnants of her sanity with clumsy fingers. She'd only counted to seven when the dungeon's heavy iron doors swung open and she heard the most beautiful sound in the whole entire world.

"Whoa there, sailor, buy a girl a drink first."

Echo.

Ivy flung herself toward the voice as far as her chains would allow. Echo was here, in the Drakharin fortress. Echo had found her. They would escape. They would be free.

"You call this a frisk? Ha!"

And just like that, Ivy's heart began to sink. She settled back against the wall, shackled wrists hugging her knees. There would be no escape. Echo was here as a prisoner.

"Hands!" Echo shouted. "In places!"

Ivy closed her eyes. The sound of at least two pairs of boots scuffing against stone and a cell door opening and closing was enough to kill the hope that had sprung in her heart. Echo wasn't a savior. She was as trapped as Ivy. When the dungeon's main doors clanged shut Ivy said, "Echo?"

A muffled curse drifted through the darkness before Echo's face appeared between the bars of the cell opposite hers.

"Ivy?" Echo said, hands clutching the bars. "Are you okay?"

Ivy crawled forward, the raw skin on her knees keenly aware of every bump and ridge through her jeans. She met Echo's eyes across the walkway between them, and tears stung her own. She thought she'd cried herself out hours before, but there was a well inside her that stubbornly refused to dry up. Echo smiled, though it was a bit wobbly at the corners. She had the unflappable composure of those who have lived too long in too short a span of time, and Ivy felt a twisted sort of envy at her ability to keep cool under pressure.

"I'm fine," Ivy said. She wasn't—not even close. "What are you doing here?"

"Would you believe me if I told you I was here to rescue you?" Echo said.

"Say it," Ivy hissed, "and I will smack you."

Echo snorted. "From all the way over there?"

"I swear to the gods, I will find a way." The tendrils of madness that had wrapped themselves around Ivy's mind slowly dissolved, forced back by their comfortable banter. It was strained, but it was familiar. Ivy clung to it, letting Echo's voice be her rock.

"Why are you here?" Ivy asked. "For real."

"Long story short, the Dragon Prince hired some jerk to hunt me down for stealing some crap," Echo said. "I just wish I knew how they found me."

It was an innocent enough statement, curious without the expectation of an answer, but bile rose in Ivy's throat. She remembered the sound of Perrin's choked screams and garbled words, thick and wet, as if he had been drowning in his own blood. She dug her nails into the soft flesh of her forearm as she recalled the part of Perrin's interrogation that stung most of all. She'd screamed, called him a liar, a traitor, a coward. It hadn't mattered to her that he'd resisted as long as he was able, that he'd told them selling information was one thing, but handing over children was another. He'd gone quiet hours ago, and Ivy tasted the sour venom of regret for the things she'd said to him.

"The bracelet," Ivy said, eyes closed tightly against the

memory. "The one Perrin gave you. He tracked it. He didn't want to, but they tortured him. They made him do it."

Echo spit out a curse and fumbled at her wrist. What sounded like leather and beads smacked against the floor. Ivy let the moments pass in silence, and slowly, the memory of Perrin's cries faded into nothingness. She listened to Echo breathing, letting the constancy of the sound steady her. After a few minutes, she felt almost sane again.

Echo sighed, the noise soft in the quiet of the dungeon. "You know, I'm getting real sick of people tossing me in prison cells."

"What?" Ivy asked. "Who else tossed you in a prison cell?"

"Altair," Echo said. "Naturally."

Ivy plucked at the straw beneath her knees. "I want to say I'm surprised, but I'm not. Not even a little bit. Not at all."

Echo's laugh was tired but genuine. "Yeah, yeah. Now shut up so I can figure out how to get us out of here. That handsy guard stole my tools." Grabbing the bars of her cell, she shouted, *"And your amenities leave something to be desired!"* With a huff, she settled back against the wall, crossing her arms and kicking her legs out in front of her.

Ivy went quiet, pressing her forehead against the cool metal of the cell's bars. It wasn't comfortable, but it reminded her of where she was and whom she was with. Echo was here, and together, they would escape. They had to. They couldn't not. The seconds ticked by, and the silence thickened, as if the air itself were coagulating with Ivy's despair.

"So," Ivy said. She needed to hear something, anything, besides that infernal drip. "What's the plan?"

Ivy heard more than saw Echo shift restlessly.

"I don't know," Echo admitted. "Weep. Panic. Die horribly."

The laughter that bubbled its way out of Ivy's throat was tinged with no small amount of hysteria. "Great pep talk."

"You're welcome," Echo said. "I tried really hard with that one."

Silence fell again, and Ivy began to count the drips. *One drip, two drips, three drips.*

"Ivy?"

"Yeah?"

"What happened to Perrin?"

The memory of Perrin's screams as Tanith asked him again and again to tell her about Echo roared back to life. For a moment, the blood Ivy smelled was fresh, and the fire that burst from Tanith's hands lit up the whole room. She buried her fingernails into her palms, and the pain brought her back to herself.

"I think they killed him." Her voice sounded like a stranger's. With any luck, the numbness she was beginning to feel would take her soon so she wouldn't have to think or feel or fear anything anymore. "He hasn't moved in a while."

Echo scrambled to her knees and snaked a hand through the bars, reaching out for Ivy. At least Echo's hands were free to do that. Ivy pulled at her chains, rattling them like some vengeful ghost. No matter how desperately she needed to feel Echo's hand in her own, to feel assured that she wasn't going to die alone, forgotten in a cold, dirty cell, the shackles held her back.

"I can't," Ivy said, swallowing around the growing lump in her throat. "I can't reach you."

And then she was crying, tears burning little paths through the layer of soot and blood on her cheeks. Echo whispered soft, soothing nonsense, but Ivy couldn't hear anything over the sound of her own sobs and that god-forsaken drip.

CHAPTER TWENTY-TWO

"Ivy," Echo said again. She'd been calling her name for a solid ten minutes, but Ivy was inconsolable. The sound of her crying had faded to a quiet sniffling, but she refused to speak.

"Ivy," Echo said again in a harsh whisper. "It's gonna be okay, I promise. The Ala and Altair were looking for you when I left. They'll find us. I know they will."

Ivy mumbled something so quietly, Echo couldn't quite catch it. "What was that?"

Raising her head to meet Echo's eyes through the bars, Ivy cleared her throat and spoke, voice raw from crying. "I said, they won't come after us. Not here. And Altair threw you in a jail cell, so why would he come looking for you?"

"Because in Altair's twisted little world, he's the only one who gets to mess with his own people."

"But you're not his people."

Under normal circumstances, Ivy would never have said

something like that quite so bluntly, but a day in a Drakharin dungeon would take a toll on anyone's tact. And even if the words were harsh, Echo couldn't deny that they were true. Altair didn't care about her. He *tolerated* her. And now he was probably glad she was out of his hair.

"Yeah," said Echo, sitting back against the wall. "And he never lets me forget it."

Ivy's face softened, and her big black eyes were clearer than they'd been minutes earlier. "I'm sorry," she said. "I didn't mean—"

"No, I know. It's fine." Echo sighed. "And you're right, he won't come looking for me. I could rot, for all Altair cares, but he *will* come looking for you." Echo glanced at the pile of robes that Ivy had assured her was Perrin. "And him."

Ivy nodded listlessly and looked down. "If you say so."

The moments passed in silence. Echo felt her hope dwindle, dripping away, drop by drop, like the leak that had been driving her insane since she'd noticed it. How Ivy had been down here as long as she had, listening to that lonely, persistent drip, without going mad was a mystery.

The guards had rotated shifts twice since she'd been dropped off, so when the heavy iron door creaked open again, Echo didn't bother looking up. She busied herself braiding tiny pieces of straw plucked off the dungeon floor. A single set of footsteps approached. Only when they stopped in front of her cell did she look up. Caius stood on the other side of the bars, peering down at her, green eyes inscrutable. He'd washed away the blood on his hands, but the fabric of his tunic was darker where Ribos had leaned against him. The blood was probably still tacky to the touch.

"Missed me already?" Echo asked. She resumed braiding

the straw, but her hands were shaking too much to make it even. "You seemed so busy before, what with all the blood and the horror and the dying."

Caius eyed the main door. The Firedrakes were on the other side, separated from this room by four inches of solid metal, but he kept his voice low anyway. "There's been a change in management."

"And what does that have to do with me?" Echo said, dropping her mangled straw.

"My contract's been cut short." Caius jingled a ring of skeleton keys at her through the bars. "As far as I'm concerned, that means you're free to go."

Echo pushed herself to her feet, knees creaking in protest. *Seventeen and already too old for this crap.* "Can I ask why?"

"I was hired by the Dragon Prince to bring you in. There's a new Dragon Prince now. I can't say I'm a huge fan of her methods."

"Tanith?"

Caius looked mildly surprised. "How did you know?"

"I have these things I like to call eyes and ears." Echo flexed her ankles, trying to get her circulation back in working order. "You know, she doesn't exactly seem like the subtle type."

"Tanith has been called many things over the years, but subtle was never one of them," Caius said, keys dangling from his fingers.

"I ask again," Echo said. She could almost taste her freedom. Ivy had gone still, watching their exchange closely. "What does this have to do with me?"

"This has everything to do with you."

"An answer that's not really an answer. Lovely. At this rate, we'll be here all day." Echo wrapped her hands around the bars of her cell door, peering at Caius. "But it's cool. Take your time. It's not like I'm going anywhere."

"I'm not interested in playing games with you, Echo. You know far more about the firebird than you want me to believe. You knew more than my own scholars, and they've spent decades looking for even the smallest clue as to its whereabouts. I believe that you're on its trail, and I need to know what you know. Now."

Echo would sooner have dashed her own skull against the bars of her cell than sold out the Ala and the Avicen to some Drakharin. Not after what they'd done to her friends. She opened her mouth to tell him exactly that when he held up a hand, silencing her.

"The fate of both our peoples may depend on your next words, so consider them carefully."

Ivy was very quiet in her cell, as if she were holding her breath, listening intently.

"Tell me why you want it," Echo said. "Tell me why I should give a damn."

Caius leaned in, studying her, his green eyes hard as jade. When he spoke, there was a quiet urgency to his voice. "I want to end this war. I'm tired of fighting. Tired of battle. Tired of bloodshed. But Tanith . . . she feasts on it. If the firebird can put a stop to all this, to the war that has devastated our people for centuries, then I would find it. I want peace, Echo. More than wealth, more than glory, more than my own life, I want peace."

And just like that, Caius unlocked her cell, letting the door swing open with a loud squeal. "And unless I'm sorely mistaken," he said, tossing her the keys to Ivy's cell and manacles, "I think you want that as well."

Echo looked at Caius, at the dark hair brushing his forehead, at the slight crease between his brows, at the faint scar at the edge of his lip, almost imperceptible in the half-light of the dungeon.

Akrasia, she thought. *The state of acting against one's better judgment.* She had a feeling that the next three words out of her mouth were the most important words she would ever speak.

"Yes," she said. "I do."

CHAPTER TWENTY-THREE

*F*etch my brother.

Tanith's words rang in Dorian's ears as he stalked through the keep, flanked by the two Firedrakes she'd assigned to him. He sank his teeth into the tender flesh on the inside of his cheek to keep from screaming. *Fetch.* As if he were a dog.

Though it gnawed at him deeply, Tanith had been right about one thing. As captain of the royal guard, he had sworn fealty to the Dragon Prince. Unfortunately, that title now belonged to Tanith, and he was expected to follow her orders as faithfully as he had followed Caius's. As if allegiance were a transferrable entity.

His first stop, Firedrakes in tow, had been Caius's study, only to find the lifeless body of one of the guards under his command. Ribos had been a loyal soldier, steadfast and true. He'd had a love of ginger tea and lemon cakes and was as quick with a barbed joke as he was with a kind word. And now he was dead, another sacrifice at the altar of Tanith's ambition.

Fetch my brother.

It had been her first order to Dorian, spoken with a taunt dancing in her sanguine eyes. He supposed she'd done it to remind him of his place. He was hers now, and she would not let him forget it. The Dragon Prince had demanded that he fetch Caius, and he would do just that.

Never let it be said, Dorian thought, *that I am not a man of my word.*

Dorian brushed past the pair of Firedrakes guarding the dungeon's door. He rounded the corner and skidded to an abrupt halt. Caius stood in the narrow pathway between the cells, with the Avicen girl and the human. And they were free.

"Dorian," Caius said. "Nice of you to join us. I see you brought friends."

"It's funny." Dorian drew his sword, keeping it at a low angle. The Firedrakes behind him followed suit. "Tanith sent me to find you to make sure you were on your best behavior. It's almost like she didn't trust you not to stir up trouble."

"It's funny," Caius replied. "She had two of her lackeys follow you around. It's almost like she didn't trust you to do as you were told."

Dorian couldn't have fought the grin that tugged at his lips even if he wanted to. Caius returned the smile, and Dorian's heart sputtered out a sickening little tune.

"Funny, that," he said. Dorian spun, knocking one Firedrake's sword from his hands with a single swift blow. The other dodged the attack, and her blade ripped through Dorian's tunic, scraping at the arch of his hip bone. Dorian brought the butt of his sword down on the guard's helmet, and she crumpled in a pile of shining armor. Disarmed and unprepared. Not much of a fight. Tanith would have been so disappointed. From the corner of his eye, Dorian saw Caius unsheathe the knives at his back, running one through the neck of the Firedrake on his right, the other through the vulnerable opening where the plates of armor met at chest and shoulder.

It ended before it had truly begun. Caius absently kicked a Firedrake's boot before stepping over the fallen body at his feet. "Tanith was right to doubt your loyalty."

"You're my friend, Caius." Dorian bent down to tear a scrap of crimson wool from the cloak of a fallen Firedrake, wincing at a sharp pain in his abdomen. The Firedrake's blade must have cut deeper than he'd thought. He wiped the blood from his sword with the scrap of cloth, taking a moment to appreciate the poetry of it all. He met Caius's eyes, flinging the cloth to the side. "My loyalty was never in question."

"Of course not." Caius smiled. "I am eternally in your debt, but now I have to leave."

"I'd guessed as much," Dorian said. "Where are we going?"

"We?"

"Yes. We. As in *you* and *me*." Dorian gestured at the two girls who'd kept a safe distance from the fight, but had curiously not chosen to flee. *Nowhere to go,* he supposed. "And them. For some reason, which I'm sure you'll explain in due time."

"Yes, of course," said Caius, sparing a glance over his shoulder. Echo gave a faint little wave. Ivy was looking even paler beneath the soot and blood on her face. "But, Dorian, you have to understand . . . if you come with me, you might never be able to return. What I'm about to do is nothing short of high treason."

Dorian rolled his eye. "Caius, I just killed two of Tanith's soldiers. I think it's safe to say the treason boat has sailed."

"You can tell them I did it," Caius said. "No one would—"

Dorian held his sword up to Caius's mouth, silencing him, blade hovering but not touching. He *had* just run it through two bodies. Contact would have been unsanitary. "I'm going to stop you right there."

Caius lifted a single eyebrow.

"I have said it a thousand times, and I will say it a thousand times more until you get it through your thick skull," Dorian said, lowering his sword but keeping it in his hand. He had a feeling they would need it before they were clear of the fortress and the long arm of Tanith's rule. Enunciating each word carefully so its meaning wouldn't be lost on Caius, he said, "You. Are. My. Friend. And I will follow you anywhere. Now let's go."

CHAPTER TWENTY-FOUR

The land beyond the keep's walls was eerily quiet. Moonlight skittered across a sea speckled with starlight. They made it all the way to the shore before Caius noticed that Dorian was nursing a limp, leaving a bloody trail behind them with each step. It was too much to ask to have escaped unscathed, but Dorian was a fighter and he would soldier on. Tanith would notice their absence soon enough, and her Firedrakes wouldn't be far behind.

"Dorian, if you would be so kind." Caius waved a hand at the foamy waves that marked the border between sand and sea. "Water is more in your wheelhouse than mine."

Dorian knelt along the shore, at the seam where the in-between pulsed, shadow dust in hand. "Where to?"

For what felt like the first time in his life, Caius had no answer. Tanith knew him better than anyone, save Dorian, and she certainly knew every inch of Drakharin land as well as he did, if not better. Every hideout, every safe house, every remote stronghold. If they stayed within Drakharin borders, it would be only a matter of time before she found them. Caius could feel their eyes on him, waiting, expectant. He was meant to be a leader, and he had no idea what to do. Maybe Tanith was right. Maybe he wasn't fit to lead, not anymore. Maybe he had lost his edge. If he couldn't lead three people to safety, how could he hope to lead an entire nation to peace?

He looked down at his hands. To think, he'd washed Ribos's blood from his skin a mere hour ago. He couldn't leave the Drakharin to Tanith's tender care. He couldn't fail the motley band of fugitives that needed him now. And he couldn't ignore the message Rose had left behind, scribbled on a map so many years ago. That map was sitting on the desk in his study, and he was plagued by a bitter stab of regret for leaving it there. Now he had nothing left of her but memories. The firebird was out there, and he was going to find it. For his people. For Rose. Thankfully, if there was one lesson he had learned during his reign, it was how to delegate. Caius cleared his throat. "Echo?"

"Yeah?" She squinted into the distance, scanning the hill behind them, checking to see if they'd been followed. They had been. Golden armor glinted in the distance. The Firedrakes would be on them in minutes.

Caius could hardly believe what he was about to ask, but everything about the past day had defied explanation. "Where to?"

Echo turned to face him, eyebrows raised. "You're asking me?"

With a sigh, Caius said, "Obviously."

He could hear the Firedrakes gathering in the distance.

They were running out of time. If he were captured now, if they were dragged back to the keep, then it would all be for naught. He would lose the only lead he had to find the firebird, and though Tanith might spare his life, Caius knew she wouldn't shed a single tear over ordering Dorian's execution. Echo and Ivy meant less than nothing to her. Capture would mean their deaths, and enough blood had been spilled already.

Echo shared an incredulous look with Ivy. "Why should I take you anywhere?"

The guards were nearer now, their footfalls getting louder and louder as the seconds ticked by.

"You want to take your chances with them?" Caius asked.

"Well, I don't exactly trust you," Echo said. Her eyes were riveted to the hill over which the Firedrakes would soon appear. The set of her shoulders was tense, as if she was ready to flee. But like Caius, she had nowhere to go, unless they went together.

"Nor I you," Caius said, "but beggars can't be choosers, can they? Your enemy has now become my enemy, and the way I see it, that makes us allies. And the firebird is bigger than you and I."

"Echo," Ivy said, tugging at her sleeve, "can't we just go home?"

"No." The word was laced with sadness. Echo swallowed thickly and shook her head. "Altair already threw me in a jail cell once today; I don't think he's going to be overly thrilled that we've started conspiring with Drakharin."

"Altair imprisoned you?" Caius asked. "I thought you were on their side."

"Yeah, so did I," Echo replied. "I've had a really long day."

"Echo," Ivy said, "I'd hardly call this conspiring." Her white feathers quivered. "Wait. Will there be conspiring? What are we conspiring about?"

Dorian looked up at them from where he knelt. "This is all well and good, but we really need to get going." His voice was strained, and he had a hand pressed to his side. Even though it was dark, Echo could see something staining his pale skin that looked a lot like blood.

"So," Caius said, "what's it going to be?"

Echo hesitated. He was losing her. The conflict was written on her face, as plain as day. They were meant to be enemies, but those distinctions were nowhere near as clear as they'd been the day before. If he failed to convince her that he was on her side—for now, at the very least—then the slim hope he had of finding the firebird would shrivel to nothing.

"You can take your chances with me," Caius said, "or you can stay and find out what the Dragon Prince has in store for you. All our fates rest with you." He extended his hand to Echo. "Well?"

"Echo . . ." Ivy took a step closer to her, fear and concern etched on her face.

Echo dragged her gaze from Caius's hand to his eyes. They could hear the Firedrakes cresting the ridge. It was now or never. Depending on Echo's decision, they would live to fight another day, or they'd meet their end here, on the shores outside the keep where Caius had been born. He and Dorian were capable fighters, but not even they could stand against the might of a full battalion of Firedrakes.

The Firedrakes were now close enough for Caius to make out individual figures on the hilltop. There were more than a dozen of them. After several agonizing seconds, Echo nodded.

"You know what they say." She stared at Caius for a beat before placing her hand, small but strong, in his. "The devil you know."

CHAPTER TWENTY-FIVE

"Any day now." The silver-haired Drakharin—Dorian, Caius had called him—was holding the portal open, his one eye fixed on the approaching Firedrakes. With Caius's hand in hers, Echo hoped to every god in the heavens that she wouldn't regret what she was about to say.

"Strasbourg."

The word was scarcely out of her mouth before the darkness of the in-between rushed up, crashing against them. The Firedrakes' shouts were eaten by a heavy silence. The impact stole the breath from Echo's lungs, and if it hadn't been for Caius's solid grip on her hand, she would have been wholly untethered, set adrift at sea in the midst of a raging storm. She'd never traveled through the in-between with more than one other person at her side, and the force of it nearly made her collapse, knees turning to jelly as the ground fell away from beneath her boots.

As suddenly as it began, it was over. Cold, hard pavement

materialized beneath her. Even though Echo hadn't moved an inch, it was like stumbling while standing still. Her eyes fought to adjust to the light. She focused on what she could hear and feel rather than what she could see: Solid stone beneath her feet. A church bell tolling the nighttime hours. The soft whisper of a river slapping the base of a bridge.

"Where are we?" Ivy asked.

Echo recognized the queasy hitch in Ivy's voice. The last time she'd heard it, the two of them had gorged themselves on a bag of Halloween candy Echo had stolen from the Kmart at Astor Place. Ivy had puked up a rainbow of masticated gummy worms. Echo wasn't the only one who'd struggled with their journey.

She held up her hand to shield her eyes. The streetlamp above was glaringly bright after the darkness of the in-between. Her vision prickled, and she blinked away the bursts of light exploding behind her lids. She recognized the bridge. It was one of the oldest in Strasbourg. Bridges made for excellent thresholds, being themselves monuments to the in-between, and age had made this one strong. Jumping between gateways without knowing one's destination was always a gamble, but some thresholds were so strong they managed to shine through the darkness at the person on the other side. Dorian had found the bridge just as it had found him.

"We're in Strasbourg," Echo said. "The Ponts Couverts in the center of town, to be specific."

"A wise choice," Caius said, as if he couldn't quite equate Echo with wise choices. Both he and Dorian seemed unruffled by their jaunt through the in-between. Echo hated them for it, just a little. "Strasbourg is situated in one of the few neutral patches of Western Europe. Neither the Avicen nor the Drakharin patrol it regularly."

"True," Echo said, brushing off bits of straw that still clung to her jeans, "but that's not why I wanted to come here."

She was beginning to learn that Caius's confused face was that of a person who was not accustomed to confusion. It was almost endearing. Almost.

"No?" Caius asked. "Then why?"

"Jasper," Echo said.

Without another word, she turned on her heel, slipping Ivy's arm into her own and trusting the Drakharin to follow. And they would. If they were desperate enough to follow a human girl into what could have been an Avicen trap, they clearly had nowhere else to go. They couldn't go home, but then again, neither could she.

They made their way through Strasbourg's narrow cobble-stoned streets, empty of wandering eyes and curious pedestrians at such a late hour. Echo counted the number of times the bells at the top of the cathedral rang. It was approaching midnight. Though Taipei felt like a lifetime ago, it was still only the middle of the week. The denizens of Strasbourg were tucked in their beds, safe and sound and completely unaware of the unusual quartet roaming their streets.

Echo spared a glance at their Drakharin company, whose leather tunics were strangely at home with the old-world feel of Strasbourg's architecture. Night painted the streets in shades of blue and black, and Dorian's fair hair shone like a beacon. Caius, with his dark hair and clothes, blended with the shadows.

"Where are you taking us?" Caius asked. His long legs caught up to her with ease.

"Jasper's." Echo could have volunteered more information, but she was feeling difficult. It was immature, but she couldn't quite find it in herself to care.

Ivy slipped her arm from Echo's, falling back a few steps. She'd kept a healthy distance between herself and the Drakharin since leaving the keep. Dorian looked in Ivy's direction, and she tensed, crossing her arms stiffly. Something had happened between them, Echo realized. She made a mental note to ask about it later.

Since arriving at the bridge, Dorian had remained silent, as though he were perfectly content to let Caius do all the talking. His face was drawn and pale, and the wound he'd been clutching earlier was still bleeding. Echo hoped he wouldn't leave a set of bloody footprints in their wake. A trail of blood leading from point A to point B would have been a touch too conspicuous. Caius had offered to help him, but Dorian had brushed his hand away, muttering something in rapid Drakhar that Echo couldn't understand. A strange pair, those two.

"Right," Caius said, keeping his voice quiet so it wouldn't carry in the still night air. "Jasper's."

He was close enough to Echo that his arm brushed against her shoulder every few steps. She wasn't quite sure why her heart wanted to beat in time with his stride, but she elected to ignore it.

"Who is this Jasper?" Caius asked. "Friend of yours?"

"Jasper doesn't really have friends," Echo said. "But he does owe me a favor. And since he's usually happiest when he's on the wrong side of the law, he's our best bet for finding a place to crash until we figure out a game plan."

They were nearing the cathedral that Jasper called home,

his nest perched in one of its spires. She was glad the bells had stopped tolling. The trip through the in-between had left her with a persistent ringing in her ears that probably wouldn't fade for hours.

Echo chanced a peek at Caius. His eyes had a faraway look to them.

"Is he Avicen?" he asked.

"Nominally."

"What does that mean?"

Echo wrapped her arms around herself, burying her hands in her armpits. It was spring, but the night air was cooler than her leather jacket was made for. "It means the only side Jasper's on is his own."

"You said he owes you a favor." Caius didn't seem bothered by the cold. Lucky him. "How did someone like that wind up in your debt?"

Echo let herself smile. "I saved the one thing he cares about more than anything else in this world."

"What's that?"

"His life."

Caius looked at her as though she were a puzzle he was trying to solve. "There must be a story behind that," he said. "Perhaps you can tell it to me sometime."

Echo shrugged. "Perhaps."

"Is he a thief, then?" he asked. "Like you?"

The question sounded vaguely judgmental, but when she shot a dirty look at Caius, she found him smiling. It was tired and ragged at the edges, but a genuine smile. Not a grin or a smirk. It made him seem younger. As quickly as the smile had appeared, it was gone. It had been a wisp of a smile. A fleeting not-smile.

"Don't knock it," she said, turning her gaze front. She must have been more tired than she realized, if she was letting her mind busy itself with musings on Caius's smile. "A girl's gotta eat. And yeah, he's a thief. Among other things. Jasper's more of a career scoundrel."

"Well, any port in a storm, I suppose."

Echo leveled another glare at Caius. He held up his hands in mock surrender. "Joking," he said.

"Not laughing." She pulled away from him as they emerged onto the plaza surrounding the cathedral. Caius had kept close enough to her that she felt colder when she stepped away, losing the nearness of his body heat.

Shoving her hands in her pockets, Echo walked up to an ornately carved door, the figures in the pietà above its lintel gazing down with unseeing eyes. There was something about churches that she found unsettling. Everything seemed overly concerned with death, as if someone had forgotten that the basis of the religion for which they'd been built was a rebirth.

"This is it." Echo waved her hand in front of the door, feeling the faint buzz of energy that signaled the presence of magic. It felt like a weak electric current, almost as though she'd been rubbing her socks on a carpeted floor. She had been to Jasper's only a few times, but she remembered the ward on the door that doubled as an alarm. If Echo kept poking at it, Jasper was bound to respond. Eventually. Hopefully. If he was home. The thought that he might be out hadn't occurred to her until that moment.

"Echo?" Ivy drew up behind her, peeking over her shoulder. "What if he's sleeping?"

"He won't be," Echo replied. "Jasper's a bit of a night owl."

The seconds ticked by in tense silence, and Echo felt the cruel pinch of hopelessness in her stomach. Even if he was home, there was no guarantee that he would answer. And why would he? If Jasper checked the small security cameras pointed at the door—the very ones Echo had helped him rig—and saw her there, with two Drakharin, one of whom was busy bleeding all over the place, he would be wise to turn them away. Her desperation crescendoed. Desperate times called for desperate measures. She ran out into the plaza, eyes fixed on the cathedral's steeple.

"Jasper!" Echo shouted at the top of her lungs, the sound bouncing off the walls of the buildings bracketing the plaza. "Jasper, open the goddamn door!"

Ivy, Caius, and Dorian stared in stunned silence.

"Jasper!" Echo yelled again, and Caius moved so quickly that he had one hand plastered over Echo's mouth and the other wrapped around the back of her neck to hold her still before she even saw him approach.

"What are you doing?" he hissed. "Are you trying to wake the entire city?" The hand at the back of her neck tangled in her hair, and his nails dug painfully into her scalp. "In case you haven't noticed, the rest of us don't exactly blend in."

As if the moon itself wanted to help Caius prove his point, the clouds cleared just enough for his scales to catch the faint bit of light that peeked through, refracting it into a million tiny rainbows scattered across his cheekbones. He became, for a brief instant, the loveliest thing Echo had ever seen up close. But then the clouds returned, and all she saw was his anger, the sharply angled planes of his face making him look even more severe.

His hand was still covering her mouth, so when she

spoke, her words were muffled. Caius retracted his hand, slowly, as if he didn't trust her not to start shouting again.

And really, he shouldn't have.

"Jasper!"

"You rang?"

Four pairs of eyes snapped to the now open door, where a figure stood silhouetted by soft yellow light. Dorian had his sword drawn, though it trembled in his hand as if his grip wasn't quite secure. Ivy looked as though she couldn't decide if it would be safer to run toward Jasper or away from him. Echo batted Caius's hands away, brushing past him as she walked to the door.

Jasper stood in the doorway, arms crossed over his slender chest, sinfully lovely even when annoyed. The warm brown of his skin glowed prettily in the gentle orange light of the streetlamp. His smooth, short hair-feathers were waves of purple, green, and blue. Jasper was a peacock, through and through. He was so striking that even the scowl on his face seemed more like adornment than genuine irritation. His well-worn jeans and white T-shirt were simple enough not to clash with the rest of him—a deliberate sartorial choice. If Echo had a dollar for every time Jasper claimed that beauty was his cross to bear, she could have treated them all to a lovely steak dinner.

"What the hell are you doing here?" Jasper asked.

"Hello to you, too." Echo smiled, far too brightly. Jasper's frown deepened. He would not be charmed. Not by her. Not tonight.

"Interesting company you're keeping," Jasper said, eyes roving over the two Drakharin behind her. Echo wouldn't swear to it, but she thought they lingered on Dorian longer than was necessary. Like any good thief, Jasper had an eye for shiny, pretty things. She supposed that Dorian, with his silver hair and sparkly blue eye, could be considered both shiny and pretty.

"Yeah, funny story about that. How about I tell it to you inside?"

Jasper stared at her as if she'd sprouted an extra head. "No," he said, and turned away. Echo grabbed his arm, holding him in place.

"Jasper—"

"I said no, Echo." He looked pointedly at her hand on his arm, but she refused to move it. He was their last hope, and she wasn't about to give up that easily.

"You owe me."

Jasper met her gaze with a hard stare, golden eyes unblinking. Just when she was beginning to think that maybe there was no honor among thieves, that he would turn them away, tell them there was no room at the inn, Jasper sighed. He rolled his eyes so hard she could almost hear them rattling around in his skull.

"Picking up macarons is one thing, but this?" Jasper gestured at the four of them. They must have made for a sorry sight. After a moment's hesitation, he heaved a weary sigh.

Sweet victory, Echo thought. Jasper was squishier on the inside than he would ever admit.

"Fine," he said with such an air of martyrdom that she wouldn't have been surprised to find his likeness mounted on the cathedral's walls alongside the saints. "Come in. And wipe your feet before you enter. You all look like crap that's been dragged through mud and then set on fire."

CHAPTER TWENTY-SIX

I f someone asked Dorian how his life had gotten to this
point, he wasn't entirely certain that he'd be able to give
them an answer. Not a satisfactory one, at least. They were
ushered up a long flight of stairs by a flamboyantly colored
Avicen who kept lamenting the inevitable ruin of his carpet.

Dorian dug his fingers deeper into the flesh on both
sides of his wound. Perhaps he was dreaming. Perhaps he
would wake up and find himself in his own bed, down the
hall from Caius's chambers, and laugh about his wild nightmare later. But a very real pain flared through his gut, and
he didn't wake.

When they reached the top, Dorian was so light-headed
he was only vaguely aware of the voices around him. He
must have lost more blood on the climb than he had on the
walk from the river. Echo was leading a circle of introduc-
tions around him. He hardly noticed anything beyond the
hand Caius placed on his back to steady him. Resting his

head against the doorjamb, he let his eyes droop closed and focused on not passing out. Collapsing in a puddle of his own blood would lack a certain dignity.

"And who is this tall drink of water?"

It took Dorian a solid minute to realize that the Avicen was talking to him. He blamed the blood loss. He opened his eye to find all four of them staring at him. Caius was closest, brows drawn together in worry. Echo looked at him the way one might look at a wounded animal by the side of the road, concerned but not overly invested in its survival. Ivy stared openly at his wound. Judging from the speed at which she was blinking, it must have looked even worse than it felt. Jasper was appraising him with an amused tilt to his lips that was almost a smirk. It probably would have been had Dorian not been bleeding all over his formerly pristine white carpet.

Caius's lips were moving but sound wasn't reaching Dorian the way it should. From the shapes Caius's mouth was making, he might be saying his name. Dorian closed his eye again and sound rushed back, as if his body could focus on only one sense at a time. How very economical. Without his sight to distract him, he heard Caius ask, "Dorian, are you all right?"

Dorian respected Caius. Admired him. Occasionally felt more for him than was entirely appropriate in a royal guard. But sometimes, even he had to admit that Caius wasn't always the sharpest knife in the armory.

"Are you dying?" Jasper asked. As if it weren't obvious.

Dorian's answer was a wordless groan. He brought his other hand up to his wound, and little flecks of red spattered on the carpet. *No*, he thought. *There is no way this looks worse than it feels.*

Caius was using both arms to support Dorian now, and for that, he was grateful. Sliding down the door and onto the floor in a graceless, bloody heap was becoming a very real possibility.

"He needs medical attention," Caius said, wrapping an arm around Dorian's waist.

That's nice, Dorian thought.

Jasper moved toward them, and without thinking twice, Dorian pressed himself against the wall as if he were trying to push through it. The cluster of scars on his eye socket pulsed with an intensity that matched the wound in his side. He closed his eye, and for a brief and terrible moment, he was back on that battlefield, with a brown-and-white-feathered Avicen leaning over him, bloodied knife in one hand, dead blue eye in the other. Caius's arm tightened around him. It was enough to pull him back to the moment. Dorian drew in a shaky breath. The metallic scent of his own blood was oddly comforting.

Jasper paused, hands raised in front of him as though he were trying to calm a rambunctious colt. Dorian had enough wherewithal left to take offense.

"I have supplies," Jasper said. "I can patch him up, but it won't be pretty. I'm no healer."

"You are," Echo said, turning to Ivy. "You're apprenticed to one, at least. Can you help him?"

Ivy's gaze darted from Echo to Dorian. When her eyes met his, Dorian couldn't read what he saw there. Ivy nodded slowly. "Yeah, I can help."

Dorian's injury-addled brain must have been playing tricks on him, because there was no way Ivy had just offered to help him after the way he'd treated her. No one was that good. No one Dorian knew. He tried to stand, tried to convince them that, no, really, he was fine, but he swayed on his feet, falling against Caius's chest. It was all very unseemly.

Jasper said something to Caius, but all of Dorian's attention was on the task of not throwing up on Caius's chest. Or his boots. Or any part of Caius, really. It wasn't until he felt himself being moved, more than half carried by Caius and Echo, that he realized they'd been talking about laying him on Jasper's bed. Dorian desperately wanted to protest. He was no fainting maiden to be coddled. Except maybe he was, because the next thing he noticed was the soft dip of a mattress beneath him.

Hands peeled back the layers of his clothing, and cool air prickled the skin on his bare chest as his shirt was cut off. Dorian tried to bat them away.

"I don't need your help," he slurred. Maybe if he said it aloud, it would magically become true.

"The gaping hole in your torso ruining my Egyptian cotton sheets says otherwise," Jasper said, emerging from what Dorian assumed was the bathroom with Ivy, arms laden with various medical supplies. He hadn't even seen them leave.

Dorian flinched when a cold rag was pressed to his forehead, wiping away the sweat beading at his hairline. A cup was held to his lips, and a hand, too small to belong to Caius or Jasper, helped him hold his head up.

"Drink this," Ivy said, tipping the cup slightly. Bitterness exploded on his tongue, and he fought not to gag. A hint of mint lingered beneath the medicinal taste of whatever she'd given him, and it made his stomach roil in rebellion. Ivy set the cup aside, turning to Caius and Echo, who hovered like mother hens. Dorian had the sneaking suspicion that Echo was more worried about Ivy than him.

"Give me some room to work, please," said Ivy. Caius, Jasper, and Echo obeyed without question. Ivy's white feathers were still covered in dirt and blood, but she sounded more sure of herself than Dorian had heard her since the warlocks he'd hired had dragged her before him. How different she seemed now, free and in her element. Something knotted in Dorian's stomach that had nothing to do with his wound.

He blinked blearily, but it was less of a struggle to keep his eyes open than it had been moments before. Whatever Ivy had made him drink was disgusting, but effective. Her small hands were fast yet methodical as she unrolled a generous length of gauze and set about cutting it into manageable strips. When she began to clean the wound, her fingers were gentle and efficient. The rest of her was as grimy as when they had fled Wyvern's Keep, but her hands and forearms gleamed white, her skin and feathers clean and spotless. She'd washed her hands, so as not to pass along an infection. Dorian was oddly touched. He had been cruel to her. He did not deserve her kindness. He wasn't even sure he wanted it.

"Why?" Dorian asked.

The sound of his voice startled her, and she flinched, fingers scraping the edge of the wound. Dorian hissed in pain. Ivy mumbled a terse apology, keeping her eyes on his wound.

"Why what?" she asked.

He lifted the arm opposite her, heavy from the combination of blood loss and medicine, to gesture loosely at his injury. "Why are you helping me?"

Ivy worked in silence for several minutes, and Dorian gave up the hope of getting an answer. She didn't owe him one. He let his eye drift shut and focused on not wincing as she picked small bits of dirt out of the wound.

"I'm a healer."

At the sound of Ivy's voice, quiet but steady, Dorian opened his eyes. She said no more, as if that simple proclamation was answer enough. The medicine continued to work its magic, and Dorian's vision cleared enough for him to see that the bruise on her cheek had blossomed to an angry shade of purple. He had put that there.

"I know," he said softly. "I know, but I—" He gestured at the bruise on her face.

"I haven't forgotten," Ivy said. She smeared a salve over the wound. It was bracingly cold at first, stinging upon contact before fading to a slight chill. The flesh around the wound numbed as she gently layered strips of gauze atop the salve.

"So why?" He didn't ask what he really wanted to. *Why are you being this kind? How can you be this kind?*

"Because," she said, reaching for the tape on the bedside table, "there's enough cruelty in this world without me adding to it."

Ivy tore off a few strips of tape and applied them to the edges of the gauze, securing them with a gentle press. Wiping her hands on the towel Jasper had provided, she stood, surveying her work with one final nod. Without another word, she turned and walked away. She hadn't made eye contact, not once, and it left him feeling terribly, undeniably small.

CHAPTER TWENTY-SEVEN

As Echo watched Ivy, she felt someone's gaze settle on her. She turned to find Caius watching her. He'd gravitated to the high-backed leather chair beside the mantel, and he didn't just sit in it. He sprawled, taking up space as if he owned it. Echo was perched on the corner of a too-soft sofa, feeling dwarfed by the openness of Jasper's loft. Fatigue had settled deep into her bones, but at least she had on clean clothes. After her first shared job with Jasper had resulted in an unfortunate incident with a septic tank, she had carved out a tiny space for herself in the bottom drawer of his dresser. She'd spent an hour picking mud out of his hair-feathers, and she strongly suspected it was gratitude that kept Jasper from complaining about her claiming the space for herself. Echo stretched the sleeves of her sweater over her thumbs and met Caius's gaze. Until this moment, she hadn't seen him in artificial light, and it was quite the view.

Small lamps dotted the loft, their bulbs covered with

stained-glass shades that cast the room in soft reds and purples. Back at the keep, Caius's eyes had looked like emerald flames, catching the light from the sconces on the walls and dancing with it. Now, they were so dark they were hardly green at all, as though the swirling black of his pupil had swallowed the iris whole. Echo stared for a minute before she realized what she was doing. Tearing her eyes from his, she felt the traitorous heat of a blush creeping up her cheeks. She turned away to hide her flush, watching Ivy tend to Dorian.

"Your friend is talented," Caius said.

There was something about being here with him that made Echo's tongue feel too large for her mouth. She simply nodded and kept her eyes forward. Jasper was loudly rearranging cutlery in the kitchenette, signaling that he was giving her some privacy. What for, she had no idea, but that was par for the course. She usually had no idea what motivated Jasper to do the things that he did.

"He's a strange one, isn't he?" Caius's voice was soft, conspiratorial even.

"Jasper?" she asked, finally looking back at him. He was trying to make small talk. *What fresh hell?*

Caius raised an eyebrow as if to say *Who else?* The blush returned, heat crawling up the back of Echo's neck like a spider.

"Yeah," she said. "Yeah, he is."

"I'm curious," Caius said, leaning forward to unbuckle the leather straps of the harness that held the two long knives on his back. "I'd like to hear about the time you saved his life. You seem so young to be having such adventures."

Echo felt a prickle of annoyance at his words and held on to it. It was better than blushing. "I'm not a child."

If embarrassment had not been beneath a hardened Drakharin mercenary, Echo would have sworn that the flash of emotion that crossed Caius's face was just that. But she blinked and it was gone.

"I meant no insult." Caius laid the knives on the floor beside the chair. Echo hated herself for noticing the way his chest strained against the bloodied fabric of his tunic. When he looked up at her, the hint of a smile he wore was almost sheepish. "But you *are* young. Too young to be spending your nights on the run from Drakharin soldiers, surely."

"I don't feel young," said Echo. It hadn't been the first time she'd been forced to run for her life, but the muscles in her legs ached in a way they never had before. A dull twinge settled into her lower back, creeping its way up her spine and across her shoulders. A faint throb had begun behind her eyes, and she knew she would be nursing a monstrous headache soon.

"The young never do," he said softly. She didn't know how to respond to this version of Caius. Antagonism she understood, but this newfound camaraderie was strange.

"How old are you?" Echo asked.

"How old do I look?" Caius's lips twitched into a small grin. If he was tired, he wore it well.

"A lot younger than you probably are."

He was quiet for a few moments, and the ping of Jasper's microwave made her jump.

"About two hundred fifty," Caius said. "The years start to blend together after a while." He shrugged, as if the notion were the most normal thing in the world. "And how old are you?"

There was something about him that seemed both young

and old at the same time. He lacked the gravitas of the Ala, who had always reminded Echo of a great oak tree, aged and eternal. In the face of two hundred fifty, any number Echo could have produced would have felt paltry by comparison, but the real answer seemed woefully inadequate.

"Seventeen."

Caius blinked, slowly, as though opening and closing his lids took a bit of effort. "Seventeen," he breathed. "Remarkable."

"If you say so."

"You still haven't answered my question," Caius said. "About Jasper."

"Oh." Echo had already forgotten it. The way Caius sat—no, sprawled—with his dark green eyes and his darker brown hair and his angular cheekbones made her slow, as if her brain had gone a bit rusty. She shook her head, as though the simple motion would clear it. It didn't.

"Me and Jasper," she said, though she didn't quite like the way that sounded. Jasper had flirted with her, but he flirted with anything with a pulse. There was no such thing as *Echo and Jasper*. She didn't know why it mattered to her that Caius shouldn't believe there was, but it did. "About a year ago, we were both hired to steal the same thing. I got it. He didn't. His employers didn't like that very much."

"What was it?" Caius stretched his long legs out in front of him, crossing them at the ankles. Echo busied herself with wondering what white-furred animal had died to make Jasper's rug.

"A harp."

"A harp?" Caius sounded almost amused.

"A harp."

"Must have been some harp."

"Supposedly, it was magical," Echo said. "Legend had it that if you played it aboard a ship, you could call mermaids to do your bidding. But I don't think mermaids even exist."

"They do."

And just like that, Echo's world rearranged itself. It seemed to be doing that with alarming frequency these days.

"Did it work?" Caius asked. "The harp?"

Echo shrugged. "I didn't stick around to find out. I was busy pulling Jasper out of the ocean. His employers threw him overboard when he told them I'd stolen it from right under his nose."

"The Avicen aren't overly fond of water," Caius said. He made it sound clinical, as if he were reciting from a textbook.

"Some are, some aren't," Echo said. "Jasper can't swim to save his life. Literally."

"But you saved it for him." Caius looked her over as if he was appraising her. She didn't like it. "That was noble." He made it sound more like a curiosity than a compliment.

"It seemed like a good idea at the time," she said.

"I'm sure it did."

They fell into a silence that wasn't entirely uncomfortable. Echo gazed around the room, at the paintings on the walls—all stolen, all famous, all hideously expensive—and the little touches that made the loft feel like a home. A record player sat in the corner, vinyl albums stacked haphazardly next to it. A row of Japanese netsuke lined the windowsill, a tiny army carved of ivory. All stolen. Muted voices drifted from the kitchenette, where Ivy had joined Jasper.

Caius spoke before Echo could make a break for the kitchenette. "I'm sorry you were dragged into this mess."

She blinked. "Really?"

"Really."

"I just . . ." The words refused to come easy. There was so much she wanted to ask. "Why?"

Caius breathed long and deep before answering. "Because it isn't your mess."

"And it's yours?" Echo asked. "I thought you were just the hired muscle."

That small smile found its way to Caius's face again. "We all have our jobs to do. The parameters of mine have simply changed."

Echo raised her eyebrows. "And now they include teaming up with a bunch of Avicen?"

"There are some things more important than taking sides," Caius said. "The . . . previous Dragon Prince tasked me with finding the firebird, and it's a cause I happen to believe in."

The clinking of ceramic cups from the kitchenette cut through the silence, but Echo couldn't have torn her eyes away from Caius if she wanted to. The fact that she didn't was problematic.

"The Dragon Prince," Echo said. "What was he like?"

Caius looked down at his interlaced fingers. A few locks of hair fell in front of his face, and Echo's fingers twitched with the urge to brush them back. She sat on her hands. He didn't look up when he said, "Bit of an idiot."

A mad giggle tore its way out of Echo. "What?"

"He was so busy looking for threats from the outside that he missed the one hiding right under his nose."

"Tanith?"

Caius nodded.

"Who is she?"

"His sister."

Echo drew her legs up onto the couch, crossing them at the ankles. What must that have been like, she wondered, to be betrayed so thoroughly by someone who was supposed to love you, wholly and unconditionally? Her own family—the biological one she'd run away from—had disabused her of the notion of innate and obligatory love long ago, but she'd always imagined the bond between siblings to be a sacred thing. Like her bond with Ivy. "Damn," she said.

"That about sums it up."

"What was his name?"

Caius shifted, long legs uncrossing and crossing, one hand rising to rub the base of his neck. "I don't know. The Drakharin keep the name of their ruler well hidden from those on the outside. There's power in names."

The Avicen and the Drakharin had more in common than they realized, but Echo kept that thought to herself. Mortal enemies were touchy about being compared to each other. "So I've heard."

Caius nodded again. "Thank you," he said quietly.

"For what?"

"For this." Caius gestured at the loft. "For bringing us here. For helping when you didn't have to."

"I didn't have much of a choice, did I?"

Caius's eyes went soft and distant, as if he was looking at her, and maybe also through her. "There's always a choice, Echo. Even if it's a bad one."

"And which one was this?" she asked. Ivy and Jasper had gone curiously quiet, and Echo knew they were listening.

"The good one, I hope."

Ivy and Jasper resumed their conversation, voices hushed, and Echo was glad of it.

"You aren't what I would have expected," she said. Now it was her turn to be quiet, to make the words soft enough for only Caius to hear. "For a Drakharin, I mean."

He clasped his hands over his stomach and smiled wearily. Smiling made him seem younger, as though his age matched his looks, but now, with the fine lines of fatigue setting in around his eyes, he looked older. He was too handsome to ever be truly haggard, but his shoulders sagged, and he sank deeper into the chair, meeting Echo's eyes with a half-lidded gaze.

"Should I apologize for that?" he asked.

Echo shook her head.

"What would the Avicen have you believe of me?"

"That you're a monster."

Caius arched an eyebrow. "And do you find me monstrous?"

She could have lied, but he'd see right through it. He didn't come across as the sort you could sneak a falsehood past. "'The devil is not as black as he is painted.'"

"Dante." The corners of Caius's lips curved upward just a touch. "You're well read, I see."

"I spend a lot of my time in libraries." It should have felt wrong, to expose that part of herself to Caius, no matter how tiny it was. It should have. It really, really should have.

Caius studied her for a few heartbeats more before reaching into his shirt and pulling out the locket. Echo's fingers twitched with her longing to hold it. Like Jasper, she had always been drawn to beautiful things, but this was different. This felt as if it should have been hers, and she couldn't have explained it if she tried.

"If the locket belonged to you once, how did it wind up at that teahouse in Japan?" Echo asked.

"I gave it to someone a long time ago." Caius twirled the pendant between his fingers, running a thumb over the bronze dragon on its front. "I suppose she gave it to someone else in turn. Strange to think that it found its way back to me."

Strange indeed. He was connected to everything—the firebird, the locket, the music box, the maps—in a way Echo couldn't quite piece together, but there was a finality to his tone that didn't invite further questioning. Perhaps in the morning, he'd be more forthcoming. Or, she mused, he would expect her to be as well. Maybe it was best if she didn't pepper him with questions he clearly didn't want to answer; that way he wouldn't pry into her secrets with equal curiosity. With a sigh, she moved on to her next query. "Did you keep the dagger?"

Caius slipped the locket's chain over his head and dropped it onto his lap. He must have replaced the broken one before their abrupt departure. Then he unclasped a small leather sheath on the side of his belt, removing the dagger in one smooth motion. He looked from the dagger to Echo, silent, waiting. Her fingers twitched again. She wanted to hold it, to feel the weight of the hilt in her palm, the onyx and pearl magpies against her skin. But there was one thing that had been bothering her since she'd found it.

"I don't get it," she said. "The locket had a map inside, but how does a dagger help us find the firebird?"

"I don't know." The phrase fell awkwardly from Caius's lips, as if he wasn't used to that particular combination of words.

"It's funny," she said. Caius tilted his head in place of asking what. "The magpies on the knife. That's what the Ala calls me, sometimes. Her little magpie." She didn't know why she felt the need to tell him that, either.

"Magpies." His voice was hushed, as if he was talking to himself. Echo felt positively incidental. "They make excellent thieves, you know."

There was something unbearably sad about him. For a brief moment, she thought she saw the person he might have been, long ago, before the war had taken its toll.

"They're smart, too," she said.

That ghost of a smile returned to Caius's face. "Is that so?"

Echo nodded. "And they're the only birds that pass the mirror test."

"What's the mirror test?"

"It's a way for scientists to measure intelligence. The humble magpie is the only bird that can recognize its own reflection."

Caius looked back at the dagger, turning it over in his hands. "Your human scientists do the strangest things."

"I don't know that I'd call them *my* human scientists," Echo said. "I haven't had many dealings with"—she curled her fingers into quotation marks in the air—"'my kind.'"

He responded with a quiet huff. He had eyes only for the dagger and the seven little magpies flying around its hilt. "Why did you steal it?" he asked.

"There was a map in the locket. It told me to go to the Louvre, and so I did." Echo wasn't sure how much she should tell him. She didn't trust him, not yet, and she knew that being guided to the dagger by some unseen force wasn't exactly what one would call *normal*.

Caius held the dagger at eye level, turning it slightly so that it glittered in the light. "Yes, but why *this*?"

"That's classified," Echo replied, for lack of a better response.

Letting out a small laugh, he said, "You know, we're going to have to start trusting each other sooner or later."

Echo smiled, just a little. "Baby steps." She watched him study the dagger, seemingly mesmerized by the play of light across its surface. "Why is it so special to you?" she asked, hoping to distract Caius from his line of questioning

"It's not," he said. "It just . . . it reminds me of someone I used to know."

There was a weight to his words that Echo thought she understood. "A girl?"

A different breed of smile graced his face, but there was no joy in it. "Isn't it always?"

The sum total of Echo's romantic endeavors was limited to the past two months she'd spent with Rowan. She felt young and inexperienced in the face of Caius's centuries. "So they say."

She watched him trail his fingers down the hilt, tilting it to better catch the light, the onyx and pearl of the magpies' wings and bellies glinting prettily. With a sigh, he handed it to her, hilt first. "Here. It's like you said: finders, keepers." He left off the *asshole*. It was nice of him.

Echo took the dagger, turning it over in her hands. If the music box had led her to the locket, and the locket had led her to this, then there had to be something about it that was special, something that would tell her what her next step should be. She examined the dagger closely, her gaze raking over every detail. The silver on the handle had darkened from age, but it had otherwise been well maintained. The onyx and pearl inlays shone as bright as new, and the blade was sharp enough to pierce skin. She squinted, searching for a clue.

If I were hiding something in a dagger, Echo thought, *where would I hide it?*

With methodical fingers, she traced every centimeter of its surface, from the guard between handle and blade to the rounded edge of the pommel on the bottom of the hilt. There were only so many places to conceal something in a dagger. Caius kept quiet as she searched by touch, and after a few seconds, she felt it. A seam, right where the base of the pommel was screwed on like a cap. Caius leaned forward, watching as she coaxed it loose. It was screwed on snugly, which was hardly a surprise since it clearly hadn't been opened in years. Echo held the handle tightly, grimacing as her palm went raw. She twisted and twisted and twisted until the rounded cap came off. Caius slid off his seat, coming to kneel near Echo.

"Well?" Caius asked. "Is there anything in there?"

"Oh, I bet there is." Holding the dagger firmly, she shook it, hoping to dislodge whatever might be hidden within the handle. A rolled-up piece of paper slid out, falling onto her lap. "God, I love it when I'm right." She looked up at Caius to find him smiling back at her, eyes alight with curiosity. The game was afoot, and they were playing it together. Drakharin or not, maybe he wouldn't make such a bad partner in this adventure after all.

Caius nodded at the paper in her lap. "Go on, open it. Maybe it's another map."

"Here's hoping." She set the dagger aside and slowly unrolled the paper. It was old, just like the maps of Kyoto and Paris, and one of the edges crumbled at her touch. When the paper was flat against her lap, she needed only seconds to recognize what it depicted. It was a small section of New York City. Her home. A straight line bisected the map's length, with FIFTH AVENUE written down the center in neat block letters. The numbers on the street were so small, they were hard to read, but Echo didn't need them to tell her what she was looking at. A building in the center of the page was circled in faded red ink. The Metropolitan Museum of Art. Beneath it, another four-line poem had been written in the same hand that had penned the clues on the other two maps. Caius leaned over to read it, breath ghosting on her hands.

"'The bird that sings at midnight,'" he recited, "'from within its cage of bones, will rise from blood and ashes to greet the truth unknown.'" He sat back on his heels, brow furrowed. "What the hell does that mean?"

"Your guess is as good as mine," Echo said. "But I have every intention of finding out." She met Caius's gaze. "You in?"

He smiled again, widely enough for her to notice that his teeth were almost disturbingly perfect. He nodded. "I'm in."

Oh yes, she thought. *The game is most definitely afoot.*

CHAPTER TWENTY-EIGHT

Sleep tickled at the edges of Dorian's mind, but he knew it would elude him until he all but passed out from exhaustion. He had fought against the Avicen for too many years, lost too much to them, to be able to rest in one of their nests while hiding like a common outlaw. And that was what they had become. Yesterday, Caius had been a prince and Dorian had been the captain of his guard.

How the mighty have fallen, he thought.

Dorian was on the verge of feeling sorry for himself when Jasper descended the three steps that separated the bedroom—if it could be called that—from the rest of the loft, two steaming mugs in hand. Dorian's hand twitched to the bedside table against which Caius had rested his sword.

Jasper clucked his tongue disapprovingly, as if he were a disappointed schoolmarm and Dorian a naughty student.

"Don't think I didn't see that," Jasper said, setting one of the mugs down on the bedside table. "It would be earth-shatteringly poor manners for you to whip out your sword in my home." And then, oh sublime horror, Jasper winked. "After all, we've only just met."

Dorian's mouth opened and closed, but there were simply no words.

Jasper shook his head and smiled. "Too easy." He settled on the edge of the bed, dangerously close to Dorian's left hand. It wasn't his sword hand, but it would do in a pinch. He hadn't realized that his fingers had curled into a tight fist until he felt the tiny pricks of pain from his nails digging into his palm.

"Relax," Jasper said. "I'm not here to hurt you."

The thought was so absurd that Dorian couldn't not respond. "As if you could."

In hindsight, it wasn't his wisest choice of words. Jasper poked the bandage Ivy had so carefully applied to his wound, and Dorian hissed as the muscles in his abdomen jumped.

"There, now that that's settled." Jasper offered the mug to Dorian. "Drink this. Doctor's orders."

Dorian accepted the mug with tentative hands. If Ivy had wanted to harm him, she'd had ample opportunity, but still. He sniffed the contents of the mug dubiously.

"It isn't poisoned." Jasper rolled his eyes. "Gimme." He snatched the mug back, quickly but carefully, and took a sip. "See? Perfectly safe." He stuck out his tongue, gagging. "Gross, but safe."

Jasper returned the mug and watched as Dorian took a small sip. It was bitter, but not nearly as intense as Ivy's last concoction. The aftertaste was vaguely citrusy this time. It wasn't pleasant, but Dorian choked it down, mindful of Jasper's golden eyes on him.

It had been a long time since Dorian had seen an Avicen male up close, and he'd never seen one quite like Jasper. Everything about him screamed *peacock*. The angles of his face were graceful yet masculine, a sharp counterpoint to the riot of color that was his hair, if one could call Avicen feathers hair. Jasper's were the familiar blues and greens and subtle golds of peacock feathers, but also deep purples and bright fuchsias. His skin gleamed a warm brown, complementing the molten gold of his eyes.

"Like what you see?" Jasper asked, voice low and dark and all too intimate. It was a bedroom voice.

Dorian sipped Ivy's home-brewed tea and refused to dignify that question with a response. The mug just barely hid the flush on his cheeks. Having skin as fair as his was far more curse than blessing.

Jasper smirked and took a sip of his own tea. After a tense few minutes, he said, "Quite a shiner our resident healer's got."

It wasn't a question, so Dorian said nothing.

"Hard to believe a gentle soul like that could have done anything to deserve it." There was a lightness to Jasper's tone that didn't quite match the hard look in his eyes. Dorian shifted, as much as he could in his current state, and wondered how Jasper knew. He'd been trying to listen in on Caius's conversation while Ivy and Jasper had been in the kitchenette. Perhaps she had told him.

Almost as though he could hear Dorian's thoughts, Jasper said, "I'm good at reading people. Between the two of you, your body language tells a hell of a story."

Dorian grunted into his tea and looked at the seating area over the cup's rim. Caius and Echo were deep in conversation, tones too hushed for Dorian to overhear.

Jasper followed his gaze. "Hmm."

Dorian went still. He hadn't meant to be so transparent. "What do you want?"

Jasper's half smirk returned. Dorian recognized it for what it was. A mask. A face to slip on to keep one's secrets secret.

"I wasn't aware I needed a reason to be in my own bedroom," Jasper said.

If that was how he felt, Dorian would happily relinquish the bed. Gritting his teeth against the pain, he tried to lift himself up. Jasper laid a single hand, warm from the mug he'd been holding, on Dorian's chest, and pressed. Dorian fell back against the mattress with a shameful lack of resistance, tea sloshing in his mug.

"Down, boy," Jasper said. "I didn't mean it like that."

It was almost an apology. Not that Dorian wanted one. He sipped at the remnants of the tea and prayed for an end to the conversation.

"Besides"—Jasper smiled, teeth pearly white and predatory—"it'll be a cold day in hell when I complain about having a hot piece like you in my bed."

Dorian choked, sputtering tea down his front. Judging from Jasper's grin, it was precisely the reaction he'd meant to elicit.

With a quiet laugh, Jasper pushed himself off the bed. Looking down on Dorian—in more ways than one—he said, "Drink all of that before you fall asleep. I suspect our little dove has a stern mistress hiding beneath all those pretty white feathers."

And with that, he was gone. Dorian was left alone, covered in tea and the unholy pink of his own blush.

CHAPTER TWENTY-NINE

The porcelain of the bathroom sink had appeared white before Ivy laid her hands on it. Next to the paleness of her skin, it looked like more of a cream color. Breathing deeply through her nose, she relinquished the iron grip she had on the sink, prying her fingers away from the cool porcelain one by one. She wanted to be proud of how she'd maintained her composure while tending to Dorian's wounds, but all she felt was hollow.

Looking at her reflection didn't help. Her skin was pale, but that was nothing new. What *was* new was the purplish bruise on her right cheekbone, the burns that formed patterns on the soft skin of her chest, and the legion of scratch marks on her face, a reminder of Tanith grabbing her by the feathers on her head and smashing the side of her face against the rough-hewn stone of her cell. The interrogation had been brutal, and the bruise Dorian had given her paled in comparison. Ivy swallowed thickly and closed her eyes. The darkness only made it worse. It made her want to remember things, like the sound of Perrin's screams and the eerie silence that fell after he'd drawn his final rasping breath. She opened her eyes. At least the girl looking back at her was clean now, even if Echo's clothes hung a little loosely on her. It was a low bar to live up to.

She needed to not be alone. Alone was bad. Alone left her with her thoughts, and they weren't very good company at the moment. Smoothing her feathers as best she could, she squared her shoulders and went out into the loft.

Jasper was in the bedroom with the tea she'd mixed for Dorian using the best ingredients she could find in his cupboards. For someone who wasn't a healer, he was remarkably well stocked, but the tea would do little more than alleviate the pain. While she watched, Jasper sat on the bed beside Dorian.

Interesting, Ivy thought. She was surprised Dorian allowed it.

She left them to it, padding to the couch, where Echo and Caius were sitting. He was kneeling by Echo's feet, their heads bent together over a scrap of paper on her lap. They looked unusually chummy.

"Am I interrupting something?" Ivy asked. At the sound of her voice, Caius sprang up and backed away from Echo, gracefully falling back into the chair when his calves touched the seat behind him.

"What? No," Echo said in a rush, scooting to the other side of the couch and shoving the piece of paper into her pocket. Part of Ivy wanted to ask what was written on it, but an even bigger part just wanted to curl into a tiny ball and sleep for five years straight. She'd ask about it in the morning. Echo patted the seat next to her. "Here. Sit."

Ivy lowered herself gingerly, her body reminding her of every ache and pain. Echo's frown was a mix of sympathy and anger. Her protective streak was a mile wide, and Ivy warmed a little to see it.

"How is he?" Caius asked, nodding toward the bed. Dorian's fair skin turned an interesting shade of pink at something Jasper said before walking away.

"I did the best I could with what I had," Ivy said.

Echo stared at the bruise on Ivy's cheek. "How'd you get that?"

Ivy's hand fluttered to her face, hovering over the bruise. She debated not answering—the situation was awkward enough as is, with two Drakharin camped out in what amounted to an Avicen safe house—but her eyes gave her away when they slid, involuntarily, to Dorian.

Both Echo and Caius followed her gaze. Ivy saw the moment they put two and two together. Like a cat ready to pounce, Echo tensed, but Ivy placed a hand on her knee to still her. Caius fell very deliberately silent.

"Don't," Ivy said.

Head snapping between Dorian and Ivy, Echo sputtered, "But he— But you— But I can't just—"

"You can and you will," Ivy said. "I don't want to fight right now, so just leave it."

"Thank you," Caius said. "You didn't have to do that."

Talk to Dorian? Heal Dorian? Not kill Dorian or otherwise cause him additional grievous bodily harm? Ivy wanted to ask Caius which one he meant. Instead, she simply replied, "I know."

Caius nodded at them both, pushing himself out of the chair and making his way to Dorian's bedside. He rested his hand on Dorian's forehead, and Dorian stirred, already in the grip of the healing tea. Caius sat on the floor, back resting against the bed. He, too, closed his eyes. Echo watched him, as attentive as a hawk.

"I don't like this," Ivy said.

Echo looked at Ivy, eyebrows raised. "What part of this exactly? The part where we're on the run from the Drakharin, or the part where we're hiding out in a thief's house in Strasbourg, or the part where you and I are evidently sharing a couch for the night?"

Ivy pinched the bridge of her nose, willing back the headache she felt tingling right behind her eyes. *When you put it like that* . . . "If I had to pick just one . . . I don't like that we ran off with two Drakharin. I don't trust them."

"Well, they got us out of the keep," Echo said with a shrug. "Maybe they're not so bad."

Ivy knew that tone of voice. It reminded her of the time Echo had found a mangy cat in the subway tunnels beneath Grand Central, the ones the Ala had told them never to play in. Echo had wrapped the cat in her jacket and presented it to the Ala, big brown eyes earnest as ever as she innocently inquired, "Can we keep it?" They would not be keeping Caius. Or Dorian. Especially not Dorian. Ivy rested her head in her hands and focused on breathing in and out. She was staying under the same roof as a man who'd helped imprison her.

A hand on Ivy's arm pulled her from her thoughts.

"Are you okay?" Echo asked.

The short answer was no. The long answer was also no. But no got them nowhere. No was useless.

"As okay as I can be," Ivy said. "I didn't know your life was so exciting."

Echo laughed, but the sound was all wrong, fragile and worn. "This is extreme, even for me."

Ivy picked at the tassels on one of Jasper's throw pillows. "Echo," she asked, "are you sure we can trust them?"

Echo slouched deeper into the couch, as if she were trying to burrow a hole to the other side. "Sure? No, not sure. But I have this feeling. . . . My gut says that Caius means what he says. I don't know why, but I believe him."

Ivy was far from sold. Her skepticism must have shown on her face, because Echo said, "You don't have to do this, Ivy."

"Do what?"

"You can go home. No one will blame you for anything. You got taken; it's not your fault. Everyone loves you." The *unlike me* was silent, but it was there all the same. "Even Altair."

Ivy frowned. "What kind of friend would I be if I left you alone with two Drakharin and the Avicen you once described as the shadiest person you know?"

"I heard that." Jasper was in the kitchenette, but the loft offered little by way of privacy.

Ivy ignored him. "Why does this mean so much to you, Echo? I mean, I get why the firebird is important, but why does it have to be you? Let someone else do this."

Echo shook her head, eyes downcast. "It needs to be me," she said softly.

"But why? Echo, you're only seventeen. I know you don't feel like a kid, and that's fair—you grew up too fast, we both did—but you don't have to do this."

"You don't understand." When Echo looked up at her, eyes raw, Ivy's heart broke. "You don't know what it's like."

"What *what's* like?" Ivy asked. "Talk to me."

"They look at me like I shouldn't be there. Like they would be happier if I wasn't," Echo said. Ivy didn't need to ask who *they* were. Altair. Ruby. The Avicen like them. Everyone who had ever looked at Echo as though she were lesser. "But if I do this, if I find the firebird, if I help them end this war, then they can't say I don't belong. They can't say I'm not one of them."

"Oh, Echo." Ivy took one of Echo's hands in her own. "You do belong with the Avicen. You belong with me and the Ala and Rowan and your little army of sticky brats. Yeah, Altair's a dick, but he doesn't speak for all of us."

Echo sniffled and rubbed her nose with her sleeve. When she spoke, she almost sounded like herself. "Strange how you ended up as an outlaw, and Rowan's the one in a uniform."

Ivy smiled, for Echo's sake. "Yeah, who saw that coming?"

"Crazy world we live in." Echo rubbed her eyes. "I saw him in his uniform, you know. When he busted me out."

Nuzzling her head against the sofa, white feathers sticking up at all sorts of angles, Ivy yawned. "Yeah? How'd he look?"

"I prefer him out of it."

Ivy forced herself to laugh, just a little. "I bet you do."

Echo flopped backward on the couch, pulling Jasper's throw blanket across the both of them. The sofa was built for three people sitting, not two teenage girls reclining, but they made it work. Ivy wrapped the blanket around herself like a shield. Echo was trying to be strong for her, and so Ivy would do the same.

"We're gonna make it home," Ivy said. "Both of us."

Echo kept her eyes down, focused on her hands. "I don't know if I can even call it that. Not now."

Ivy reached across their legs to seize Echo's hand. She squeezed it tight. "You belong with us, Echo. Never doubt that. If I can't get you to believe that, maybe Rowan can. You know he and I don't always get along, but he loves you, even if he hasn't said it yet. You're one of us, whether you like it or not. Just try to remember that." She brought her other hand up, pinkie raised. "Promise? For me?"

Echo's smile was more a halfhearted twitch of the lips, but it was something. She linked her own pinkie with Ivy's. "Promise."

CHAPTER THIRTY

Echo crouched deeper in the coat closet. It was dark, and the smell of old wool was thick on the air. This was her safe space. The place where she went when the monsters outside were too real to ignore. She balanced her flashlight on her knee and turned the pages of a hopelessly outdated encyclopedia. It was so old, the chapter on the Berlin Wall referred to the structure as "still standing." Echo had read it cover to cover enough times that the pages had gone soft like fabric. Its words were imprinted on her brain, but still she read on. She reached up to push her bangs out of her face, and that was when she realized she was in a dream. Echo hadn't had bangs since she was seven. She'd let her hair grow out after running away, and it was only ever tamed when the Ala forced her into a chair to trim the ends.

The nightmare was a familiar one, and as the dream unraveled, she knew what to expect. There was the crunch of gravel in a driveway, the familiar growl of an engine on its last legs, the metallic slam of a car door closing. The sharp tang of whiskey and the cloying scent of stale cigarettes clinging to the air no matter how many windows she cracked. The closet door yanked open so fast and hard that its hinges groaned in protest.

But when the door opened, it wasn't the backlit figure of her mother—drunk, and reeking of whatever bar she'd stumbled home from—that she had been expecting.

"Hello, my little magpie."

The Ala reached a hand down to Echo, black feathers glinting in the soft light behind her. Over her shoulder, Echo could see the mismatched furniture and haphazard piles of throw pillows that decorated the Ala's chambers. The wave of homesickness that hit her was so powerful, she felt as if she might drown in it.

"Ala," Echo said. She pulled herself to her feet, aware of how small the closet was. Or had she grown in the seconds it took for her to stand? One could never quite trust the internal logic of dreams. "What are you doing here?"

The Ala squeezed Echo's fingers and drew her out of the darkness. With her long skirt whispering against the Persian rug, she guided Echo to the center of the room. "I'm here because you needed me."

The glow of candlelight was hazy, as if Echo were looking at everything through a lens smeared with Vaseline. There were no sharp edges. The corners of the shelves and tables were worn down and blurred. The more Echo fought to bring it all into focus, the faster it slipped away. The Ala's fingers untangled from hers. Echo reached a hand out, but the Ala shook her head and stepped back.

"I want to go home," Echo whispered.

There was such sadness in the Ala's eyes. "I'm afraid you can't. Not now. Not yet. You have miles to go before you sleep, Echo dear."

"Don't you quote Robert Frost at me."

The Ala smiled. "That's my girl. But back to your original question. Do *you* know why I'm here?"

Echo frowned. Poking at the world of the dream made the room quiver, as if the walls were threatening to cave in. "You saved me. Back there, in the closet. From my effed-up childhood."

The Ala shook her head. "No, Echo. You saved yourself. And I wish you hadn't had to. But you must understand, I cannot save you from the past. Only you can do that."

Echo pressed the heel of her palms into her eyes. How was it that anyone could be this tired while they were sleeping? "That doesn't make any sense. Why do I need saving from something that's already happened?"

"Just because it's in the past doesn't mean it's over. Remember what I taught you, Echo."

"And what's that? You know, it wouldn't kill you to stop being cryptic for like five seconds."

"Your future is your own. Remember that, and you will find your way."

The Ala's form began to go soft at the edges, like the blurred furniture and hazy candlelight. Echo was losing her.

"Ala, wait!" Echo flung a hand out, but the Ala's feathers slipped through her fingers like smoke.

The walls of the Ala's chamber disintegrated, giving way to a light that swallowed the smell of melted wax and the feel of the rug beneath her feet. The light was so bright it felt as if Echo were staring into the heart of the sun. She brought a hand up to shield her eyes. One by one, the sounds and smells and textures of the world around her materialized. Wet grains of sand squished between her bare toes. A spray of ocean water misted her face, and she tasted the salt of it on her tongue. Nearby, waves crested and crashed, dashing against rocks. Overhead, gulls sang their mournful lullaby. Behind her sat a modest wooden cabin, smoke cheerily piping from its chimney. It was a beautiful sight, but unfamiliar.

A screech cut through the gulls' soft cries. Echo looked up, squinting against the cloudy brightness. A bird, fat and dark, soared toward the beach, a black blemish against the gray-blue sky. Her heart pounded against the walls of her chest in time with each flap of its wings, and she knew that if it reached her, she would die.

Echo tried to run, but her feet sank into the sand. She couldn't move. The tiny waves that had lapped at her ankles so gently before boiled when they collided with her skin. The bird's silhouette got bigger and bigger, closer and closer, until Echo could just make out the streaks of white under its wings.

The bird approached, feathers turning to flames as if something had ignited it from within. Echo screamed, but the sound was little more than a pained whimper as acrid air seared her lungs. She wanted to beg, to plead, to open her eyes and wake up and leave this nightmare behind, but the sand formed shackles around her ankles. No matter how vigorously she struggled, she couldn't break free.

The bird swooped down, talons extended, with a screech loud enough to shatter glass. Its beak was nearly level with her eyes. Echo held up her arms, and the bird scratched at them in a rage, its beak ripping at her skin. She tried to scream, but her voice had abandoned her. The sand beneath her turned to ash, and the salty tang of seawater was replaced with the hot, coppery taste of blood. Every breath she drew was smoke. She was dying. The sky around her burned, and she burned with it.

CHAPTER THIRTY-ONE

Beneath Caius's feet was solid ground, but he was surrounded by perfect, velvety blackness, darker than the darkest night. The in-between.

A weight settled against his chest. He reached for it, fingers brushing the metal of the locket he'd given to Rose a lifetime ago. He traced the jade and bronze on its face, the gentle dips and swoops of the dragon that adorned it. It was only when the dragon began to peel away from the pendant, flapping its wings as it took to the air, that Caius realized he was dreaming.

The tiny dragon hovered before him, wings churning air as it quirked its head. Its bejeweled eyes blinked, as if it was asking a question.

"What do you want?" Caius said.

The dragon gave a mighty flap of its wings, buffeting Caius with a hot breeze that was stronger than it should have been able to produce. He'd asked the wrong question, but he still didn't know what the right one was.

"Why am I here?"

Because this was a dream, and in dreams, anything was possible, the dragon winked at him. The right question, then.

"I don't understand."

But you will.

The voice was not the dragon's, nor did it belong to anyone living.

"Rose?"

The voice went silent.

The dragon flitted around Caius, beckoning him to follow. A hole opened up and the warm light of the morning sun penetrated the darkness. The dragon flew through the opening, and Caius followed.

He was in a library, but not one he had ever seen before. There were books everywhere, piled high on mahogany desks and packed tightly on shelves. The ceiling was painted with clouds, white and puffy on a sea of pale blue. The room's deep reddish-brown paneling shimmered in the sunlight. Windows peeked out on a city Caius didn't recognize. There were buildings outside, human-made, that touched the sky, like steel and concrete steeples.

"Where am I?" Caius asked. The dragon flitted around his head.

Home.

"This is not my home."

Not yours. Hers.

And then, one by one, the books on the shelves burst into flames, bits of singed paper floating on the air like autumn leaves. The shelves crumbled as the wood popped and crackled, and the fake clouds in their fake sky slowly began to melt. With a keening wail from the little dragon, its wings caught fire, thin membranes crumbling into ash.

Smoke seared Caius's throat, and the scent of burning paper and melting glue made his stomach churn. Covering his mouth and nose with his sleeve, he choked out a single word.

"Why?"

So you will learn.

"Learn what?"

What will happen if you do not find it.

"Find what?" Caius wheezed. "The firebird?"

Yes. The word held an echo, as though it were spoken by many voices all at once.

His eyes watered as the library around him burned. A part of him knew that one could not die in dreams, but another part feared that if he perished here, he would never wake up. There was something dark at the end of the aisle, something that refused to catch fire. Choking down lungfuls of smoke, he stumbled toward the figure.

It was a woman, silhouetted by flames. Her long hair whipped around her face, obscuring it from view. The fire around her was as bright as she was dark. Caius couldn't make out much beyond her softly curved form against the blaze, but she stood still, unafraid. She held a hand out to him, beseeching, pleading, offering. When Caius reached for her, tongues of fire licked at his hand. His skin blistered and peeled, but he felt no pain as he touched her skin. Her flesh was strangely supple, like overripe fruit, and cold as ice.

Like a corpse, he thought. When he tried to snatch his hand away, the woman's grip tightened, refusing to let go.

"What are you?" he asked. "What is all this?"

The consequence of your failure.

The smoke cleared, just enough to let him see the hand that held his own. The skin was mottled and gray, sallow the way skin turned in death. The stench of rot mingled with smoke, and though Caius breathed through his nose, he could still taste it on his tongue. He tried to yank his hand away, but the corpse held on, delicate fingers digging into his flesh hard enough to bruise.

Death touches us all.

He watched in horror as the rot spread from the corpse's hand to his own. His flesh sloughed off his bones, falling to the floor with wet, meaty slaps.

"How do I stop this?" he asked, frantic. "How do I find it?"

The only response he received was a great, yawning silence.

"Answer me!" he shouted.

The muscles in his arms, his chest, his legs atrophied as the decay spread. He tried to demand an answer again, but his tongue shriveled in his mouth. The voice was gone, the dragon was gone, the library was gone, and Caius was dying, dying, dead.

CHAPTER THIRTY-TWO

"Caius, wake up. Caius!"

Caius blinked blearily to find Echo crouched in front of him, silhouetted by the early-morning sun streaming in through the loft's stained-glass windows. For a second, he was back in his dream, with the woman on fire and burning books all around him. He swallowed thickly, the sour taste of his own breath doing little to quell the unease in his stomach.

Echo cocked her head to the side, expression soft. "Are you okay?"

Caius shook his head, as if he could knock loose the cobwebs of his dream. "Yes," he lied. "I'm fine."

"Oh." Echo looked down at the floor, eyelashes dark smudges on her cheeks. "Did you sleep okay?"

"No," he said. "Did you?"

"Not really." Echo met his eyes once more before standing,

enthusiasm slipping on like a well-worn mask. "Up and at 'em. I cooked."

Jasper piped in from the kitchenette, "Consider yourself warned."

Echo stuck out her tongue at Jasper's back. Caius rubbed the sleep from his eyes and pushed himself up, stretching when he got to his feet.

"You seem chipper this morning," Caius said. A small, curious part of him wanted to find out if she was like this every morning.

Her eyes narrowed, and he had his answer. People wore all sorts of masks when they wanted to hide themselves, and cheer was the one Echo had chosen for today.

"Guess I'm just a morning person," she said. The lie was obvious. She was silent, waiting for him to call her bluff.

He didn't. All he said was "After you."

Without another word, Echo led the way to the small round table around which Dorian and Jasper sat. Ivy stood by the counter, arms wrapped tightly around herself, staring at the waffle iron as if she could will it to work faster. She looked cold, even though the kitchen was warm.

Dorian tried to rise as Caius approached, but the motion made him wince. Caius rested a hand on Dorian's shoulder, pushing him back down before taking the seat next to him. Jasper watched them, lips hidden behind the rim of his mug, eyes giving away nothing. The scent of coffee was strong, and Caius's stomach lurched.

Echo shoved Ivy over with a bump of her hips, busying herself with plates and cutlery. "I made waffles."

"And not just any waffles," Jasper said.

"Damn right." Echo slid a plate in front of Jasper, who in

turn slid it in front of Dorian. It was piled high with crumbling waffle bits dappled with small brown chunks. Dorian looked at Jasper, who simply arched an eyebrow in response. The dynamic between the two of them had shifted since the night before.

Interesting, Caius thought.

"What is it?" Dorian asked, poking at the pile of food with his fork.

"Bacon waffles!" Echo chirped. She had a frilly floral apron tied around her waist, leaving Caius to ponder why Jasper owned a frilly floral apron in the first place.

Dorian remained dubious. "Bacon waffles?"

Echo leveled him with a glare that dared him to question her culinary choices one more time. "Bacon waffles."

"I'm sorry, is there an echo in here?" Jasper said, entirely too pleased with himself.

Puns, Caius thought. *How droll.*

Echo slapped Jasper's wrist with a dirty spatula. "Yes, bacon waffles. And you want to know why?" She shoveled a sizable serving onto another plate. "Bacon next to waffles? Good. Bacon inside waffles? Great."

"Listen closely," Jasper said, leaning in to Dorian. It was gratuitous, as his stage whisper was loud enough to be heard by the whole table. "You can hear the sound of your arteries clogging."

Echo handed Caius and Ivy their plates, though she hadn't touched her own. Ivy remained standing, poking listlessly at her waffle. Of the five of them, Jasper was the only one who had the audacity to look well rested. Dorian wouldn't eat until Caius did, and so, despite his better judgment, he took a bite.

Four sets of eyes looked at him expectantly. He chewed, self-conscious. The waffle was both too salty and too sweet, but he choked it down anyway. "Delicious."

Echo's smile flashed by so quickly Caius wasn't certain he'd even seen it. She placed the last plate in front of Jasper. He eyed it warily, sipping his coffee.

"Try it, Jasper. They're good, I promise."

Jasper peered up at her, unconvinced.

"Don't you trust me?" Echo asked.

"When it comes to food, yes." Jasper cut into the waffle with cautious movements, as if he expected it to bite him back.

"Wait a minute," Echo said. "What *don't* you trust me with?"

Jasper kept his eyes on his plate when he said, "Most other things."

"That's the last time I make you bacon waffles."

"Thank the gods for small miracles," Jasper said, dropping his fork. "So, are you going to tell me what you're running from and also what you're running toward?"

The question was met with silence. Dorian looked at Caius. Caius looked at Echo. Echo looked at Ivy. Ivy looked at no one.

"Anyone?" Jasper asked. "I'm sheltering what I'm assuming are refugees from both the Avicen and the Drakharin in my home, I think I have a right to know."

The silence continued.

"Or you could all just leave," Jasper said. The short feathers on his arms ruffled slightly.

Removing her apron and setting it aside, Echo took the lead. "We're looking for something. Something a lot of people want, but it wouldn't be safe with them, so we have to find it first."

"We?" Jasper waved his mug at the four of them. "This motley crew of misfits? Tell me, what could possibly capture the interest of a Drakharin mercenary, his loyal manservant, an Avicen healer, and a human pickpocket?"

Dorian tensed. Caius could tell he desperately wanted to argue the "manservant" part of that question, but he held his tongue. Echo didn't.

"Pickpocket?" The word was so salty Caius could almost taste it.

Jasper plowed on. "The only thing that could possibly bring all of you together is something major. Now, someone tell me what it is, or I find out which side is offering the best price for your heads."

If it hadn't been for the hand Caius laid on Dorian's arm, Jasper would have had a fork protruding from his neck. Echo looked ready to jump into the fray, but her eyes darted from Dorian to Jasper as if she wasn't sure whose side she was on. Caius hoped his next decision was the right one.

"We're going to find the firebird," he said.

Of all the reactions Jasper could have had, his bark of laughter really shouldn't have come as a surprise.

"You're joking." Jasper set his mug down and looked from Caius to Echo, taking in their solemn faces. "Echo, please tell me this clown is joking."

Caius resented the clown bit, but if Dorian could hold his tongue in the face of Jasper's jabs, then so could he.

"Nope," Echo replied. "This is officially a joke-free zone."

"The firebird is not real," Jasper said slowly, as if he were talking to idiots. A sneaky, vicious part of Caius thought that he just might have been. "The firebird is a bedtime story. It's our version of the Holy Grail. It doesn't exist."

Caius removed his hand from Dorian's arm, praying that Dorian would curb his violent impulses for a few minutes more.

"We have reason to believe it does," Caius said. He met Echo's gaze and wished he knew her well enough to read what he saw there. "Echo?"

He didn't miss her hesitation. She trusted Jasper as far as she could throw him, but if it was between trusting him and going on the run, this time with no place to hide, the choice was simple. So simple it wasn't really a choice at all. Echo looked at him, a question in her eyes, and he nodded. She reached into her back pocket, sliding out a map with frayed edges. She smoothed it down on the table.

"The firebird is real," Caius said. "And Echo knows the way." *Hopefully.*

Jasper studied the map for a solid minute before he looked up at Caius. "And you're sure?"

"I would bet my life on it," Caius said. "I *am* betting my life on it."

Jasper held his gaze with his strange golden eyes. Caius waited for his answer.

"Good," Jasper said. "I want in."

CHAPTER THIRTY-THREE

Echo blinked, once, twice, three times, not quite sure she had heard him correctly. "Come again?"

Jasper enunciated his words carefully, as if she were being deliberately slow. "I. Want. In."

Echo had heard him right the first time. It still made no sense. "Why?"

"I pride myself on my ability to read people." Jasper gestured toward Caius, who sat there, as unreadable as stone. "And there isn't a shred of doubt in this man. If he thinks it's real, I'm inclined to believe him."

"Yeah, but I know you, Jasper, and I know that you don't do anything without a reason." Echo pushed away from the counter, crossing her arms. "What's in it for you?"

"Are you kidding?" Jasper's smirk blossomed into a full-blown grin, blinding in its loveliness. "I make a living acquiring elusive items for an extremely select clientele, and *nothing* is more elusive than this. Finding the firebird would be the biggest score the world has ever seen. I want my finger-prints all over it."

"You won't get to keep it," Echo said. *Not unless you pry it from my cold dead hands,* she thought. She tried to not con-sider what it meant that those words had become a running theme in their relationship.

"Not the point," Jasper said. "Imagine what wonders it would do for my reputation. I want to be known as the guy who found the firebird. What happens to it afterward is your business. Avicen-Drakharin politics are not my department."

Ivy had thus far kept her peace, but at Jasper's words, she said, "Do you really not care about the fate of your people?"

He shrugged. "They're hardly my people."

"You're Avicen," Ivy said, as if that alone should have been enough.

"So?"

Ivy scowled. "Does loyalty mean nothing to you?"

"Look," Jasper said, propping his elbows up on the table. He was so nonchalant, they might as well have been dis-cussing the weather. "I understand loyalty well enough. It's admirable, really, it is. But loyalty won't put food on my table or a roof over my head. I do what I have to do."

Ivy's scowl deepened, but she said nothing.

Caius cleared his throat. "Jasper, a word?" He rose, walk-ing toward the bank of windows on the far side of the room. Jasper waited a beat, as if to refuse the request on princi-ple, but with a sigh, he followed Caius. Echo wanted to tag along, but Ivy's drawn face gave her pause. Dorian stewed in his own tense silence, his eyes glued to Caius's back. Leav-ing the two of them alone was probably not the best idea.

Echo was flipping through her mental Rolodex of awkward conversation starters when Dorian spoke.

"You changed my bandages while I slept," he said. He wasn't looking at Ivy so much as in her general direction.

"Yes," Ivy said. She started fluttering about the kitchen, picking up plates and forks and dumping them in the sink.

Dorian cleared his throat, very quietly. "Thank you." He looked at Ivy then, at the angry bruise on her cheek. "And I'm sorry."

Ivy nodded, just once, then turned her back to him and began washing dishes.

If someone had told Echo that one day she'd witness a Drakharin humble himself before Ivy—quiet, unassuming Ivy—she would have laughed. But seeing it happen now? Not laughable. Not even close.

CHAPTER THIRTY-FOUR

Jasper spoke before Caius had the chance to. "I don't like being ordered around my own home."

Caius might not have been a prince any longer, but he couldn't forget a century's worth of ingrained behavior any easier than a leopard could change its spots.

"My apologies," he said. It had been a while since he'd had to utter an apology, and never had he offered one to an Avicen. He felt rusty.

Jasper sat on the edge of a windowsill, its gothic arch coming to a point high above his head. Fragments of colored light dappled his skin as the sun shone through the window's stained glass. The effect was so striking, Jasper might have planned it. He seemed like the type who would.

He also appeared to be less than mollified. "Another thing I don't like is having my motivations questioned in my own home," he said, "which I have a feeling you're about to do."

Caius shook his head. "No, I believe what you said was true, though perhaps not the whole truth."

Canting his head, Jasper looked every inch the bird his feathers mimicked. "Is that so?"

"I may not know you well, but I know that a man like you does nothing for free." Caius met Jasper's eyes, but they were unreadable. The Avicen had the best poker face Caius had seen in years, a self-satisfied smirk glued in place. "If you're going to help us find the firebird without laying claim to it, I assume you'll expect compensation of a different sort."

Jasper smiled. "Now we're talking. Echo's a good thief, but she doesn't quite get how this game works."

"She's a child," Caius said.

Jasper snorted. "I don't think Echo's ever really been a child. But that's neither here nor there. You're right. I don't make working for free a habit. What have you got to offer?"

Caius cursed his sister for stealing his throne and the royal treasury that went with it. He didn't have much to offer—a new and uncomfortable feeling—but Jasper didn't need to know that. When in doubt, improvise.

"I would give you my share of the Drakharin's reward," he said. There was no reward, but once he'd returned triumphant and taken back his crown, he'd have more gold and jewels at his disposal than even Jasper would know what to do with. *If* he returned. And *if* he reclaimed his title. The number of ifs in the scenario was unsettling. "I was never in it for the money anyway."

With a soft chuckle, Jasper shook his head. "Never promise to pay with money you don't have."

Caius shrugged. "It's all I can offer you."

"Is it?" Jasper asked, gaze drifting to a point beyond Caius's shoulder. "Money isn't the only valuable currency in the world."

Jasper tilted his head toward the kitchen area, where Echo and Ivy were tidying up, but Caius knew they weren't what interested him. Jasper was staring at Dorian, golden eyes guarded but keen. Caius tried to see his friend as Jasper did. Scarred skin impossibly fair. Gray hair with a soft luster that made it look almost silver. A single blue eye, as clear as the sea at morning. Jasper's nest was a testament to his appreciation of beautiful things, and Dorian was lovely, even with his scars, even if he never recognized it in himself.

"I see." Caius turned back to face Jasper. "But some things aren't mine to give."

Jasper smiled, and Caius found he didn't much care for it. "Oh, I think some things are more yours than you realize."

Dorian's affection was far from secret, but Caius had no desire to divulge the details to a thief he'd only just met, a fact he telegraphed with a meaningful silence.

Jasper unfolded his slender legs and stood. "I'll help you. After all, some rewards are far more precious than gold or jewels."

Jasper extended his hand, and Caius merely stared at it. He had vowed to find the firebird, but what Jasper was implying left a foul taste in his mouth. The seconds ticked by and still Jasper did not move.

Slowly, Caius reached out to shake Jasper's hand. It felt like sealing a deal with the devil. His captain might not have been his to give, but Dorian would follow Caius's orders, no matter how distasteful he found them. Dorian might never forgive him, but what was friendship in the face of peace? Caius had promised to put an end to this war, and that was precisely what he would do, whatever the cost.

CHAPTER THIRTY-FIVE

By the time Jasper and Caius returned, Dorian was ready to jump out of his skin. The tension in the room was so thick, he felt as though he could walk on it. Ivy was doing her best to ignore him, a compulsion that Dorian didn't mind at all. Echo busied herself with a quiet running commentary designed to soothe Ivy's nerves. As she mumbled about the cherry blossoms in Japan and her favorite bakeries in Strasbourg, Ivy responded with absent nods at appropriate intervals.

Dorian caught Caius's eyes, asking, without words, if his conversation had gone well. Caius looked away, just a hair too quickly, and Dorian frowned. His scar tingled beneath his eye patch.

"So, what's the plan?" Dorian asked, mostly because no one else would. Again he tried to make eye contact with Caius, and again Caius avoided his gaze.

Echo pointed to the map on the table. "The plan is we

follow this trail of bread crumbs to the firebird. According to this handy-dandy map, our next stop is the Metropolitan Museum of Art."

"The Met?" Dorian asked. "Isn't that in New York? As in, the central seat of Avicen power?"

"Yeah," Echo said. "But, you know, no pressure."

Caius looked at Dorian for the first time since taking his seat. "I didn't realize you were familiar with human museums. Or art."

The question made Dorian bristle. "What?" he asked. "I read."

Echo carried on, and Caius's attention drifted back to her, both of them oblivious to Dorian's hurt feelings. "Grab your gear, Jasper," she said. "We should leave ASAP, scope out the place. You know how it goes."

Caius rose from his seat. "I'm going with you."

"Not wearing that you're not," Jasper said. He went to the wardrobe on the other side of the loft and began pulling out items that would blend with humans far better than the bloodied clothes both Caius and Dorian still wore.

Caius ignored Jasper. He waited, patiently, for Echo to speak, as if he expected her to argue. She didn't disappoint.

"Jasper and I can do this alone."

Ivy's quiet intake of breath escaped everyone's notice but Dorian's. He glanced at her from the corner of his eye. He caught her looking back at him for a quick second before her gaze flitted away, settling on the floor as if it were the most interesting thing in the world.

Caius, unaware of the small drama unfolding next to him, said, "We're all in this now, Echo. We do this together, or not at all."

"You know, I liked you better when you weren't being bossy," said Echo. "Are you sure you can keep up?"

Caius smiled. "I caught you once, didn't I?"

Gods spare me, Dorian thought, trying to ignore the pang of jealousy he felt. They were flirting. At a time like this.

"Not to interrupt whatever *this* is," he said, waving a hand between Echo and Caius, "but, shouldn't you be more concerned about venturing behind enemy lines, Caius?"

"None of the Avicen know me," Caius replied. His eyes flicked between Echo and Dorian. The message was clear: Tread lightly. Give nothing away. They had no idea who he was, and he intended to keep it that way. "I'm good at evading attention when I want to."

"So, it's settled," Jasper said. "The three of us have an after-hours date at the Met." He had returned with a pile of clothes thrown over his arm. There was a sweater on top that matched the blue of Dorian's eye. Jasper had considered his choices carefully. As his words sank in, Dorian's stomach did something strange and acrobatic.

"The *three* of us?" Dorian asked.

Caius turned to look at him, as though he had forgotten that Dorian was there. "Dorian, you're in no condition to go."

Dorian struggled to his feet, his wound screaming in protest. He was unable to bite back a soft hiss of pain. He wanted to smack the sympathy right off Caius's face. "My place is at your side."

He'd been saying those same words for a hundred years, and he'd say it for a hundred more. It would be nice if Caius listened for once.

"I'm sorry," Caius said, "but it would be best if you stayed, let yourself heal. It wouldn't do to have you worsen your injury." He settled a hand on Dorian's shoulder. Dorian wanted to shrug it off but refrained. "I'll be fine."

There were a myriad of things Dorian wanted to say, but he settled on, "It's my job to make sure that you are."

It was the truth, albeit the abridged version. Not that it mattered. He'd already lost. If Caius ordered him to stay, he would stay, even if it tore at him in a way that hurt far worse than the sword that had bit into his flesh.

"Am I staying, too?" Ivy asked. She sounded small and scared. It was Dorian's fault, and he hated himself for it.

Echo looked at Ivy, then Dorian. Her indecision was as plain as day.

"It's safer here," she said, but she was assessing Dorian as though she wasn't entirely certain that that was true. Echo didn't want to leave Ivy alone with him. Ivy didn't want to be left alone with him. Dorian wished that he had the moral high ground to be offended, but he had given that up when he had tossed Ivy, alone and scared, into a cell. When he had struck a prisoner who had no hope of hitting back.

Dorian was so preoccupied with his guilt that he almost missed the way Jasper was appraising him.

"I'll stay," Jasper said.

"What?" Caius and Echo replied, as one.

"I'll stay," Jasper repeated. "And make sure everyone plays nice. You don't need me, Echo. Breaking into museums is old hat for you. Go, find whatever it is you're looking for. I'm only in it for the endgame anyway. Take whatever supplies you want." He smiled, his gaze settling on Dorian. "Free of charge."

"I don't need a babysitter," Dorian grumbled.

Jasper's smile widened, and Dorian was reminded of a fox baring its teeth. "Maybe I do."

CHAPTER THIRTY-SIX

It was strange, traveling alone with Caius. Having been raised on a steady diet of horror stories about the Drakharin's cruelty, Echo kept expecting to feel uncomfortable in his presence. She couldn't reconcile the ghoulish figure of the Avicen tales with the person who offered her his hand on the shore of the Ill River beneath the Ponts Couverts.

"I don't get why we had to come all the way back here," Echo said, placing her hand in his. The magpie dagger tucked into her boot was a comforting weight against her skin. Caius wrapped his fingers around hers, and Echo was keenly aware of the calluses on his palm. "I saw what you did at the Louvre. You could have turned any old doorway in that cathedral into a threshold."

Caius summoned the in-between, black tendrils emerging from the ground like smoky weeds. Echo was grateful for the bridge that hid them from view. Daytime Strasbourg was a bustling smorgasbord of tourists and locals, and the river was at the heart of it all.

"Creating a gateway from a man-made door without the help of shadow dust takes a great deal of energy," Caius said, black smoke swirling around his ankles. "Magic is like a muscle. Abuse it, and it'll abuse you later."

"Smart," Echo said.

Caius nodded, eyes half closed. He was focused on summoning the in-between. "Just because you have power doesn't mean you have to use it. It's a lesson I wish my people understood."

Echo wanted to respond, but the black cloud rose, engulfing them completely. The ground dropped out from beneath her, and she was falling, Caius's hand her only anchor. She held it tightly, and when he squeezed back, her stomach lurched in a way that had nothing to do with the in-between. Echo wanted to blame the bacon waffles, but she knew they were innocent.

Soon enough, light penetrated the darkness, and they reached their destination. They stood upon a patch of grass, shielded by the cast-iron archway of a bridge on the east side of Central Park, close to the Met. The feel of dirt beneath her boots was a solid, welcome comfort.

Dropping Caius's hand, Echo doubled over as the contents of her stomach did an unhappy jig. Now, that was most definitely the bacon waffles. *Why did I ever think bacon waffles were a good idea?*

"Are you all right?" Caius asked.

Her stomach somersaulted with an audible gurgle, as if it wanted to answer for her.

"Yeah," Echo said. "Just give me a minute."

Though all she saw were his boots—the only part of his original outfit to survive Jasper's wardrobe intervention—she could feel his eyes on her.

"Sorry," Caius said. "Sometimes I forget."

She focused on breathing in through her nose and out through her mouth as her body struggled to find equilibrium. "Forget what?"

"How fragile humans are."

Echo gave him what she considered her best side eye, though it was spoiled by the fact that she was hunched over and battling the unique brand of motion sickness that accompanied long-distance travel with another person leading the way.

"You know, you have a real way with words," she groaned.

"Sorry," Caius said. "Again."

Echo waved it off as a second bout of nausea threatened to overwhelm her.

"No," she said. "I get it. You're a bajillion-year-old demigod, I'm a puny mortal."

"Well, I don't know about demigod." Again, that little smile that was almost not a smile. A ghost of a smile. A blink-and-you'll-miss-it smile. He bowed his head as a cyclist passed them. The shade beneath the bridge shielded his scales from the late-afternoon sun, but they were still visible. It must've sucked not being able to walk in the daylight among humans, Echo thought. She'd spent so long envying the Avicen their vibrant plumage that it was easy to forget that their feathers—and Caius's scales—came with a price.

Caius slipped a pair of sunglasses out of his pocket and put them on. The aviators Jasper had lent him—with a solemn warning to return them in once piece—just barely covered the scales on his cheekbones.

"How do I look?" he asked.

How strange, Echo thought. A Drakharin mercenary, worried about his appearance. Truly, she had seen everything.

"Like a native New Yorker," she said.

Jasper's jeans hugged Caius's slender hips in a way that should have been criminal, and his black wool jacket contrasted nicely with his tanned skin. The military cut suited him. The nausea passed, and Echo straightened. A persistent breeze pulled a few strands of hair loose from her braid.

"So what's the deal with you and this new and terrifying Dragon Prince? You sold your loyalty to the old one, but not this one?" Echo said. She shoved her hands in the pockets of her leather jacket, stepping onto the paved walkway beneath the bridge. Caius had deposited them exactly where she'd told him to. The path would lead them to Museum Mile and East Eighty-Fifth Street, a few blocks from the Met's entrance.

He fell in step with her, shortening his strides to match hers. "We had a difference of opinion."

"I've gathered that you don't support wiping out the Avicen," Echo said. "Considering how you managed to spend an entire night in the home of one without so much as insulting his decor."

Caius had a little not-laugh to go with his little not-smile. "It wasn't easy. Not with that white carpet." But the not-laugh and the not-smile faded as he spoke. Echo was sad to see them go. "Tanith thinks the only way to win is in a fury of fire and blood. But fire only brings about death, and blood only brings about more blood."

It was an impressive answer, but Echo was oddly dissatisfied with it. They'd reached the main path, and the proud stone facade of the Met was visible across the park. The skin between her shoulder blades tingled, as if someone was watching her, but when she turned, all she saw were a few joggers and a hot-dog vendor. Altair probably had someone out looking for her, and she knew the paranoia wouldn't dissipate until they were clear of New York. She scanned their surroundings as she asked, "Do others agree with you? I've never heard about any peace talks between the Avicen and the Drakharin."

The sun beat brightly down upon them. Caius kept his head bowed. The few scales the sunglasses didn't shield glittered, sort of like a fish in sunlight. "That's because there haven't been any."

Echo waited for him to volunteer more information, but when he simply walked in silence, she asked, "Why not?"

Caius let his answer percolate. They were nearly to the park's exit when he finally spoke.

"War is like a drug," he said. "You spend so long chasing victory that you become blind to the fact that you'll never find it. It had never even occurred to me that peace was possible, not until . . ."

He let his words trail off. His voice had the same strangled quality to it that it had the night before, when he'd given her the dagger.

Echo hazarded a guess. "Until the girl?"

"Yes."

"Must have been some girl."

"She was."

Caius fell quiet again as they approached Fifth Avenue. Echo let him have his silence. She couldn't help but wonder about the woman who had captured his heart. She couldn't imagine Caius—stoic, serious Caius—in love.

When they reached the Met's front steps, Echo came to a stop. A crowd of tourists clustered at the foot of the grand staircase, posing for pictures.

"An hour before closing time," Caius said. "What now? You're the expert."

The heady excitement she always felt before a job rose. Echo tried to control her face so that she didn't give away just how pleased she was by his words. When the little not-smile flashed across Caius's lips, she knew that she had failed. *C'est la vie.*

"Now," Echo said, plopping down on the steps. "The fun part starts."

CHAPTER THIRTY-SEVEN

Ivy was sure she'd lived through more awkward situations than this, but she couldn't seem to think of any. After Caius and Echo left, Dorian pressed his lips tightly into something she couldn't quite call a pout even if it was perilously close. He spent a considerable amount of time sitting on the edge of Jasper's bed, wiping his sword down with supplies Jasper had conjured up from the depths of his closet. If he cleaned it any more ferociously, she was sure the steel would begin to erode.

She was content to let Dorian stew in his own juices, but Jasper had other ideas. From her seat on the sofa, cradling a warm cup of tea in her hands, she watched the scene unfold. It was better than TV. Besides, it wasn't like Jasper even owned a television. His loft—with its plush white carpet, stained-glass windows, and stolen art collection—was entirely too posh for something so pedestrian.

Jasper held a sweater out to Dorian. It was a pretty corn-flower blue that looked incredibly soft, even from this distance.

"Try it on," Jasper said.

Dorian didn't bother looking up from the sword on his lap. "No."

"In case you forgot, the shirt Caius cut off you last night is currently sporting a sword-shaped hole in it," Jasper said. "Kind of like you."

Ivy didn't want to laugh, but Jasper made it difficult to resist. He was easy to be around, and Ivy appreciated that. She needed a buffer between herself and Dorian, and Jasper had been more than willing to keep them both distracted.

"Besides," Jasper said, dangling the sweater next to Dorian's face, "this shade of blue brings out your eyes. Sorry. Eye."

If looks could actually kill, Jasper would have been brought down by Dorian's dark stare. Ivy thought he might be teasing the Drakharin for her benefit as much as for his own amusement. Dorian appeared to be on the verge of doing something truly regrettable, but he gingerly laid the sword aside and took the sweater from Jasper's hands.

Interesting. Maybe he wasn't so easy to read after all.

"Attaboy," Jasper said. "Let me help you."

Dorian jerked away from Jasper's hands. Ivy caught the way Dorian's jaw clenched, and his eyes narrowed, ever so slightly. He was in pain. The part of Ivy that had drawn her to apprentice as a healer poked at her persistently as if trying to convince her to help him. The part of her that wanted to see him suffer squashed it down.

"I don't need your help," Dorian said, though it was clear to Ivy, and probably also to Jasper, that he did.

To call Jasper's sigh exasperated would be to call a hurricane a spot of rain. "There's no shame in accepting help when you need it, Dorian."

With a glare, Dorian relinquished the sweater. "Fine," he gritted out through clenched teeth.

Jasper took the sweater from Dorian's hands and, with a gentleness that surprised Ivy, helped him pull it over his head. Ivy was beginning to think that all parties involved would escape the ordeal unscathed when Jasper said, "It's funny. I'm usually better at taking clothes off than putting them on."

Dorian sputtered. It was the only word Ivy could think of to describe the noise he made. A flush so deep it was almost scarlet crawled up his neck, painting his incredibly fair cheeks a lovely shade of crimson. Ivy almost sympathized. Her own white skin had a tendency to broadcast her embarrassment just as loudly. Between Dorian's violent blushing and the tufts of silver-white hair sticking up at odd angles it was hard to believe that he'd ever been terrifying. Jasper smoothed the Drakharin's unruly locks down while Dorian made a sound that was somewhere between a gurgle and a gasp. Ivy hid her smile behind her mug.

"You're cute when you blush," Jasper said.

Shockingly, Dorian didn't come back at Jasper with a pointed barb or a surly retort. He simply blushed even more furiously and pushed his arms through the sleeves of the sweater with a small pained exhalation. Jasper winked at Ivy over Dorian's shoulder.

What a ham, Ivy thought.

Blowing on her steaming tea, Ivy settled back against the sofa. Its purple cushions were just the right amount of squishy. She took a sip of her tea and watched the two of them bicker.

Yup, she thought, *way better than TV.*

CHAPTER THIRTY-EIGHT

Caius watched Echo study the blueprints Jasper had provided, planning a way inside. She was so earnest, so focused, that he left her to it. After they'd made camp on the steps, she had pressed a crumpled pile of green paper currency in his hand and ordered him to buy her a hot chocolate while she schemed. He had stared at the bills for a solid thirty seconds before moving on in search of a street vendor. It was the first time someone had so blatantly ordered him around in decades. He had gotten himself a hot chocolate, too. It was surprisingly nice.

Getting in would be the easy part, but there was something fascinating about the way Echo pored over the map, nose scrunching every so often in concentration, errant strands of hair stubbornly falling in front of her face. She had been at it for about fifteen minutes before Caius finally spoke up.

"I can transport us in," he said.

Echo's head shot up, startled, as if she had forgotten he was there. They were sitting on the Met's front steps, right in front of the museum they planned to burgle. Echo had been endlessly amused by the idea of planning a heist right under the guards' noses. Caius thought it was a needless risk, but she had been so enthused that he'd felt forced to indulge her.

"What?" she said, stretching her legs. She'd spread the blueprints out on the step above the one on which she sat and had been still for so long that her joints must have been unhappy.

Caius waved the paper cup in his hand toward the vendor selling sausages wrapped in bread from a cart on the sidewalk. Echo had called them hot dogs, but as there were no dogs involved in their making, he didn't understand why.

"I had a lovely chat with that man over there while you were busy scheming. He said his favorite attraction in the museum was the Tomb of Perneb. Apparently, it's situated on the ground floor of the museum, where it gets a significant amount of foot traffic." He took a sip of his cocoa, feeling rather proud of himself. Perhaps he was better suited to the life of an outlaw than that of a prince. "Egyptians didn't view their tombs as monuments of death—they saw them as places of transition between life and what lay beyond."

Echo nodded slowly. "Meaning, a tomb would be the perfect place to access the in-between."

He raised his cup in a toast. "Precisely." He swirled the last bit of chocolate sludge around the bottom. "It's the same principle behind travel over natural thresholds, like intertwined cherry blossom trees. The cycle of life and death gives them power. That was a rather impressive escape, by the way."

She blushed, accepting his compliment with a shy smile. That was nice, too. She took a hurried sip of her hot chocolate. "How did you know?"

"Dorian told me," he said.

Her smile wilted. "Of course."

"You don't like him very much," he said. The sun was setting behind them, and the tall buildings lining the avenue cast a sea of angular shadows on the sidewalk.

"He hit Ivy."

Caius stared into his cup. Powdery chunks of chocolate slid to the bottom. "I know. And that's not like him. Dorian is like a brother to me. I know him. He's not the sort of man who does things like that."

"Are you defending him?" Any trace of shy sweetness was long gone.

"No." He set his cup down and watched the last of the daytime staff depart. The only people inside now would be night guards. "No, I'm not. It's just . . . this war takes its toll on people, even good men like Dorian." Echo frowned, but Caius continued. "And he *is* good. But war makes monsters of us all, and the people who least deserve it pay the highest cost."

Echo sighed, and her shoulders sagged, her anger seeming to dissipate with the motion. Modest progress, but still progress. Caius was struck by the overwhelming desire to know what was going on behind her eyes, to know what she was thinking. He rolled his head, letting his gaze wander from hers. There were more important matters at hand than his fledgling fascination with a thieving human girl.

"That is why this war needs to end," he said. "There are

no victors in a conflict such as this. Just death and destruction."

Echo looked at him for a beat, then nodded, shifting her gaze to some point beyond his shoulder. She bit her lower lip absently. "You know," she said. "You talk a lot in generalities. I mean, I get that you're a bigger-picture kind of guy, but you have to have some personal stake in this. It can't just be for the greater good." She turned back at him, pinning him to the steps with a look that was more astute than Caius was comfortable with. "Nobody's that good. Nobody's that selfless."

Caius examined the contents of his cup, imagining that he could read the chocolate dregs at the bottom like tea leaves.

"Not even opportunistic mercenaries?" he asked.

"You don't seem like any merc I've ever met before."

"Hang out with many, do you?"

"Friends in low places and all that." Echo cocked her head to the side. A crisp breeze picked up a strand of her hair, made it tickle the bridge of her nose. She pushed it behind her ear, but it stubbornly slipped loose. With a sigh, she added, "And don't think I haven't noticed that you dodged the question."

He smiled. "Has anyone ever told you that you're infuriatingly clever?"

"Often," she replied. "Now spill."

He dropped his eyes to the chocolate sludge, willing it to give up its secrets. But unlike tea leaves, it had none to give.

"The woman I told you about last night," he said. "She was a soldier, but not by nature. She was conscripted for service, and it cost her everything." It was the truth, unencumbered by details. He continued, words stretching in the late-afternoon sun after being silenced for so long. "She was good, in a way so few people are. She liked to sing. Had the loveliest voice I've ever heard. She was fond of puzzles and couldn't abide the taste of pears." The corners of his eyes stung, and he was glad Jasper had lent him sunglasses. "I thought that was endlessly funny. She always smelled like pears, but she couldn't stand the taste of them."

Echo let the silence between them marinate for a few moments before asking, "What was her name?"

Outside of his dreams, Caius hadn't spoken her name since the day she died, the day Tanith brought the cabin down around them in a fire she convinced him was for his own good. He breathed that single syllable into the air. "Rose."

If Echo chewed her lower lip much more, she would make herself bleed. He was beginning to learn her little habits, those small things that were uniquely hers. Biting her lip was a tell. She was uncertain about the course of their conversation. Caius couldn't really blame her. "When did you meet her?" she asked.

"A long time ago," he said. Rose's name had been carried aloft on the wind, and it had taken some of his reserve with it. It was easier to speak to Echo now, easier to breathe. "Longer than you've been alive. Longer than your parents have been alive. Speaking of which, where are your parents? Don't seventeen-year-olds normally have those?"

"Normally, yeah."

Caius waited for her to speak. If he pushed her, he had a feeling she would clam up, hiding the details of her past like an oyster jealously guarding a pearl.

She sighed. "I don't have parents. Well, I did once. But I left home a long time ago and never looked back."

"Why?"

Echo was silent, staring at the blueprints as if she could singe them with her eyes. She kept her gaze downcast when she said, "They weren't very nice people."

A woman pushing a stroller walked past the steps, a rosy-cheeked toddler trailing after her. Echo watched them pass, a look of such wistfulness on her face that Caius's heart ached for her, just a little. He had only vague memories of his parents. They had been distant, as noble families tended to be, but never cruel.

"I'm sorry," he said. It was inadequate, but it was all he had.

She waited a beat before answering, watching the mother and her child cross the street. "Yeah," she said. "Me too."

He hadn't meant to upset her. Upsetting her was upsetting to him in a way that, in itself, was more than a little disconcerting. He wasn't sure he wanted to begin puzzling out why. He wanted to fix it, so he went with the only thing he knew would put a smile on her face.

"So," he said, ignoring the way her eyes were still cautious and a little bit steely. "Tell me about these blueprints."

CHAPTER THIRTY-NINE

The Tomb of Perneb was more claustrophobic than Echo remembered. As the black wisps of the in-between faded into the tomb's sandy stone walls, she brought a hand up to steady herself. When her palm connected with the soft wool of Caius's jacket, she yanked her hand back. He quirked an eyebrow at her, as if he wasn't at all bothered to be sharing personal space. She took a step back, pressing herself against the wall.

"Well, this is cozy," she said, shouldering past Caius. "Let's go." When she exited the tomb into the Egyptian wing, she breathed in deeply. Her thoughts were less scattered with some distance between herself and Caius. He disarmed her, and she hated it. Behind her, he barely made a sound as he exited the tomb, and she felt his presence at her back like a hovering ghost. She dropped to her knees, sketching out the same Avicet rune she'd used at the Louvre to put the guards to sleep and deactivate the cameras.

Caius was silent as she cast the spell. Echo snuck a surreptitious glance at him. The dim blue glow of the museum's security lights illuminated the planes of his face with the gentleness of a lover. It wasn't the worst view in the world. Guilt tickled at her conscience. She had a boyfriend. His name was Rowan, and he was wonderful, and she shouldn't be making eyes at some random mercenary she had picked up on her travels.

"Echo?" Caius asked, one brow arched. He was looking right at her. So maybe she wasn't half as subtle as she thought she was.

"Yeah," she mumbled. "I was just . . . thinking about our next move." She cringed inwardly. *Real smooth.*

He nodded, but not as if he bought it.

Oh, well, Echo thought.

"That was a nice charm you worked," he said. "With the Avicet rune. Clever and clean."

She willed herself not to blush. Her traitorous skin did not oblige. She pushed herself to her feet, brushing imaginary dust off her jeans. "Thanks."

"Right," he said, gazing around at the granite sculptures surrounding the tomb. "So, any idea what we're looking for?" Caius looked back at Echo. "You know, I never asked you how you found the dagger at the Louvre. I assumed you knew what you were looking for, but that map doesn't tell you much beyond general location."

And that was the tricky part. She couldn't begin to explain how or why the locket had pulsed in her hand that night, leading her straight to the dagger. Every step of this quest for the firebird seemed to bring on more questions than answers. But if it had worked once before, then maybe it would work again.

"I need the locket." She'd watched him slip it on that morning, tucking it into the neck of the borrowed shirt. He'd kept it with him at all times after taking it from her, and Echo burned with a ferocious curiosity to figure out why he guarded it like a dragon hoarding treasure.

He narrowed his eyes, just a hair. "Why?"

She hadn't even told Ivy about the way the locket had showed her the path to the dagger as clear as day, its pull growing stronger the closer she got. But if she was going to work with Caius to find the firebird, she would have to start trusting him at some point. Trust, she knew, was a funny thing. It had a habit of biting people in the ass more often than not. But she had to work with what she had, and what she had was Caius.

"It's how I found the dagger," she said. "It led me to it." She waited, drumming her fingers on her thigh.

With a sigh, he pulled the chain over his head. He held the locket in his hand, but he didn't offer it to her. "How?"

Oh, if only she knew. That would have been nice. That would have been just peachy.

"I don't know," she said. "It just kind of drew me toward it."

Caius studied the locket. "I don't feel anything."

"Look, dude, I don't know how to explain it. I just know that it worked." Echo held out her hand and after a lengthy moment, he placed it in her palm. The second it touched her skin, a surge of energy went through her, stealing the breath from her lungs and weakening her knees. Caius caught her by her elbow, and the locket throbbed even harder.

"I'm fine," she gasped. "I just . . ."

And she was off, striding down the hall, locket vibrating in her palm. Any other day, she would have slowed down to appreciate the architecture of the Met's lobby, with its high domed ceilings and plentiful skylights, but the locket's pull grew stronger with each step, propelling her forward.

Caius jogged to catch up to her, his long legs easily keeping pace. He looked down at the locket in her hands. "What is it—"

She held up her free hand. "Shush."

A small part of Echo, the tiny bit left of her that wasn't in the thrall of the locket's siren song, marveled at the fact that he did indeed shush.

A fallen guard, knocked out by her spell, blocked the entrance to the Greco-Roman sculpture hall opposite the Egyptian wing. She stepped over his prone form, half blind to the majesty of the room. Moonlight filtered in through the skylights, making the bleached white sculptures of forgotten gods and goddesses shine as if from within. It was stunningly beautiful and absolutely irrelevant.

"It's here," Echo said. She broke into a run, swerving around a massive Ionic column in the center of the long corridor. The next room held even more sculptures, but the glass display cases lining the walls were what captured her attention. "It's here, Caius, I can feel—"

She skidded to a halt in front of one of the cases so suddenly that Caius crashed into her. He grabbed her arms to steady them both, and his hands felt like burning brands through the leather of her jacket. She pulled away from him, and the fire abated, but she could still feel heat rolling off him in waves.

"Echo." She could hardly hear Caius past the ringing in her ears. "Echo, where—"

"Here." She laid her palms flat on the glass case before

her, peering in. An ancient marble urn dominated the center of the display. Dancing figures were carved into its sides, bound together by swirling vines, and its lid appeared to be fused shut. One of the figures held a key in its upraised hand. This was it. Echo knew it as surely as she knew her own name.

"Break it," Echo said, stepping aside. "Break the case. It's in the urn, I know it."

"Are you—"

"Just break it, Caius."

He looked at her as if she were a woman possessed. She *was* a woman possessed. But whatever his reservations, they were nothing compared with the fire she felt when she laid eyes on the urn.

"Give me my knives," he said.

Echo reached into her backpack and pulled them out. He had thrown an unholy fit when she had insisted on carrying them, but one couldn't walk around Manhattan openly armed. She handed them to Caius. Trying not to bounce on her toes in her excitement, she watched as he fastened the leather straps across his chest and unsheathed only one. He smashed through the case's glass with the hilt of the knife; then he sheathed it and grabbed the urn.

"Are you absolutely sure?" Caius asked. "I need you to be certain before I deface a culturally significant artifact."

"Oh, for the love of—" Echo elbowed him with all of her strength. The urn slipped through his fingers and smashed to the ground, bits of marble scattering across the floor. A flash of silver drew her eye. There it was. A skeleton key, small and unassuming. The only adornment of which it could boast was a vine twisting around the bow and stem, tiny thorns dotting its surface. Echo pushed past Caius and picked up the key.

It was a rush, heady and wonderful, and Echo laughed. She could feel Caius watching her, probably wondering if she had completely lost her grip on reality. And maybe she had, but she didn't care. The locket ceased its painful pulsing, and the key felt like sunlight in her hands. She turned to him, and her laughter fizzled. She held the key so tightly its thorns dug into the soft flesh of her palm. She looked up at Caius, and it was as if she were seeing him for the first time. He was beautiful, had always been beautiful, but this time, the locket surged once more as if to agree.

CHAPTER FORTY

"That was easier than I expected," Echo said. Caius watched her studying the key. Her earlier intensity simmered beneath the surface, and he could see her body thrum with the energy of it. She turned the key over in her palm to run a finger along the delicate inscriptions it bore. "That's weird. I think these are Drakhar." Not a language one would have expected to find in a human museum. She offered the key to Caius. "Can you read it?"

Their fingers brushed when he took the key from her hand, and a shock ran up his arm, stronger than static. Echo yanked her hand back, flexing her fingers.

"Sorry," she mumbled.

"It's all right," he said, rubbing his palm on his thighs. The back of his neck still tingled. "Let me see."

He squinted at the runes written on the key's stem. They were old, older than Caius even, but he knew them. "'To know the truth, you must first want the truth.' I've seen that before."

Echo peered over his arm at the key. Even with his jacket on, he was hyperaware of her hair brushing his shoulder. "Where?"

He shook his head, puzzled. "It's an old Drakhar saying, but it comes from somewhere very specific. It's written above the entrance to the Oracle's cave."

"An Oracle?" she asked, eyebrows inching up. "Really?"

"Really."

Echo whistled, long and low. "My life just keeps getting weirder and weirder," she said. "And have you met this Oracle before?"

Caius nodded. "Once."

"Why?"

He wanted to tell her. He wanted to tell her who he was. He wanted to tell her that visiting the Oracle was the first thing he had done as the Dragon Prince, just as every prince before him had. He wanted to tell her what the Oracle had told him. In that moment, he wanted her to know him, all of him. Yet all he could say was "That's personal."

Echo held his gaze for a beat before shrugging. "Whatever. Back to Jasper's and then off to see this Oracle of yours?"

Caius's teeth sank into the flesh of his cheek, considering his next words. The Oracle knew who he was. If they went to her, there was a chance—and a large one at that—that his deception would be exposed, that Echo would see him for who and what he truly was. Wanting her to know him, the real him, was a nice thought, but only in the abstract.

The reality of it would shatter their fragile partnership. He'd already figured out that she wasn't the kind of person who put her trust in others easily, and the depth of his lie would stretch the bounds of forgiveness, he was sure of it.

Echo poked him in the side with a gentle elbow. "Earth to Caius. You still with me?"

He cleared his throat and offered her a quick nod. "Yes, sorry." She canted her head to the side, waiting for him to answer her original question. The Oracle. They had to go see her. While he could have ventured to the Oracle's alone, he felt, deep in his bones, that he needed Echo to find the answers he sought. The maps had come to her, and though he couldn't decipher why, he knew that she was tied to this quest, as inextricably as he was. There was no way around it. He would tell her the truth. Soon, but not now. He looked down at her, slipping on a small smile he didn't quite feel, and nodded again. "We'll leave tomorrow. The Oracle isn't going anywhere."

They walked back through the sculpture hall at a much slower pace than they'd entered. Marble gods stared down at them, beautiful enough to break the hardest heart. The guards were still out, the cameras were still down, and Caius was one step closer to the firebird. Perhaps they would reach the end of this journey together, unscathed. He pivoted, turning in a slow circle. "I almost don't want to leave."

Echo practically skipped down the hall, still holding the key tightly. Face breaking into a lopsided grin, she asked, "Why not?"

He smiled again, and it was real this time. He spread his arms wide and said, "Art."

"Do the Drakharin not make art?" Echo asked.

"They do," he said. But Drakharin art had never moved him the way these works did. It had never screamed its presence at him, had never demanded that he recognize its immediacy, its fragility. He looked at Echo to find her looking back at him. There was something in her, some sense of cosmic impermanence that mirrored the museum's paintings and sculptures. "But it's all about battles and victors and commemorating something awful and bloody. There's no beauty. No softness. No . . . art."

Echo's grin flashed across her face. There and gone. "There's no art in Drakharin art?"

His smile was pulled from him, against his will, a hostage of Echo's charm. He doubted she knew just how charming she was. He thought about telling her, but she seemed like the kind of person on whom compliments were wasted.

"When you say it like that, it sounds so eloquent." He came to a halt in front of a decapitated Aphrodite. Even without a head, its presence was so strong, so mighty, that he was convinced that if he only stood still and watched long enough, he would see the delicate drapery on its chest rise and fall with breath.

"Some things demand to be noticed," said Caius. "They grab you and shout, 'I am here! See me!'"

He could feel Echo watching him. "And does Drakharin art not do that?"

When he turned to her, she was looking back at the statue, but a few strands of her hair swayed slightly, as if she'd snapped her head around fast.

"No," Caius said. "I don't think we know how to do that."

"Why is that?" Echo reached a hand out to Aphrodite's stone foot. She peered up at the statue, her fingers hovering close but not touching. She was so perfectly still that she could have been carved from marble. There was something monumental about her. He was beginning to understand what drove a certain breed of man to make art.

When he spoke, his words were soft and quiet, so as not to disturb the absolute stillness of the moment. "We live too long. We remember too much. We don't know what it's like."

Echo turned back to him, exhaling a light sigh. It was as though the room breathed with her. "What what's like?"

"Forgetting," he said. "The fear that we will die and no one will remember that we were ever there. That someday, everyone we know and everyone who knew them will be gone and forgotten, and no one will be left to remember our names."

Echo frowned, but her face was lovely still. "That's so sad."

"And that's why it matters. Humans make art to remember and be remembered," said Caius. "Art is their weapon against forgetting."

"That's beautiful." Echo was standing very close to him now. He noticed, for the first time, the faint dusting of freckles across her nose. There were a great many things he found beautiful just then. He was searching for the words to tell her just that when the shadows around them exploded.

CHAPTER FORTY-ONE

Echo knew who it was before the darkness coalesced into shape, black feathers fluttering around a figure at the opposite end of the corridor, blocking the way to the lobby. There was only one person who could wrap themselves in shadows like that. Ruby emerged from the darkness, her cloak dragging over the marble.

"Hi, Ruby," Echo said, slipping the key into the zippered pocket of her jacket. "Fancy meeting you here."

Ruby's smile was as false as ever. "Echo, always nice to see you. But I have a feeling you'd much prefer to see who I brought with me."

A figure stepped out from the shadows behind Ruby, and Echo's heart stuttered in her chest. "Rowan?"

He looked almost exactly as he had when she'd left him in the Avicen cells. The bronze armor had been swapped for jeans and a black hoodie, but the concern in his eyes and the tight set of his jaw were the same.

"Echo?" Rowan asked. "What are you doing here?" His gaze darted between Echo and Caius. "With a Drakharin?"

"Get back," Caius said. He shoved Echo behind him, drawing both knives from the sheaths on his back. It felt like hiding, but Echo was glad to have him as a buffer between herself and Ruby. A Drakharin shielding her from Altair's favorite lackey. If Ruby didn't kill her, the irony would. Rowan's gaze bounced between Caius and Echo as he tried to puzzle out why and how their strange alliance had come to be. Echo wanted to explain it to him, but she didn't think Ruby would tolerate a lengthy chat.

"Caius," Echo said, placing a hand on his arm. "It's okay. Rowan's a friend. He won't hurt me." She tripped over the word "friend," hating the way it felt on her lips, regretting how it made Rowan flinch when she said it. He was staring at her so hard, she felt as though she would break. There were a million things she wanted to tell him, but she didn't think any could quell the feeling of guilt that curdled in her stomach. She was standing side by side with a Drakharin, letting herself be protected by him. To Rowan, it must have looked like betrayal.

Caius shot her a quizzical glance, but he didn't argue. He jerked his head at Ruby. "And what about her?"

Ruby drew a wickedly long sword, and the sound Echo made was embarrassingly close to a whimper. There was a reason Ruby was Altair's favorite recruit, and it had nothing to do with her sterling personality.

Echo swallowed. "Um, not so sure about her."

Ruby glided toward them as if she had been waiting for her close-up. "Hiding behind your new boyfriend now, are you? I want to say I expected more from you, but it would be a lie."

Rowan recoiled as if struck.

"He is *not* my boyfriend," Echo said in a rush. The situation was deteriorating faster than she could handle. Half of her was happy to see Rowan, to know that he was looking for her, that he cared enough to come after her. The other half almost wished he hadn't. Getting in and out of the museum should have been simple. This . . . this was not simple.

Caius kept his eyes on Ruby, long knives held at the ready, but he angled his head toward Echo when he said, "Really? That's what you're worried about?"

"The truth is very important to me, Caius." So maybe her priorities needed work. She looked back to Rowan and Ruby. "What are you two doing here?"

Rowan stepped forward, placing a hand on Ruby's arm. She didn't look happy to be held back, but she didn't fight him.

"The wards were tripped when you got back to the city," Rowan said. "Altair had us tracking you. He knew I let you out, so he said I had to bring you back. It's my . . . penance." He inched forward warily, but when Caius gripped the hilts of his knives as if preparing to strike, he paused. "Echo, *what* is going on?" He gestured to Caius. "And why are you with him? What happened to Ivy?"

"Ivy's okay," Echo said. "Rowan, I know this looks bad, but I can explain." She tried to step around Caius, but his arm shot out, blocking her path. Rowan looked at Caius's arm as though he wanted to rip it off.

"We didn't come here to listen to your excuses, traitor." Ruby brushed past Rowan but left a comfortable distance between her own sword and Caius's blades. "I knew it was a mistake taking you in. The Ala should have drowned you like the runt you are."

The muscles in Caius's back tensed at Ruby's taunt, and for some insane reason, that struck Echo as the most miraculous thing that had happened all day. Rowan said nothing in her defense, and Echo tried not to think about how much his silence hurt.

Ruby raised her sword, but stayed where she was. "To be honest, I should thank you. You led me right to the next step in finding the firebird. Altair will be pleased. He'll be even happier when you've been arrested. Escaping from the cells was one thing, but this?" She waved her sword at Caius and Echo. "This is a whole new level of wrong."

Echo's throat tightened, and she hated Ruby more than she ever had. She looked at Rowan, but he'd averted his gaze, choosing instead to stare at the floor. "Rowan?" she asked. "Were you sent here to arrest me?"

Rowan dragged his eyes up to meet hers. "Yeah, technically, but—" He groaned low in his throat, raking his hands through his feathers. "Altair just wants us to bring you back. I'm sure it'll be fine."

With a snort, Ruby shook her head. "Don't lie to her, Rowan." She turned back to Echo, pale blue eyes glinting in the darkness. "Our orders are clear. We're to bring you before the council. The charges leveled against you are almost impressive. Withholding secrets pertinent to the security of the Avicen people. Breaking out of prison. And now, I'm sure cavorting with the enemy will be added to the list." She tilted her head to the side, never breaking eye contact with Echo. "Do you know what the penalty for treason is?"

Without a word, Echo shook her head.

Ruby smiled, slow and predatory. "Death."

No one in Echo's lifetime had ever been charged with treason among the Avicen. She'd never thought to ask what happened to people who turned against their own. The Avicen were the closest thing she had to family, to home. They'd taken her in, and it would be hard to convince them that she hadn't betrayed them, not with two Warhawk witnesses to testify that she'd been seen with a Drakharin. Rowan might have tried to cover for her, but Ruby would relish the opportunity to see her fall from grace, even though death did feel a bit extreme. Perhaps Ruby's loathing ran deeper than Echo had realized. The Ala had only so much influence, revered as she was. If the council sentenced Echo to death, even the Ala's powers would be limited. Echo might be able to escape, but she'd live the rest of her life on the run, constantly looking over her shoulder to see if there was an executioner on her tail. But if she returned to the Avicen with the firebird, if she proved that she'd been on their side the whole time, then maybe, just maybe, she'd find clemency. But the Avicen would never forgive her if she returned empty-handed.

Rowan was looking at her with desperation in his eyes. She could imagine how he felt. Powerless. She knew the feeling well. He was about to speak, perhaps to plead with her, when Caius backed away, shoving Echo along with his body. "Echo, run."

She let herself be pushed, but she stood her ground in a different way. "What? No, I'm not leaving you here."

Rowan's hands twitched into fists. "Echo, this is crazy. Come back with us. I'll talk to Altair. Everything will be okay."

Ruby laughed, and the sound was like knives on the

wind. "Honestly, Rowan. She made her bed, and now she's going to sleep in it." And then she leaped, feathered cloak cutting through the air like real wings, ignoring Rowan's shout for her to stop.

"Echo!" Caius yelled. "Run!"

Echo stumbled back, suddenly very, very aware not only that she was unarmed but also that she was less than useless in a fight between two trained warriors. Ruby's sword sliced down toward Caius. He raised his knives, and the sword glanced off one of his blades with a metallic whisper.

"Echo. Run. Now." Caius kept his eyes on Ruby, who was circling him like the vulture she was.

Rowan looked as lost as Echo felt. "Echo, stop. You don't have to do this. You can come home."

But he was wrong. She had to find the firebird, even if it meant joining forces with someone Rowan had been taught to hate from childhood. It was the only way to set things right, to get her friends out of danger, to make sure no one else got hurt because of a conflict no one alive could even remember starting. She couldn't go home, not until she found what she was looking for. Not while she was labeled a traitor.

"I'm so sorry," Echo said.

Before Rowan could respond, she bolted, throwing herself down the hall so fast her feet barely touched the ground. She dug into her pocket for the small pouch of dust Jasper had given her, but she wasn't Caius. She couldn't conjure gateways out of thin air with just any threshold. The closest useful gateway was the bridge in Central Park they'd used earlier that day. Her feet pounded against the floor, but she didn't hear another set of steps behind her. Rowan hadn't followed her. He'd stayed behind, probably to help Ruby fight Caius.

With the sound of steel clashing against steel ringing in her ears, Echo skidded to a stop, breath coming in harsh pants. She stood before the information desk in the lobby. A sleeping guard was bent over a crumpled-up newspaper, pen still dangling from his loose grip. He'd been doing the crossword puzzle. The museum's doors were feet away, but she couldn't move. She couldn't do it. She couldn't leave them behind. She'd seen Caius fight back at the keep. He was good. Beyond good. Rowan didn't stand a chance.

A vengeful little voice whispered that if their roles had been reversed, Caius would have left her. That he would have taken the key and run. But she knew that little voice was full of crap. Echo slid the dagger from her boot and turned back, breaking into a run. It was like Caius said. They did this together, or not at all.

Echo ran as if she had wings on her feet, skidding around a corner and knocking over at least one priceless artifact, adrenaline singing through her veins. When she rounded the last corner, her breath caught. Ruby was sprawled on the floor, groaning in pain, while Caius towered over Rowan, knives still in hand.

"Caius, no!"

At the sound of Echo's shout, Caius paused, turning to look at her. Behind him, Ruby pulled herself to her feet. Her sword arced through the air, and Echo ran as she never had before, tackling Ruby with a wordless yell. She had just enough time to see surprise flash across Caius's face before they fell to the ground in a tangle of limbs and feathers.

Echo's blade was lodged in Ruby's back before she even realized she'd raised it. Ruby twitched beneath her, sword forgotten as her hands scrabbled at the marble floor, fingers slipping in her own blood. Echo pulled the dagger free from between Ruby's shoulder blades, and the wet squelch made her stomach heave.

"Echo, we have to go." Caius's voice was muffled by the ringing in Echo's ears. Her hands were slick with crimson, and she didn't know what to do with them.

Caius grabbed her by her upper arms and hauled her to her feet. Her boots slid in the puddle of blood that was forming beneath Ruby's still-twitching body, and she fell against Caius's chest. He wrapped an arm around her—Echo hadn't even seen him sheathe his knives—and half carried, half dragged her back toward the lobby. She twisted in Caius's arms to peer over his shoulder. Ruby was nothing more than a black pile of feathers. Rowan crawled over to Ruby's body, hands hovering uselessly over the wound in her back. He looked so lost.

Echo's feet felt as if they belonged to someone else, and she stumbled as Caius led her back toward the Tomb of Perneb. Her legs were clumsy, as though she'd forgotten how they worked. Caius pulled her along, out of the sculpture hall, through the lobby, and back to the Egyptian gallery, and when he finally stopped at the tomb's entrance, Echo closed her eyes. The last image she had of Ruby was seared into her retinas. She knew it was a sight she would never forget, no matter how hard she tried. All she could think, even as Caius summoned the black smoke of the in-between, was that Ruby's blood had been as red as her name.

CHAPTER FORTY-TWO

Echo barely remembered getting back to Jasper's. She was certain that she'd been covered in blood and that Caius had all but carried her out of the Met, but beyond those general brushstrokes of a story, the finer details of the picture were grainy, half-focused images. She remembered the curve of Rowan's back as he knelt over Ruby's body, the inky swirls of the in-between as Caius conjured them a way out, and the nave of the cathedral, where he must have taken them. She wanted to laugh at his resourcefulness when it came to finding handy thresholds—a nave, who knew?—but she couldn't feel anything beyond a yawning emptiness inside, a chasm that had been hollowed out in her chest. She felt as if she had been the one left to die on a cold marble floor. It was a selfish thought. Another thing to add to the bottomless pit of regret that had taken up residence where her stomach used to be.

The images began to crystallize after they arrived at the cathedral. Ivy, shining and white, big black eyes clouded with concern. Jasper's worry made noticeable through his uncharacteristic silence. Dorian had nearly bled out on his Egyptian cotton sheets, and Jasper had quipped the whole way through, but when Echo burst through his front door covered in someone else's blood, he hadn't once lamented the state of his impractical furnishings. It was fascinating, the way they treated her. As if she was traumatized. She must have been, but how would the traumatized know? How could they tell? How could they see anything objective past the impenetrable force field of their own trauma?

Echo curled into a ball and rubbed her face into the pillow. It was memory foam or something like it. Her hands knotted together under the blankets. Someone had scrubbed them clean, leaving her skin dry and raw. She slipped them free of the blankets, looking at her knuckles, then at her open palms. Her skin was grayish in the darkness. Not a speck of blood remained. It was strange to think that they'd been slick with it just hours ago. Or had it been days? Time had become elastic, stretching loose and snapping tight.

She brought her fingers up to her lips, remembering the way Rowan's had felt against her skin when he'd helped her escape from Altair's jail. The way he'd looked at her as if she mattered more than he could have said in that moment. The warmth of his breath as he spoke. She wondered what he would think of her now. If he would ever be able to forgive the girl who had buried a knife in someone's back. The girl who was officially a traitor and a murderer. She let her hands fall back onto the blankets. Rowan was at home in the

Nest—*his* home, not hers; it could never be hers, not now, not after what she'd done. And she was here, an ocean away, huddled under a mound of blankets.

Jasper's loft was too high up for the orangey glow of Strasbourg's streetlights to reach them, but the stained-glass windows caught the bare bits of starlight that pricked at the sky. Echo didn't know what time it was, but it must have been late. Sheets rustled elsewhere in the loft as someone shifted in their sleep. She pulled the covers up to her chin and wondered about their sleeping arrangements, since she'd evidently claimed Jasper's giant bed for herself. Ivy must have tucked her in, but she couldn't really remember that, either. She studied the sleeping form on the chair beside her bed, the only person she could see from her cocoon of blankets.

Caius.

He must have started the night off sitting like a normal person, feet on the ground, legs stretched out, but he'd twisted as he slept. He was cradled in the chair, long legs draped over one arm while his back rested on the other, head slightly bowed so his bangs brushed the scales on his cheekbones. He reminded Echo of a statue, beautiful and serene.

From that moment in the Met—when something had fractured deep inside her—Caius had been her one constant. Through the broken shards of her memory, she remembered the feel of his hands as he hauled her up, grip as strong as iron, but strangely gentle, as if he was trying to hold the broken bits of her together even though it was futile. She was Humpty Dumpty, and she'd already tumbled from the wall.

She wasn't sure what it was that glued him to her side.

Kindness, perhaps. Or maybe guilt. She had, after all, saved his life. The moment he'd picked her up, he'd begun to feel like her anchor. Like a piece of driftwood she clung to in her sea of guilt and despair, knowing that if she let go, she would drown.

She closed her eyes and tried to will herself to sleep. Since getting back, she'd heard only scraps of conversation. The inscription on the key, the one Caius recognized, was explained. His voice had drifted in and out as he told the others about the Oracle. Something about the Black Forest, and a cave, and how they would all wait until she and Dorian were up to snuff before departing.

She would have gladly traded places with Dorian in an instant. A sword wound seemed easy compared with this. In one way, out the other. Nice and clean. There was nothing clean about how she felt, little pieces of herself scattered around like broken porcelain. She drew in a shaky breath, trying to quell the unease in her gut. This was what guilt—real, undeniable guilt—felt like. It was a weight settling on her rib cage, crushing her with the force of a pile of stones. She wondered if it would ever let up, if she would ever scrub the image of the blood on her hands from her mind. If she even deserved that kind of reprieve, or if the magnitude of her sin was so great that she would carry it with her always.

Echo hadn't even realized she'd started crying until she felt the brush of callused fingers on her face, wiping at her cheeks. She opened her eyes, lashes sticky with tears, to find Caius crouched beside the bed. She hadn't heard him rise, but there he was, eyes nearly black in the darkness.

"Hey." The word sounded strange coming from his mouth, as if it wasn't something he ought to say. Echo swallowed past the lump in her throat. Caius didn't seem to mind her silence. "We were worried about you."

She wasn't sure when their strange little group had coalesced from "us" and "them" into a single, cohesive "we." Stranger things had happened, she supposed. His soft, kind eyes tugged at something inside her chest, a reminder that her heart was still there despite how empty she felt.

Caius's fingers traced the lines of her face, from cheekbone to chin, his touch as soft as a feather.

"If you're feeling up to it," he said, "we're going to head out soon. The Oracle will tell us what we need to do next."

Again with the "we." He sounded so confident, but Echo had a feeling that it was feigned certainty, put on for her benefit. The notion that he was trying to make her feel better, even in a minor way, made the tiny, broken things inside her flutter, as though maybe they were considering gluing themselves back together. She liked the way his voice sounded in the dark, soft and low, as if it was meant just for her. She closed her eyes and buried her face in the sheets.

Caius heaved a sigh, but it wasn't an angry or frustrated one. It was, perhaps, a little bit sad. As if he, too, mourned the loss of whatever part of her had been left to die alongside Ruby. He stayed there, cradling her face for a minute more. The edge of the bed dipped as he balanced his other hand on it, pushing himself to his feet. Echo wanted to ask him not to leave, to keep his hand where it had been, tracing her cheek with his thumb, but she didn't have the words.

His voice drifted to her through the darkness as he

settled back into the chair. "Get some rest, if you can. It'll be a long day tomorrow."

Echo listened for the barely audible sound of his breathing and paced her own to match it. Sooner than she thought possible, she drifted into slumber, lulled by the rhythm of Caius's breath, in and out, in and out.

CHAPTER FORTY-THREE

Caius looked around as the swirling black tendrils of the in-between faded into the station platform. It was grimly industrial. In the early-dawn light, a single smokestack towered above the trees, painting the sky charcoal with its noxious plumes. His eyes drooped shut as he stretched, groaning through the symphony of popping joints in his shoulders and arms. He'd spent the past day and a half sleeping in a chair by Echo's bedside, all the while pretending not to see the quizzical glances Dorian kept sending his way.

The Black Forest was visible from where they stood, the tops of the trees jutting into the sky, but their destination lay deep within it. The station sat on the edge of the forest, but it was still a day's walk from where they needed to be, two if they stopped to rest. With Dorian injured and the rest unaccustomed to arduous hikes, they would have to move slowly.

The others got their bearings around him, and he watched as Echo inhaled deeply, one hand resting on her stomach. She had come back to herself in stages, and the effort it cost her to shake off her disorientation long enough to point out the Appenweier train station on a map had been noticeable. Beyond hushed exchanges with Ivy and Jasper about food and logistics, she hadn't spoken much. After Caius had brushed her tears away in the night, she'd avoided his gaze, eyes darting to the side every time he looked at her. He didn't need words to know what was wrong. He'd been similarly withdrawn after his first kill, all those years ago, and then, his victim had been a stranger. An Avicen soldier who'd fallen afoul of Caius's blade. But Echo had known the person she'd killed. He offered up a silent prayer to any god that might be listening that it would be the last time her hands were stained with blood. Taking a life was no easy thing to bear. It changed a person in fundamental ways, as the pieces of one's old self fractured and re-formed to accommodate a new and horrible truth: the world would keep on spinning, no matter how guilty or wretched a soul felt. You had to go on living, even when there was a dead body in your wake.

The brisk dawn air seemed to give Echo back some of the vigor she'd lost. He was glad to see the subtle pink in her cheeks as her hair whipped around her face, but she was still pale and drawn, shoulders hunched in on herself as though she could hide where she stood. In a short span of time, she'd lost everything—her home, the trust of the people she considered family. She hadn't explained to Caius her relationship to the Avicen, but it was clear, from the way she interacted with Ivy and Jasper, that they were *her people,* more so than humans. And when word reached the Nest that she'd spilled Avicen blood, he supposed they would gladly sentence her to death. Regret swelled in his chest, not for himself, but for Echo. She may have been a thief, but she was no murderer, not by nature. A sudden chill bit at his skin, daring the wool of his jacket to try to stop it.

"Honestly, Caius, you couldn't get us any closer?" Jasper said, flipping up the collar of his coat.

Caius swallowed a retort unfit for polite company. As much as he would have liked to argue with Jasper, the station was bleak and deserted, emphasizing just how cold it was.

"As I explained to you earlier," he replied, "the area surrounding the Oracle's cave is null. The in-between cannot be accessed from within her borders."

"I get that there's a magical no-fly zone." Jasper rubbed his hands together before shoving them into the pockets of his coat. "I'm just a touch disappointed that this was the best you could do."

Caius inhaled, counted to five, then exhaled. "My apologies, Your Highness."

"Apology accepted."

Caius rolled his eyes. Only Jasper would have the gall.

Kicking aside a filthy chunk of stubborn spring snow, Jasper sniffed haughtily and added, "Too bad I'm fresh out of dead bodies to hide. This place would be perfect."

Dorian snorted. Caius shot him his best glower, and Dorian cleared his throat, tucking his chin into his collar. The coat Jasper had lent Dorian was a deep navy, much the same shade as his eye patch. Caius hadn't failed to notice that Jasper didn't bother to color-code the clothes he passed on to him.

"Echo, you didn't tell me it would be cold," Ivy grumbled, pulling her hands into the sleeves of her jacket. "I didn't think to pack my winter wear when I was kidnapped."

And just like that, the last vestiges of Dorian's small smile died. Wordlessly, he unbuttoned his coat and slipped it off. He held it out to Ivy, who stared at it, blinking rapidly. Caius knew he wasn't the only person holding his breath. Something delicate was happening, and he had no desire to disrupt it.

With a trembling hand, Ivy took the coat. Dorian turned away, walking toward the station steps. Ivy looked from the coat to Dorian's retreating form. Her dark eyes were shiny.

"Thank you," she said.

Dorian paused. He nodded, without looking back, before heading down the platform steps. Caius met Jasper's eyes from across the platform, and Jasper shrugged.

"Are we just going to stand around staring at each other all day," Echo said, "or are we going to get this show on the road?"

Caius turned and was surprised to see her looking at him, holding his eyes for a few seconds before heading toward the station steps. It was the first thing she'd said to him since New York.

CHAPTER FORTY-FOUR

The moment they crossed the wards surrounding the Black Forest, Dorian felt the faint hum of magic in the atmosphere. The farther they walked, the less he noticed it, but it was there all the same. Brittle twigs and paper-thin leaves crunched beneath his feet, and the crisp forest air made puffy little clouds of his breath. The branches of the birch trees around them danced in the light wind, leaves rustling. The chalk white of their bark was painted a soft buttery yellow in the early-morning light. It would have been lovely if Dorian's mood hadn't been so foul. His still-healing wound and the sight of Caius shooting strange, searching glances Echo's way made for a dire combination. He trudged along, hardly noticing when Jasper sidled up next to him. How strange it was that he should be so comfortable in the presence of an Avicen, but there was something about Jasper that defied convention.

"Penny for your thoughts?" Jasper asked, reaching behind

Dorian's ear. With a flick of his wrist, he produced a shiny copper coin.

Charlatan, Dorian thought, fighting back a smile. Jasper was a pest, but an effective one. The more he pushed at Dorian's walls, the harder it was to stay irritated.

"My thoughts are my own," Dorian said. He tore his eye from Caius's back. There was little use in studying the set of his shoulders, or the angle of his gait, or the way his eyes lingered on Echo a beat longer than they had the day before. Caius was walking away from him, in more ways than one.

Dorian met Jasper's gaze, and he knew that Jasper had been watching him watch Caius. *A clever charlatan. The very worst kind.*

"And even if my thoughts were for sale," Dorian said, "I doubt you could afford them."

Jasper smiled, toothy and winsome. It was a refreshing change from the smirk he wore as faithfully as Dorian wore his eye patch. To each his own mask.

"Behold," Jasper said, rolling the word around on his tongue as if it was something to be savored. "It speaks."

Just to spite him, Dorian said no more. They walked in a silence that shouldn't have been amicable, with Dorian being who he was and Jasper being who he was. Dorian was beginning to suspect that somewhere between Japan and Germany, he had completely lost control of his life.

He looked at Jasper from the corner of his eye. The Avicen seemed at home in the woods, despite his complaints, bountiful as they were. Dorian wasn't sure if Jasper's jewel-toned feathers were always brighter in the light of day, or if his eyes were always that shade of gold bordering on yellow, or if his skin always held that touch of bronze that stood out against the backdrop of dusty-white birch trees. He especially wasn't sure when he'd started noticing the vibrance of Jasper's many colors to begin with.

"You know," Jasper mused, "I wouldn't have actually sold you out, right? I just wanted someone to tell me what the deal was."

Dorian shrugged. "I had my doubts."

With an indignant gasp, Jasper laid a hand over his heart. "You wound me, sir. I'll have you know I *do* have a moral compass." He paused. "Even if I'm the only one who can read it."

Again, Dorian had his doubts. He cast another glance at the sea of birch trees around them. They needed a watchful eye on the forest to see if their enemies had found them, but he was beginning to realize that an Avicen threat of an entirely different sort was walking right beside him.

"Why are you here?" Dorian asked.

"I told you," Jasper said, rolling his neck with a studied grace, eyes drifting shut slowly. He looked like something out of a painting. "I'm in it for the glory."

"Caius and Echo almost died the other day." Dorian scanned the trees. He needed to not be looking at Jasper. "It seems like a great deal of trouble just for glory."

Jasper hummed, twirling the coin between his long, elegant fingers. "I have my reasons. Besides, anything worth having is never easy to get." He settled his yellow-gold gaze on Dorian, quiet and searching. Dorian decided not to read into Jasper's words. It was better that way.

"And what about you?" Jasper asked, hands dancing as he made the coin disappear and reappear in his palms. "Why are you here?"

"Duty," Dorian replied. The answer was instinctive. While it wasn't a lie, it was—arguably—not the entire truth.

Jasper's eyes fixed on a spot in front of them. Dorian didn't need to follow them to know that he was looking at Caius. "Is that all?"

"It's enough."

And, because the gods had not seen fit to smile on Dorian as of late, Jasper saw right through him. "I think we both know that isn't true."

Dorian looked away, bereft of a response. He hated to think that his feelings were so transparent, but Jasper was right. Not that he would deign to admit such a thing aloud. The Avicen's ego didn't need the help. He trudged on, watching the trees, trampling dry grass beneath his feet.

"And maybe it's just because I'm so self-serving," Jasper continued, "but it seems a strange thing, to devote one's entire life to someone who can't see what's right in front of him."

"Caius would give his life for me," Dorian said, almost too quickly. He knew that it was true, but he also knew, no matter how badly he would have liked to cling to the lie that had sustained him for so long, that it simply wasn't enough. Not anymore. Perhaps it never had been. Perhaps he'd been dishonest with himself for so long that he'd come to believe his own lie.

There was a knowing wistfulness to Jasper's slow smile. "But it's not his life you want, is it?"

Dorian had an answer for that, but he didn't feel much like sharing it. He slid his hands into the pockets of his borrowed jeans and walked on in silence. The birds of the Black Forest chirped while Dorian kept his peace.

"Yeah," Jasper said, pocketing the coin. "I didn't think so."

CHAPTER FORTY-FIVE

Echo surveyed the ruins before them. They had been an abbey once, though the front wall had collapsed, and the interior had long since been picked clean of anything of value. But there were still three solid walls, and nature had reclaimed it, granting it something of a roof from the branches of an overgrown oak tree. Echo assumed that Caius had chosen it as their camp for the night because it was dry and defensible, not because it was pretty.

"You're joking," Jasper said as Dorian walked the perimeter, carving runes into the dry earth with the tip of his sword.

"No," Caius replied, gaze raking over the ruins. "Not joking." He caught Echo's eyes for the space of a single heartbeat before she turned away, wrapping her arms tightly around herself. There was too much knowledge in his eyes, too much understanding. It had comforted her before, how he seemed to know when she needed to be left alone and when she needed comfort, but now it was just disconcerting. She didn't like that he had learned to read her so well after so little time.

Jasper dragged out his sigh for so long that Echo wondered how he had any air left in his lungs. "Why did I ever agree to come on this wild-goose chase?"

"I thought you were in it for the glory," Dorian tossed over his shoulder with a tiny grin that was halfway to becoming an actual smile.

"Glory is overrated," Jasper replied. "I think I'd much rather have a soft, warm bed, thank you very much."

Echo listened to their banter for as long as she could. Dorian had grown more comfortable around the two Avicen in their little party. She felt as though she had missed something vital over the past few days. Even Ivy had begun to thaw. Dorian was obviously trying, and Ivy had always been the forgiving kind. She was a good person. Better than Echo.

Jasper was laughing at something Ivy had said, and the sound turned Echo's stomach. She couldn't acknowledge that the world was full of things like mirth when she felt as if she were decaying from the inside out. With a mumbled excuse, which she didn't care if they believed, or even heard, Echo turned away from the camp. Picking her way over fallen logs and bits of broken abbey wall, she walked deeper into the woods, silent and alone. An owl hooted in the distance, and another answered it, their unearthly cries filling the sky with song.

The Black Forest slowly fell quiet as twilight descended, as though even the birds kept their silence to appreciate it. The setting sun peeked between the trunks of trees on the horizon in violent shades of purple and red. Echo understood why the Brothers Grimm had found inspiration here for their twisted tales. It was dark and magical, menacing and beautiful, and it made her heart hurt to look at it. It wasn't long before she heard quiet footsteps behind her. She didn't need to turn around to know that it was *him*.

Caius said nothing. He moved to stand beside her, but he seemed content to let her choose if she wanted to talk or not. She let several moments tick by in silence as they watched the sun slip beneath the line of trees in the distance. The sound of leaves whispering against one another was almost like a language, but an ancient one. One Echo couldn't understand. The words hovered on the air, on the edge of meaning. Present, but utterly incomprehensible.

"Psithurism," she said.

Next to her, Caius shifted, boots crunching on dry leaves. She could feel his eyes on her.

"Psithurism?" he asked.

"The sound of the wind through the trees."

"I didn't know there was a word for that," he said.

"There's a word for just about everything if you look hard enough." Her breath made little clouds in the cold forest air, as if her voice had shape and substance.

"Echo, I—"

She cut him off. "When I was twelve, I developed a crush on a boy. Rowan." Beside her, Caius tensed. Putting two and two together, she assumed. After all, there were only so many Rowans in the world, and Caius had recently made the acquaintance of one. "We grew up together. I liked him, and I was so sure that he liked me, too." He had. There was a chance—even a small one—that he still did, but Echo knew that she'd ruined any possibility of a future with him after taking the life of an Avicen. The enormity of her crime was simply too grand. "But you know what Ruby did?"

She didn't wait for Caius to answer. "She told him I was contagious. That if he touched me, he would catch what I had, and it would molt his feathers right off his flesh. I couldn't understand why she did it or what I'd done to deserve it."

Echo was incredibly aware of Caius's eyes on her, tracing her profile. She wanted to look at him, but she also didn't want to look at him. She didn't know what she wanted, but now that she'd started and the words were out, falling from her lips of their own volition, she couldn't stop them.

"Most of the other Avicelings steered clear of me after that. But that wasn't even the worst part. Not really. Ruby had never liked me, and I didn't exactly go out of my way to be nice to her, but . . ."

This was the part Echo had never shared with another soul. Not the Ala, who had held her, rubbing soothing circles on her back, when Echo had run to her, face streaked with tears, after Rowan had told her what Ruby had said. Not even Ivy, from whom she kept no secrets.

"There's this fountain in the Nest, one that supposedly grants wishes. I went to it and threw a penny in. I thought about wishing for Rowan to fall in love with me. Or about making everyone forget what Ruby had said. I even thought about wishing for feathers of my own. But I didn't ask for any of those things. Do you know what I wished for?"

Caius's voice was soft and maybe even a little bit sweet. "What?"

"I wished that Ruby would die. I wished that she would die, and I would never have to see her again. Talk about a self-fulfilling prophecy." The words sat bitter on Echo's tongue, and she swallowed them down with a broken laugh. She laughed because it was better than crying, but the laugh was all jagged edges and sharp corners, and it cut up her insides as it clawed its way out.

"For what it's worth," Caius said, "I wish you hadn't had to do it."

Echo thrust her hands into her jacket pockets. Her fingers were cold, as if the tips were slowly going dead. "I don't think that's worth anything."

"I know, but it needed to be said anyway. I should have been faster; I shouldn't have needed your help."

"Don't," Echo said, shaking her head. "Don't make this about you."

"That's not what I—" From the corner of her eye, she saw his hand reach out to her before falling away. "Echo, you did what you felt you had to do."

"Did I? Did I have to do it?" Echo toed a log over with her boot. Little worms, unhappy to be exposed to the fading light, wriggled their way into the ground, seeking darkness. "I could have left you there. But I didn't. I went back. I was scared for Rowan, but I was worried about you, too. And I don't even know why. We aren't friends, Caius. I barely even know you. But I couldn't watch Ruby hurt you. I stabbed a person in the back for you. Literally."

She turned to Caius. Standing there, in the dying light of the early-evening sun, he didn't look two hundred fifty. He looked dark and silent and sad. She was keenly aware of her own pulse, of the way his hair just barely brushed his collar, of the scales on his cheeks, of the sound of the nighttime forest coming alive. It was beautiful and terrible, all at once.

Ever since she'd found that music box, Echo's world had tilted on its axis, just a few degrees, but enough so that everything was different. She saw colors differently, smelled things differently, heard sounds that she had never deigned to notice before. It was as though she was experiencing the world for the first time, and everything was new. But nothing was newer to her than Caius. He was the sound of the nightingale welcoming the evening, the moon peeking out from behind a cloud, the secret shadowy parts of the Black Forest that she was only just discovering.

But she didn't deserve this novelty, this great and terrible beauty, not when she could still feel Ruby's blood on her hands, seeping into her pores, drying under her nails.

"Why do I feel like this?" she said. "I did something terrible, and I did it for you, and I don't understand why."

A change was happening beneath the surface of her skin, as monumental as the shifting of tectonic plates. Something inside her was building to a crescendo she couldn't begin to fathom. She rubbed her fingers against her temples and squeezed her eyes shut. She didn't want to feel like this. It was too much. Too confusing. Too disastrous. She wanted to be the person she'd been before she'd taken a life, before she'd set off on this cursed journey. She wanted, more than anything else, to forget. To forget the pain and the guilt and the regret that threatened to drown her. She wanted to feel something, anything, besides the ache inside her heart.

When Caius didn't answer, she reached for his hand, fingers brushing along his knuckles. She needed to feel the warmth of another person. She wanted to let him be her anchor. Caius looked down at their joined hands. His hair fell in front of his eyes, hiding them. This time, she didn't quell the urge to brush it away. Her fingers traced the line of his temples, the uneven texture of his scales. His eyes fluttered shut, and he leaned his cheek into her hand. He let her explore the contours of his face for a moment before pulling his hand away. No more than six inches separated their bodies, but it felt like a vast expanse. He wrapped his arms around himself. On anyone else, the gesture would have made them look smaller. It just made him look tired.

Echo took another step forward, crowding into Caius's space. He tensed but didn't step back. Their chests brushed with every indrawn breath.

"Help me, Caius," she said. "Help me forget."

He parted his lips, but no sound came out save a barely there hitch in his breath. A tiny part of her wished that he would push her away, tell her to stop, but more than that, she prayed he wouldn't. She needed the silent comfort of feeling another person's body against her own without the weight of words between them. She didn't think she could bear what he would say. If he spoke, he would water the nasty little seeds of betrayal that had taken root in her heart when she wasn't looking, and they would blossom into something she couldn't deny, and bend toward him, a flower angling for the sun.

"Echo, I—"

When she pressed her lips to his, balancing on the tips of her toes to reach him, she felt something inside her click into place. She grabbed the open collar of his jacket for balance. His hands slid up her arms to circle her wrists, steadying her. Caius's lips were warm and slightly chapped. They parted, welcoming her own. It was a soft kiss, searching and hesitant. Echo's pulse roared in her ears. She pressed her body flush against his, soaking up every bit of warmth he could offer. When she felt his tongue slide against her bottom lip, she thought she might explode.

He pulled back first, trailing his lips over her cheekbones, the bridge of her nose, the ridge of her brow, his fingers tracing the skin of her wrists as though it were as delicate as the spindly membrane of butterfly wings. Echo could feel herself dissolving where he touched her, disintegrating into a pile of ash at his feet. On a good day, she would have been embarrassed about that, but today was not a good day. She felt herself becoming someone else, someone she didn't recognize. *War makes monsters of us all,* Caius had said. Echo wondered, if she were to look in a mirror now, who she would see.

She slipped her fingers under Caius's shirt, warming them against his skin. His hands dropped to wrap around her waist, and he arched into her touch. A strangled sound escaped him, like a man gasping for breath after drowning. Breathing heavily, he shuddered in her arms and squeezed his eyes shut, forehead falling to rest against hers. Her touch was light, but Caius reacted as though he hadn't been touched in years. Maybe he hadn't. Echo flattened her palm against his lower back, right above the waistband of his jeans. Her skin felt aflame.

"Echo." It was a whisper, breathed into her hair.

She reached up, closing the inch that separated them to brush her lips against his. He made that desperate strangled sound again. This was what she needed. A distraction. A way to feel something besides regret. But after a few seconds, his hands dropped from her waist. He followed the line of her arms to grasp her forearms, pushing her away from him. The distance was practically negligible, but it was enough for Echo to curse the cold that settled between them. He'd been so warm. He let his head drop, close enough for his bangs to brush her cheekbones.

"Not like this," he whispered. "Not like this."

CHAPTER FORTY-SIX

Even after he pulled away, Caius could still taste the subtle mint of Echo's lip balm. She sagged against him, forehead falling against his chest. When she spoke, her words were muffled by his jacket.

"I did it for you."

Caius stroked the soft skin on the undersides of her wrists with his thumbs. "I know."

She rubbed her face against the space between his collarbones. He could feel a slight dampness on her cheeks through his shirt.

"Why did I do it?" she asked.

"I don't know."

"I mean, would you have done the same for me?" Echo peered up at him, brown eyes bloodshot and shiny. She lifted her head just enough so that Caius's skin tingled with the fleeting warmth of her cheek. Something quite like pain seized at his chest. He would have. Without a moment's hesitation.

"Echo—"

And then she was crying. Caius wanted to cry with her, but he had run out of tears so long ago. There was nothing he could do for her beyond sliding his hands up her arms and around her shoulders, pulling her closer, smoothing the mess of her hair. She sobbed her guilt against his chest while he whispered soft Drakhar nonsense into her ear. She didn't understand his words, but the sound of his voice seemed to soothe her. After a while, her sobs faded to hiccups and then, finally, to silence.

Caius held her as he sank to his knees, drawing her down with him. He rested his back against the trunk of an oak tree, stretching his legs out in front of him. Echo pulled her knees close to her chest, burrowing into the space between his arm and his body, her thighs resting against his own. She fit against the curve of him as though she'd always been there.

They sat like that long enough to watch the sun dip below the horizon, the stars pricking their way through the velvety indigo of dusk. The only noise to keep them company was the sorrowful song of the thrushes nesting in the trees as they bid farewell to the sun. Caius closed his eyes and listened to the quiet sound of Echo's breathing.

He hummed a lilting tune into her hair, the same one he had heard in his dreams for so many years. She shifted in his arms, hair brushing the sensitive skin of his throat.

"How do you know that song?" Echo asked. "The magpie's lullaby. I thought it was an Avicen thing."

"It is." His chin slid against her forehead when he spoke, but she didn't seem to mind. "Someone taught it to me, a long time ago. The girl I told you about."

"Rose . . . she was Avicen, wasn't she?" Echo shifted, and her hair tickled his cheek. "What happened to her?"

He hesitated. Some wounds were not so easily reopened. Her breath ghosted, warm and soft, against his collarbone.

"There was a fire," Caius said, brushing away an errant strand of Echo's hair. "She died."

Two sentences. That was all it took to sum up their story. The neatness of it felt like another death. Echo's arm tightened around Caius's waist. Just like that, his darkest secret, the one known only to him and his sister, was bared to the dying light of the Black Forest.

"And the fire," Echo said, fingers drawing small circles on the skin at his side. His shirt must have ridden up when he sat down. It was the nicest thing he'd felt in years. "Was it an accident?"

Caius shook his head, rubbing his cheek against Echo's hair. "No. Someone found out about us. They said Rose was a spy."

"Was she?"

Shrugging the shoulder opposite Echo, Caius answered as truthfully as he could. "I don't know. I like to think so. If she was, then maybe her death would be easier to bear."

He couldn't see Echo frown, but he could feel the set of her jaw against his clavicle. "Is it?"

Caius's shaky exhale stirred the hairs atop Echo's head, and she squirmed slightly, as if tickled. "No," he admitted. "Not really. Not at all."

"I'm sorry," Echo whispered. With her lips brushing his throat with each word, he felt it more than heard it. He shivered and tightened his arms around her. Night continued to settle, painting the forest violet.

"It was a long time ago." If Caius kept saying it, then maybe it would begin to mean something.

"It must hurt." Echo shifted again, stretching her legs out next to his. She reached for the key that hung around her neck, stroking it lightly. She'd slipped it on that morning, along with the locket, before they left Jasper's. "Remembering."

And it did. But the only thing worse than remembering the feel of Rose in his arms, the softness of her black and white feathers, the sound of her voice when she sang quietly to herself, would be forgetting it.

"Memories make us who we are," he said. "Without them, we are nothing."

Echo hmmed in response. The distant sound of birdsong gave way to the gentle chirping of crickets in the dark and the lonely hoot of an owl in the distance. A chill was beginning to set in. It was late spring, but remnants of winter clung to the forest like a lover reluctant to say goodbye. Caius whispered a soft Drakhar spell into Echo's hair—it was a simple thing, a spell to keep warm. The words came without him having to think about them—he'd said them enough during long, cold nights of battle and bloodshed. The feeling of Echo in his arms was much nicer than that.

The part of himself that craved the touch of another person, the feel of warm skin against his own had died with Rose, burned out of him with Tanith's flames. But Echo had burrowed her way inside, past decades of stone walls, and found the dying embers of the man Caius had been. She was bringing him back to life, slowly, as if coaxing a stubborn fire. He stroked the soft hair at the nape of her neck and breathed in time with the rise and fall of her chest as she dozed off. Soon enough, he, too, fell asleep. For the first time in days, he did not dream of fire.

CHAPTER FORTY-SEVEN

Echo blinked awake to the sound of birdsong. Larks crooned at the rising sun while warblers sang their lullabies. She settled deeper against Caius's chest and breathed in. He smelled, just faintly, like wood. And apples. It was cozy. When he'd talked to her in Drakhar the night before, it was the first time she'd ever really heard it spoken, aside from a few indistinct bits of conversation between Caius and Dorian and the words inscribed on the key. The Avicen claimed it was a guttural language, with inelegant vowels and harsh consonants, but when Caius spoke it, whispering words into her hair, it was melodic, almost lyrical. It was beautiful.

Her first time waking up next to a person of the opposite sex wasn't quite what she'd expected. In her fantasies, there had been no stubborn sharp-edged stones digging into her thighs, no gnarled twigs stabbing at the sliver of bare skin between her jeans and T-shirt, no awkward cramps in her neck from falling asleep mostly upright. And in those fantasies, the person resting beside her had always been Rowan.

Echo shifted so she could see Caius's face. He looked younger asleep, softer. His dark lashes were stark brushstrokes against his cheekbones, scales barely visible in the dawn light. She let her eyes roam over him, trying to commit each detail to memory. This quiet reprieve wouldn't last, but she didn't want to let it go. She closed her eyes, resting her temple against the curve of Caius's shoulder. She wasn't sure if she was imagining it or if the locket and key dangling from the chain at her breast were actually thrumming in time with the thumping of his heart. Even the dagger in her boot felt warmer through the fabric of her jeans, but it was nothing compared with the heat radiating off Caius. When she was held against his side like this, it was almost too much. She slid down, pressing her ear against his chest. *Thump. Thump thump.* It was a good heartbeat. A solid heartbeat. It felt as though her own were skipping a few beats to match it.

There was a sense of rightness to being in Caius's arms. It was the sort of rightness she'd never felt before, not even with Rowan. It was almost like . . . belonging. Like home. Echo squeezed her eyes shut and rubbed her cheek against his chest, feeling the soft scrape of wool against her skin. But she had to remember that Caius was not her home. She already had a home.

Do you? a nasty little part of her whispered.

Shut up, Echo whispered right back.

She turned in the circle of Caius's arms and looked around. Drakhar runes had been drawn in the dirt nearby, alternating with a line of stones to form a circle. Dorian must have come after them in the night to cast a protective ward.

Heat pricked at Echo's cheeks at the thought of another person finding them like this, wrapped around each other with a familiarity they shouldn't have felt. But as embarrassing as the thought of Dorian and his judgmental one-eyed gaze was, Echo was glad it hadn't been Ivy who found them. Her best friend had stuck with her through a decade's worth of questionable life choices, but even the most tolerant of people had their limits. Echo snuggling with a Drakharin mercenary just may have been Ivy's.

When she pulled away from Caius, slipping out from under the jacket he'd wrapped around her in the night, the brisk morning chill came as a shock. Echo walked away from Caius without a backward glance even though something deep inside her screamed at her to turn around, to crawl back into his arms and nestle into his warmth. She trampled through the underbrush, heading back to where the others had camped for the night. It took a herculean effort, putting one foot in front of the other, keeping her eyes locked forward, but it was the right thing to do. It had to be. Yet with every step she took closer to the Oracle, to the firebird, to whatever great and unknowable destiny loomed before her, she was beginning to feel more and more as if she had no idea what was right anymore.

CHAPTER FORTY-EIGHT

The walk was longer than Caius remembered. They'd spent the entire day and the better part of the night navigating the forest's increasingly uneven terrain, and it was nearly midnight by the time they reached the waterfall hiding the path to the Oracle's cave. It was modest, at least when compared with the Triberg Falls on the other side of the Black Forest. Unlike Triberg, this waterfall wasn't crawling with tourists and their cameras. No human or Avicen had heard of it, and few Drakharin knew of its existence. The location was a secret, albeit a poorly guarded one. It was meant to be passed down from one Dragon Prince to the next, but most of the nobles of the court knew where to find it. Curiosity motivated many a Drakharin to seek out the Oracle's services, though officially, they were limited to the elected prince.

Caius tried to imagine Tanith here, in all her golden glory, glittering among the soft green willows still lush despite the frost tickling at their leaves. He couldn't. This was no place for fire and steel. He glanced back at the rest of their party. For all her big-city charm, Echo carved out a place for herself in the forest as if she belonged, taking to it as naturally as a bird to air.

He'd woken alone with the faint scent of her shampoo clinging to his shirt. As much as he ached to close the distance between them, he couldn't. For every step he took toward her, she took one farther away. For hours, they'd marched on in relative silence, though every now and then, Caius overheard Jasper's quiet voice attempting to needle Dorian into conversation. It had taken them longer to reach the falls than he had anticipated. Dorian's injury had been aggravated by their journey, slowing their progress, though his captain would never admit it. The sun had set hours earlier, and the moon was high in the sky. The words on the map, scrawled in Rose's hand, echoed in Caius's mind.

The bird that sings at midnight, he thought, remembering the familiar sight of Rose's handwriting on the crinkled page, *from within its cage of bones, will rise from blood and ashes to greet the truth unknown.*

It was a lovely rhyme, if more than a little ominous. It told Caius nothing useful, but then he'd never had much of an ear for poetry. With a sigh, he climbed the mossy stone steps leading to the falls, the others clambering behind him with less grace.

"Ugh." Jasper retched. "Water."

"That does tend to accompany waterfalls." Dorian's smile flashed, brilliantly. Dorian, of all people, joking with an Avicen. Caius could hardly believe it. Perhaps he and Echo weren't the only ones to have been changed, irreparably, by their journey.

Jasper returned Dorian's smile with one of his own. "And here I was, thinking that was just a vicious rumor."

"Toughen up, Jasper," Echo said, holding out a steadying hand to Ivy as her friend slipped on cold stone. Echo's eyes flicked up to Caius's, but she didn't hold his gaze for long. "This our stop?"

"Yes," Caius said.

Echo breezed past him to duck beneath the falls, her arm brushing against his sleeve. His heart thudded in his chest as if it were trying to pound its way out.

Jasper sidled up next to Caius, still hopelessly pretty despite his grimace. "We have to go under that?"

Caius answered by doing just that, bowing his head against the falling water. Jasper's plaintive protest—"But my plumage!"—was swallowed by the damp, dark silence of the cave tucked away behind the falls. Loose pebbles and crumbling moist earth bordered an underground lake. The water refracted scraps of moonlight that fell between the gaps in the stone overheard, sending light skittering across the lake's surface like stars.

Echo stood on a long, narrow dock, near where a small boat bobbed in the water. Brows knitted in concentration, she stared across the lake that separated the falls from the rocky shore that led to the Oracle's cave. The rotting wooden slats groaned under Caius's feet, but Echo didn't turn as he approached. He moved to stand beside her, not close enough to touch, but close enough that he could feel the hum of her presence across the inches that divided them.

"We're close, aren't we?" She didn't face him as she spoke, arms crossed and eyes searching. Caius studied her profile, her features half in shadow.

"The entrance to the Oracle's sanctum is right across the lake," he said. "The boat will take us there. It'll only hold two, so I'll ask Dorian to stay behind with Jasper and Ivy."

Echo frowned, shaking her head slightly. "No, not like that. It's something else. I can feel it, like a balloon that's been blown up too much and is about to burst." She looked at him then, eyes shiny with the reflection of light off the lake's surface. "What did she tell you when you came here? The Oracle, I mean."

With a little puff of laughter, Caius said, "To follow my heart."

Echo arched a single eyebrow. "That's it?"

"That's it."

"Wow. Useful."

"Hardly."

She held his gaze for a moment longer, silent, contemplating. He wanted to ask her what she was thinking, what she feared, what she wanted, but Jasper's grumbling and Ivy's soft voice drifted to the end of the dock, reminding Caius that they weren't alone.

In the blink of an eye, the spell was broken.

"Great." Echo started toward the boat. "Let's hope she's got something better than fortune-cookie wisdom for us this time around."

"Wait." Caius grabbed her arm before she could go any farther. She snatched it back as if his hand had burned her. It was the first time they'd touched since that morning. Echo glowered at him but stayed put. "Before we go," he said, "there's something you need to know."

She nodded slowly, as if she was ready to dislike what he was about to say.

Smart girl, he thought. So much of Echo reminded him of Rose. She was intelligent and brave and fiercely protective of the people she loved. And like Rose, she burned so brightly it was hardly a surprise that he was drawn to her flame. He hoped her story had a happier ending, that he could give her the peace he hadn't been able to give Rose. If war had taught him anything, it was that it took the people who deserved long and happy lives and gave them short, brutal ones instead.

Caius pushed the thought away. "The Oracle doesn't impart her wisdom for free," he said, peering across the lake. He could just barely make out the entrance to the Oracle's cave. "We have to pay for it."

"Yeah, well, I left my euros in my other pants," she said.

He huffed out a laugh. He was glad she hadn't lost her sense of humor. "If only it were that easy. The Oracle doesn't want money. She'll want a sacrifice, a gift that has special meaning to you. Something that you part with at great cost."

Her hand rose to wrap around the locket. "This is the only thing I have with me. I'm guessing it's more valuable than the dagger and the key, but I don't know."

He placed a hand over hers. "No," he said. "You keep that."

She looked up at him. "Why? You said it was yours, a long time ago."

"Because I want you to have it." He unsheathed one of his blades. Tanith had given them to him years ago, before their relationship had begun to sour after his election to Dragon Prince. He loved the delicate carvings on the blades, the fine craftsmanship that had gone into their making. He'd never been in a fight without them.

"I'll give her these. That should suffice." He traced the figures carved into the steel. "They're not something I part with easily. Assuming the Oracle decides they're a worthy sacrifice on my part."

Echo raised an eyebrow. "And if she decides they're not?"

Caius slid the blade back into its sheath. "Then she chooses something that is."

"And that's a bad thing?" Echo said. "So we let her pick what she wants. What's the big deal?"

He studied her, taking in the delicate angle of her chin, the hair that fought its way out of her ponytail, the wary set of her eyes. He'd thought he was willing to give anything up to find the firebird, but he was starting to realize that there were some things he'd rather not lose.

"The big deal," Caius said, "is that it might not be something you're willing to sacrifice."

CHAPTER FORTY-NINE

Echo was silent as they traveled across the lake, their boat propelled by an unseen force. Every now and then, she looked back at the shore. Ivy, Dorian, and Jasper grew smaller and smaller as she and Caius approached the other side. The sense of unease that had been growing in the forest swelled, suffocating her with its immensity. As she was carried farther away, she quashed the fear that she would never see their faces again. When the boat bumped against the shore, she was jolted back to reality. Ominous melancholy could wait. She had an Oracle to see and a firebird to find.

Echo stepped out of the boat, and her boots slipped on the loose pebbles of a shore that was hardly worthy of the name. They stood on a tiny spit of land, about twenty feet across, covered in rocks, with the occasional weed stubbornly growing between the cracks, facing a wall made of large stones. Caius reached out a hand to steady her, and even through the leather of her jacket, his touch was warm. Warmer than it had any right to be. Echo shrugged out of his grip, pretending not to see the hurt that flashed across his face. She looked around, taking note of the complete and utter lack of an entrance to the Oracle's sanctum. Moss crawled along the boulder before them, though a space about three feet wide was left bare, with a series of runes etched into the stone. Echo couldn't read them, but she'd seen them before. She touched the key that hung around her neck, fingers brushing cool silver.

"Well," Caius said, "this is where the entrance *should* be." He leaned forward to read the inscription aloud. "'To know the truth, you must first want the truth.' Just like the key." He pressed a hand against the boulder, running his palm over its surface. "This wasn't here before. The runes were, but they weren't carved on a giant wall of stone."

Echo stood close to him, their arms just barely brushing. "How did you get in last time?"

"There was a door. I knocked." Caius's fist hovered over the stone as if he were considering doing just that before dropping back to his side. "I'm fairly certain this wall is designed to keep people out, not let them in."

"To keep people out, huh?" Echo pulled the dagger from her boot. "I have an idea." As the danger of her situation had increased with each passing day, she tried not to imagine home. The thought of never seeing her library again, never smelling its stale books or seeing her fairy lights dangling from her stolen shelves was too much to bear. But home was where she had designed her own door meant to keep people out, not let them in. With Caius's gaze on her, she pricked her index finger with the tip of the blade. She pressed her finger to the wall and whispered, "By my blood."

The familiar feel of magic crackled in the air, and with a loud rumble, the boulder slid to the side, revealing a room lit by candles. The walls were lined with shelves from floor to ceiling, packed with the most unusual assortment of objects Echo had ever seen. Crowns, signet rings, and loose jewels were strewn about like debris. A medieval harpsichord collected dust in the corner beside a broken violin and a crate full of rusting handbells. There was an entire shelf devoted to porcelain cat figurines and another lined with skulls, some human, some animal. One wall was covered with clocks of varying shapes and sizes, all surrounding a grandfather clock that listed slightly to the side. Candles blazed on every available surface, wax dripping freely onto the floor. The only other exit was a wooden door, reinforced with a dark metal latticed frame, on the opposite side of the room.

"Fascinating," Caius said.

"*Creepy* is the word I'd go with." Echo set a cautious foot across the threshold. "I can't believe that actually worked."

He followed her in, and the boulder slid back into place behind him. "I don't think our visit is as unexpected as we thought it was."

Caius walked around the room, investigating the Oracle's collection, and paused in front of the wall of clocks. There must have been dozens of them, but they were all set to the same time. A quarter to midnight.

The bird that sings at midnight, Echo thought. *Whatever that means.*

"What *is* all this stuff?" she asked. She poked at one of

the skulls on the shelf in front of her. It looked as if it had belonged to a cat, but it was hard to tell.

"Gifts," Caius replied. "The Oracle trades her wisdom for them." He waved a hand at the hoard of objects around them. "She's been at it for a while, as you can see."

"And what did you give her when you came here?" Echo asked.

He walked over to a pile of weaponry in the corner opposite the harpsichord. He sorted through the items, sending a few helmets clattering to the ground, along with a shield and about half a dozen throwing stars. After a minute of rummaging, he pulled out a dented broadsword. "This. It was my first sword. My father gave it to me when I was just a boy. I was too small to handle it then, but I grew into it." He ran a reverent hand down the dull blade. "I never thought I'd see it again."

The skin on the back of Echo's neck prickled with gooseflesh, and she had the uncanny feeling that they weren't alone. Just then, a new voice spoke, coming from everywhere and nowhere.

"But I knew you'd come back."

Echo spun around, bringing up the dagger in her hand. A figure stood in the center of the room, face obscured by a hooded black cloak. The only part that Echo could see was the hands, the backs of which were covered in feathers of every color from indigo to chartreuse. As they tapered toward her fingers, the feathers gave way to iridescent scales, like the ones on Caius's cheekbones. The Oracle bore the markings of both Avicen and Drakharin, and Echo had never seen anything like her before.

If the Oracle was as old as Caius said, Echo doubted the

dagger would do much damage, but it made her feel better. The unease in her gut grew, though she wasn't sure why. The Oracle wasn't supposed to be a threat, but Echo hated being taken by surprise.

"Welcome to my home." The Oracle stepped forward, and Echo backed up. "Please put down your weapons. They won't be necessary." Her s's were stretched thin, like taffy.

Echo didn't turn around to see if Caius complied, but metal clattered against the stone floor. He'd dropped the sword. She kept the dagger in her hand.

"I didn't hear the door open," Echo said. "How did you get here?"

The Oracle wiggled her fingers and said, "Magic."

Warm hands settled on Echo's shoulders, and she nearly jumped out of her skin. She turned her head just enough to see Caius behind her.

"It's all right," he said. "She'll tell us what we need to know." He looked back at the Oracle. "If I recall correctly, a gift is customary at this point."

When the Oracle moved toward them, her cloak drifted over the floor, as if her feet didn't touch the ground and she was floating instead of walking. Echo tried to step away, but all she managed to do was press her back against Caius's chest. She swallowed past the fear rising in her throat. All of her instincts were telling her to flee, to hop back in the boat and cross the lake, to leave behind the Oracle and whatever secrets she held, to forget all about the firebird. But she'd never been one to run away, and she'd come too far to turn back now.

"Oh, I wouldn't worry about that, Caius," said the Oracle. "A gift will be given in due time." She slanted her hood toward Echo. "I see you've followed the trail of bread crumbs the last girl left."

The last girl? Echo shrugged out of Caius's grip. She needed room to breathe, to think. "What girl? What are you talking about?"

"The last one who came around asking questions," the Oracle said. "She didn't like the answers I gave, so she decided to pass her problems on to you. When you picked up that music box, you put in motion a series of events that led you to me. Every action in this universe has consequences. Every domino topples the next. It's been waiting so long for something to trigger its release."

"What has?" Echo asked.

"The firebird," the Oracle replied. "What else?"

Echo's pulse pounded with such force, Caius could probably hear it. "It's here? It's alive?"

The Oracle's face remained in shadow, but Echo was pretty sure there was a smirk hidden under that hood. "Oh yes. Very much so. And it is closer than you think, though sometimes, before something can rise, first it must fall." With a glance in Caius's direction, she added, "The last girl didn't bring him along. That was her first mistake."

Echo shot a look at Caius, who was staring at her, brow furrowed, as if he were seeing her for the first time. She didn't like it. None of this was proving remotely likable.

"I don't understand," Echo said.

The Oracle didn't seem to care. "Oh, you will," she replied, cool as an autumn breeze. "But I'm getting ahead of myself. The clock is ticking, and you have places to be. It's nearly midnight. Tell me, child, what did your Ala tell you?"

The sweat on Echo's palms threatened to loosen her grip

on the dagger. There was no reason for the Oracle to be so focused on her. She was just a girl, looking for a bird. "How do you know about the Ala?"

"I know more than you could possibly imagine, child." The Oracle picked up a small, yellowed skull from the shelf with the bones. She examined it for a second before gently placing it back. "It's my reason for being."

It wasn't the answer that Echo wanted, but she had a feeling it was the only one she'd be getting. She wanted to find her answers and get out as quickly as possible. If she had to play the Oracle's game to do so, then that was exactly what she'd do. She swallowed before speaking, taking a moment to calm her nerves. "The Ala said that the firebird would rise soon."

"It's already begun," the Oracle said. "You can feel it, can't you?"

The dagger in Echo's hand, along with the locket and key dangling from the chain around her neck, sent out deep, pulsating waves of heat in response.

The Oracle bowed her head in the direction of the wooden door opposite the entrance. "Down that hall, you will find a door to which you hold the key. Behind *that* door, you will find another gateway, one that you must unlock, as only you can. What you find in that room will show you the firebird. But remember, some doors are more difficult to open than others."

"Do you ever just give a straight answer?" As Echo asked the question, she almost felt like herself again. Almost, but not quite. Again, that great, unknowable thing loomed over her, and she felt powerless against it.

"No." The Oracle smiled, forked tongue flicking over her fangs. "Was that answer straight enough?"

Of course. A smart-ass Oracle, Echo thought. *Because why would this be easy when nothing else is?*

The Oracle turned to Caius, content to leave Echo staring at her, dissatisfied.

"And might I add," the Oracle said, "it's so lovely to see you again . . . Prince."

CHAPTER FIFTY

Echo froze. *Prince?*

She turned to Caius, clutching the dagger so tightly that her palm hurt, but the solidity of it anchored her. He was just a mercenary, contracted by the Dragon Prince. Not the prince himself. He was simply Caius. But the name of the Dragon Prince had been unknown, out of use for over a century, lost to time and willful forgetting.

The Oracle continued, "It's funny, isn't it? The way people always fail to see what's right in front of them." The Oracle leaned in to Echo, sniffing her hair. Echo flinched. "What's been in front of them the whole time."

"Prince?" Echo said. Caius reached for her, contrition in his eyes, as if he wanted to apologize, but she stepped back. If he had an explanation to give, Echo wasn't interested in making it easy for him. "Why is she calling you a prince?"

The Oracle made a strange hissing sound that might have been a laugh. She walked over to the harpsichord and sat down on the small stool in front of it. "Tell her the truth, Caius. That you have no intention of letting her keep the firebird. That you intend to take it for yourself. That the Dragon Prince did not hire you to steal the firebird. That you *are* the Dragon Prince."

The words were stones, sinking to the bottom of Echo's stomach. They'd come so far together. She'd killed for him, and he wasn't even the person he'd said he was. She'd *trusted* him. After a lifetime of keeping herself closed off to all but a select few, she'd opened up to him in ways she'd never expected. She'd turned her back on Rowan, put her friends' lives in danger, and all he'd done was lie to her. His betrayal cut as sharply as a knife to the chest.

"Is that true?" Echo asked. "Caius, tell me it's not. Tell me she's screwing with me, because I don't know if I can handle the alternative."

He parted his lips as if to respond, but all that came out was a shaky sigh. He ground his fingers into his temples, as though rubbing away a headache, and said, "I'm sorry."

Two words. Two small words, and Echo's world collapsed under the weight of them.

"I trusted you," she bit out through clenched teeth. Once she said it, the words ran through her mind, a mantra that twisted the knife deeper and deeper. *I trusted you. I trusted you. I trusted you.*

Caius held out a hand to her as if he was begging for forgiveness. He wasn't going to get it. "Echo, I—"

"I killed for you!"

He recoiled, as if Echo had punched him. She wished she had. She wanted to sink the dagger into his chest the way she'd plunged it into Ruby's back. She'd taken a life because of him, and he was nothing more than a manipulator, a liar. He buried his face in his hands and sighed behind them. Running his fingers through his hair, he said, "Echo, I can explain."

"I don't care what you have to say," Echo said, stepping away from him. She couldn't be near him. She couldn't even bear to look at him. All she saw was the person she'd kissed in the forest, the person who held her as she cried, soothing her to sleep. "You'll just lie to me again."

She grabbed the key and the locket at her neck, pulling hard on the chain until it snapped. She slipped the locket into her jacket pocket, but kept the key held tightly in her fist. Caius's eyes, dark and shiny with what looked suspiciously like unshed tears, followed the motion of her hand. What the Oracle had said was true, she realized. He meant to take the key from her.

"I never lied to you about anything important," Caius pleaded. "My title doesn't change anything. I meant everything I said."

A broken excuse for a laugh dug its talons in her throat and scratched its way out, dragging her innards with it. "Anything important? You didn't think the fact that you're the *Dragon Prince* was important? Oh, God, the things you must have done. How many deaths are you responsible for? How many Avicen have you killed?"

It was one thing for him to lie to her, but to try to talk his way out of it was just insulting. Echo might have been played for a fool once, but she wasn't going to let it happen twice. Not with him.

Caius took a step forward, and Echo lifted the dagger. He stopped, but said, "Echo, please, let me explain—"

"No," she said. "No, you don't get to do that. You don't have the right. I'm going to go find the firebird. Without you. You goddamn liar."

"Please." Caius moved to stand between Echo and the wooden door leading deeper into the Oracle's cavern. "Nothing's changed. Let me go with you. We'll find the firebird, just like we planned."

"Why?" she asked, shaking her head in disbelief. The nerve of him. Pretending they were still in this together, that they were on the same side. She'd been brought low before, but no one had ever made her feel like such an idiot. "Why would I let you have it? The Oracle's right. You're going to steal it. You're going to take it back to the Drakharin, aren't you? Was that your plan all along?"

"No." Caius spoke, his voice laced with desperation. "I meant what I said. I want peace. I'll use it to protect you, to protect everyone. Please, Echo."

"And how am I supposed to trust a single word you say?" She circled around him, bringing herself closer to the door the Oracle had said would lead her to the firebird. "You're a liar, Caius. I don't trust liars."

The Oracle tsked from her seat in the corner. "So stubborn, these children," she said, as if Caius and Echo weren't right there. "Fighting fate like they can stop it."

"No, Echo, please," Caius said, hands out, pleading. "I have to find the firebird. If I fail, we both lose everything. You'll lose your home. I saw it, Echo, in a dream. I know it sounds crazy, but you have to believe me."

Echo stilled. Her pulse roared in her ears. "My home? What about my home?"

Caius inched toward her as if she were some kind of

frightened woodland creature. She tightened her grip on the dagger. No way in hell was she going down without a fight.

"Your home. The library. You live there," he said. "I know I've given you every reason not to trust me, but *please*. Trust me on this."

He was close now, no more than six feet away. Echo watched him, cataloging everything the Ala had taught her about reading body language. His left leg twitched, just a tad, but it was enough to telegraph his next move. Echo clutched the key tighter, silver thorns digging into her skin, dagger raised in her other hand. When Caius lunged for her, she was ready. Catching his leg with hers, she sent him crashing to the floor, smashing the heel of her hand into his mouth. He rolled with the impact and was halfway up before Echo was on him with the knife.

"Stop." She pressed the dagger against Caius's throat. A drop of scarlet beaded on his skin.

Stop.

Echo stopped. The voice was in her mind, but it wasn't hers. She shook her head as if she could knock it loose from where it clung to her brain.

"Try to take this key from me one more time," Echo said. The tremor in her hand made a thin trickle of Caius's blood track down his neck, so vulnerable, so pale. "And I swear to God, I will kill you."

No, you won't.

"Shut up," Echo hissed.

Caius held up his hands, placating. The sadness in his eyes was deep enough to drown them both. "I didn't say anything."

His is not the life this blade was meant to take.

Echo shook her head again, while Caius looked on in confusion.

"I don't understand," she whispered.

You do, the voice said. *You just wish you didn't.*

Caius's lip was bloodied from where she'd smashed her hand into it, gashing it against his teeth. She remembered the feel of those lips on hers, not hesitant and unfamiliar as they had been in the forest, but soft and slow as they shared unhurried kisses in a cabin by the sea. It was not her memory.

"No," Echo said. The blade quivered against Caius's throat again. She was distantly aware of him asking whom she was speaking to, what she meant, but all she could hear was the voice in her head.

You know what you have to do, it whispered.

"Echo," Caius said. "What are you—"

The room shook, stealing his response. A few of the cat figurines fell to the floor, shattering into tiny shards of porcelain. The Oracle sprang to her feet, snaking out a hand to catch one of the skulls before it hit the ground.

"I suggest you bring this quarrel to an end," the Oracle said. She pointed at the wall of clocks, her sleeve falling back enough to show that the scales and feathers ran all the way up her arm. "It's nearly midnight, but the firebird isn't the only thing that is almost upon us." She made her way to the boulder and pressed her ear to the stone. "Young prince, your sister is here."

As if on cue, a woman's voice shouted on the other side of the door through which they'd entered. "Caius!"

The room trembled once more with the force of the shout as something heavy buffeted the sanctum's walls. Even within the Oracle's chamber, the air crackled with heat.

"It's Tanith," Caius said. "She must have followed us here." He started to move. Echo eased up on the knife enough to allow him to rise to his feet, but still kept the blade at his throat. "If she finds you, she will kill you."

Wisps of smoke leaked through the cracks around the stone door, and Echo could smell the stench of something burning on the other side. Tanith. The Dragon Prince's sister. *Caius's* sister. She had found them, and they would all die, burned to cinders in her fire.

No, said the voice. *Not if you stop it.*

"How?" Echo asked, pulling the blade away from Caius's throat, slowly, slowly, slowly. He rubbed his throat, but didn't move toward her. With Tanith calling out to him, he kept his eyes, dark and green and as lovely as ever, on Echo alone.

The firebird. Go, find it.

The key in her hand pulsed with a heat so strong Echo almost dropped it, but it may as well have been glued to her palm. She doubted Caius could take it, even if she were to give him the chance.

"Caius!" Tanith called. She was closer now, voice on the other side of the sanctum's stone door. "Caius, where are you?"

When Echo spoke, her words were meant for Caius, voice in her head be damned. "My friends. They're out there."

"I'll protect you," he said, drawing the two long knives from their sheaths. "I won't let her hurt you."

Tanith had never laid a finger on Echo, but the voice in her head exhaled a quivering, fearful sigh. Echo shook her head, hair flying about her face. "No." The key in her hand throbbed mightily. "Protect them."

She spun on her heel, throwing open the wooden door, running toward the answers she hoped to find. A long corridor separated her from a door at the other end, and her boots pounded hard against stone as she ran toward it, Caius calling after her.

Run, Echo, the voice in her mind whispered. *And rise.*

CHAPTER FIFTY-ONE

The sky was red.

Not the warm red of the sunset Ivy had watched over the crumbling walls of the ruined abbey as the day gave way to the dark blue of night. Nor was it the happy red of freshly picked apples, plump and ripe and delicious, or the vibrant hue of maple leaves in autumn. No, this was the red of newly spilled blood, dark and thick. Or maybe the red of charcoal as it burned. The air was clogged with the scent of ash and smoke. A body slammed into Ivy, pinning her against the sharp stone of the cavern wall behind her. She looked up, but a field of navy blue and silver blocked her view of the sky as it erupted into flames.

Dorian.

Ivy pushed at his chest, but he didn't budge. He had thrown himself between her and whatever had poured through the hole in the sky that had set it alight. She could smell the ozonic tang of the in-between, more powerful than she'd ever experienced. Whatever gateway had just opened in the sky had to have been massive. Large enough for an army.

The entrance to the cavern exploded inward as a fireball smashed through it. Stone rained down, pelting Ivy and Dorian with jagged little pebbles. The force of the explosion cracked Ivy's head against the wall, and her vision sparked with a display of pyrotechnics to rival the one surrounding her. Dorian had his hands on either side of her face, cradling her head between his palms. His lips were moving, and his one eye was searching Ivy's for some sign that she understood, but all she could hear was a shrill ringing in her ears. She had never had a concussion before, but she strongly suspected that this was what one felt like.

Dorian pushed away, sword in hand, spinning in a blur of blue and silver. Not even the ringing in Ivy's ears was loud enough to drown out the unmistakable clash of steel against steel. Her brain struggled to make sense of what she was seeing. Dorian, locked in combat with two soldiers, sword whistling through the air as he danced back, deftly dodging the shining golden blades that matched the soldiers' shining golden armor.

Firedrakes. Dorian was fighting Firedrakes. And no matter how they lunged and parried, he kept himself in front of Ivy, using his body as a shield between her and their blades. He was protecting her. A Firedrake rushed toward them, but Dorian's sword slid through a chink in its armor with a spray of blood that marred his fair skin with a bright red splatter.

Ivy fought to get to her feet, fingers scrabbling at the stone behind her, as more Firedrakes poured through the cavern's entrance. She tried to shout at Dorian, to warn him, but her voice was lost in the cacophony of falling stone and the roar of the fire. Four Firedrakes replaced the one Dorian had killed. They were going to die here, no matter how swift or strong or skilled Dorian was. There were so many of them and only one of him.

The Firedrakes set upon Dorian at once. Though he held off three, one slipped through the pack and circled the rest, sword leveled directly at Dorian's back. Ivy's entire world narrowed down to that one blade as it sailed through the air, golden and graceful. She screamed a warning, but she knew it would be too late.

A figure crashed into Dorian, moving so fast that Ivy saw only the quickest flash of feathers—blue and purple and green—before Dorian was knocked aside. It was Jasper. But Jasper hadn't joined Dorian on the stone floor of the cavern, still cold despite the fire raging all around them. The sword that protruded from Jasper's front was slightly off-center, impaling him like a bird on a spit.

Jasper's mouth opened and closed in soundless shock. Dorian stared at him, face pale and stricken beneath the blood that dotted his skin like scarlet freckles. Even the Firedrake holding the sword that had run Jasper through looked the tiniest bit surprised to find an Avicen on the end of it. But the pulsating pain in Ivy's head, vicious and powerful, would not be ignored. It clawed at her, dragging her down into the deep. The last thing Ivy thought, before the darkness opened up and swallowed her whole, was *Interesting.*

CHAPTER FIFTY-TWO

Echo ran, but the hallway seemed impossibly long. Behind her, the Oracle's army of clocks chimed midnight, and the key and dagger blazed in her hands with a force so strong she stumbled. She fell to her knees, assaulted by a searing pain in her head. It brought with it a kaleidoscopic mess of images that made little sense. Visions of places she knew—the library, the Ala's chamber in the Nest, Grand Central—mixed with sights she'd never seen and locations she'd never been. A cabin by the sea. The beach she'd set foot on only in her dream. Echo struggled to her feet, the pain so severe she thought it might split her skull. She leaned against the wall, pushing herself onward to the door at the end of the hallway.

The sounds of a battle raged behind her—the loud metallic clang of blades colliding, the angry roar of a raging fire—but she was in another world, one that contained nothing but the door at the end of the hall and the memories that crashed into her, one on top of the other, flashing by with dizzying speed. Snippets of a life, of hers, and lives that were not hers, couldn't possibly be hers. Echo shouldn't have remembered them. She hadn't lived them, hadn't made those memories, hadn't seen what those eyes had seen. She ran without seeing what was in front of her, struck blind by the chaos of her own mind.

—shadow dust in her hand, smearing a doorjamb as it opened into the blackness of the in-between—

"*. . . the magpie is the only bird that can recognize its own reflection . . .*"

—a man's hands, made strong through years of swordsmanship, in hers, but they were not her hands, they were Avicen hands, and on the backs of her arms were feathers, neatly striped, black and white, like the wings of a magpie—

"*The bird that sings at midnight . . .*"

—a voice, talking about magpies, and it was hers, but it was also not hers, not always, in a richly furnished nest atop the tallest spire in a cathedral, stained-glass windows painting the light that drifted through them, excellent thieves, magpies—

"*. . . from within its cage of bones . . .*"

—the long line of a slender back, half covered by a tangled bedsheet, a delicate speckling of iridescent scales down the ridges of a man's spine, lovingly lit by moonlight streaming in through her window, and she traced the line of scales, counting them, one by one, drawing patterns on his skin as he slept—

"*. . . will rise from blood and ashes . . .*"

—the Ala speaking, voice light and airy, calling Echo her little magpie—

"*. . . to greet the truth unknown. . . .*"

—lips brushed her neck, and arms snaked around her

waist, solid and strong and safe, and she knew, without the tiniest shred of doubt, that she was loved—

"Memories make us who we are. Without them, we are nothing. . . ."

—fire crashing through her window like a hurricane, someone she knew, someone she loved, shouting her name, while she was burning, burning, burning—

Echo reached the end of the hallway and slumped against the door, fumbling to fit the key in the lock. Other memories, less familiar, more removed by time and distance battered at her. Memories of her own flesh, covered in feathers in shades of azure and gold and crimson. The sight of her own knuckles, speckled with scales that glittered under a field of stars. Her skin felt as if it were bursting at the seams with a hundred souls jockeying for place inside a single body.

The key slid home, and Echo flung the door open. She fell through it with such force that she collapsed to her knees and stared at what the Oracle had said would show her the firebird.

A mirror. It was a mirror. She gazed into it, chest heaving with ragged breaths, hand clutching the dagger in a viselike grip, onyx and pearl magpies digging into her palm.

Echo looked into the mirror and saw only herself.

It was her. Echo was the firebird. The firebird was Echo. She wanted to laugh, but all that came out was a strangled sob.

She closed her eyes. Images of entire worlds flashed by, freeze-frames and stilted moments, scrambled to the point of illegibility. Echoes of lives she had never lived, in places she had never seen. Echoes within echoes within Echo. As they shifted and coalesced into globs of colors and splashes of sound, one memory stood out: a cabin by the sea and a man by her side—he was so much younger in the memory, as if his shiny newness hadn't yet been worn down by time and tragedy. Caius. He had known her before. No, not her. Another person, someone whose memories mingled with her own.

Yes, whispered the voice that had stilled her hand when she'd held the dagger to his throat, and Echo knew what she had to do. Her eyes fell shut and images flickered behind her lids. Ivy's face lit up with a smile. Dorian's hesitation in response to kindness he couldn't understand. Jasper, wearing a grin that knew too much. Rowan's face, full of tenderness, and maybe even love. And Caius, smiling at her as if he'd only just remembered how. She could save them. She could protect them from the dangers that threatened to bring their world crashing down, from Tanith and her fire, from the war that promised to swallow them whole. She could do it. She could make things right. But before she could rise, first she had to fall. She met her own gaze in the mirror and raised the dagger high. She gritted her teeth and clenched the hilt tightly.

"By my blood."

Echo drove the blade down, and it sank into her skin, sliding between the bones of her rib cage with a painful scrape. She had only a fraction of a second to register that the blood leaking around the hilt was her own when the door flew off its hinges in a whirlwind of smoke and flame.

The last thing she saw before her eyes drifted closed, welcoming the dark oblivion of death, was Caius, mouth moving as he shouted her name just as Tanith's flame engulfed the room and Echo with it. This was it. This was how her life ended. In blood and ashes.

CHAPTER FIFTY-THREE

"The firebird is not a *what*," the Oracle had said. "It's more of a *who*. You, Rose, are its vessel."

Rose sat in front of the fireplace in her cabin, knees drawn up to her chest, blanket wrapped around her shoulders, and turned the words over in her mind. It was amazing how a simple statement could change a life forever.

She teased the dying fire in the hearth with a poker. Caius had gone out for more wood, and she hadn't decided how much she wanted to tell him about her trip to the Oracle. He hadn't known where she'd gone when she'd left four days prior, only that she was following a lead on the firebird. If it hadn't been for Caius, she never would have known of the Oracle's existence, never would have followed the feeling in her gut that told her she would find answers there.

They'd been sharing stories, cuddled under a blanket in front of this same fireplace. He'd told her all about his election the year before and his journey to the Oracle. They'd laughed over the bit of inane wisdom she'd imparted—*Follow your heart, honestly*—and traded lazy kisses, treasuring the rare bit of stolen time they had together. It wasn't often that Caius managed to sneak away from the keep without a retinue of guards to accompany him, and those moments were precious. They were sacred, and she had violated his trust in a way she wasn't sure he would forgive.

Rose sighed and rested her chin on her knees. She loved Caius. There was no doubt in her mind about that, but there was a part of her that missed the simplicity of her mission before she'd given him her heart. Find the firebird, the Council of Elders had instructed her. She remembered the look of absolute conviction in Altair's eyes when he'd taken her aside and told her to do whatever she had to in order to complete her mission, up to and including seducing the Dragon Prince for information. Rose had always been confident about what she had to offer: beauty, intelligence, a quick wit. She wasn't surprised that Caius had succumbed to her charms. What *did* surprise her was that she had fallen for his. Altair must have suspected something was amiss when she stopped sending him reports the last time she was in Japan, but that was a problem for another day.

The front door banged open as Caius entered, arms full of freshly chopped wood. He delighted in the simple domesticity of life in her little cabin by the sea, and Rose found his naïveté unspeakably adorable. He may have been a prince, but he was so young, so hopeful. The truth would shatter him. The knowledge that the firebird—nothing more than an object of scholarly fascination for him—required Rose's death to manifest would be too much for him to handle. It was too much for Rose to handle. The Oracle's next words rang in her mind, as if on an endless loop.

"To unleash the power of the firebird, you must prove yourself worthy," the Oracle said. Rose had traipsed through the forest looking for the falls for two days. Her feathers had been matted down with mud, and she'd had little desire to prove her worth to some metaphysical being straight out of legend.

"What do you mean, prove myself worthy?" Rose asked. "What exactly does that entail?"

The Oracle sat on the small bench in front of her harpsichord and toyed with the keys, playing a familiar tune. The magpie's lullaby. The song all little Avicelings were sung before bedtime.

"The vessel must offer a truly selfless sacrifice," the Oracle told her. "The ultimate sacrifice."

She'd turned to Rose, though the hood of her cloak left her face hidden. "You must ask yourself what you're willing to lose for all of that power. The firebird will bring about an end to this war, but it might not be the end you desire. There may be peace, or perhaps destruction. Would you lay down your life for such power?" The Oracle turned back to the harpsichord, fingers hovering over the keys. "Or *his*?"

Rose didn't need the Oracle to specify whom she was talking about. She watched as Caius fed a fresh log to the fire and held out his hand for the poker. Rose offered it to him, and he used it to push the log into place. The fire crackled back to life, and Caius settled on the pillows strewn about the floor beside her. She held out the blanket so he could slip underneath it.

Wrapping his arms around her waist, he dropped a kiss

on her temple, nuzzling her black and white feathers with his nose, and said, "How was your trip? Did you find what you were looking for?"

She smiled at him and knew that she couldn't tell him. The truth was a burden she had to bear alone. "No. Just another dead end."

Caius bumped his forehead against hers, planting a chaste kiss on her lips. "Maybe next time."

Rose closed her eyes and breathed him in. "Yes," she whispered. "Maybe next time."

She may have been the firebird's vessel, but her destiny was her own. If dying by her own hand to unleash it meant that the people she loved would be hurt, then she wouldn't do it. Another vessel would be born, the Oracle had promised. It might have been selfish, but Rose knew she wasn't willing to sacrifice Caius or what they shared for the sake of power.

After leaving the Black Forest, she'd spent two days planting a trail of clues for the next vessel to follow. Let someone else deal with fate. Rose was young and in love and if she had nothing else, she had this moment, snuggled under a blanket with Caius. Their dalliance was dangerous and, one way or another, their tryst would end with her death, either at the hands of her people or his. It was only a matter of time until Rose's secrets died with her, but the firebird would live on. And like a phoenix from the ashes, it would rise again.

CHAPTER FIFTY-FOUR

Echo fell, dagger still clutched in bloodstained fingers, and Caius felt as though he'd been stabbed as well. He thought his heart had died with Rose, in a blaze of Tanith's doing, but at the sight of Echo's body, crumpled to the floor like a broken doll, it pounded against his ribs as if it were beating for the first time in a hundred years. Blood seeped, thick and crimson, from Echo's wound, soaking the fabric of her shirt, and rage and hopelessness, the likes of which Caius hadn't felt in over a century, boiled in his veins.

Fire burst forth from Tanith's fists, racing up her arms all the way to her shoulders, glinting off her golden armor. "Where is it, Caius?"

The heavy scent of smoke seared his nostrils. *No,* he thought, staring at Echo's still chest, willing it to rise with an intake of breath. She looked dead, but he couldn't be sure. *Please. Not like this. Don't take her the way you took Rose.*

"The firebird, Caius," Tanith said. "Where is it?"

"Now you want it?" His voice was salt rubbing at the raw skin of his throat. He could barely see past the smoke hanging heavy in the air.

"Now that I have reason to believe that it's real. Yes." Tanith never had much of an appreciation for life's little ironies. "There's no point in resisting, Brother. I have two dozen Firedrakes waiting outside. I'm sure Dorian is fighting bravely, but there are too many of them. You don't stand a chance."

Caius gripped his knives tightly. He had to get her away from Echo. He wouldn't let himself believe she was dead. Not now. Not here. Not like this. "How did you even find us?"

Tanith rolled her eyes, though her guard remained up. "I know you, Caius. I had sentries posted all the places I thought you might turn to in your hour of need. Did you honestly believe I wouldn't think to keep watch on the Oracle?"

It hadn't occurred to him until that moment. He'd been so caught up in the chase, in Echo, that he'd been blind to the possibility that Tanith was one step ahead, though, of the two of them, she'd always been the better strategist. He should have known. *You fool. You goddamn fool.* But all was not lost. Not yet.

"I can't let you have the firebird," he said. "I can't. I won't."

"Don't be a fool, Caius." Tanith drew her sword, its steel glowing red as an ember. It would burn its way through whatever it touched. She stalked toward him, naked blade in hand, picking her way through the mess of shattered stone and warped wood. Her blood would decorate his knives tonight. As strongly as he'd tried to fight it, he had always known, in a deep, dark part of his heart, that this was the only way it ever could have ended between them.

"I am doing this for our people," said Tanith.

"Our people? Ribos was one of our people, as was every Drakharin you killed for standing between you and your delusions. Don't you dare speak to me of our people." Angry tears stung Caius's eyes, already watery from the smoke. "You *slaughtered* them."

"I did what had to be done," Tanith hissed. "I did what you couldn't. What you wouldn't. They were losing faith in you, in the seat of the Dragon Prince. I gave them a purpose, a direction."

"Does that help you sleep at night?" Caius circled his sister, never letting his eyes stray from her. He was almost to Echo. *Don't be dead. Please don't be dead.* "Do you actually believe your own lies?"

"My conscience is clear, Caius."

For years, the rift between them had grown, but he had never given up hope that one day, he would be able to cross it, that he would have his sister by his side again as an ally, a friend. Even after what she'd done to Rose, he'd held on to that slim hope, but he could no longer pretend that forgiveness was possible. She'd taken everything from him. He had loved, truly loved, so few things in his life, and Tanith had systematically destroyed each and every one.

"You won't win," he said. "I won't let you."

Tanith squeezed her eyes shut for half a second, flaring her nostrils as she huffed out a frustrated breath. The tip of her sword lowered, just an inch.

"Don't do this, Caius. You may not believe it, but you are my brother, my blood, and I don't want to hurt you. That was never the point of this. Don't fight me. You have no title. You have no army. Your allies are dead or dying. You have nothing."

"No," Caius said, balancing one of his long knives in his hand. "I have this." He threw the blade. Tanith raised her sword to deflect it, sending it careering off to the side. He had less than a second to release the other knife, but it was enough. The second blade flew straight and true, burying itself in her shoulder. It drove clean through to the other side, pinning her to the wooden wall behind her.

Tanith screamed, and fire erupted around her, fueled by her fury. The flames roared with her, filling the room with scorched air. It wouldn't buy him much time, but it would be enough. It needed to be enough. Caius scooped Echo up, trying to ignore how limp she felt in his arms, and ran, Tanith's rage bellowing in his ears.

Smoke and the scent of burning flesh clogged the air. Flames licked at his feet as the traces of Tanith's power crackled all around him. He stumbled over a pile of rags. The Oracle. Her body, crumpled on the stone floor, was still smoking, robes smoldering with little puffs. The stench of sizzling flesh made his throat seize and his stomach churn.

Outside, the lake was gone. All that was left was a dried-up crater, littered with bleached fish bones. The Oracle's power must have sustained it all, and that power had died with her. A distant part of Caius mourned her and feared for the friends they'd left on the other side of the lake, but he could barely think past the body in his arms. Echo was so limp, so quiet, so small. How had he never noticed how small she was before?

Caius ran past the dry basin of the lake and the unmoving bodies of half a dozen Firedrakes. Dorian must have fought them off, but Caius couldn't see past the smoke to look for him or the others. Once he reached a place where he could summon the in-between, he would find them and bring them to safety. He told himself that Echo would blink her eyes open, injured but alive, and she would be okay.

As soon as he set foot beyond the cave's entrance, the rocks flanking the now dry waterfall glowing like charcoal embers, he looked up, just in time to see the sky rip open. Great black clouds spewed forth a battalion of Avicen Warhawks, screaming their battle cries into the cold darkness of the Black Forest. Altair. It had to be. He had found them, too. He must have been tracking them. The Oracle's death had brought down the wards around the forest, their enemies had followed their trail, and the war was upon them.

CHAPTER FIFTY-FIVE

Rising from the dead was not the thrill ride Echo had anticipated. She floated, weightless, in a sea of darkness. The only thing making her aware of the fact that she had a body at all was the pain. It was intense, blinding, and everywhere at once. Slowly, unimaginably slowly, her mind rose to the surface, seeking out the single, weakly glowing speck of light in the distance. Her body shed death like a snake molting. There was nothing poetic about the process, nothing that felt remotely transcendental.

But no matter how hard and how far she stretched, the light stayed right where it was, distant, unreachable. Her chest was on fire. She wondered if this was what it felt like to drown. It hurt. It hurt so badly that a tiny part of her wished she could have just stayed dead.

Wake up.

Again, that voice, but this time Echo knew who it was.

"Rose?" Echo's voice sounded, for all intents and purposes,

like an echo in her own head. Her life was a pun now. Great.

Time to wake up, Echo.

"Where am I?"

Not where you should be.

"But . . . how?"

No time for that. Your friends need you.

She'd had enough of this double serving of cryptic. "How do I get out of here?"

The laugh, crisp and clear, bounced against the walls of her skull.

You're the firebird, Rose said, voice as soft as the petals from which she'd taken her name. *Fly.*

Oh, Echo thought. She didn't need to ask how or why or where. She knew, almost as if she'd always known. She stretched her wings, as if she'd been born to do it, and flew.

CHAPTER FIFTY-SIX

Hearing was the first sense that returned to Echo as she pulled herself up from the muck of death, stubborn and sticky as fresh cement. She heard steel clashing against steel. The bark of trees crackling and popping as they burned. Voices shouting their triumphs and howling their defeats. Her head throbbed with every sound. It was so loud. So unthinkably loud. If she could have moved her hands, she would have clapped them over her ears. Earmuffs. She needed earmuffs, but all she had was a bed of unforgiving pebbles digging into her spine and the nauseating scent of sizzling flesh in her nostrils.

Rising from the dead sucked. Rising from the dead in the middle of a battle sucked even more.

Echo cracked her eyes open, and they immediately began to water. Smoke permeated the air along with some-thing else, something she recognized. Squeezing her eyes shut, she grasped at the familiar scent, trying desperately to place it. It was acrid and sharp, like ozone. Her eyes flew open. The in-between. The Black Forest was supposed to be a null zone. Caius had said so. No thresholds could be accessed within its borders. But when she pulled herself upright, willow branches catching in her hair, she saw the hell that the sky had vomited up.

She had never seen a war before, but this had to be what one looked like. Warhawks clashed with Firedrakes, limbs and weapons tangled in a bloody mess. Altair, towering above it all like a bronze god, cut his way through the sea of bodies as if they were matchsticks. She caught a glimpse of Dorian's silvery-gray hair before he was overcome by no fewer than six Firedrakes. He disappeared beneath them, swarmed by his own people. Echo scanned the crowd for a flash of Ivy's white head or Jasper's peacock feathers, but all she could see was a mess of broken bodies and fire, everywhere fire.

Her gaze landed on Caius. He was in the middle of it all, cutting down Warhawks and Firedrakes alike. He'd lost his knives somewhere along the way, and Echo recognized the sword in his hand. The Dragon Prince fighting with an Avicen blade. She hadn't seen that one coming, but then, she also hadn't seen herself dying by her own hand and rising from the dead with a strange energy surging through her. It was a day for firsts.

Caius fought on, sword glancing off a fallen Warhawk's armor. The Warhawk's cloak was as white as the others, his bronze armor identical to that worn by his comrades, but Echo would have recognized the set of his shoulders, the curve of his jaw, and those golden speckled feathers anywhere. Altair had led his troops into battle, and Rowan— loyal, brave, beautiful Rowan—had followed him. As if he could feel her eyes on him, he turned, catching her gaze, brows drawn tight over hazel eyes. Rowan shouted for her, but the roar of the battle swallowed his voice, scattering his words aloft on the scorched air. He looked at her as though he had never seen her before, as though she were something new and strange and terrible. Just as Caius lifted his blade, ready to cut down Rowan for good, a crack, loud as lightning, sounded from the mouth of the Oracle's cave.

Fire billowed from the entrance as if the cave were belching it out. Tanith stood in its archway, arms raised as she called flames to do her bidding. She was going to burn the entire forest down around them. Echo felt as small and helpless as she ever had. They didn't stand a chance against Tanith. They would die here, in the Black Forest, burned to a bloody crisp.

Cowering behind the drooping branches of the willow beneath which she'd been placed, its green leaves yellow in the light of Tanith's fire, Echo was seven years old again, hiding from the monsters outside. But she heard Rose's voice whisper the words she'd spoken as Echo had floated in that black netherworld. *Your friends need you.*

She was not seven years old, and she was not alone. She would not hide, not from Tanith, not from Altair, not from anyone. Not if she could help it. Not when her friends needed her.

Echo summoned every ounce of courage she had and hauled herself to her feet. She expected to feel the sharp bite of pain where the blade had pierced her chest, but looking down, she found that her skin had healed, leaving only the faintest pucker of a scar. *Well, that's a fun new skill.*

She felt the moment Tanith spotted her. They were too

far apart for Echo to be able to make out her eyes, but she remembered them, red and furious, even if the memory didn't belong to her. It was like looking into a distorted mirror, showing glimpses of someone else's life as though it were her own, when Tanith had brought Rose's cabin burning down around her. A ferocious thrill of hate cut through her.

Yes. Rose's voice echoed in her head. *You know what to do.*

Echo raised her hands the way Tanith had. She didn't question it. She didn't second-guess herself. She simply held out her palms, summoned the fire she felt burning beneath her skin, and thought, *Burn.*

From the corner of her eye, Echo saw Caius turn from Rowan, who was blessedly still breathing, staring at her as if she were something from a nightmare. Caius ran, trying to place himself between Echo and Tanith, but Altair muscled his way through the tangle of bodies to reach him first. His sword arced through the air toward Caius. Time crawled to a stop, and Echo saw it happen in slow motion. Altair brought his blade down, aiming squarely for the center of Caius's chest. Again, she thought, *Burn.*

Flames poured from her open palms, black and white, as crisp and clear as a magpie's feathers, so different from Tanith's riotous reds and yellows. The blaze strengthened, first in stuttering pulses, then growing stronger and stronger until it burned as bright as the sun and as dark as night. The violent pounding of her heart was like wings beating against her bones. Power simmered beneath her skin, fighting to be free, but Echo's body was a cage, and she held the power of the firebird within. She laughed, and her fire surged forward. Flames twisted and twined through the air, colliding with Tanith's blaze. But Tanith didn't so much as flinch.

The black and white flames flickered with Echo's uncertainty. She poured everything she was, everything she had been, and everything she thought she would ever be into her fire, but it wasn't enough. Tanith was too strong and Echo's power was too new, too weak. Tanith's blaze battered Echo's until her brilliant flames muddied into a sad gray.

In the distance, Caius fell to his knees, Altair's body lay behind him, feathers smoking. Caius stared at Echo, expression open and raw. Something deep and secret twisted in her gut. Her blaze strengthened, and she felt Rose push inside her mind. Tanith fought back, and Echo fell her to knees, fire dying in her open palms.

She couldn't die now, not again. She wasn't ready. She wasn't done. She needed to see Ivy one last time, to tell her that she was glad to be her friend. And Rowan. There were so many things she had to say, so much that she owed him. She had to thank him for freeing her, to apologize for Ruby, for betraying his trust, for running away from him. She wanted to tell the Ala she loved her. The last thing Echo heard before she passed out was the rustle of feathers, like wings on a breeze. The black of the in-between surged over the forest, and then there was nothing but silence.

CHAPTER FIFTY-SEVEN

The first thing Jasper noticed was the pain. Pain was good. Pain meant he was alive, but it also meant that he wasn't going to be happy about it. His head throbbed worse than the time he'd tried to match a bar full of warlocks drink for drink. The muscles in his abdomen jumped, spitefully, with every breath he took. He laid a hand on his stomach, and his fingers slid through something warm and wet. Blood. *Well then.*

The second thing he noticed was that it was not cold, hard stone beneath him, but the plush white of his own carpet. It was most assuredly ruined now. He would have to import an entirely new one.

The third thing he noticed, after opening his eyes, was a raven-feathered Avicen looming over him.

"Oh, good," the Ala said. "You're up. I was beginning to think I'd pulled a corpse out of that fire."

"Whaaaa . . ." Jasper was usually capable of greater

eloquence than that, but for the life of him, he couldn't seem to rustle up any.

Behind the Ala, Ivy's white-feathered head bent over a very still body as she wrapped Echo's palm with a thick white bandage. Jasper's heart lurched. He tried to sit up, despite the rather vociferous protestations of his aggrieved abdominal muscles. With a single black-feathered hand, the Ala pushed him back down.

"She'll live," she said. "But you won't if you don't lie still."

Lie still. Jasper could do that. Nay, Jasper could excel at that.

"You, with the eye patch," the Ala called, looking over her shoulder. "Ivy looks like she could use an extra set of hands." And then, sweet, immortal delight, she clapped twice. "Hop to it."

Oh, how Dorian would love that. Even more splendidly, Dorian hopped to it, coming over to kneel beside Jasper, arms laden with clean gauze.

When Dorian pressed a bandage to the wound right below his ribs, Jasper bit back a yelp. What hurt even worse was the fact that Dorian mumbled a quick apology before letting his eyes drift over to where Caius was struggling to sit up beside Echo.

No, Jasper thought. *None of that now.*

"Would you be surprised to know," Jasper croaked, drawing Dorian's attention, "that this is the first time I've wound up on the business end of a sword?"

Dorian's quiet little laugh was bells on Sunday morning. "Just a bit, yes." He looked at Jasper then. There was a softness in his eyes that made Jasper's insides do all sorts of terrible things. "And you took a blow meant for me."

"Are you sure?" Jasper asked, voice sandpaper-rough. "That doesn't sound like me at all." He coughed, and blood tickled his throat. "But then, I suppose I haven't been feeling much like myself lately."

"You saved my life," Dorian said, swapping out the bandage for a fresh one. The one he laid aside was an alarming shade of red. Jasper decided he was better off not looking at it.

"And you saved our little dove," Jasper replied, craning his neck to see where Ivy was still tending to Echo. "I saw what you did back there."

Dorian's lips twitched in a way that wasn't entirely happy but was entirely appealing to Jasper on a level that should have been disturbing. "Yes, well, I owed her one."

Dorian spared another surreptitious glance over his shoulder. Jasper followed his gaze. Caius was holding Echo's hand, the one that Ivy was not bandaging.

Nope, Jasper thought. *Bad Dorian.*

He laid a hand atop Dorian's. It increased the pressure on his wound, but the feel of Dorian's skin, warm and callused beneath his own, was worth it.

"You see him," Jasper said. "But does he see you?"

Dorian turned away from Caius, silver bangs falling over his eye as he bowed his head. "No," he whispered. Jasper had a feeling that this was perhaps the first time Dorian had ever admitted it aloud. "He never has."

There was a whole host of comments Jasper had stock-piled in his arsenal, locked and loaded and ready to launch at the slightest hint that Dorian was willing to admit the futility of his unrequited love, but each and every one of them was rejected in favor of silently lacing his fingers with Dorian's. When Dorian didn't pull away, Jasper's insides quivered.

Dorian was silent for a moment, his blue eye resting on their joined hands. Then, slowly, painfully, he raised his gaze to Jasper's. "Do you?"

Jasper thought he knew where this was going, but he needed to be very clear on one thing. "Do I what?"

"See me." Dorian swallowed. Jasper must have lost a lot of blood to be so easily hypnotized by the motion of Dorian's throat.

Jasper answered by raising their linked fingers to his mouth, brushing his chapped lips over the scarred skin of Dorian's knuckles. A pink flush crept up Dorian's pale neck. Jasper was as enthralled with the blush as he had been the first time he'd seen it. But unlike the first time he had seen that hint of scarlet taint Dorian's cheeks, he had an over-whelming desire to be the only one to make Dorian blush like that, deeply and often. And that was when Jasper knew that he'd lost a war he hadn't even realized he'd been fighting. Resistance was futile. Surrender, inevitable. He pressed another kiss to Dorian's hand, just to see that pink darken a shade.

"I'm sorry," Dorian said, shaking his head, Christmas-tinsel hair fluttering with the movement. "I guess I haven't been feeling much like myself lately either."

Dorian drew his hand back, and the smooth glide of skin on skin was nearly too much to bear. Jasper had long ago decided that his heart had little use beyond its biological function, but as Dorian pulled away from him, he knew that his was as breakable as anyone's.

CHAPTER FIFTY-EIGHT

E cho stirred, feeling the scratch of carpeting beneath her head. Bells tolled, and she'd never been happier to hear them. She was alive, even if just barely, and someone was wrapping linen around her burnt hands. Ivy's voice floated through the black, and the Ala's answered it. They were alive too. Echo kept her eyes closed and let the familiar sound of their conversation wash over her.

Now that she was out of the Black Forest, away from the Oracle's sanctum and the power of her own reflection, she was beginning to feel like herself again. Her wounds had mostly healed, save for the burns on her hands. The fire she'd called had scorched her, too. It didn't seem fair that her newfound power should turn on her like that, but it bothered her infinitely less than the sensation of another person lurking at the back of her mind, like an actor waiting in the wings.

Rose.

When Echo had opened that door inside her, letting the firebird out of its cage, Rose had come along for the ride, clinging to the power that could have been hers had she only made the choice to welcome it. She'd been a vessel, too, just like Echo. And now, she was occupying a darkened corner of Echo's brain, not merely with her presence, but with everything that made her *Rose*. What Rose knew, Echo knew, even the secrets she'd kept until the day she died. What Rose felt, Echo felt. She remembered being happy once, a long time ago. She remembered the way Caius had kissed her the first time, standing on the beach by her cabin with the ocean lapping at their feet. She remembered nights spent cuddled together in front of a fireplace, talking about their hopes and fears. All of it was as real to Echo as her own memories, her own emotions. It was too much.

When she cracked her eyes open, she was greeted by the sight of three people leaning over her. Three of the most important people in her life. The Ala. Ivy. And now, strangely enough, Caius. They were all staring at her. This was how animals in zoos must have felt. Lying there, with all those faces peering at her with equal parts concern and curiosity, was suffocating. When she struggled to sit up, no fewer than three sets of hands—black, white, and a featherless tan—moved to push her back down. It was all too much.

"Stop," Echo said, voice breathier than she would have liked. "Everybody, stop. Stop touching me, stop staring at me, stop inhaling my air."

Ivy sucked in a breath, and Echo could have sworn she actually held it. *God bless your heart, Ivy.*

The Ala's face slipped into something approaching neutrality, but Echo could see the wonder in her eyes.

"It was in you the whole time," the Ala said. "I should have known."

Echo pushed herself up to a seated position, back resting against Jasper's ridiculous suede couch. When Caius steadied her with a hand on her lower back, she didn't stop him. His hand lingered there, settling right above the waistband of her jeans. Echo was acutely aware of every minute detail of the texture of his skin. Ivy's eyes darted down to Caius's hand, but she kept her thoughts to herself.

"How could you have known?" Echo asked. "I still don't even understand how or why this is possible. I remember everything about Rose. She was the firebird's last vessel— she's the one who left the maps behind for me to find. And there are other images, things I don't understand. How do I have those memories?"

The Ala ran a hand through her feathers and sighed. Echo had never seen her look so tired.

"When you were out, I meditated to try to make sense of all of this, and I had a vision. The firebird, I believe, is a transferable entity," the Ala said. "And each person who comes into contact with it leaves a sort of psychic fingerprint. Since Rose was the most recent vessel before you, her voice is the loudest. I'm sure it helps that you've given her a reason to shout." She looked pointedly at where Caius's hand rested. "The firebird was within the both of you all along. It was your sacrifice that released it. For whatever reason, Rose decided to leave it alone. You chose to unleash it. If my understanding is correct, and the firebird is a being of pure magic, of raw energy, then it needs something to contain it in order to exist in this world."

"I don't get it. Why send me on a scavenger hunt around the world? Why not just send me straight to the Oracle?"

Ivy broke her silence at last. "Maybe it wasn't about the destination. Maybe it was about the journey."

Echo blinked. "Come again?"

Ivy fiddled with the hem of her shirt, eyes downcast to watch her hands. "Maybe if things had been too easy, you wouldn't have been the person you needed to be when the time came. You sacrificed yourself to save us." She looked up, and Echo recognized the look in her eyes. She was holding back tears, the corners of her lips quivering slightly. "And you didn't have proof that you'd come back, but you did it anyway. That was really brave." She sniffled and brought her arm up to wipe her nose on her sleeve.

Echo reached out to take Ivy's hand, bandages be damned. She hadn't felt brave. She'd just been desperate. All this talk of vessels was making the dull ache in her head throb even harder. She rubbed at her temples, hoping it would help quell the pain. "But why me? I mean, I'm just a girl. I'm nothing special."

The Ala laid a gentle hand on Echo's cheek. "Oh, my little magpie, you've always been special. I don't think it was a coincidence I found you in that library. I think we were meant to find each other, you and I. The same way you and Caius were meant to find one another. Without him, you never would have known about the Oracle."

Echo raised her eyebrows. "So you're saying this is like a destiny thing?"

The Ala shook her head, black feathers ruffling slightly before settling. "Your fate is your own, but I think everyone in this world is given a role." She looked at Echo with a weight in her eyes that Echo wasn't sure she wanted to bear. "Your role is to be the firebird. How you choose to play it is up to you. The fire you called is proof of that."

The fire. *Shit. Shit, shit, shit.* She hadn't meant to hurt people indiscriminately; she'd just wanted the fighting to end.

"Rowan," Echo whispered. "And the others . . . are they okay?" She'd only wanted to stop Tanith, to stop Altair, to stop everyone from ripping each other apart.

The Ala nodded. "The fire passed over them without burning, like you didn't want to hurt them."

"I didn't," Echo said. But it hadn't been her choice. She hadn't thought about it. There was power coursing through her veins, and she wasn't sure she could even begin to make sense of it. She squeezed her eyes shut. The realization of how close she'd come to hurting the people she loved curdled inside her. Caius rubbed circles on her back, and his touch helped her push the thought away.

Echo shook her head, as if she could dislodge her fear. She couldn't. What she could do was ignore it and focus on something else. "How did you know where to find us?"

The Ala smiled, and it was so lovely, so familiar, that Echo wanted to weep. "Tanith and her forces followed you. And we followed them."

Caius ran a hand through his hair and sighed. "I guess none of us were nearly as subtle as we thought we were."

He sounded vaguely ashamed, and Echo patted the hand that rested on her waist. That small smile graced his lips, and she wanted to smile back, but the weight of her next question was too heavy to allow for something so light.

"Okay, so if I'm the firebird, that means I'm supposed to

stop a war. How the hell do I do that?" said Echo. "I'm just one person."

"One needs only a single match to start a fire, Echo," the Ala replied. "It is a heavy burden you bear, but never forget that you do not bear it alone."

The Ala placed a hand on Ivy's arm and stood. Ivy looked like she wanted to protest, but she only blinked, too rapidly, in silence. The Ala nodded at Caius and added, "I'll give the two of you some time. I'm sure you have much to discuss."

Echo watched them walk away. Caius's hand fell from her back, but he scooted a few inches closer to her. It was strange to think of him doing anything that could be described as scooting.

"How do you feel?" he asked.

Laughing hurt, but Echo did it anyway. "Like I died and came back to life. So, you know, not bad."

Caius's mouth went soft at the edges. Sympathy made him dangerously pretty. She had to look away. He looked away, too.

"I still don't understand what happened back there," he said.

Echo looked at her hands. Fire had poured out from those palms. "I don't think I do, either."

Caius turned back to her. He opened his mouth. Closed it. He looked as if he was debating what to say. Lips pressed into a thin line, he shook his head. Whatever it was, he either wasn't going to say it, or he couldn't find the words. His hand rose to hover in front of Echo's shirt. Someone— Ivy, she presumed—had torn it open about a third of the way so that the puckered skin of the scar on her chest was visible. Caius curled his fingers into fists, as though he didn't trust himself not to reach out and touch it.

"You healed." He shook his head, astonishment in his eyes. "You're the firebird. And you rose, from blood and ashes, just like Rose wrote."

"Yup," Echo said. She waited a beat before adding, just for good measure, "And you're the Dragon Prince."

"*Former* Dragon Prince," Caius amended, though Echo detected a note of embarrassment in his voice. "Once Tanith usurped me, it wasn't *technically* a lie."

She fixed him with her best dubious stare.

He winced. "I'm sorry. I know that isn't enough, but I don't know what else—"

Echo held up a bandaged hand, silencing him. "I can only deal with so many revelations at a time, and this whole firebird thing kind of trumps your secret identity by a long shot. For now, consider yourself forgiven, but don't think I'm going to forget it."

"That's more than I deserve," he said softly.

"Oh, I don't know, I think you've maybe suffered enough for one day. Your own sister did try to kill you."

"She tried to stop me. If Tanith truly wanted me dead, I'd be dead. Or, at the very least, maimed. She's my twin, and I'm still her brother. That means something to her."

"And does it mean something to you?" she asked.

Caius sighed, long and weary. "I don't know."

Echo wanted to wrap her arms around herself, but that would have felt too much like cowering. From what, she wasn't sure. From the people who would be hunting her now that they knew she and the firebird were one and the same. From Caius.

From the fact that she had risen from the dead. From herself. From her destiny. *Pick a door,* Echo thought, *any door.*

"What happened in that room?" Caius's voice was barely above a whisper, but the sound of it snaked around Echo's rib cage, squeezing. "Before Tanith. What did you see?"

"A mirror," Echo said. "Just a mirror."

Caius ducked his head, hair falling over his eyes and brushing his scales. She wanted to smooth his bangs back for him, to feel the silk of his hair between her fingers again. Now it was her untrustworthy hands curling into loose fists; the pain caused by the burns on her palms helped quell the urge. When he spoke, he kept his gaze lowered. "And them?"

He looked at her then, and Echo didn't turn away.

"I remembered," she said. "I remembered things I shouldn't, because they're not my memories. It's weird. I remember it like I was there, like I was Rose. I remember *you*. I remember loving you because she loved you."

Hope and sadness and something new, something just for her, warred in Caius's eyes. Invisible hands wrapped around her heart and twisted, as if they were trying to wring it dry of blood. He looked like a man who wanted to hope but didn't quite know how.

Echo didn't know who moved first. All she knew was that she was kissing Caius, and Caius was kissing her. Something inside her that had been misaligned was slowly setting itself right, gears clicking into place one by one. It was thrilling and terrifying all at once.

Schwellenangst, Echo thought. *The fear of starting something new.*

Caius kissed her as if he knew her already, as if pressing his lips against hers were an old habit, as easy as breathing.

He kissed her like he remembered her. And a small part of her, a part that Echo was beginning to realize was not her at all, remembered him. As Caius sank his fingers into the hair at the base of her neck, Echo could have sworn that she felt Rose sigh.

At the faint tickle of another person inside her head, she pulled away. Caius moved back, reluctantly. His fingers traced a path from the shell of her ear to the curve of her jaw and came to rest there. It was nice, but as soon as she had the thought, she wasn't sure if it was hers. She shook her head, dislodging Caius's hand.

"I'm sorry," she said. "I just . . . how do I know where I end and Rose begins? How do I know what's me and what's her?"

The corners of Caius's mouth turned up ever so slightly. "You're you, Echo. You always have been and you always will be. Nothing will change that."

He couldn't have known how desperately she wanted to believe him, yet he looked so sure of himself, so sure of *her* that she didn't have the heart to tell him she didn't. But because her reality had become a smorgasbord of life-altering events, the problem of sharing head space with Caius's dead girlfriend wasn't the only serving of strange on her plate. *Time to compartmentalize.*

"So," she said. "What are we going to do now?"

Caius's hand traveled toward Echo's, inching closer, giving her time to retract it. She didn't. His fingers closed around hers. He turned her hand over in his and said, "Damned if I know."

Her laugh was tired and quiet. She looked around the loft because she needed a minute to digest it all. Ivy and the Ala had retreated to the kitchenette, making tea, probably. It was one thing Ivy had inherited from the Ala. Making warm beverages in a crisis. Jasper was still stretched out flat on the floor, with Dorian's hands holding a bandage to his abdomen.

Echo's fingers twitched with the urge to tighten her hold on Caius's hand despite the pain. She glanced at where Dorian had his head bent over Jasper's. They were so different. Dorian, with his fair skin and his silvery-gray hair. Jasper, all golden brown and a riot of color, ever the peacock. But as Jasper raised Dorian's hand to his mouth, pressing a gentle kiss onto his fingers, they looked right together.

The sight of them made something ping inside Echo.

"Maybe this is how I do it," she said.

"Do what?" Caius asked.

"End the war. Bring everyone together."

Caius's expression sailed past dubious to land squarely on shocked. "The Avicen and the Drakharin would never unite."

"Wouldn't they?" Echo flung out a hand, gesturing at the open expanse of Jasper's nest. "Look at us. Ivy worked her healing magic on Dorian after that psycho chased us out of Wyvern's Keep. Dorian's busy holding Jasper's guts in." She shook her head, sighing. "You saw the Oracle's arms. She had both scales *and* feathers. Maybe the Avicen and the Drakharin had a common ancestor. They share the mythology about the firebird, don't they? Maybe it didn't used to be this way, Caius. The Avicen and the Drakharin were one, once. Maybe they can be again."

Caius's smile was sad, but still lovely. Kind of like the rest of him. She was fairly certain that thought did not belong to her. "It's a beautiful dream, Echo. But that's all it'll ever be. I'm too old to believe anything else."

Once more, the hands around Echo's heart clenched.

"Well, maybe it's time the dreamers started calling the shots," she said.

Caius brought their joined hands to his mouth and held them there, brushing his lips against her fingers, and Echo spied the telltale shine of tears in his eyes.

"They won't like it," he said, mouthing the words against her skin. "People like Altair. Like Tanith. They'll fight until there's no one left standing."

"But does that mean we don't try?"

Caius's voice was soft with wonder. "You know, you sound just like her."

Like Rose. Echo wasn't sure how she felt about that. In that moment, he didn't look like a two-hundred-fifty-year-old almost immortal. He didn't look like a prince elected to bear the burdens of an entire nation's hopes and failures. He simply looked like Caius. Serious green eyes, hair so brown it was almost black, the faintest hint of a smile he wore around the edges of his lips when he didn't remember to frown. Echo wondered if this was the way Rose had seen him, if the amalgamation of these traits was the reason she'd fallen in love with Caius a century ago.

With a small sigh, he lowered her hand and gazed around the room. "So. Here we are. A flame-throwing thief, a deposed prince, an apprentice healer, an ex–royal guard, and a career scoundrel taking on a war on two fronts." The sadness seeped out of Caius's smile like a puddle drying up in the sun. He laughed, and Echo wanted to bottle the sound and save it forever. "What could possibly go wrong?"

"Honestly?" Echo replied. "Probably everything."

CHAPTER FIFTY-NINE

"They'll be looking for you," the Ala said, watching Echo lay out her few belongings on Jasper's bed so she could pack. Echo wanted to sit next to her, to lean her weary head on the Ala's shoulder, as she had so many times before, to let herself be comforted by those strong arms. But that was something a child would have done, and the time for childish things had passed.

"Tanith," the Ala continued. "Altair, if he survived. Their enemies. Their allies. Anyone with a vested interest in the firebird's power."

"I know," Echo said. She shoved her belongings into her bag with a surprising amount of calm and tried not to think about the things she was leaving behind: the Nest, the home she could never return to, or Rowan, the boy she couldn't— wouldn't—burden with her newfound power. The dagger lay next to the backpack, gleaming prettily against the white of Jasper's sheets. She would pack that last.

"You can't stay here."

"I know," Echo said.

She looked around the loft, airy and bright at the top of the Strasbourg Cathedral. Sunlight streamed in through the stained-glass windows, painting the white carpet—dirty as it was—a thousand shades of orange, purple, green, and blue. It was so very Jasper. How quickly it had begun to feel like a home, with so many people—Avicen, Drakharin, and human—packed into it.

The others puttered about the loft, gathering the few things they would need on the run. Dorian and Ivy were packing whatever medical supplies they could scrounge up, while Jasper lay on the sofa, sulking. Ivy and the Ala had worked miracles on his wound, but he needed time to heal. Time they didn't have.

Caius met her gaze from across the room. He smiled at her, eyes soft and warm, and Echo couldn't not smile back. Dorian called his name, and Caius looked away. There was the faintest echo of a presence inside her head, demanding attention. Rose. Echo closed her eyes and breathed deeply. Rose faded, like the ghost she was.

The Ala smoothed her honey-colored skirt over her thighs. "What will you do?"

"The same thing I've always done," Echo said, swinging her backpack over her shoulder. She held the dagger in her hand, onyx and pearl magpies catching the light. If she angled it just right, they looked like they were flying. "Run when I have to, and fight till the end."

FOLLOW THE FIREBIRD
IN BOOK TWO OF
THE GIRL AT MIDNIGHT SERIES

AVAILABLE IN JUNE 2016

ACKNOWLEDGMENTS

Writing a book is a bit like embarking on a quest to throw a magical golden ring into an active volcano. You start off alone, wondering how you're ever going to make it to the end, and along the way you wind up picking up friends who make your journey possible.

I'm so incredibly lucky to have been given the opportunity to work with inimitable Krista Marino at Delacorte Press, who is more wizard than editor. Her unwavering faith in the book, even when it felt like mine was failing, sustained me, making sure that Echo got where she needed to be by the final page. Publishing your first novel is by turns thrilling, overwhelming, and terrifying, and I feel so fortunate to have a wonderful team at Random House who worked to make *The Girl at Midnight* the best it could possibly be. And an extra special thank-you to Alison Impey, Gail Doobinin, and Jen Wang for designing such a beautiful book. I mean, just look at it. Go ahead. Ogle it. Appreciate the pretty. I'll wait.

Are you back? Okay, good. Let us proceed.

There's that saying that sometimes in art, you must kill your darlings, and as a debut writer, that can be difficult. The urge to be precious with your book babies is strong. You want to pet them and love them and cherish them forever, but you really need someone in your corner who will help you do what needs doing, even when it's scary. My agent, Catherine Drayton, has always been ready with both tough love and pep talks, dispensed with great wisdom as needed. Thank you so, so, so much for looking at this story and seeing something special there, even (especially) when I couldn't. And thank you to the staff at InkWell Management, especially foreign rights rock stars Lyndsey Blessing and Alyssa Mozdzen, for all their hard work.

I wouldn't be who I am—as a person and as a writer—without the ladies of the Midnight Society. Calling you critique partners and beta readers doesn't do you justice. Amanda, I don't even know if I'd be writing novels if it hadn't been for those stories we wrote by passing notes, oh-so-stealthily, to each other in French class. Idil, I may have racked up a mountain of debt in grad school, but since the experience was the start of a beautiful friendship, I don't regret a single penny. If not for our lunch at Yo! Sushi that fateful afternoon, Echo would probably never have been born. Laura, your enthusiasm was sometimes the only thing that got me through the day. The fact that you were excited for this book made me know I had to finish it, even if just for you. Also, I was kind of afraid you would hunt me down if I didn't. I'm doubly grateful that you introduced me to Robin Lange—thanks for the Latin translation, Robin! And, Chelsea: You were the first person to read *The Girl at Midnight* from start to finish. When you emailed me to say you'd devoured it in one sitting, staying up late into the night to reach the end, I cried. Real, human tears.

To paraphrase Virginia Woolf, a woman needs a room of her own to write fiction, but even more importantly, you need to have a roof over your head and food on your table. If not for my family's love and support, this story would probably never have made it from my brain to the page.

Like Echo, I was a lonely child, but I knew that so long as I had a book in my hands, I was never truly alone. I'm incredibly grateful to the writers whose stories kept me company, reminding me that the world was a wondrous place, full of adventures, if only you were brave enough to look, and to the teachers (Hi, Dr. Meade!) who encouraged me to write my own.

And lastly, I would like to thank *you,* the reader, for going on this journey with me. The fact that you even picked up this book at all will never stop boggling my mind, and I'm honored and humbled that you chose to spend those precious hours of your time with Echo and her friends.

ABOUT THE AUTHOR

Melissa Grey wrote her first short story at the age of twelve and hasn't stopped writing since. After earning a degree in fine art at Yale University, she embarked on an adventure of global proportions and discovered a secret talent for navigating subway systems in just about any language. She works as a freelance journalist in New York City. To learn more about Melissa, visit melissa-grey.com and follow @meligrey on Twitter.